Published by Jo Pilsworth and The Hunter's Arrov

Discover other titles by Jo Pilsworth and The Hunter's Arrow:

The Diaries of the Cŵn Annwn

The Diaries of the Cŵn Annwn
Alpha (planned publication May 2016)
Beta (planned publication August 2016)
Yr Ddraig (planned publication May 2019)

The Hellfire Pack
Cysgodion (planned publication Summer 2018)
Merysekhmet (published Spring 2017)
Toho (planned publication Spring 2018)
Medved (planned publication December 2018)
Ma'iitsoh (planned publication early 2019)

E-book Edition 2016, License Notes

Book cover designed by Jo Pilsworth.

DEDICATION FROM JO

The Hunter's Arrow Ltd was a dream made possible through friendship. Without those friendships, the stories which we hope you will enjoy would never have come together. So, thanks go to the following:

Tracy Andrews

Donna DeBoard

Bethan Thomas

Gabriela Collazo

Angela Keys

Melissa Keyza

Katlyn Stone

Aiden Williams

I am fortunate to have such creative and innovative friends. If we have learned anything it is that a dream can come true. We are much more than our detractors might say, and through our stories, we have proven just how wrong they are. I look forward to writing with you for many years to come.

I also want to thank those non-writers, who have told me how much they enjoy what I have written from the early days of writing online role-play and fan fiction, to now. Your encouragement and support means the world to me.

Finally, my thanks to Karen Nethercott, Marta Jenkala and Miss TN Kiersnowska: three teachers from St Anne's Convent School. In your own way, you started me down the journey of writing.

My friends, you all rock!

ALPHA: TABLE OF CONTENTS

PROLOGUE

November 2014

I have walked this world for 410 years, with 170 years having passed since I assumed the role of Alpha of this Pack of Cŵn Annwn. In that time, I have seen the world change dramatically from an agrarian society to one where common words include terms like 'global warming' due to the pollution levels engendered by mankind's activities in less than a couple of centuries. I have found my Mate, I have lost close family, and throughout, I have remained true to my promise to my Goddess.

I harvest souls

My duty lies with my Goddess, who has tasked me with bringing her the souls of evil-doers. But there is more to my role than that. For all the evil in the world, there are innocents, and as the gatekeeper to the Underworld, not the Hell that modern religions would suggest, but a place of rest, my Goddess has charged me to bring those for whom a reward for their suffering is due. For them, there is the choice of rest, or rebirth. Most choose rest, and paradise for each is different.

And, I don't necessarily wait until those who commit evil have reached the end of their 'natural' lives. Like I said, I harvest souls. When evil has been done, and another life ended prematurely, there are even more grounds for the harvest to be, shall we say, early. As with any transaction involving evil, there is a downside. Well, there are several downsides, not least of which is that those who would do evil tend to not wish to surrender their souls for judgement. The other key downside was something I had seen with the former Alpha of my Pack. When my sire was murdered, the balance that should have existed was lost. I must find my Mate, my balance, or I will risk the same fate.

I was born Gabriel Black, although for the last few centuries, I have been known as Gavril Negrescu. These are our tales of my Mate and my Pack, our sorrows and our triumphs. Perhaps one day, evil will be no more. I am not holding my breath.

CHAPTER 1: A MEETING OF MATES

"Brawd, you need some time out, some time away from the Pack. That last harvest was particularly difficult for you. Don't deny it." The muscular build of the man speaking seemed at odds with the concern in his voice. The object of his conversation turned to face him from the windows of the well-appointed study. "Gabriel, why don't you accept the invitation to visit the Carpathians? The way that Romanian goes on about it, it might be just what you need, clean air, and a change of scenery.

"You know, Bran, it is amazing how life can change in a relatively short span of years. Our homeland has gone from being largely agrarian, to a hub of mining." Gabriel's voice was soft, but there was no mistaking that his friend's use of the word 'brawd' was more from their long-standing friendship, rather than from blood brotherhood.

Throwing his tall frame into the chair opposite Bran, Gabriel looked broodingly at the flames burning cheerfully in the grate, warding off the slight chill in the air.

"I can see a time when those slag heaps will become mountains themselves: man-made mountains, to be sure, but just as prominent on the landscape. The trick will be make sure that the Pack benefits from the change of circumstance." The laugh was self-deprecating. "I may be relatively new-come to being the Alpha, but I must ensure that the declining years of our former Alpha are not used as an excuse to encroach on our land, by incoming industrialists."

"Be that as it may, Gabriel, you need to relax. You know the risks you are running right now, unmated as you are." Bran's voice was a warm, musical, deep rumble. "If needs be Owain and I will pack you up like baggage and take you there. I am sure there are more civilised ways to travel, and if you want your host to see you as his peer, I might suggest you use them."

For a brief moment, Gabriel's rich brown eyes sparkled with something like humour. "My 'host' as you suggest is just like all the other industrialists. All hail the progress of the Industrial Revolution, a time of change, of betterment." Again Gabriel laughed. "Provided you have the money and the connections."

"Aye, that may be, brawd. And may I point out that you have both, courtesy of your canny handling of Pack business." Bran stood up. "Come on, by now, your bags are packed, and you can go. Owain and I can hold the fort for you in the meantime."

"Goddess, you are so very close to nagging me, Bran." Gabriel sighed. "Very well. I know you are right. Damn, but I thought I might have another hundred years or so before the cynicism started to affect me, but perhaps not. I don't know. There is something about this visit to the Carpathians. It is like I am feeling a pull." Gabriel shook his head. "It is more than that. If I didn't know better, I would say it is our Goddess' will that I leave our blessed land."

Gabriel stood. "Have the baggage sent on. I know where this hunting lodge is located, and I will flash myself there. I will tell my host that I will meet him there, that I have other business to attend to in Europe. At least that way, I won't have to endure his chattering the whole time."

Bran slapped his Alpha and friend on the back. "The trip will do you good. I feel it in my bones. Go visit these Carpathian Mountains and you can come back and tell us how they compare to our own Welsh hills. There will be no contest, of course."

The two laughed, the laughter of old friends, of an Alpha and one of his trusted Betas as both finished their wine, and Bran left the room. Gabriel smiled at his friend's insistence, but he had known that Bran only spoke out of concern for him. It was the nature of the Cŵn Annwn. It was the Alpha's duty to harvest the souls of those who did evil to their fellow man, and convey them to the Goddess for judgement. If they passed, well and good. But more often, they would not pass. A harvest was not carried out lightly, not least because each harvest came at a cost. Whilst the Goddess may take the souls from him, Gabriel knew that a small fraction would be left, and that gradually, those fractions would start to take its toll. That was how it happened to the previous Alpha, his own dam, until such time as the burden drove her insane, and he had had no choice but to Challenge her for leadership of the Pack.

Yes, Bran had the right of it, Gabriel thought to himself. Perhaps there was a reason, a plan in the Goddess' mind that he should travel to Eastern Europe. Gabriel laughed as he made his way past the kitchens of the Pack home in Snowdonia, to his own rooms upstairs. Who knew? Perhaps his Mate awaited him. Gabriel shook his head. It was unlikely. He would just have to learn to cope with the role imposed on him. He was the Alpha, and until he found his Mate, there was no other option.

-x-

It had taken ten days to sort matters out at the Pack, such that he could leave to visit the 'hunting lodge' to which he had been invited. Ten days was also a reasonable time for it to take to travel to Europe and across, if one rushed, so Gabriel took pains to arrive looking travel weary.

Of course, the lodge was anything but the simple home his host claimed. It was a showpiece to the man's wealth, a way of demonstrating clearly to his Romanian neighbours and the native Roma who worked his estates that he was a man of wealth and power, and that they should look up to him. Gabriel resisted the temptation to recoil from the embrace of his host, the slightly sour smell from his soul mixing with the taint of a lack of washing. Even as so much had advanced in the Industrial Revolution, the simple concept of washing seemed to elude many.

As a Cŵn Annwn, with his alternative forms of spectral hound and wolf, Gabriel had sense of smell far in excess of his host's, which meant that the barrage of smells was almost overwhelming. More so than that was the other side that his senses as an Alpha told him. The servants, Roma mostly, were treated as little more than chattel, to be bought and sold, not treated as the souls that they were in truth. And Bran had thought that this trip might refresh his outlook? It was going to be a long few days, that much was certain.

His host was determined to show him the lay of the land. "I have ordered my lupari to organise a wolf hunt." He boasted. His eyes had gleamed in the anticipation of impressing his Welsh guest. The man was one of the pre-eminent bowyers of the land, the latest craze amongst the higher echelons of society, amongst other things, which was why they did business. His European contacts provided a good source of the yew wood needed for bow staves and in turn, that gave him a reason to travel frequently to England, and thus impress the rest of his circle with his London contacts.

He missed the look of scorn on Gabriel's face. A wolf hunt? More than likely, it was his own starving farm workers who had stolen the missing livestock, rather than the wolf, but he had observed the tendency of hanging hunting trophies around the lodge. Gabriel made no mention of the harsh memories such sights brought back to him, of his own sire's murder when running as a wolf and how his killers had not even attempted to save his pelt, letting their common dogs tear the black wolf to shreds, whilst unbeknownst his cub had watched from the tree line.

"A wolf hunt sounds like an excellent idea." Gabriel told himself that he had to 'play nice', and maintain the persona that his host expected to see. Perhaps the hunt might give him the chance to slip away, to see more of the wild mountains around the estate?

Watching the hounds milling around, for a moment, Gabriel put the thoughts of his sire's death to one side. His host wanted to impress him. He would just have to hide his personal distaste, he thought, as he pulled on his leather riding gloves. Declining the assistance offered to him to mount the loaned gelding his host had provided, Gabriel swung himself easily into the saddle. He was only too well aware that his tall, muscled frame had caught the eyes of the mamas in the party, eyeing him as a potential marriage prize, even more so once his host mentioned the extent of his holdings in England and Wales. Well, he was unmated, that was true, but that didn't mean he wanted to be paired off with one of the hopeful young ladies. Thank the Goddess that they would be gone, since the evening festivities were not deemed suitable for ladies of good breeding. Rumour had it that there would be … gypsy dancers? That would not be suitable fare for a young lady of good breeding, but, and there were titters of laughter, the men must be allowed their entertainment, and if necessary … sow their wild oats before settling down. The fact that several mothers had looked at him pointedly had been difficult to ignore, particularly when there was no sign of his having a wife.

The gelding danced under him in a circle, not sure what to make of the scent of the rider on his back. Laying a gentle hand on the animal's neck, Gabriel smiled, communicating wordlessly that he meant no harm to the horse, and that they must pretend to just be the same as all the other riders. A snort from the horse told volumes, and brought the first genuine smile Gabriel knew had crossed his face in a long time. Maybe Bran had been right, as the call was given to follow the lupari and their dogs.

Knowing that his mount was familiar the lay of the land, Gabriel relaxed his hands on the reins, using them for show, and maintaining his seat through his lower body muscles. His fellow guests and his hosts would not know that he had been taught to ride at a time when the King of England might call muster of his subjects, and as landowners, his sire and others would ride. Gabriel had been taught to fight both on foot and in the saddle, and had been riding that way for the last two hundred years or so. His style of riding also left him free to pay more attention to his surroundings and the very amusing running commentary that the gelding was providing, once it realised that it had been given a rider who understood 'horse'. Gabriel smiled to himself. Let his host think that the smile was for the spectacle being provided by the hunt.

Then, something changed. Had he been in wolf form, Gabriel knew his hackles would have risen as the tone of the hunting dogs' barking changed. They had a quarry, but then as the whines attested, their quarry was proving elusive. Extending his own senses, Gabriel tried to sense whatever it was that had the dogs in such confusion. He could smell wolf, but it was something else, and yes, as the dogs started to whine, and the lupari's actions demonstrated that the hunt was not progressing as they expected, the scent disappeared. Not faded. It disappeared, as if it had not been there in the first place.

The smile returned to Gabriel's lips. This was interesting, not least because something seemed to pull inside his own soul. This way that the scent of the hunt's quarry continued to change? This was significant. This was more than significant, but why? What did it mean? Was it something that affected his Pack? Gabriel shook his head mentally. No, this was not a danger to his Pack. Danger? No, that wasn't the right description, so what was it?

He became aware of his host's blustering red face, and the angry words being exchanged with the lead lupari. The scent was lost. The dogs could not find it no matter how much the lupari wielded their whips. It was gone. Gabriel's host was clearly angered, and he could understand why. After all, the hunt had been arranged with the sole intent of demonstrating to his 'English' guest how skilled his lupari were, and how well his host understood that it is important to impress one's guest. Gabriel smiled, attempting to diffuse his host's clear ire.

"It is of little matter." He kept his tone calm, projecting the hint to those around him that it was not amiss that the quarry had been lost. "I am sure that another day you will be more successful." In an attempt to distract his host, Gabriel waved towards an area through which they had ridden. "I am more than happy to see some more of the land itself. Perhaps it might even consider purchasing some property out here." The latter had been a spontaneous thought, but it seemed right somehow.

"Of course, of course. Let me show you what the land has to offer. I have heard tell that there is a property up for sale further into the mountains. The gentleman who owned it passed away recently, and his daughters have no use for the property, being well married themselves. They may well wish to sell. I can make enquiries for you, if you wish, Mr Black." Gabriel forced himself to nod politely to his host.

"That would be more than acceptable. Why don't you show me the area around this property?" He suggested. "One doesn't wish to buy a pig in a poke, after all. I take it the property is suitable for a family." Gabriel grinned to himself, knowing his words would have been overhead. That should distract anyone. The well-presented, and clearly wealthy Welshman was thinking of 'family'. There was hope for the unmarried young ladies yet.

At least by the evening, the young unmarried ladies had retired to wherever it was that young ladies retired. Quite frankly, Gabriel was just glad it was one less group for him to put on a display of 'unwed, wealthy Englishman'. Just the thought of being considered English was enough to turn his stomach, assuming the miasma of personal odour of the other gentlemen did not do so first. Wine was flowing freely, and several of those were more than slightly drunk. If they managed to stand it would be a miracle. At least it meant, as the promised troupe of Roma dancers whirled into the room to the sound of violins scraping a tune, none of the dancers need fear being attacked by their 'betters'. Alcohol had an interesting contraceptive effect after all, since penetration was required for a Roma girl to fall pregnant. As Gabriel toyed with his glass, watching those around him, he couldn't help but think that it was small recompense for having to stomach the inept pawing of a drunken 'nobleman'.

Just as he was wondering how long it would be before he might slip away from the over-crowded room, something changed, and it took all his hard-won control to continue to appear bored, relaxed and just enjoying the entertainment.

His own mind was anything but relaxed. A scent. It was the wolf, but it was something else; it was much more than something else. What was it? Glancing at his host, Gabriel noticed the way the man's thick tongue slurped around his lips, as he watched one of the dancers. Gabriel's eyes followed his look, knowing that what he himself wanted to do was find the one who bore such an intriguing scent. There was someone in this room, one of the dancers he was sure, and she was not the Roma that she pretended to be. She was so much more than that. And then, just like on the hunt, the scent was gone. No, not gone, fading. She had left the room. It was a female, and if her scent was so familiar, was it because she was also a shifter? Might that explain the strange pull of her scent? Gabriel knew that he had to find out what it was that was so important. That's what it felt like. The scent was pulling him. Something he had to do. Something he had to know.

Nodding politely to his host, Gabriel murmured that he just needed a breath of fresh air. His host nodded, at the same time, beckoning one of the dancers to come closer. This seemed to be an open invitation to others in the room, as each male made a choice. One stood, or rather stumbled to his feet, heading towards the kitchen. Gabriel's wolf howled inside him. No, he was following the female who had left. He could not be allowed to lay a hand on her. If necessary, the wolf inside Gabriel insisted that it would kill. Wouldn't that shock all those aspiring Mamas? Without wanting to make his pursuit obvious, Gabriel followed the scent of the female. It seemed to weave around him, drawing him closer, but at the same time, it was clear that she had fled because she had scented him. A vague recollection filled his mind of long dark hair, of a dance that seemed to call to him, and she had swirled her skirts, dipping a shoulder to give a tantalising glimpse of breast. Why did she flee? Did she not realise that he would not hurt her? But then, this human male was following her path, his intent clear. Goddess forbid that perhaps the female thought that Gabriel would be of a like frame of mind?

Outside now, and her scent … vanished? Gabriel smiled watching the drunk human try to work out where the 'blasted wench' had gone. "Probably diseased anyway." He mumbled as he pushed past Gabriel, not even registering in his sodden brain that he had just insulted the evening's guest of honour. Gabriel couldn't care less. The scent had reappeared. A shifter who had the ability to disappear? That was one of the Goddess' gifts to her Cŵn Annwn, that they might better hunt their quarry. How could a mere shifter share that same ability? Yet it was the only explanation for her ability to hide her scent in this way.

There. It had reappeared. The pull to find the female and her intriguing scent was becoming stronger. He had to find her, but why? When the realisation hit him, Gabriel laughed, the first genuine laugh in many a month, in far too long. That was why he had to find her. Why had he not realised it before? With that thought it mind, it was clear what he needed to do, as he allowed his own visible form to disappear from sight. She must have a means of leaving and he just needed to ensure that when she left, she would not do so alone. Invisible, his footsteps were noiseless as he followed his hunch on where she had left her means of leaving. Sure enough, a soft neigh gave away the fact that she was close. Hiding in the shadows, Gabriel smiled as the female's form was revealed: one of the dancers, wearing the traditional simple white blouse and red skirt. The tinkling coins attached to the skirt, designed to catch the light as she danced made a soft counterpoint to her steps as she danced towards her waiting horse.

The female gasped, as Gabriel's arm shot out, barring her path. His finger on her lips warned her not to make a sound, as he examined the face of the young female Roma. Her scent filled his senses as he smiled, confirming in his own mind what he thought. No one could describe this moment, he realised, the moment when he encountered one female whose presence in his life was as necessary to him as breathing. One female destined to make him feel whole, in the way that his sire and dam had been in the long-past days of his youth. One female to be his predestined Mate. And yet, she didn't struggle, but stood still, her eyes fixed on his face. As Gabriel's head dipped down, his lips seeking her tempting mouth, as his arm pulled her closer into his embrace, she did not fight him. Rather her free hand fingered his dark hair as her lips softened beneath his kiss. It felt as if a Bond flared into life between them, a tangible bond which might only grow stronger over time.

Sweeping her into his arms, Gabriel deepened the kiss, luxuriating in the feeling of holding his Mate close. As their lips parted, the Roma female's finger traced his lips. "She spoke true. My angel said that you would come. She said that I would find a male who needed me, who would know me. May I know your name?"

Gabriel smiled. "I am Gabriel, Gabriel Black. And you, inima mea? How shall I call you?" It didn't occur to him until later that the endearment in her own tongue slipped from his lips so easily, proof if it was needed that she was the one for whom he had searched whether he realised it or not.

The female laughed softly. "Gabriel Black is an ordinary name, and you, sir, are not ordinary. I think I will call you Gavril Negrescu. It sounds more regal, sounds more like the man I have just met. I am Aaleahya." She smiled again. “Aaleahya Mic Daciana, my Lord.” A soft laugh escaped her. “My angel, who told me her name was Mallt-y-Nos, said that I would find you one day, a male would be the other half of my soul. But why are you with the ones who would hunt me?”

Gavril rolled the name around his tongue, wanting to laugh at her feeling that his own name, his birth name was not regal enough.

Her name was a simple name. Aaleahya of Daciana, an older name for the region. “Well, no more are you just Aaleahya Mic Daciana either, inima mea. Rather you are Aaleahya Mic Daciana-Negrescu.”

Pulling his Mate close, Gavril luxuriated in the peace that seemed to fill him. This was what was missing. This was what his sire had provided to the previous Alpha of his Cŵn Annwn pack. This was the balance that he sought.

He heard her mention the name of the Goddess, and knew that what he felt, what he had hoped might be, was confirmed. Why he had to travel so far, why his Mate should be weeks away from his homeland, he did not know. But she was the one chosen for him by the Goddess, and for that he was glad. No distance was too great to feel this sensation of coming home.

He laughed softly at her question. Why was he with the ones who would hunt his Mate? "I was drawn here. You drew me here, but I had to find you." Pulling her close to him, sheltering her in the crook of his arm, Gavril stroked her hair, his fingers caressing the line of her jaw, and the slender line of her neck

He could not get enough of her, of her scent, of the feel of her in his arms. “My Mate.” The affirmation whispered through his mind and along the nascent Bond between them.

Almost shyly, Aaleahya’s fingers traced his lips again. “Take your pleasure of me, my Lord. My angel said that you would need me. Take what you need.” Though her words were selfless, Gavril could feel the thrum through the nascent Mating Bond. She was nothing but a Roma. How could she be destined for this magnificent male, clearly of the same class as the landowner whose lupari hunted her in her wolf form.

“He will hunt you no more, inima mea.” Gavril’s face hardened for a moment, at the potential danger to his Mate, his predestined Mate. “He will hunt you no more or he will face my anger.” Another kiss to take away the harshness of his words. “Show me where you live, inima mea. I need to feel you close to me.”

Aaleahya nodded. "It is a little way, in the forests. A cave." The whisper was hesitant. Again there was that doubt in her mind. Her home was little more than a cave. Certainly not the fine home that this male must occupy. A night with him was all she might hope, and then, she sighed. "A night with you will be my gift to you, my Lord." She whispered.

Gavril didn't try to correct her. He wanted to show her since she knew clearly that she would meet him, but did not understand the nature of the Bond that would exist between them.

"Take what you need of me, my Lord. I am your servant to command. What do you wish to do? Where do we go? I live in the forest and have for many years."

Gavril felt also that he too wanted to just stand with his Mate in his arms, but practicality must play its part. His host would have wondered at his sudden disappearance if he didn't use his rooms. Yet, at the same time, he wanted nothing more to slip away with his Mate, to explore the forest she called home.

"I must return here in the morning, or it will result in more questions than I wish to give answers to a herd of humans." Gavril didn't hide the scorn he felt for them from his voice. "For now, show me your home, my Aaleahya."

Gavril scooped Aaleahya into his arms, holding her, knowing that this moment is for them alone. Then looking into her eyes, he raised his head, and softly, the throbbing howl that told his Pack what has happened filled the air. Too soft for humans to hear. Aaleahya's horse let out a soft whinny in response, and Gavril smiled. "Tonight will be our night and for us alone. Tonight my Mate will be just mine. Not the Pack's. Not even the chosen of the Goddess."

Again, Gavril smiled as he pressed kiss to Aaleahya's soft lips. "Tonight will be for us to learn about each other, and make permanent the sacred gift of being Mates."

Her horse was tethered nearby, and followed them, as Aaleahya's quiet voice directed his steps. The distance was of little consequence to him as Cŵn Annwn Alpha.

Gavril wondered again why his Goddess had made it necessary for him to travel so far to find his Mate, and the only reason that made sense was that she wanted him to move as a Pack. His own Cymru was changing, had changed already. It was no longer a place where wolves or even large dogs might be welcome. The once clean hills were polluted through the actions of man, the rivers contaminated by the outflow of their mines. Whatever the purpose his Goddess had seen for his Pack in this land of forests and mountains, she also knew that it was a home that would suit them physically and mentally.

Eventually, Gavril reached Aaleahya's cave. With a wave of her hand, the branches screening the entrance parted, and they entered. Allowing her lithe body to slide down him, as her feet touched the packed dirt floor of the cave, he seized her head between my hands, and captured her lips, kissing her with the passion that he had longed to show her before. Her mouth opened beneath the pressure of his lips, allowing him to taste her, to breathe with her.

There was that certainty in Aaleahya's mind again, that he could not possibly be hers to keep, no matter what the angel had told her. But she could give him one thing that would be for him and him alone. Taking his hand, she led him to the pallet of furs. "It is not much I know, but please …"

"Let me show you what you don't know, inima mea." Gavril's voice was soft but his need for her apparent in the hoarse tone of his words. On this night of all nights, he would not tup her against the wall as she seemed to expect. This night, he wanted her to know what she meant to him, the gift that she was giving him was immeasurable in his mind, and yet she didn't realise it.

As Gavril raised his head and looked again in her eyes, he could not help but wonder at this feeling of calm, of light coursing through him. Yes, he had delivered the recent harvest of souls to his Goddess, but as had happened before, it was as if a taint remained. With Aaleahya in his arms, that taint was gone. Gavril felt more as he had done before he became Alpha of the Cŵn Annwn.

"What are you doing to me, my love?" Gavril asked, trying to understand what was happening. No description of the relationship between the Alpha and the Mate could have prepared him for this sensation.

A home was a cave indeed, screened from view by vines. The earthen floor of the cave was firm, clear evidence of this being her sanctuary. As Gavril looked around, he observed comfortable but very basic simplicity. To one side, a pallet bed had been formed on a shelf of rock, the moss and bracken covered in a layer of furs. As her feet touched the floor, Aaleahya had watched him. Gavril could feel the uncertainty in her mind, as with a smile, she approached him.

As Aaleahya dipped her eyes, Gavril realised that she felt embarrassed about this place. Her sanctuary. Her home. So it lacked the fine furnishings of his own home in Cymru or the 'lodge' in which he was a guest, but it did not matter. The Pack had profited from the Industrial Revolution, as it would be known but that had not always been the case. Well cared for slate miners worked harder and thus, both they and the Pack benefitted.

He suppressed a groan as her lithe body pressed against him and he could feel her legs parting.

"Never feel shame for who and what you are, my love. A cave or a mansion makes no difference to me. This is your place and that is all that matters."

He had no intent on tupping her against a wall. Lifting her into his arms, he walked the short distance to her fur covered pallet. Laying Aaleahya down gently, he knelt by the side of the pallet. For the feeling of peace that she had brought me, Gavril wanted this night to have the right memories for them both.

One hand caressing her face, the other eased the simple blouse she wore upwards, revealing her slender form. Slipping his hand behind her head Gavril lifted her torso gently, easing the scrap of fabric out of the way. Her skirt next. The decorations tinkling softly as the red fabric formed a puddle at the end of the bed. Gavril smiled.

Seeing Aaleahya's eyes turn to the gold colour of her wolf, as she tried to push the buttons of his shirt through the holes, his own grumble was one of content as she ripped them from the material. The sounds of the buttons hitting the stone echoed in the cave. Then she was running her fingers along his masculine chest tracing the ridges of his ribs and stomach, as she stared at the muscles, licking her lips involuntarily or perhaps it was from the want that seemed to perfume the air. The words 'mine' were echoing in Gavril's mind loud and clear. For this one night, for herself, Aaleahya allowed herself to dream that this magnificent male might be hers to keep. One night but it would suffice. She traced a circle around the brown flat discs on Gavril's chest, knowing that she was smiling when Gavril gave a sharp intake of breath; a sound coming from this virile male, which told her that her efforts were welcome. There was a power in knowing that her touch was giving him pleasure.

As Aaleahya's scent changed, Gavril's own wolf knew her wolf wanted more, and he was more than happy to oblige, as Gavril felt his eyes change to the gold of his wolf. Growling, Gavril's left hand reached for Aaleahya's breasts as his right slipped between her thighs, his fingers exploring the warmth, the liquid rush of her arousal. Growling again, Gavril's head followed his right hand as he inhaled the scent of his Mate before tasting the honeyed sweetness of her core. Her arousal filled his senses like a drug. Her soft cry as his tongue drank in her arousal only served to push him further.

Raising his head, watching his Mate, Gavril switched his attention to her breasts, his mouth drawing her nipples to sharp peaks in turn while his fingers tugged and massaged the ever more tender flesh. Her whimper for more was all he needed. Withdrawing his fingers, he kicked free of his pants before manoeuvring himself to position above Aaleahya. His knee pushed her thighs wider apart as his head dipped again, and he feasted again on her nipples, rosy, flushed with blood from his earlier attentions.

With a howl of pleasure, he drove himself into Aaleahya's core, her own scream echoing his howl.

Aaleahya had known that the first time would either be a time of pleasure or a time of pain. She had heard enough stories from other Roma girls of what it was like to be forced, but this was different. Even if this male was not hers to keep, she could give him this one thing that was for him. She could give him … whatever it was that she needed to give to this male, to her Mate.

What was her Mate is doing to her, what is he making her feel, she wondered to herself? The touching and licking was driving her wolf wild, leaving her whimpering for more from him. She could feel his strong nimble fingers on her breast. His warm mouth was suckling, bringing her nipples to stiff peaks. The sensations! His fingers tugged on her swollen flesh, the pleasure-pain of his fingers making her core tighten and heat with liquid warmth. She could smell her own arousal heavy in the air, all the sensations had her whimpering with need.

Aaleahya watched with glazed eyes as Gavril kicked free of his britches, inhaling deeply as she gasped seeing his erection jutting from body. His mouth was once again on her nipples going from one to the other. She heard him howl as he pushed inside her tight core and she released her own scream at the intrusion. He stopped a moment and let her get accustomed to his width and girth. Wrapping her long legs around Gavril's waist, Aaleahya lifted her hips towards his as her Mate leant in, kissing her, and devouring her mouth with his. He moved slowly at first but she growled, moving her hips faster and harder against him, letting him know that he didn't need to hold back, that she would meet him with exactly the same passion.

Aaleahya's scream coupled with the tightness surrounding him, demonstrated to Gavril that she had managed to escape the fate of so many at the hands of men like his host and the drunken dinner guest. Pausing, to let her flesh become more accustomed to the feel of intrusion, again, the scent of her wolf told him that, inexperience be damned, her wolf wanted more, and her wolf wanted it hard and feral.

Gavril's own wolf was more than happy with that suggestion. As he dipped his head, his attentions returning to her breasts as he drove hard into her, Gavril heard the start of a soft whine from his Mate. Pausing again, he let her become accustomed to the barrage of sensation.

This time, he explored her mouth, his tongue dancing with her tongue, locking them together, pulling her closer to himself. Releasing her mouth, Gavril's lips nibbled their way around her mouth, teasing, tantalising, before he laved the long column of her neck, the pulsing of her blood beckoning to him. He needed to taste more. Swirling his tongue against her neck, Gavril lowered his head, feeling his fangs lengthen, wanting to mark his Mate, wanting the world to know that she was his. Within him, his wolf howled, shivering in anticipation of this clear and visible demonstration of their possession of their Mate.

Waiting, driving in, withdrawing from Aaleahya, only to drive in again, Gavril could feel her muscles starting to tense. His fingers found the sensitive nub of nerves, pinching at the moment of her climax, as his head dipped down, as his fangs tasted the wine of Aaleahya's veins and the nascent Bond between them flared as their souls wove together, never to be apart.

Feeling Aaleahya's fingers wind into his hair as she screamed her release, coupled with the taste of her blood, filling his mouth, the essence filling his soul with the peace and the calm that was his Mate's gift, Gavril knew that he had received a precious gift indeed.

Raising his head, seeing her eyes dilated from her pleasure, he licked the small wound on her neck closed, knowing that a scar would form from this first taste of her. Leaning on one arm, not wanting to withdraw from her just yet, his hand stroked her face softly, through the edge of her hairline. Gavril lowered his head and kissed her reddened lips, slowly, lingering and tasting, before he returned to just watching her, stroking the soft skin under his fingertips.

The feeling of satiation filled Aaleahya's body as it released its last pulse. She felt his soft tongue licking the bite mark. Her own wolf was lying in surrender just as she had. She felt complete for the first time in her life. Gavril's fingers were gently stroking her face, a feather like touch causing her skin to rise in little bumps all over. His head dipped lower to Aaleahya's, and he was kissing her once again. She could feel him still inside her, and she didn't want him to leave. Clenching her core's muscles, she mewled against his mouth as the sensations raced through her.

Her wolf inside was wanting to bite and mark him also. Moving her head from his lips, her tongue lapped at his shoulder and neck finding just the right place to leave her mark. She pushed Gavril onto his back with him still inside her as she began to move her hips up and down, her hands on his stomach, raking them up his chest, her fingers pinching his nipples as she rode, her hips fluid as if she was riding her own horse. Leaning down, her hair forming a veil as Aaleahya found the mark again smiling against his scented skin. She bit down marking him as her own, drawing his sweet coppery blood into her mouth, murmuring, “You are also mine.”

Gavril couldn’t help but smile as he felt Aaleahya's fangs pierce his neck, and the pull as she took her own drink, his wolf more than happy with the situation. They were both more than happy to be marked by their Mates, to know the pleasure of being joined to another soul.

"I have no problem with that, my love." Gavril murmured at her declaration that she has claimed him. "No problem with that at all."

Taking her lips again, Gavril savoured the taste of his blood on her tongue. "Iti dau inima mea." he murmured, the words of her own language, coming to him as part of their union. "I give you my heart." He repeated in English.

Rolling them to the side, still joined together, Gavril continued to watch his beautiful Mate, his hands on either side of her face, stroking, needing to touch, and needing to feel. He wanted to stay with her, but he knew that he had to return to the home of his host during his stay here. He didn’t want to, but he had to return, if only so that he might prepare for bringing the Pack to this new land, chosen for them by their Goddess.

Aaleahya was realising that one thing about being Mated not only by flesh but by soul is that she could sense and see what was going on through the other’s mind. She could see the turmoil going through his head. He wanted to stay with her but he had obligations he needed to fulfil first, his obligation to the owner of the mansion, to the one who hunted her relentlessly.

She also felt the revulsion from her Mate at the thought of returning there. She laid her hand gently on his shoulder, whispering, “Go my love. I know it is not what you wish to do. But you have others that need you also. Go and do what you must. I will be here waiting for your return.” She kissed him passionately. “Go now before I change my mind.”

Aaleahya’s words and the touch of her lips against his reminded Gavril of a way that he could use his host's prejudice to their advantage, whilst making sure that his Mate would be safe from anyone's interference, in this time of women being perceived as the weaker sex.

Laying a finger against her lips, Gavril smiled. "I have a better idea, my love." Holding her close, he took them both to his own bed in the Pack's house in Cymru. Unwrapping his arms from his Mate, Gavril called one of the female Pack members, and asked her to bring male and female 'travelling' clothing. She returned quickly, her arms full of the frills and furbelows required by a lady of gentle breeding.

Holding the chemise up to Aaleahya, Gavril smiled. "Time to dress you as befits my wife, who will be arriving on the overnight train from England. Just in time to help me start looking for our family's new home and base of operations in the Carpathians."

Aaleahya was clearly stunned to find herself in another land and to be able to smell others similar to her. Gavril called a pack female asking for clothes in which to dress he. Aaleahya squealed when she realised that she was not clothed, growling low at Gavril for not giving her a warning.

As she looked around in awe at the opulence in this domicile, Aaleahya could not help but remember the difference between this place and her cave. She turned her head when the she-wolf brought in some beautiful clothes, gasping in surprise at how soft the material was, and smiling as she threw her arms around her Mate's neck kissing every inch she could reach. She hurriedly pulled on the under garments then looked quizzically over the dress wondering how the fine ladies put these clothes on. Aaleahya was used to the loose blouses and skirts of the peasant not the fine fabric such as these clothes were. She looked at her Mate helplessly then asked him if he could help her to dress.

Gavril had to laugh softly at his Mate's confusion, as it became clear she did not realise just who or what the Cŵn Annwn were, and that Gavril led a Pack, rather than just being on her own,tha as she had been.

However, her irritation at his humour was evident at the tapping foot, whilst she poked at the dress. Picking it up, Gavril helped her into the underskirt, followed by tying the watch-spring cage around her waist. He left out the boned corset, knowing that it would be one restriction too many, before handing her the petticoats. Finally, he passed her the velvet skirt, and its matching bodice.

Standing behind her, as his hands touched her skin, a frisson went through Gavril, and his smile widened. Shifting his hands from her shoulders so that they spanned her waist, Gavril gently kissed Aaleahya's shoulders.

"My love, I think there is something else you should know."

Aaleahya's was shocked when Gavril murmured to her that there was something else she should know. She worried there was another female in his life and, with a soft growl, she considered that she really hated to have to kill one of his pack if that was the case. Walking out of his embrace, hugging herself, she looked up at him, her eyes blazing.

“What else should I know?” Aaleahya demanded of Gavril, the tapping foot returning as evidence of her irritation with his smile.

Before he could tell her, Aaleahya railed at him asking if there was another female, a tirade she couldn’t seem to stop. It was if she was not just quite herself.

Gavril thanked the Goddess that this is not the first time he had been faced with a female Pack member with these symptoms. He knew only too well the meaning of Rule #1 of Longevity: walk with care, particularly if you value your longevity. For a near immortal being, that was saying something.

Holding his hand out to Aaleahya, he had a soft smile on his lips. "Well, there is another female involved, my love, but not, I believe, in the way that you think." Enfolding her hands in his own, Gavril whispered. "Feel, my love, don't look. Just feel."

Aaleahya saw red when Gavril told her there was another female involved but not in the way she was envisioning. It was only when she closed her eyes and heard and felt the little heartbeat within herself that the realisation of what he meant hit her. Opening her eyes, Aaleahya looked to her Mate and with large smile, asked him for confirmation of what she had felt. “I am expecting a little one?”

She wrapped arms around his neck hugging him tightly. “I never thought. Oh, Gavril, please forgive my outburst. I couldn't stop myself.” Aaleahya was laughing and crying at the same time. “I am going to be a mother.”

Allowing the joy he felt at this proof positive that their Mating is true, Gavril returned Aaleahya's embrace. "We are going to be parents, my love."

Wiping the tears of joy from his beautiful Mate’s face, Gavril kissed her long and tenderly, communicating without words his joy that in a matter of hours, he had not only found his Mate, but that his Mate was giving him a gift that he had not thought would be his to cherish and to enjoy. Others in the Pack had produced young. There was no impediment after all. But until he had a Mate, the chances of Gavril sharing this precious gift of parenthood had been unlikely. No more. He would be a father.

"Thank you, my love. Thank you for this blessing that is your gift to give."

Aaleahya would never have guessed that her life would change like it had. Mated and mother to be in a matter of hours. “Does this change things? Gavril, are we still returning to the mansion? I know you need to finish things there, and if you feel I should accompany you I will." Aaleahya saw a mirror and walked towards it, unable to even recognise herself as she looked at the image that was peering back at her. There was a strange woman there, like one of the ladies she had seen at the home of her persecutor. Is this really her? Is this the woman she must be for her Mate?

Gavril saw the way that Aaleahya looked at her reflection in the mirror, garbed as she was in the clothing lady of gentle breeding. As much as his life has changed in the last day, he realised that Aaleahya's had changed even more. No more, at least in public, the free spirit that she had been. Now, she would have to present an appearance of conformity, in a world where the females were not expected to even think for themselves. Yet, his Mate, his Aaleahya, had a role to play: a role given to her by the Goddess.

"I think that finding you was my Goddess' way of telling me that the Pack needs to move. Cymru has changed beyond recognition almost, from the land of my youth, to the industrial landscape it is now. Just as much as you, I need to run within forests and the mountains, so moving is no great hardship."

Gavril moved to the window of the room, looking out over the neat miners' cottages in the distance, and the nascent slag heap which would, one day, become one of many man-made mountains. "At the same time, I want to ensure that those who look to us for protection are not left at the mercy of less honest folk. So, I will need to come back here. Call it prescience, but I would prefer to keep our finances based in England, in London. If the Goddess wants us to move the Pack, it can only be because there will be turmoil, in which lives will be lost, and there will be souls for us to gather."

Turning back to Aaleahya, he held his Mate in his arms, silently begging the Goddess that amongst the souls to be harvested would not be that of his Mate or his child. "I know this is a lot for you to take in. It has been less than a day since we met, and so much has happened." Gavril smiled gently at Aaleahya. "And now, I am asking you to just accept even more change, perhaps even bribing you with pretty clothes." Pressing a kiss to her head, he posed the question on his mind."

"Will you stay at my side, my love? Do you want to stay at my side?"

Aaleahya was thoughtful at Gavril's words. She carried his child now, her Mate's child. Her place was at her side, not just because that was the 'done' thing but because she knew that her Mate would need her. The way that her angel had spoken to her had made it clear that this was not just because this male needed female company. No, the angel had made it clear that she was more to him that a few nights' distraction from his duties.

Coming to stand near to Gavril, she leaned her head against his back, taking in his scent, her eyes seeing for the first time the view beyond the window.

“I could no more leave you, my love, that I could leave half of my own body. I am your Mate, and that means my place is at your side, raising our child so that she will understand what we are and what her own role in our world must be.” Pressing her lips to Gavril’s back, Aaleahya repeated her sentiments, “Whatever the future must bring, my place will always be at your side.”

The relief that Gavril felt at Aaleahya’s decision was apparent to all. With a low howl, he summoned the two in whose care he would entrust his Mate and their child, his own childhood friends and joint Pack Betas, Bran Cadwgan and Owain Cadwaladr. He also requested that the Pack’s Healer, Angharad, the female who had brought clothing for Aaleahya joined them, since he wished her also to accompany his Mate.

"Bran and Owain will accompany us, ostensibly escorting you on the train. I will meet you at the station this morning." Gavril smiled. "You will be tired, of course, having come on the overnight boat and train, all the way from England, with only your personal maid for assistance, particularly given your 'delicate condition'."

"In the meantime, I will join my host for breakfast, and inform him that I have decided to move some of my business interests to the Carpathians, and ask him to suggest property that I might purchase as a home for my wife and family."

Moving to hold Aaleahya close, Gavril kissed her again. "Of course, provided you are happy with this little subterfuge. I want to make sure that no one connects you with the 'gypsy dancer' at dinner tonight. My host mentioned a house in the mountains that had fallen vacant, after the old man who owned it passed away recently. From his description, it would fit in with the image I must present in order for the Pack to function without interference."

Again, Gavril waited for Aaleahya's response to his plans to turn her world upside-down.

Aaleahya felt as if her head were spinning with the speed of change around her. In her heart and soul, she knew that her place was at Gavril’s side, at her Mate’s side, so her nod was to confirm what she felt. “Make your arrangements my love.” She murmured, kissing his cheeks. “You had best go now. I will see you in the morning.”

She watched as Gavril smiled, and disappeared before her eyes. She could feel him still, she realised, and she marvelled that such a thing was possible.

For his part, once more, Gavril found himself in a hunting lodge in the Carpathians, in the room assigned to him. At least his host had learned not to have a servant up waiting for him, he thought, as he tried to compose his mind to rest. Ten hours was all that he needed, and then he would be able to hold his Mate in his arms again.

The following morning, Gavril was not surprised that his host was delighted that Mr Black had decided to purchase the property in the Carpathians that he had suggested. Of course, his delight dampened slightly on hearing that Mrs Black would be joining her husband, having travelled overnight on the train in the company of trusted servants. It went without saying that Mr Black must borrow his own carriage, said his host, to fetch his wife from the station. Gavril had nodded. Yes, that would be appreciated, not least because his wife was, well, you know …

Gavril hid his smile as his host had turned bright red with embarrassment. Perish the thought that the 'p' word was mentioned in polite society. Clearing his throat, his host had suggested that perhaps Mrs Black would prefer to remain in her own rooms for a couple of evenings, since she was sure to be tired from the journey, particularly in her condition …

Nodding, Gavril agreed to his suggestion, whilst relishing the thought of spending time with his Mate and not having to worry that his host would have come up with a new plan to introduce him to others in the area, and demonstrate that he knew a male who had connections with the royal family of England.

When the train pulled into the platform, Gavril was waiting, desperate to see Aaleahya, and at the same time, contemplating why it had felt like a lifetime to be parted from her, rather than a matter of hours. Such was the nature of a new mating, when the Bond was still growing and becoming established. And a child. It was hard to think that two days ago, he had not met his Mate, and now he had both Mate and a child on the way. Gavril knew that Aaleahya had been flashed to the train by Bran, with Owain and Angharad in attendance. With them having a private section on the train, there was little risk of them being seen, but caution was still exercised, particularly with one as precious to the Pack as the Alpha's Mate and child. Still, Gavril could see Aaleahya's tension as she had descended the steps of the train carriage, holding herself carefully, as she tried to accustom herself to the more lavish clothing as befitted the rank society had now assigned to her. Holding out his hands to his Mate, Gavril had smiled at her in reassurance, wanting more than anything to hold her in his arms. Again human society norms dictated that those of their perceived rank did not indulge in such public displays of affection. He had to content himself with pressing a kiss to her gloved hand, before placing her hand on his arm to escort her to the carriage.

Of course, once in the carriage, it was a different matter. Owain had laughed. "We will sit outside, brawd." He had commented. "Give you and Aaleahya some private time." He had shivered dramatically. "Just as well we dressed for the weather." He added, as he climbed up beside the driver, who was looking a tad uncomfortable at being sandwiched between the two tall, large manservants of his host's guest.

Angharad had laughed. "I shall sit inside." She declared. "You can freeze out there. I am going to take a nap. Trust me, Gavril, I shall be too busy thinking of what I must do to establish a new herbal garden in this house you are buying to care what you and Aaleahya do …" She laughed again, a light sight, demonstrating her personality. "… Within reason, of course."

Gavril's focus was already on his Mate. Wordlessly, he had communicated down their Mating Bond how he admired her, loved her, and had missed her even for such as short separation. For her part, Aaleahya relaxed in his arms. Her finger drew circles on his chest as she posed the question on her mind. "This new house you are buying, will I be permitted to use my own Roma clothes when I can't be observed, my Lord." She gestured to the outfit she was wearing, a supposedly comfortable travelling dress. "This is all very well and good, but it is constricting. I don't want our child to be squashed." She smiled in amusement at her Mate. "I promise that when I must, I will play the part of your lady, but just once in a while."

Gavril had taken her hand. Removing her glove, he had kissed each finger, sucking slightly on the fingertip. "You may dress how you wish, my love." He confirmed. "Whilst, yes, there are occasions when you must look the part of a lady of wealth, I, too, would prefer you to be comfortable. We may have to pretend to be human, but we are also practical.

All too soon, they arrived at the Lodge. Aaleahya shivered slightly, recalling the previous evening and the way that one of the guests had thought that he might just avail himself of her body, because she was 'only' a Roma. "Fear not, my love. You are Mrs Black, the heavily pregnant wife of Gabriel Black." Gavril reminded her. "No one will touch you, and for a male to approach you without my permission would be considered very bad form indeed."

Sure enough, their host had been awaiting their arrival and greeted them on the steps of his home. A perfunctory pressing of lips to her gloved hand was all the greeting he made, before he turned them over to his housekeeper. He had had Mr Black's possessions moved to another, larger room, in anticipation of their arrival. Gavril nodded to Bran and Owain, who carried Aaleahya's trunk between them. His mind-linked message to them was succinct, asking them to check the room and then to stand guard on the door. He needed Aaleahya to rest. He wanted to hold her in his arms whilst she did. Knowing his friends would bar entry to all made that much easier.

Two days, and so much had changed already. What more could there be to come?

Diary extract: Gavril Dracul Negrescu

With Aaleahya's pregnancy becoming more and more conspicuous, it was essential that I concluded the purchase of our new home, and that we moved away from the prying eyes of our host, and now, my business partner.

He believed that I had wished to diversify my interests, and had thus bought into the large inn that he ran in the Carpathian Mountains. I had explained that my family had come from the Welsh mountains, and this seemed a way that I could both satisfy my business needs and maintain some sort of link with my origins. Yada, yada, yada. The man was becoming more irritating, the more I had to deal with him.

Of greater importance to me was that our new home should be ready before Aaleahya was due to give birth to our first child. Our new home was substantial, by any standards, but it had been chosen for the simple reason that its size and the size of the estate that came with it was sufficient for the whole Pack to stay, if needs be, and also sufficient that, in this land which was not friendly to wolves, we still had space to run, and space to cement the bonds of Pack.

There were gardens, so that there was no need for Aaleahya to wander far, if she did not wish to do so. I ensured that her beloved Bella, the horse she had been riding when I had met her, had a place in the refitted stables. In short, if there was anything I could do to make my Mate feel more comfortable in this world in which she found herself, I was prepared to do it or have it done.

Then, a matter of weeks before the birth, Aaleahya saw me harvest a soul for the first time. My, now, former business partner had ordered another wolf hunt. His lupari made the mistake of allowing their hunt to cross into our lands. At that point, all bets were off. This land was belonged to our pack. It was for us so that we might run in safety without having to worry about being hunted. That on its own was not enough for my business partner to die. It was the very way that he felt it was acceptable to conduct his affairs. He was 'better' than his employees and dependents. They should be glad of their jobs, of their livelihoods, as grim as they were. When threatened with eviction, they should be glad that he gave them a second chance to work themselves, almost to death. For all these things and more, he was to die.

CHAPTER 2: CHANGING TIMES

1877: The regions which used to be individual states such Aaleahya's homeland of Dacia have formed into an independent country, gaining their independence from the Ottoman Empire. Does that mean more peace, or less?

Gavril contemplated the flames burning in the fireplace in his study. The thick curtains had been drawn against the chill in the air, and as he put pen to paper in a journal, and awaited the birth of his daughter, he couldn't help but wonder how all these changes around them will impact on her, and other younglings.

Of course, as Cŵn Annwn, crossed with werewolf, their daughter's longevity would be a bit longer than the average human and thus, she will only be considered a child by the time the century changes as humans measure the years.

Still a father can ponder.

It is all very well having to conform to society norms, which in the time that the Pack moved to the Carpathian Mountains, were perhaps even more strict in terms of what should and shouldn't be done. However, when it comes down to it, Gavril was Alpha of the Cŵn Annwn. One of their three forms is that of wolves. And wolves need to run, as a Pack.

Once he had confirmed the purchase of our new home, and sorted out the details of the business partnership that 'Gabriel Black' had with his former host in this area, Gavril knew he needed to take the Pack for a run. It would not be long before a run would become difficult for Aaleahya. Already, by the time they moved into our new home, her pregnancy was very noticeable when she was in her human form. In her wolf form, it was not so much, and certainly, it seemed as if she could move easier in her wolf form.

They waited until early evening, so that there was enough light for them to familiarise themselves with the terrain of the Pack's new home, both in daylight and in darkness. This was not a hunt for food, or for souls. It was a run for pleasure and for the enjoyment of being Pack.

Shame that Gavril's business partner had to spoil it.

Damn fool had decided to let his lupari have another go at organising a wolf hunt. He was determined to catch this rogue wolf whom he claimed had devastated his livestock herds. Given that said 'rogue wolf' was heavily pregnant and hadn't been out on a decent run in weeks, Gavril doubted his Mate was to blame. Still, when they heard the hounds, it did not take the brains of a genius to realise what was happening. It meant they had a quandary.

In the few weeks that Gavril had been working closely with the man, it had also become obvious that his attitude made him a prime candidate for a soul harvest: the way he conducted his business affairs, the way his tenants were made to suffer for the mistakes of others, the levels of desperation Gavril had seen amongst his employees. All these things added up against him. That he had repeatedly tried to kill Gavril's Mate? That was personal, but still as relevant.

Their duty had to come before their pleasure.

While Angharad led the lupari on a merry chase, the rest of the Pack cornered Gavril's business partner. The stink of fear that came off his sweat was almost nauseating in its sweetness. He may not have known the identity of his attackers, but he did know that four wolves against one human was not likely to go in his favour. Then his horror was compounded, when Gavril shifted to his human form. Cowering, with his back against a tree, he begged for an explanation, as Gavril stalked towards him, wearing just his traditional leather trousers. He could see his business partner, and yet it was not that man. It was someone ... something, different.

Yes, he was right there.

"You have been judged, my friend." Gavril informed him. "For your crimes against your fellow man, you must pay the price demanded by the Goddess."

"What do you mean, Black? Of which crimes do you speak? I have killed no one." He stammered.

Interesting that he should immediately think that they had come because he had killed someone.

"It is not my decision to make." Gavril smiled. Pushing him back against the tree, Gavril forced his head to one side, baring his neck. His scream as Gavril sank his fangs into his neck, taking in his essence, was silenced quickly. Calling Angharad back to the mansion, Gavril left his body to be found, first cleaning and healing any trace of the neck wound. Instead Gavril's erstwhile host was left with a broken neck, a common enough accidental death in a forest such as this.

"Take care of my Mate." he ordered the others. "I will take this one to the Goddess now. The less I soil myself with his essence, the better."

It did not occur to him until later, that this was the first time Aaleahya had seen him take a soul.

The man's essence sat within Gavril like a bad meal, leaving a sour taste in his mouth. Since becoming Alpha, he had harvested many forms of evil to convey them to his Goddess, but this one? Gavril supposed it could be argued that if he had NOT known the effect of what he did, it would have been a mitigating circumstance. But he knew. By the Goddess, did he know!

When Gavril returned home, having delivered the soul to his Goddess, he found that he needed more than ever to hold his Mate in his arms, and to feel the peace and calm that was her gift to him.

Only a few weeks, and their child would be born. It was quite a thought, and something they both anticipated eagerly.

- x –

Aaleahya was humming to herself as she wandered around the gardens of her new home. It still surprised her, this ease with which her Mate had purchased a home for the Pack, and finding out that they were a Pack, a tribe like the one into which she had been born herself. This home that Gavril had bought seemed to be like a palace, but in reality, it was perfect for the Pack, with rooms for all the couples and their own children. With a smile, Aaleahya patted her own substantial belly. Her little girl would be due any day, she knew, as her belly hindered her movements. Her walk had changed to a waddle as she moved. Her own gift from the Goddess, the ability to grow and accelerate the growth of plants had increased along with her pregnant body, hence her pleasure in wandering through the gardens.

Thinking about Gavril, Aaleahya recalled the day she had watched him harvest a soul for the first time, since it was the day that she started to appreciate what her role in her Mate's life meant in truth. When Gavril had returned from the Goddess, the smell of evil was heavy around him, and Aaleahya realised that she could smell the evil taint in his blood. She had laid a hand on his arms, and then flashing her clothes away, she had stood before him, her belly protruding out with their child. She placed his hands on her belly so that he could feel the treasure that they had created together. As she did so, Aaleahya could feel the residual taint leaving her Mate, feel it being funnelled through her and her own light erasing it. There was something though, something more, about their daughter. Call it a foretelling, Aaleahya didn't know, but it seemed to her that their child was destined for great things, like her father. She had smiled at Gavril. "I think our daughter is going to make a name for herself helping others as she grows older."

Gavril had smiled at her words, conscious that he could feel the innocence and goodness of their daughter's soul radiating from his Mate's womb. Yet that feeling was tempered. Something was in the air; the world was changing, and for just a second, Gavril felt a frisson of cold down his spine. Silently, he prayed to his Goddess. Of all the souls that he would harvest, he begged that the souls of his Mate and daughter would not be amongst them.

The call came when Aaleahya was enjoying the late sunshine, taking in the fragrance of the rose garden. She had planted it with Gallica roses, their perfumes heavy in the air, made richer from the warmth of the sun. Bending slightly to snip at one faded flower, the sharp pain caught her by surprise. "Gavril …" Her scream was both mental and physical. "Something is wrong. I need you. I am in the rose garden."

Her Mate was at her side in seconds, coming swiftly to her side and taking in the confusion in her eyes, the certainty that something was wrong. Surely this pain couldn't be normal? Scooping her into his arms, Gavril carried her to their rooms, not wishing to flash them there in the face of the fear and tension radiating from his Mate. It was not the first time he had observed a member of his Pack giving birth, but he did realise that it was Aaleahya's first pregnancy. Having lived away from her tribe for several years, she may not be familiar with the way things would progress. Projecting assurance down their Mating Bond, he laid her gently on the bed which Angharad had prepared. "Our daughter is ready to be born, my love." He murmured, seeking to calm her nerves.

Aaleahya seemed reassured that Angharad would be attending the birth. In the weeks since she had first met the Cŵn Annwn Healer, they had become firm friends. It would help ease her concerns to have a friend present, as Angharad had well known. Another pain ripped through Aaleahya's body, and her back felt as if it were on fire. She curled slightly in an attempt to ease the pain, as her body took over the process, the contractions coming faster and stronger. The urge to push was strong. Angharad nodded, having checked Aaleahya's body for progress. Smiling at them both, she announced. "It is time, my Alpha. Your young one will be with us shortly."

Aaleahya clenched her teeth, sweat seeming to pour from her face. She wanted to switch to her wolf, but felt that if she did so at this stage, it might harm her child. At Angharad's words, she bore down, pushing with all her might to help bring their daughter into the world. She pushed until she felt she could push no more, knowing that the pressure of the child's head between her legs meant that it would be soon, very soon. Angharad went to the bottom of the bed, telling Aaleahya to bring her knees up close to her head if she could and spread them wide. Aaleahya tried to focus on her words and do as she had been told, as yet another contraction hit her. She cried out in pain, as she felt a sharp sting of tearing tissue as the head of her child crowned.

Gavril took her hand to give her comfort. Aaleahya bit her lip, wanting to show her Mate that she could be strong for him. As she felt the urge to push again, Aaleahya grabbed underneath her legs, trying to raise her knees further. Her face was scrunched up and her body felt soaked with sweat and blood. She heard a pop and then the pain was gone, and her daughter was being caught by Gavril. Aaleahya was laughing and crying at the same time, as Gavril swatted his daughter's bottom, to force her to breathe. She was so beautiful, Aaleahya thought with the love of a mother for her newborn. Wanting to reach out her arms, Aaleahya was surprised to find her arms felt weak, as they fell to her sides. Then darkness.

"Gavril, something is not right. I need your help." Angharad's voice was sharp. Gavril placed his daughter in the crib by the bed and watched as Angharad pressed forcefully on Aaleahya's deflated belly, muttering a curse under her breath. "She has not expelled the afterbirth. Your Mate needs our help. She's stopped pushing." Gently, the Healer inserted her hand and forearm into the birth canal. The blood pooling on the bedclothes was a sight for concern. Gavril was used to the sight of blood, given the number of battlefields on which had had harvested souls, but this was different. This was a battle to save the life of his Mate. Angharad's triumphant cry as she tugged the afterbirth loose was followed by her muttered swearing. "Too much blood, Alpha. I need you to support your Mate and help me to stop this."

Instantly, Gavril's mind forced the link wider between his mind and that of Aaleahya. He forced her to see the image of their daughter lying in the crib. He pushed the love he felt for her, willing her to come back to him. Another part of his mind sent energy to support Angharad's work. Surgeon, they would call them in the modern age, for what they had to do now. His mind worked to cauterise, to seal off the flow of blood from damaged vessels, to repair the damage caused by the afterbirth refusing to come loose naturally.

"Stay with me, inima mea. Don't leave me now. Not when I have only just found you." He poured his love down their Bond, willing, hoping that Aaleahya would hear him. The Goddess could not have brought her into his life just to take her from him, Gavril thought. "Don't leave our daughter without her mother. She needs you. We both need you." His words were like a chant, flowing through his Mate's mind, even as he knew that physically, they had stopped the bleeding. But, was it enough. Removing one hand from Aaleahya's forehead, Gavril used his own fangs to tear into his wrist, bringing the vein close to Aaleahya's mouth. It was the only thing that he could think to do now. Would it be enough?

Aaleahya could hear the distant crying of her daughter and she heard Gavril through their link, telling her to come back. She was so tired, but the crying of their child brought her around. She felt pressure on her belly and then the pressure eased. She could hear Gavril begging her to not leave them. Leave? She wasn't going anywhere; she was just tired, wanting to embrace the calm of sleep.

A sweet tangy coppery taste filled her mouth as her Mate's life blood flowed down her throat. She could feel the power starting to grow inside her. She was no longer tired and wanted to open her eyes and hold her daughter. As her eyes fluttered open, she was staring into a vast pool of dark brown eyes, filled with love and concern. "Good day, my Lord." She smiled weakly. "I did it. I gave you our daughter. How is she? I would like to hold her."

Aaleahya could hear her child's insistent crying indicating her hunger. The sound was having an effect on her, as her nipples hardened with each cry from the newborn. Gavril placed the baby in Aaleahya's arm and she held the baby to her breast. The child began to suckle instantly having no problem at all. Aaleahya could feel each tug as she suckled, and could not help but think that this sensation was so different to when her Mate suckled her breasts. She kissed the top of the head, noticing a soft spot where her skull was no fully together. She looked at her Mate, asking him if this was natural. It was her first child and she hoped that it was the first of many more to come. As Aaleahya looked up at her Mate, the light of love that she felt for her family, for her Pack, shone in her eyes.

Gavril could see the exhaustion in Aaleahya's face. Given the amount of blood she had lost, it was not surprising that she was tired and wanted to sleep. That the sleep would have been the sleep of death was not something that he wanted to consider and it was certainly not something that he would tell her now. For that matter, telling her of the repairs to her womb that he had to make, repairs which might prevent a natural conception, were not his priority either. All that didn't matter. He had his Mate and he had his daughter.

Give both a gentle kiss, Gavril suggested that he moved them both to his own room so that Aaleahya might change into fresh, dry garments and be more comfortable. It would also remove them from the smell of blood in the air. Gavril didn't want to tell Aaleahya how close it had come, how close to losing her.

Smiling at them both, he asked her the most pressing question of all, at least for the moment. "So what are we going to name our little angel?"

With their daughter still nursing when Gavril picked them up, Aaleahya smiled and she recalled the name she had wanted for her daughter.

"Ekaterina. It means innocent in my language, but if you would like to call her something else, then please tell me what you would have named her." One thing puzzled Aaleahya. She could recall the smell of blood in the room, but could not work out from where it had come. This was her first child and she had not been around others in the tribe when they bore a child.

Gavril smiled at the suggestion of a name for their daughter. "Ekaterina mic Daciana-Negrescu. Such a big name for such a little angel." Placing his Mate and daughter down on the bed, he kissed her again, his lips lingering, communicating his love for her. "Cati, we would say in my native tongue, our own little kitten, born to a pair of wolves." He kissed Aaleahya again. "Thank you for the gift of my daughter." He laughed. "I can't believe that I am a father."

CHAPTER 3: A GROWING FAMILY

The biggest problem for a Pack of Cŵn Annwn living as humans, in the human world, is that eventually, the locals notice little details such as the fact that they don't age, they don't appear to suffer from the usual maladies that affects humans, that they are good at what they do, whether than it hunting, riding or fighting.

It leaves the Pack with two choices. They can either remove the evidence and witnesses, which is not their first choice, particularly if an innocent soul is involved. The other option is that they integrate with the local population.

Yes, the humans are let in on the secret; they know that their neighbours are 'different'. They are permitted to know that there may be more to their neighbours than meets the eye, but that the Pack are there to protect. Rather than be seen as something to be feared, they become a treasured part of their community. They Pack helps, they offer succour, they protect those who look to them. They take pride in what they do, because those that they protect have given them a sacred trust.

Still, it is very amusing when their human friends will tell outsiders that Gavril, for example, is the son of the man who bought Negrescu Hall as the Pack home became known. How else could you explain the fact that he had not aged? However, one thing remained. Woe betide anyone who thinks that they can harm those who look to the Pack for protection. Just because the Pack chooses to live in peace does not mean that they are a peaceful species.

They are harvesters of souls. Never forget that.

Gavril would often reflect that laughter is the best medicine and smile at the memory of Ekaterina's baptism. To appear a part of the community, it had been a Pack tradition to have the young blessed in whatever religious faith predominated in an area. That meant chapel in Wales, but it was Roman Catholic in their new home.

The only problem was that Ekaterina did not like the cold water that was dribbled on her head by the priest and promptly relocated herself from the priest's arms to her mother's arms. The look on the young priest's face was a classic, particularly as he was new to the area. The Pack's guests, both human and Pack, didn't help, because there were smothered laughs all around, since they knew what had happened.

It didn't hurt that the young priest was open minded, and was willing to accept Gavril's word that they were not some spawn of Satan. He realised that it was actually in his flock's interest to have someone looking out for them. Gavril had smiled again, suspecting with some truth that there were be many an evening spent in theological debate. Many an evening did pass that way and it was interesting to discover that a human priest did not differ that much from a Cŵn Annwn when the need to protect came into play.

He was killed in WW2, one of the many friends of the Pack lost, still trying to protect those who looked to him. That was war, and a waste of a good human.

- x –

Gavril would also recollect the day that his daughter found her protector in another young member of the Pack. At six months old, she was trying to walk already. She was crawling at three months. The Pack loved her dearly and she had found her own personal guard who accompanied her everywhere. Aaleahya had told him how the youngling had tried to bully the younger Ekaterina only to find that the Pack's 'Princess' could bite back. Aaleahya had laughed telling Gavril the tale, and how she had told the youngling, Sandu, that if he tried pulling a stunt like that again, she would thrash him herself. Without a doubt, Ekaterina would be a fighter, but then that was hardly surprising, given her parentage.

However, since then, Sandu became her personal protector and growled in warning if anyone tried to approach his charge. He would bare his teeth even at her sire, his own Alpha, which demonstrated to Gavril and Aaleahya that the bond between Sandu and Ekaterina perhaps went deeper than just the protector of their daughter.

Aaleahya admitted that it surprised her each day watching her daughter develop so quickly. It did not seem long before she had gone from crawling to walking, or another favourite activity of taking rides on her mother's trusted horse, Bella.

Ekaterina would reach a hand out to Bella, and demand that "Mama, ride.". Aaleahya would smile and reply that yes, they would ride. It would be a slow and cautious ride around the garden, with Sandu not that far behind, taking care not to spook the horse that his charge rode with her dam.

Gavril had found Sandu's protective nature amusing, but at the same time, he could not help but wonder why the Goddess chose to reveal the nature of the link between his daughter and her protector. There was little doubt in his mind. When Ekaterina and Sandu were mature, they would be Bonded Mates. Why it was essential for them to know this now? Well, that was the mystery.

Perhaps the clue might have been in the way that the world was changing around them. The English Royal family was following a tried and trusted dynastic pattern and had married into most of the royal families of Europe. The Queen of England had become a recluse after the death of her beloved Albert. But all those family bonds meant little in the face of the acquisition of power. Russia was a case in point. Time and time again, Gavril led his Pack into Russia, harvesting those who would harm their fellow man. That such individuals fell on both sides of the political divide only reflected those changes elsewhere.

Gone were the days when evil and greed were the purview of the wealthy. Now it was the former 'downtrodden masses' who might display evil and greed. Sometimes Aaleahya would accompany him and there came a time when, as she matured, that Ekaterina would ask to come with her sire, despite his reluctance to expose her inherent good nature to such evil. As Gavril put it, to see an adult laugh at the fear or tears of a young girl before he attacked her was not something that he wished his own daughter to witness. The brutality of a soul harvest was something he would not wish her to witness and yet, she was Cŵn Annwn. He could not hide from her what was within her very nature, as much as he wanted to do.

Aaleahya had noticed also the change around them, a miasma of pain and suffering of the desire to inflict pain and suffering on others. She knew that her Mate was trying to protect them all. For her own part, Aaleahya was being cautious. The Roma had always had a different status in the land of her birth, but she was now Mated. For all intents and purpose, she was a native of her Mate's land, but there were still those who might try to profit with the authorities in revealing the truth, or for that matter, tell a member of a race seen as slaves by many, that their silence had a price.

Gavril would sit back in his chair, the door of his study open, listening to the sound of younger voices in the gardens. He would listen to the giggles and whispers and wonder where the time had gone. It seemed only yesterday that his daughter had been a babe in arms. He would look up at the painting hanging in his study, of Aaleahya and Ekaterina sitting in the garden and he would thank his Goddess again for the gift that he had been given.

For her part, Aaleahya knew that Ekaterina had asked her sire if she might accompany him during the soul harvests. It was becoming harder to tell her no. Aaleahya had accompanied her Mate, and had seen the evil that was lurking just out of reach. It seemed to her that the souls he was collecting were becoming darker. Her own powers to cleanse the taint were coming forth more and more often to clean that stain from her Mate. She knew the time would come when Ekaterina's own powers would reach adult strength, even as her own continued to grow in order for her to support her Mate. As much as Aaleahya wanted to protect her little girl, the fact was that

Kat was no longer little. It turned her mind to thoughts of perhaps having another child. There was a need in her to hear the sweet sounds of younglings around her.

Gavril had dreaded the day when Aaleahya might broach the subject of having another child. His heart bled for his beautiful Mate, who should have had a houseful of children. Instead, he had to find a way of telling her that because of the problems from Kat's birth, all those years ago, and the desperate measures that he had to take to stop her from bleeding to death, it meant the chances of her conceiving naturally were virtually zero. Holding his Mate close one night, he had wondered how to broach the subject, but then Aaleahya was his Mate for a good reason. She could feel his turmoil, and knew that there was something which caused him pain. Such was her nature, her first instinct was not anger at what Gavril had done, but rather it was to sooth him.

"I don't want to risk losing you, inima mea." Gavril had murmured into her hair. "It was so close the last time. I nearly lost you." He repeated what was, after all, the truth. Had Angharad not been as experienced as she was or had he not had to deal with severe injuries before, Gavril acknowledged the hard truth: he might have lost his Mate and the light of his life.

Aaleahya knew that her Mate was trying to be gentle with her and she knew deep down that they would not be able to have more children, thus making Kat their one and only child who must be protected. She tried to hide her tears from her Mate but he lifted her chin up, kissing away the tears which were falling.

"I have you, my love and we have our little Kat." Gavril murmured as he kissed her tears. "And whilst natural conception may be impossible, who knows what might happen in the future. Perhaps the Goddess will be gracious and grant us other young.

Diary Extract: Gavril Dracul Negrescu

War. The world thought that, with the end of the Great War in 1918, the conflict to end all conflicts, that we would see peace for all time. The killing fields of Northern Europe, whilst a plentiful source of souls for the Cŵn Annwn to harvest, were still a harsh sight. In the time that I have walked these lands, I have seen conflict after conflict. What is it that causes men, and women, to desire the things that belong to another, be it gold or gems, be it land. To me, the fact that the Cŵn Annwn lack neither is almost a side effect. Knowing the truth behind a soul's intentions means we cannot take advantage of those humans who live around us. It would be, as I have described before, like a constant feeling of indigestion. When I entered into a business partnership with a man from the Carpathian Mountains in 1877, the year that my daughter was born, I did so because he had a business that worked well with the needs of my Pack. I had no idea at the time that he would become a soul for me to harvest, thus making me the sole owner of our former partnership businesses.

The net result was that, by the time war broke out again in Europe and spread again around the world, the Negrescu Cŵn Annwn were wealthy in any way man would care to measure.

Politics is starting to have an impact, even in our corner of the Carpathians. In many respects, I and the Pack, are protected by the fact that locally, it is known that I am neither Christian, nor Jewish nor any of the other local nationalities. For Aaleahya, it is perhaps a bit more difficult, with the rising nationalistic attitudes potentially making it difficult for her, with her Roma blood, even if she chose not to live with them. Instead we have let it be known that we are of Welsh origin.

And, yes, I have paid the appropriate bribes where needed. It is ironic that, as a harvester of souls, I am seeing more and more a switch in the definition of evil. Wealth and evil are no longer an exclusive pairing. Greed, envy, coveting another's property. All these things are hiding beneath those nationalistic attitudes.

After the horrors of the Great War, it would be nice to see some peace, but I was not holding my breath. I will need to put a protection strategy in place, not just for those humans who look to us, but for my own Pack. I thanked the Goddess that we are able to do this.

I would soon find the true cost of war, in a way that would change me forever but for now, all I and my Pack could do was watch and wait for the turmoil we knew was coming.

CHAPTER 4: THE HIDDEN COST OF WAR

Aaleahya had heard the rumours whispered in the winds. Romania had entered into a secret treaty, fighting a war against the Austrian-Hungarian for a piece of territory called Transylvania. She used to visit there with those of her tribe who still lived there. She loved to roam the Carpathian Mountains in her wolf form, running through all the caves hidden on that part of the mountain. The rich plains below the mountains were where most of the Romanians made their homes, with the rich soil making farming a valuable industry.

She loved her visits there, not least because of the many friendships built through the years. Deciding it was time for another visit, she had taken Kat and Sandu with her. The townsfolk were happy to see them. There were new faces, it was true, who didn't know of them, but it was no matter. Their friends knew the truth and that was what mattered. Those were the people who knew that the Cŵn Annwn would protect them. That was what mattered.

Aaleahya had wanted to visit with a specific friend, but to her surprise, Camelia had hustled her into the house, putting a finger to her lips in caution until they were out of sight. "Aaleahya, you must go. We have new people moving into the area and they are not good men. They are talking to many people, asking many questions." She had whispered, as if she feared being overheard, even in the safety of her own home.

Aaleahya had tilted her head in query, seeing the genuine fear in her old friend's eyes. "What sort of questions are they asking?"

"They are asking if we noticed anyone sneaking in, amassing large amounts of money. They are asking who owns the large lodge and who owns the Hunter's Arrow. We tell them nothing." She assured Aaleahya proudly. "You are our friends and we have been friends for many years."

Aaleahya had glanced at Kat, who whilst she was 67 in human years, looked only in her early 20s, as did Sandu. Those who might remember her as a baby or a child were old now, or even dead. "Camelia, don't worry; we will be here for you as we always done." Aaleahya tried to reassure her old friend. She had shaken her head and implored them to stay away.

"Go, hide in the mountains. Something evil is coming and is already rearing its ugly head." Her fear was almost palpable and it was that we decided Aaleahya. As much as she loved visiting her friends, she knew that she could not put them at risk for her selfishness.

Kat was unusually quiet, as was Sandu as they returned to Negrescu Hall. Aaleahya went in search of Gavril, to tell him what Camelia had said and also to report the feeling of oppression and darkness that she had felt around the once cheerful town. She found him in a sombre frame of mind. Wrapping her arms around him, she felt the dark taint leave him once again.

"You went into Hungary, didn't you?" She asked him as he nodded his head. Gavril asked his Mate where she had been. Of greater concern was the frown on her Mate's face, a frown which even Kat was noticing.

Gavril sighed. His first instinct was to protect both his daughter and his Mate, but he knew that this was impossible. His Mate would know that he was hiding the truth from her and it would not take Kat long to work it out herself. And, where Kat went, Sandu would follow, fulfilling the duty Gavril had given him as a pup.

"War is happening. The Great War was not the 'war to end all wars' after all. The politics of Germany have spilled out. The evil in the hearts and souls of their leaders is staggering, even for me. Their fellow man are just cattle, and like cattle, they will be slaughtered as befits the needs of their regime."

Gavril enfolded his Mate and his daughter in his arms. After a brief moment, he reopened his arms, and beckoned to Sandu, before explaining his words further. "They call it the Final Solution. It is a genocidal extermination plan and it puts both of you, Aaleahya and Kat, in danger."

Sandu stood straighter, pulling free from the group embrace. "I will continue to protect them both, my Alpha." He announced formally. "You placed your trust in me. I will not fail you."

Gavril shook his head. "Would that it was that simple, Sandu. These Germans, the National Socialists they call themselves, want to exterminate a whole race. More than one race. My Mate's people, the Roma, are deemed to be a sub-species of human, and therefore they say, must be exterminated, wiped from the world so that their pure 'Aryan' race might take priority. They also wish to exterminate the Jewish race, laying a large part of the blame for Germany's inter-war woes on them. Already, in Hungary, I have seen them being loaded into cattle trucks. Too many for us to rescue or move. I am going to have to bring more of the Pack in from Cymru so that we can do something. If we can save some of the children, at least their existence will offer hope. I am going to bring some of the Pack from New York also, so that we can transfer people there. We can't save them all, but if we can save some…" His words tailed off. The sheer enormity of what his very being as Cŵn Annwn needed to do was staggering.

Aaleahya felt as if her heart stopped for a moment when she heard her Mate describe what he had seen, the extermination of whole races of people who did not meet the requirements of what was considered the superior race. That she herself might be a target did not concern her. What did give her cause to worry was that the only child whom she had been able to give her Mate might be seen as a target, just because she was half-Roma. Listening to the plans being made by Gavril and Kat, she knew that she would be at his side, helping him to save those innocent souls. Then Aaleahya noticed the look passing between Kat and Sandu, and whilst her heart sank at the danger to her daughter, it swelled with pride that Kat would volunteer to place herself in danger for the sake of complete strangers.

Gavril pulled his daughter close and tilted her face to his. The eyes that she had from her mother stared up at him, a spark of defiance visible, prepared if she must to argue that this evacuation plan was something that she had to do. Gavril wanted more than anything to protect her, to cushion his angel from what was happening, but he knew that it would be an impossible task. She was both her mother's child and his. The fact that her very essence was screaming that she could not allow the innocent to be slaughtered showed that only too well.

"I know, my angel." He said quietly. "I know what you must do, and we will work together on this. I will bring in the Cŵn Annwn that you will need to make the transports. We will have to run this almost constantly, if we are to make a difference. We can use the Hunter's Arrow and the Hall as transport points, but we also need to set up a network of points in the villages and mountains. The more the apparent disappearance seem to be happening around the country, with no discernible pattern, the greater our chances of success, and the less risk of us being stopped."

He sighed. "At the moment, the Hungarian and Romanian governments are working with the National Socialists, but if the war changes, if the Nazis decide it suits their purposes to invade, the slaughter will be even greater."

Gavril took comfort in holding his family, Mate, daughter and son by adoption. Yes, Sandu was as much family as Kat, he thought, acknowledging what he had believed when they had been little more than pups. It hurt that there could be only one reason why his angel and her Mate might be so clear so early in their young lives. There was only one reason.

Diary Extract: Gavril Dracul Negrescu (June 1942)

The madness that is War continues to rage around us. Unbelievably, there is denial in the Allied Governments that what I and the rest of my Pack know is happening in places like Auschwitz is taking place. How many lives could be saved if the Nazis are unable to transport their victims to the place, relying as they do on the rail network. But no, the bombing of the rail network in a network of camps in Poland didn't happen. The Poles were the victims of the Nazis too, given that their land was one of the earliest to be invaded. No doubt questions will be asked about this for decades to come.

With my intent to establish an underground railroad of sorts, to attempt to save at least some of the innocent souls of children, even whilst I and my Sentinels continue to hunt down the evil, I found an ally in my old theological debating partner, our local Catholic priest, whose first introduction to the Cŵn Annwn had been his attempt to baptise my little Angel, resulting in her first demonstration of her powers.

We became firm friends after that, spending many an evening over a glass of wine debating the finer points of theology and human belief patterns over the centuries. When he first moved to this area, he was young, only in his early 20s, and fresh from his seminary. He was full of idealism, but relished that he had been assigned to the rural 'backwater' of the Carpathians. It helped that he was open to realise that there was more to the world than he had experienced. So, friends we became, and have stayed, even though now, he is in his 80s, and soon, all too soon, Aaleahya will take his soul to its rest in whatever form of Paradise he will envisage.

However, over time, he had established his own network of friends, other ministers and religious leaders. When I approached him with my plan, his failing eyes lit up with the fire I remembered from his youth. As he coughed, standing, he eased himself over to his desk, grabbing pen, ink and paper.

"I know just the person for you to see, my old friend." His voice was soft, and slightly breathless. "He is a senior Rabbi now, but like me, he believes that there is more to the world than meets the eye. If anyone can convince those at risk to let you transport their children to safety, it will be him."

"Would that I could come with you, Gavril. But, this old body will let me down, and speed is more important than my feeling that I need to be involved. Take this letter to my friend, and work with him. He is old enough that hopefully, he won't be at immediate risk himself but who knows with these intolerant murderers."

He used stronger words to describe the actions of the Nazis, but it would serve little purpose for me to repeat them. Suffice it to say that the fires of an old man were rekindled that night, as between us, we put into place a plan. With his letter in hand, I travelled to see his contact. Time being of the essence, I took the old Rabbi back to my home, to meet with my priest friend. It provided him with the proof that what I had proposed might actually work. Whilst we might only save hundreds, or maybe, just maybe a few thousand children, it would be something. I returned the old Rabbi to his own home, and he set about immediately identifying those who were open enough not to fear that, by exposing their children to me and mine, they were damning them in the eyes of their religion. For the first time since the Nazis started to gain ascendency in Europe, I felt hope that the Cŵn Annwn might be able to make a difference.

We were more than harvesters of evil souls. We had a purpose that our Goddess endorsed wholeheartedly. It mattered not that those we would save from death were not 'her' children. What mattered was that we tried to prevent the loss of innocence, in a truly dark and dismal world.

The first meeting with a selected group of families took place in the Rabbi's home, in a back room, the curtains drawn against prying eyes. The level of fear was almost tangible, given that the effects of the recent laws against Jews were starting to be felt. These families all had relations in other nearby countries, relations who had disappeared. Their families had been told that they had chosen to be relocated. However, none of those families ever heard from the relatives again. In their hearts, they all knew, as did Gavril, that it meant their relatives were dead. Their fear was that it was only a matter of time before their turn came.

When their Rabbi had approached them with a way out, explaining that the Pack were 'different', they had been willing to listen. At that esteemed gentleman's suggestion, Ekaterina, Sandu and Gavril, along with the Sentinels came in together, in the area of the room which the Rabbi had cleared for that very purpose. To their credit, the parents had pushed their children behind them, and faced us, their expressions grim.

Kat had discussed with Gavril how they should manage this initial introduction. Aaleahya had stayed behind at the Hunter's Arrow to organise the 'reception' into the cellars, prior to them moving the children immediately to their newly established Hunter's Arrow in New York State. Kat approached the group of parents, her voice quiet as she explained that, she could understand their fear, since they were trusting total strangers with their children, but she promised that we would ensure no harm came to them. We knew the Rabbi had explained that their children would be taken to a place of safety, but that she would not tell them where that place was. The Pack had to allow for the fact that, if the parents were interrogated, our plans might be revealed. Such a revelation would be catastrophic, and thus would be strictly on a need to know basis.

As Gavril had suspected, Kat's soft voice, and the air of innocence that was her unique gift, won over the parents.

"My father." She indicated Gavril. "He will ensure that no one knows what we are doing here."

Gavril nodded. "There is a group approaching the building from the south of town. My Sentinels and I will ensure that they don't interrupt you, daughter." He noticed the parents' pallor, noticeable even in the dimly lit room, and on faces which were already pale by their genetics. "For all intents and purposes, you are meeting with the Rabbi for some prayer meeting, perhaps for your missing relatives?" Gavril suggested.

The Rabbi nodded. "I can do that. I thank you again, my friend, for what you are prepared to risk for us."

Gavril gave him a brief nod, before glancing at Owain and Bran. Friends from childhood for him, and now his Sentinels. It was their job protect him when he harvested souls, but they also had the ability to harvest as well, after which Gavril would absorb their 'takings', to convey the whole harvest to the Goddess. It was a more efficient way when large numbers of souls were involved.

"I count ten targets for us, daughter. We will endeavour to ensure that they do not find this house, but I suggest you both work quickly. Your mother is waiting for you." Gavril pressed a brief kiss to the top of her head, and left the room. The dark clothing worn by the three of them would allow them to blend into the poorly lit streets around the house, all the better to set their ambush for the would-be attackers.

The streets were quiet, lit only by very occasional small pools of light from the street lamps, as if their valiant attempt might drive back the greater darkness sweeping the land. Gavril and his friends approached the SS group on foot. There was no doubt that they believed they had a target, with the souls of the SS open books for any Cŵn Annwn to read. Their past deeds, their pleasure in what they had done stank to preternatural senses, and Gavril knew that his Sentinels felt the same way. Ten targets, and three Cŵn Annwn. Gavril indicated with hand signals that he would take four, and Owain and Bran could divide the remaining six between them. Rain glistened on the cobbled streets, as they inched forward, surprised that their targets were not making an attempt to hide their approach.

Again with hand signals, Gavril indicated our approach plan. They called it the 'rabbit in the light' approach, as he walked forwards, whilst Bran and Owain hid in the shadows. The sharp order to stop was ignored, of course, resulting in weapons being raised. The officer who appeared to be in command was Gavril's first target. The stink from his soul was enticing, but

Gavril kept the smile from his face. Dipping his shoulders, he let them see what they wanted to see: one man, out after curfew, and most damning of all if what was known to be a Jewish quarter, not wearing the identifying yellow star on his clothing.

"Kill the dog for breaking curfew." The officer laughed as he gave the order.

"It will be my pleasure." Gavril replied in the man's native German, a smile on his own lips for the first time, as he raised his head, allowing his targets to take in for a split second that the dark haired man before them was smiling as his eyes glowed ... red? In the blink of an eye, Gavril was standing behind the man, his arm around his target's throat. "It will be my pleasure." Gavril repeated, as he forced the SS officer's head to one side, and sank his fangs into the man's neck. As Gavril drank deeply, the images of those the officer had beaten, had killed swept through his mind, showing him that this was no simple soldier, but one who truly believed that he was performing a 'pest control' service by exterminating those he saw as inferior to the Aryan race.

As Gavril wiped his lips, he knew that Bran and Owain had taken their first targets down. Three left for him, and all had weapons trained on him. Gavril smiled again. "Cute, gentlemen." Again, Gavril spoke in their native language, "But a waste of effort."

At that point, the three of them found out why Gavril was the Alpha of the Cŵn Annwn, and he consumed three more souls. Looking at the ten bodies, he motioned to my two Sentinels. As each approached him, Gavril took the offered wrist and the requisite sample of their blood for the soul transfer to take place, and the souls leave them and join the four Gavril held so far. Ten souls, all sharing the same delight and pleasure that they would have killed not just adults, but potentially children tonight.

"They knew." he said. "They knew that children would be present. Their eagerness for the kills?" Gavril's Sentinels had worked with him for long enough to share his distaste in what they had read from these killers. The Goddess would enjoy herself indeed with this harvest.

"We need to ensure that these bodies are not found, and we need to find out the source of their knowledge that children would be present. If there is an informant, then both Kat and Sandu would be in danger." Gavril's Sentinels knew that they could never allow that to happen.

They didn't return to the house that night. but straight to the Hunter's Arrow. Kat's smile and Aaleahya's caress restored some of Gavril's humour, but his Mate knew that he needed to offload his harvest sooner rather than later. The longer that he held on to them, the greater the sensation of over-eating would be felt.

"I will be back shortly, my love." Gavril returned Aaleahya's caress. "We can talk then. Did it work?" He asked, curious at the success of this, their first evacuation in this way.

"Yes, Papa, it worked. Fifteen children are now resident at the house in New York State." Kat had a smile on her face.

"Before the next evacuation, I want to find out who informed on what we had planned tonight. That SS group had information that both adults and children were in that house, although they didn't know what we intended to do. Any information of that nature had to come from someone within the group. A leak of that nature could compromise everything that we are trying to do."

Kat and Aaleahya nodded in agreement. "Papa, as much I would wish otherwise, it is probably one of the people whom the Rabbi approached. He told me that he had said only that a meeting was being held. With their synagogue closed down, they have to meet in each other's houses."

That had been Gavril's summation also. This was not going to be an easy undertaking, but undoubtedly, the initial signs were promising. At this stage, it was all they could hope.

It took Gavril nearly a month to track down the identity of the informant, whose actions had resulted in the presence of the SS patrol group near to where we had arranged for that first evacuation. Having harvested the soul of the commander of that group, Gavril knew it had been an informant, but the man had not known the identity of the informant. However, he had known that it was another member of the Jewish community, his soul enjoying the fact that the group he was about to kill had been betrayed by one of their own.

This was not just a case of harvesting an evil soul. There had to be a reason why this individual had betrayed his compatriots, and that was something Gavril had to find. His instructions from his Goddess were quite clear on that matter. As much as part of him, the father in him, wanted revenge on the individual who had put his little Kat in danger, Gavril would not kill until he knew why this person had felt it necessary to go to an organisation such as the SS to reveal a plan to flee the authorities.

Something about the situation just didn't feel right.

It took him a month because first he had to obtain a list of the people contacted by the Rabbi, and then gain access to the SS Headquarters building and specifically to their files on the 'risks' of Jews managing to escape their 'gentle attentions'. The frustrating thing for him was that he had to make a judgement call on whether to harvest the soul of the SS Commandant, or just take his files. He had to decide on the files, because it would be just a tad suspicious for one of their patrol groups to disappear into thin air, and then have the same thing happen to the local Commandant. So, he waited until the man had left his office, and gone to enjoy his dinner, before searching for the information that he required. Well, Gavril decided to take a bit more than just the information that he required. The Commandant's office had held quite a comprehensive list of targets. The smell of carbon on the back of the sheets of paper told Gavril that multiple copies of this document existed, so he would not be able to eliminate the presence of the list completely. However, what he could do was to use the list to target those whom the Cŵn Annwn needed to evacuate from the area as a priority.

So, the traitor. Why had he done it? The man Gavril found that night was sitting in a dark kitchen. A bottle of wine, and the soft sobs told a story of grief and regret. Yes, he had betrayed his compatriots, but only because he had been told that it was either that or his wife and daughter would not be returned to him. It wasn't a case of fearing that they might be taken by the authorities. They had been taken. Gavril knew, from what he had scanned in the Commandant's office, that the man's wife and daughter would not be returning to him. Not now. They had been deported to one of the camps being used by the Nazis to exterminate the local Jewish population.

He had looked up as he became aware of Gavril's presence in the room. "Will you kill me now?" He asked hoarsely. He stood up. "I deserve to die for what I have done. At least then, I will be reunited with my girls, with my lovely wife and daughter." He came closer to Gavril. "Please, kill me now. I can't continue to live with myself for what I have done." He sobbed. "And it was all for nothing. Nothing!" He screamed the last word, his soul's torment in that wailing sound.

"Your actions could have resulted in the deaths of another thirty people." Gavril's voice was cold. At the same time, he could almost understand his rationale. Had it been his own Aaleahya and his Kat in danger, would he have done any different?

Gavril smiled suddenly, as a solution came to him. "I have a suggestion for you. Instead of seeking death, why don't you accept the greater challenge to live?" Gavril took the wine glass from the grieving man's hand. "Restitution instead of death?"

"But I deserve to die for what I have done." He stammered. "I don't deserve a second chance."

"No, you don't, but that is what I am offering you. You lost your wife and your daughter, but in a vain attempt to save them, you betrayed others to the SS. What did you think they would do with that information?" Gavril had the answer even before he spoke. He had been driven by the first stages of grieving. If he had to lose his loved ones, then why should anyone else enjoy having their families around them? "Whatever your reasons, you are now in a position to do some good, because the authorities believe that you would betray your own people. They will use you again, if they think it will serve their purposes."

The man's eyes widened, as he went from sobbing drunk to sober in a matter of minutes. "You would trust me to do this? To misinform them?"

"Do you not feel that you could do this?" Gavril asked him. "I believe that you would be able to do this, and more to the point, when the time comes, know that you will be with your wife and daughter, because restitution has been made. What is your decision?" Gavril was not surprised when he agreed. Handing him the list of potential targets, he suggested the man familiarise himself with them, and endeavour to start his misinformation project.

Whilst having a new purpose would not remove his grief, it did change the essence of his soul. There had been no intent to commit evil, but he had acted in a way that could have sent him down that dark path.

A harvest is never as straightforward as it might appear.

Diary Extract: Gavril Dracul Negrescu (Spring 1944)

The rumours were there again, the same ones that Aaleahya heard when she had visited Transylvania at the start of the war. The authorities wanted to know who in the local area had sympathies with particular groups? Who had been moving money around? Who had links outside of the local area, perhaps even in other countries? Why was it that our particular part of the Carpathians seemed so ... quiet?

The last question was easy enough. Each time an individual had appeared, and tried to cause trouble, or tried to find out if the stories about other creatures and inhabitants of the Carpathians were true? Well, that individual had disappeared. Just because we had made this our home did not mean that we were the only supernatural beings in the area, just as we were not the only ones to be harvesting souls on behalf of our deity. Just as I had seen on the battlefields of the First World War, other deities had sent their own 'teams' into the 'all you can eat buffet' that was a battlefield. For many of them, it was just the soul that mattered. Guilt or innocence, evil or pure. Both were irrelevant. I like to think that I was a bit more discerning.

CHAPTER 5: A THREAT ON THE HORIZON

Without a doubt, the Pack had links outside of the area. With the origins of Gavril's family being in the Welsh mountains and a second base in New York State, definitely that counted as links outside the area, and more importantly for some, they were links with 'enemies', at least as the war progressed. There was a method in the madness. Gavril had guessed how the war was likely to progress, and had moved a significant portion of the Pack's finances out of the country. Money makes the world go round and perhaps even more so in the 'land of the free'. What it meant in practical terms was that either Gavril or one of his Betas would transport the funds out of the country, without using human banks or similar means. Cold, hard, gold was what the Pack used. Secure, but of course, in a war, in great demand from all parties. If they could pin down a source of such wealth and more to the point, ensure that the wealth was diverted their way, well, so much the better. From what Gavril had heard, the war was not going as well as the Nazis had thought it might from their initial successes and they were hungry for more wealth, so that they might use it to develop weapons which might turn the tide back in their favour.

It sickened Gavril that some the gold 'acquired' by the Nazis was callously torn from the dead bodies of the concentration camps. Gold teeth torn from a corpse, then melted and reformed into bars. When Gavril could, he took great delight in harvesting the souls of the camp guards, some of whom were local and had known the initial tranche of incoming prisoners. That they might have grown up with the people whom they slaughtered was nothing to them. The evil in their souls was a cross between having the draw of nectar, coupled with the stench of rot. As many as the Pack harvested, there were always more ready to take their places.

Was that the nature of the human race? It would be easy enough to say that it was, had it not been for those humans whom the Pack protected in the area around the Hunter's Arrow. These were humans who had grown up knowing that the beings who operated the local inn and hostelry were different, but, not least because their priest accepted the Pack also, they saw them as protectors. Ask as many questions of them as the authorities did, and still none of the villagers would say anything about their protectors. Maybe it was self-preservation on their part. They knew that if the Pack was not there to keep them safe from the depredations of both the common solider and the more 'specialised' SS divisions, then there would be no one, and they would be at the mercy of whomever held the reins at the time. So, protect the Pack with their silence they did, even as the Pack protected them from attack.

But the questions continued. And then, in the Spring of 1944, their little corner of the world was invaded. Hungary had tried to form a treaty with the United Kingdom, and strangely enough, the Nazis did not think that this was appropriate behaviour from their former ally. To their minds, if Hungary wished to be allied to the United Kingdom and the USA, then they could take the consequences of their actions. Invasion.

Our little corner of the world was swarming with the grey uniforms of the ordinary soldier, some of whom looked barely young enough to be out of school, let alone fighting a war. With them were the black uniforms of the SS, a group feared even by their own ordinary soldier. Whilst some of them might have been in uniform purely for their age, having grown up in the Hitler Youth Movement, the 'dedication' of the SS was clear to everyone. To them, the Final Solution was just that. It was the means by which the Aryan race would triumph over the lesser humans. The lesser humans. Included in that classification were the people from whom Aaleahya had been born, even if she had not chosen to live with them. The Roma. For Gavril's gentle Mate to see cattle-trucks loaded with her people, and yet unable to help all of them brought a shadow to her eyes. Their daughter's approach was somewhat different. Some of them she and Sandu, working with both Welsh and American contingents from the Pack, managed to save. Not all, but at least some of them. But we had to be more careful each day.

Because, when it came down to it, the questions were still being asked.

April 1944

Troop billeting. The curse of being in occupied territories. Even more of a curse when your homes include a multi-room inn and a large mansion. Gavril could not deny being a person of affluence in the local area, not when his home was so well known. However, the risk involved in having enemy troops in such close proximity to the basement which Kat and Sandu used to transport evacuees was substantial. The risk to his Mate was also significant, given that her looks and free attitude marked her as Roma, even if she had chosen not to live as one of them.

But it was inevitable, and Gavril was not surprised when a clipboard bearing administrator made his arrogant way through the bar, demanding to speak to the owner.

Aaleahya had been down to the market, ostensibly to purchase vegetables, but in reality to listen to the chatter amongst the villagers and from the soldiers as she meandered through the stalls. Returning, she entered the building through the back of the bar, cautious still, not knowing who was around. She could hear Gavril's rich, deep voice talking to another person. Peeking through a crack in the door, she could see a male of small stature demanding to speak with the owner of the inn. The scent of evil hung thick around him, and unconsciously, Aaleahya's lip curled.

"Goddess, it is a German administrator." She recognised the man, but his uniform made it clear that whilst he may have been a native, his sympathies lay with the invaders. Knowing that Sandu and Kat were in the basement with the latest batch of children to be evacuated, she sent a mind-linked message to her daughter in the basement, warning her of the situation in the bar. Remaining in the kitchen for the moment, she could overhear the conversation clearly. Her anger rose a notch as it became clear that the arrogant little man was demanding that they accept a good quantity of German soldiers, whom they would be expected to feed and quarter at the Pack's own expense. Either they gave them the Pack's co-operation, or they would take what they wanted anyway.

Gavril felt his Mate return to the inn with a sense of relief, even as he worked to control his temper in the face of the arrogant turd demanding the two homes registered to him as accommodation for the invading army. Ordinary soldiers were to be quartered at the inn, but they would be expected to 'donate' Negrescu Hall as a local area HQ, quartering SS and Gestapo officers.

"Yes, I own both Negrescu Hall and the Hunter's Arrow." Gavril confirmed to the administrator. He kept his voice cold but still there was a slight tone of challenge. "You have made the position quite clear. One hundred ordinary troops at the inn and officers in my home. When might my family and I expect our 'guests' to arrive? With the war, I am sure you will appreciate that we don't keep all the rooms ready to accept guests. My wife will want to ensure that the rooms are to an appropriate standard."

Aaleahya's temper was boiling as she listened to the implicit threats being made to her Mate. She wanted to rush out and pin the odious little man to the wall, but she felt Gavril's calming pulse through their Mating Bond, informing her that she needed to remain out of sight for now. Clearly, the 'authorities' were looking for a reason to take everything from the Pack.

Hearing Kat and Sandu's steps coming up from the basement, she hurried to them, placing a finger on Kat's lips, stilling her question. Telling her daughter to be silent, Aaleahya motioned for them to return to the basement. Kat's eyes flared in defiance when she caught the scent of the putrid little man, but she obeyed her mother, conscious of the batch of refugees hiding below the floor.

Gavril was trying hard to avoid showing how much the stink of evil from this administrator was apparent to a Cŵn Annwn. He was aware of Kat and Sandu coming up from the basement and knew he had to keep the administrator occupied until they might leave. The chances of avoiding this slug from scrutinising the rooms of the inn were slim, and sure enough that was the demand made. Gritting his teeth, Gavril warned Aaleahya via their

Mating Bond of the man's demand. A message was also sent to Bran and Owain to ensure that there was no trace of the Pack's other activities.

"I believe my wife is in the kitchen at the moment." Gavril explained, indicating the door at the rear of the bar. "If you come with me, we will discuss your requirements with her."

On receipt of Gavril's message, Aaleahya moved a table over the trapdoor in the floor, placing chairs around it, and a sack of potatoes leaning against the leg. Sitting at the table, she acted as if she had been preparing the root vegetables for the large pots of gulyas cooking, filling the kitchen with a rich aroma.

"You have Roma working here?" The administrator's voice dripped scorn as he saw Aaleahya working at the table. Given that she had been in the village and had planned to work in the kitchen, she was dressed casually.

Gavril came to stand behind Aaleahya's chair. "My wife." He stressed the word, introducing her. "We run a business here and there is a marked shortage of people to work in the kitchens at the moment." Gavril stopped himself from saying that this was since the bastard Nazi soldiers had arrived and started deporting them to the camps. "It means we have little opportunity for her to dress as befits our status in the area." Gavril was blunt in reminding the little shit of an administrator that he was a major, and wealthy, land and business owner in the area.

"So exactly what will we be expected to provide for our 'guests' in terms of meals and so forth?" Gavril placed a reassuring hand on Aaleahya's shoulder, needing the physical contact with her to control his temper.

For her own part, Aaleahya struggled to control the growl threatening along with the urge to shift and kill this intruder. Her own hand came up to her shoulder, covering Gavril's hand and seeking calm from him as well as giving it in return.

"Do you wish me to accompany you, my dear, whilst we show …" She smiled, "… our guests what we have available?"

Gavril nodded. Given the assumption that his Mate was a Roma, he was not taking the risk of her being escorted to the next deportation train. "Yes, please do, my love." Gavril explained to Aaleahya, ignoring the sneer from the administrator. "Please do."

Gavril indicated with one hand the stairs leading to the guest room floors above the kitchen.

"This inn has a total of 100 guest bedrooms." He explained to the clipboard-wielding administrator. "You stated that we are to accommodate that many soldiers here?" Gavril checked his understanding of the orders.

The little shit nodded. "That is correct. You will quarter 100 soldiers, and you will provide them with breakfast, and dinner." He looked back at the rich-smelling venison stew. "Clearly, the deprivations of food availability don't seem to apply to you."

Gavril was not going to fall for his baiting. "This inn is called the Hunter's Arrow for a reason. The local area is rich in game. We hunt for our meat, as my father and grandfather did." He was also aware that the Pack needed ensure that any risk to the Pack was minimised. The Nazis interest in the paranormal was well known. Anything that might give them an edge in the war was likely to be followed up, and where possible, exploited. Gavril needed to ensure that his Cŵn Annwn were not seen as just another 'exploitable' resource. Given that they had lived in this area for as long as they had, it was likely that rumours about them existed also.

"So the provision of food is not a problem to ... hunters such as yourselves?" He asked again.

"Do you have a point to make?" Gavril kept his tone level. Aaleahya glanced at him, and he knew she could feel his simmering anger.

"This area is unusual, is it not?" The administrator purred. "Your family has been here for several generations, as we understand." It was a statement, not a question. "I am sure you are aware of the stories that have been rumoured about you. Why, for example, do you have several able-bodied men here? Why have they not enlisted for the greater good of the Reich?"

Gavril smiled. "Perhaps because, until last month, if they were going to enlist anywhere, it would have been with the Hungarian Army." Gavril suggested politely.

"An army which used to be allies of the Reich." The man snapped. "Conscription of able-bodied men remains an option, may I remind you."

"I am sure that it does, but if that were the case, then your soldiers would not be able to enjoy the hospitality of the Hunter's Arrow." Gavril pointed out in a reasonable tone. "Come, let me show you the rooms we have, and you can tell me how I am to quarter your soldiers. Are they to be one man to a room, or do you intend them to share?" He knew damn well that for a common soldier, one room each was to be considered quite luxurious.

Gavril could feel Kat on the periphery of his awareness. "When I have taken this little shit upstairs, I need you and Sandu to finish the current batch of evacuations." he told her. He reinforced the instruction with an Alpha's command. "We can't let them discover what we are doing. Then, I need you to head over to the Hall. They are planning to quarter the damn Gestapo in our home."

Aaleahya could feel Gavril's temper rising with each question the little man puppet asked him. Shyly, she glanced his way, using her power to calm him once again, only for the little man to continue hammering with questions about how they have food. She admitted to herself that controlling her own temper was difficult, and she could not wait for this odious little official to leave. The realisation that the Gestapo would be staying in Negrescu Hall made her eyes flash with fire. Would it be necessary to move some of the Pack to their properties in Wales or New York for safety? Glancing up, Aaleahya realised that the little man with the clipboard was watching her intently as if he was trying to figure something out. She smiled politely, laying a hand on Gavril's arm again, albeit a bit shakily.

Seeing the administrator's interest in Aaleahya forced Gavril to bring his own temper under control. He was only too well aware that the man was a danger both to himself and to the Pack, but until it was clear who else he might have shared information on the Negrescu holdings, Gavril knew that the putrid soul would survive another day. Covering Aaleahya's hand with his own, he reassured her with a wordless pulse of love down their link that his temper was under control. Again, Gavril indicated that the administrator should precede them up the stairs. Little power hungry dictators like him liked to feel that they had the upper hand. Well, his 40 years of life experience will find a challenge from Gavril's own 350 years or so.

Gavril knew that the rooms of the Hunter's Arrow were more than adequate for billeting soldiers. The place was, after all, the premier inn in the area, catering for those with the money to tour Europe, prior to the war. Of greater concern to Gavril was that his family home, Negrescu Hall, would become quarters for the Gestapo, the police element of the SS, and thus, the ones who truly saw themselves as superior to all around them. This little administrator might believe that he had the upper hand over them, but Gavril knew the challenge would be the invaders into their home.

Satisfied that the arrangements at the inn met with his requirements, everyone returned downstairs to the bar area to find that the first of their new 'guests' had arrived.

"Of course, you and your staff will make sure that every need of our troops is handled appropriately." The little shit sneered at Gavril.

Gavril was more than familiar with the 'expectations' of an occupying army. "Any need within reason." He tempered his answer. "There are several young women on my staff, including my own daughter and wife. They are not there to 'service' the baser needs of our guests." His voice was quiet.

"Every need, Mr Negrescu." The administrator snapped.

Gavril raised a brow in query. "Why are you, as the face of authority in this area, trying to provoke me? I take the protection of those who look to me very seriously. I might almost think that you are trying to force a situation where you have a legitimate reason to arrest me, when all I am trying to do is find a mutually agreeable way for you to appropriate the use of my property."

He repeated his words. "Every need, Mr Negrescu." Gesturing to his waiting car, he went to leave, before turning. "As we have to make the arrangement for your other property, perhaps I might offer you and your lady a lift." He sneered. "Unless, of course, you have another means of getting there. It is about five miles from here, is it not?"

Yeah, this little shit had done his research into the local rumours. Placing his hand over Aaleahya's on my arm, Gavril smiled coldly. "My wife and I will be pleased to accept your offer of a lift."

Aaleahya knew the little man, the puppet of a Nazi master, was enjoying trying to rile them both, using his position to threaten and cajole his way into their lives. She could sense the suspicion in this little weasel of a human. Keeping her eyes on her Mate helped her to maintain her own sense of calm when the little maggot ordered the women to service the soldiers, as if they were just a group of whores. She could see the cold smile on Gavril's face, which clearly the little twerp thought was an indication that he was making headway with him. Allowing Gavril to steer her to the shiny black car and help her into the back seat, she made her point clear to her Mate.

"Gavril, I so want to spill this creature's blood and I haven't felt like this before. Is this how you feel around the evil souls you must harvest for the Goddess?" Aaleahya kept her attention and gaze on the administrator as he instructed the driver to Negrescu Hall. "I will be glad when the Goddess tells you to harvest this individual, who takes such pleasure in the pain of others."

Gavril had a half smile on his face at Aaleahya's avowal. Goddess willing, it would be sooner rather than later, once he had determined with whom he may have shared any information he had about the Pack. If, for example, he had knowledge of the Welsh legend of the Cŵn Annwn, then his life would be over.

However, given that the road to Negrescu Hall is long, twisted and mountainous, it could be just as easy for a terrible accident to befall him and his driver, particularly if it was known that he and Aaleahya had parted company with him at either the Hall or at the Hunter's Arrow. It was something for him to consider in due course.

Gavril pulled Aaleahya closer to him as they sat facing the little shit, keeping her tucked against his side. Her hands were tucked into the folds of her skirt, and she kept her eyes down, the better to reinforce the impression of the 'good' little wife.

"So, exactly how long has your family been in the area, Herr Negrescu?" The administrator asked them. The sneer was still on his face, at the obvious gesture of affection between Gavril and his Mate.

"My grandfather moved here in the late 1880s. My father and I were both born here. The records exist in the local church, if you don't believe me." Gavril kept his tone civil.

"I am sure that they do. It would be the first thing to check if there were ... questions about your origins." He replied. His voice was back to that self-satisfied purr.

"Of course, you and I both know that there is more to you than meets the eye."

Gavril raised a brow. That was the most blatant accusation the little shit had made so far. "Indeed? Would you care to elucidate your statement? I am not sure I understand what you are implying." Gavril kept his tone polite, even as his temper was rising again. Outside of the vehicle, the trees bent in a sudden gust of wind, the car being pushed along and to the side, as the driver fought for control.

The administrator did look a tad nervous. "You know what I mean." He snarled. "This area is renowned for the paranormal. Do you deny that you are one of those legends?"

Gavril laughed. "I? A legend? I run an inn, and an import/export wine business. As a result of those business being some years old, I have a reasonable amount of wealth to my name. But a legend? I think perhaps the stories of the Carpathians have gone to your head." Gavril tipped his head to one side, a smile on his lips. "So what am I? I am curious."

Aaleahya half-smiled at Gavril's mental prompt to follow his lead. Lifting her chin, she asked quietly whether the little twerp believed in vampires, scoffing at the myth that was flying around the small villages on the outskirts of the Carpathian Mountains.

"Sir I can assure you there are not any vampires." She pointed out. Using the link as she spoke, Aaleahya asked her Mate if they should send their daughter away to where she will be safe. She could feel the heated gaze of worm as he looked at her. Again her wolf reared its head and again Aaleahya fought to subdue her.

"Herr Administrator I suppose you also believe in were-wolves?" Aaleahya could not seem to help herself, wanting to find out exactly what these human knew also, not only for herself but also for her Mate's sake, although she dropped her gaze again at Gavril's question asking what the administrator thought he was.

"It is not wise to mock me, Herr Negrescu." The shit-for-brains administrator snarled. "I was appointed Gauleiter for this area because of my knowledge of local legends. I was a top academic in Budapest. I know what I am talking about, and you, Herr Negrescu, and your family were a topic of particular interest."

He sneered at Aaleahya, who, having asked if he believed in vampires and werewolves, had an amused smile on her lips. "You call her your 'wife'. I know that in private, you refer to her as your Mate." He continued to sneer. "You are not the grandson of the man who settled here in the last century. You are that man."

Gavril did not allow the half smile to leave his lips. "Really? Forgive my amusement, but having grown up in this area, you would not be the first person who accused me of being some sort of creature of the unknown. Usually, such an accusation is succeeded by a demand that perhaps I would consider selling my business to them. Is that also your intent?" Gavril asked politely.

At the same time, he swore to himself. Great! A fucking academic. An ivory tower peddler of tales, who would have gathered every little scrap of superstition, convinced that somehow it all linked together. "And you are correct. I do refer to my wife as my Mate in private. It is an English word, meaning friend. My family have always believed that one's spouse should also be one's friend."

Again, through the calm look on his face, Gavril dared him to contradict him. Fortunately, the administrator didn't have the opportunity, as the car drew up in front of Negrescu Hall. Gavril was greeted by the sight of his daughter and Sandu, both wearing riding apparel: Kat wore a white silk shirt, and the still-fashionable baggy riding trousers, popularised by the Russian horsemen. Sandu wore a similar outfit, but in more subdued colours. Kat's booted foot was tapping angrily on the gravel before the house, as she watched a stream of black-garbed SS walking in and out of our home, carrying boxes and bags, clearly intent on settling in.

"Herr Gauleiter? I didn't expect that my guests would be here quite yet." Gavril awaited his explanation, noting with irritation, the banner of the Third Reich, their swastika flag, which now hung from the balcony of the upstairs master suite.

He shrugged. "You knew they were coming. When was irrelevant. Why? Is it going to be a problem? Perhaps you had some ... indications of your real identities which you wished to hide first?"

It was becoming harder not to flatten this man. "Far from it, but a good host is always present before his guests arrive. Perhaps that is not something to which... academics are accustomed?

Entering the house, Gavril kept his arm around Aaleahya. Dressed as she was, in casual clothing, he wanted there to be no risk to her from these scum, the police arm of the SS. Sandu walked behind him, with Kat sandwiched between them. For once his daughter did not argue, aware that it was essential that they presented a united front. What had been their family room downstairs had been turned into some sort of operations centre, with the fine tables dragged in from other rooms to be turned into desks, the tiled and wooden floors showing signs of scant care being taken. The silk wall hangings had been left, but the walls were festooned with maps and diagrams. Even as Gavril looked, the doors were slammed shut. As if a closed door would stop him from seeing what they had in their files and maps?

"Is it too much to think that my family and I will still have our own quarters in this, our own home, Herr Gauleiter?" Gavril asked quietly.

CHAPTER 6: APRIL OF 1944 - THE SS IN OUR HOME

With the Officers in their lovely home making a mess doors slammed in their faces as they walked by, Aaleahya was angry to find herself separated Gavril, although at least she was with the children. They had decided it was best to introduce their daughter as his younger sister and Sandu as a family friend.

She did not like all these haughty men in her home and it was becoming harder to keep her wolf at bay. Glaring at those officers nearby, one in particular caught her attention, given his apparent fixation on Kat, paying more than a little too much attention to her coming and goings. She had also seen the look of contempt in in his eyes as he watched her with Sandu. Letting Gavril know of this development through their link, Aaleahya could not help but wonder whether the sudden separation from her Mate was a sign of things to come.

As Gavril asked the question of whether he and his family would still be permitted to live in their own home, the response was a curt, "Of course, Herr Negrescu, but other rooms will be assigned to you." That those rooms were in the back of the house, in what had been deemed by the SS to have been 'servants' quarters' suited them perfectly. Given the circumstances, Gavril would rather have kept the Pack together. In addition, to those as arrogant as these SS seemed to be, one servant looked the same as another, particularly if they were a race on whom they looked down. There was less risk of them noticing the changing headcount and faces of the Pack if they were out of sight, relatively speaking.

Of more immediate concern was that he was given no choice but to accompany the Gauleiter and a man whom he would find out was the local SS commander to what had been Gavril's own study. Giving Aaleahya a quick kiss, he told her not to worry, but to go with his 'sister' to wherever their new quarters would be. Again, they both ignored the scornful looks at their clear affection for each other.

The room had been cleared of most of the decorative items, leaving the books on the shelves. Artwork was missing from the walls, and Gavril wondered if it had been confiscated. A chair had been placed in front of what had been Gavril's own desk. Both 'gentlemen' took seats behind the desk, indicating he was to take the seat remaining to him, which he did.

Had he not been Cŵn Annwn, what happened next may well have killed him. Certainly, it would have hurt like hell, which was their intention. An electric shock, not far from a level which could stop a human heart coursed through his body, the design of the chair having hidden the wires they had attached. Or so they thought. Their intent was to prove that Gavril was something other than human, as the Gauleiter suspected. A human would not have been able to avoid a reaction to the shock. A paranormal being would. So, having read their souls, and knowing their intent, he played along.

"Beth mae'r uffern oedd bod, byddwch yn arseholes" Were his first words when he reopened his eyes, having taken a few minutes out to simulate the effect of the shock. Both of them looked surprised. "What? Welsh is my cradle language, in honour of my grandfather's origins. Of course, I am going to use for swearing, particularly as no one outside of my family speaks it here."

The Gauleiter in particular seemed annoyed. "What did you hope to prove, Herr Gauleiter?" Gavril let scorn infuse his voice. "I told you that your fixation on the paranormal stories around the Carpathians was mistaken. Did you really need to try to kill me to prove it.?"

Kat and Sandu excused themselves from Aaleahya's company, once they had been shown their quarters and left the house from the back stating they were going to the gardens to check on the vegetables which had been planted a while back. Giving the two of them hugs as they left, Aaleahya warned them to be careful. The fixated look of the young SS officer on her daughter concerned her, but Kat did not seem to share her concern. Perhaps it was just a mother's paranoia for her child, but it might be paranoia well founded, particularly as the SS officer left almost with them, saying nothing, but clearly intent on following them.

As soon as the two of them left, Aaleahya busied herself, moving from room to room cleaning the linen and freshening the rooms up. She could not help but notice clear gaps on the walls, from the paintings that had hung on the walls but were now missing along with her jewellery that Gavril had given her over the years.

She howled angrily inside her head wanting to absent herself from what had been her home. Through the Pack link, she heard that others were escaping through the mountains to other countries. Her mind was on her Mate and their children. Her half smile returned on receiving a link from Kat telling her mother that she was successful with the evacuation of the latest refugees. She implored them once again to be careful, reminding them that they are being followed. Kat laughed through the link, still young enough to be excited that she had pulled one over on the German's soldiers. Aaleahya shivered inadvertently. She was not so sure.

Having managed to convince the Gauleiter and the SS Commander, for now, that he was human, Gavril was permitted to return to his family. He knew, from what the Gauleiter had said, and the fact that, at such an early juncture, the SS Commander's involvement, that he and his family were going to be under scrutiny, and warned the Pack to be more careful.

- x -

The number of deportations, both of Jews and Roma, had increased exponentially since the Germans arrival. In only a month, it was becoming more imperative that the Pack up scaled their own activities, whilst maintaining the fiction that Gavril didn't have a problem playing host to both ordinary soldiers and the SS.

Kat and Sandu were having to play a dodging game on a regular basis. Aaleahya had alerted Gavril to the fact that Kat had picked up a Gestapo Officer's fixation in her, and that either he viewed Sandu as a rival for their daughter's affections, or something more sinister was afoot. Certainly there was nothing in the minds of the Gauleiter and the SS Commander. The German would not know, of course, that Sandu was Kat's bodyguard, rather than her love interest, although they had grown up together. The fiction that they saw themselves as brother and sister would have to suffice as protection.

Each day, as the months progressed through Spring and Summer, the process of running evacuations continued. Around them the leaves were changing colours, the damp air redolent with the smell of game in the forest. Stags were in rut, their bellows filling the air as they fought for the honour of mating. And throughout the constant cycle of the seasons, the war continued.

The Pack had moved their operations to the basement in the Hunter's Arrow, working under the noses of their occupiers, so to speak, and thus avoiding any suspicion that they would use other locations. Each night, another group would be brought in by several members of the Pack, children cautioned to stay silent during the entire process. What was the effect of this on them? Did they realise that they might, or rather would, never see their parents again? Auschwitz. The name was heard more and more these days. This was the place to which their parents were destined to travel. The place where their parents would meet their end, joining the piles of bodies there already. The children whom the Pack managed to transport were split between their original home in Wales, with a greater proportion going to our more recently established home in New York State. With America still a relatively young country, it was easier to move the children onward. Even the numbers that they moved, hundreds of children, were not enough that, when spread over a large country, would attract attention, which was the way that Gavril wanted it to be. Some of them were so heartbreakingly young. At least the older children would have a memory of their parents. But the very young? Nothing. Perhaps a vague memory of a dark-haired stranger arriving and then reappearing in a basement, before being whisked away by some magical means to another country. The Pack members didn't allow themselves the luxury of time with the transports. In and out. The risk of their activities being uncovered was too great.

Still questions were there. Gavril knew he was being watched. Aaleahya was being watched, but at least, it seemed they had decided that she was not Roma and thus not in danger of being deported herself. They shared a room in the rear of what had been their home, their lovely restful Negrescu Hall, with the gardens that had flourished under Aaleahya's gift. The flower gardens were gone now, a distant memory, replaced instead by more practical rows of root vegetables, the better to ensure that those who looked to the Pack for assistance amongst the locals would not starve as the winter months drew in.

Each night, Gavril would pick off one or two souls. Not enough to be noticed, and always accidental. Sometimes, he would leave the mark of his fangs in the corpse, and the locals played their part by whispering about the vampire legends that had been a part of Carpathian history for decades.

Once a week, he would be summoned by the Gauleiter, and the SS Kommandant, and he would be interrogated. Gavril believed they hoped they could somehow confuse him, trip him up, so to speak, with their constant questions. The question of where the source of his wealth was seemed to be a popular question. Clearly importing and exporting wine didn't happen during a war. No, it didn't because the motherfuckers who had seized his house had also seized his stocks. At least, they thought they had seized it. Not all of it. Caves make remarkably good cellars, and Aaleahya knew the local cave network like no other. The questions continued. Constant. A barrage of interrogation. Gavril thanked the Goddess that his priest friend had the foresight to create false entries in his registers for each member of the Pack. They might appear convenient, but they served their purpose. There was solid proof of Gavril being his own grandson.

But, without a doubt, it was becoming difficult. The excesses were becoming worse. The Germans were losing the war, and losers become desperate. Their drive to find a paranormal solution to their problems became almost obsessive. Care was needed, and warranted.

- x –

As the summer months waned, and the cooler temperatures of September became more noticeable, the rumours of Allied success in Western Europe became more than rumours. The Russian advance was also becoming more clear. Those Germans left in Hungary were starting to feel as if they were caught in the middle.

CHAPTER 7: PROTECTING THE PACK (JUNE 1944)

The room had been a side room used to store wet clothing. The tiled floor and the hanging racks bore testament to its practicality being a primary objective. Now it was to be used for a different purpose.

Gone were the cloaks and wooden overshoes, the practical garments useful when working in muddy vineyards and farmlands. The racks were still there. The tiled floor was still there, but when Gavril was shown into the room, the only other furniture was a table and three chairs. On the table was a pile of rope and a pulley system. The armed guards who had escorted him to the room pushed him into a chair, whilst the Kommandant and the Gauleiter themselves were occupied in slinging the rope over the hanging rack and threading it through the pulley system. A few experimental tugs on the rope, and they appeared satisfied with what they were trying to achieve.

"Herr Negrescu. So good of you to join us." The Gauleiter's false polite greeting was sufficient warning, had Gavril been only human. But he wasn't. As soon as he had entered the room, he knew what was planned. He knew it was going to hurt, and he knew that these two bastards were looking forward to the prospect of seeing if they could make him scream.

At a gesture from the Kommandant, the two guards used their weapons to prod Gavril to a standing position, and push him to where the rope hung from the rack and pulley system. He was ordered to turn, so that his hands, which had been bound behind him, were positioned just under the end of the rope. Gavril felt the tugging as the rope was attached to the cuffs around his wrists, and mentally, he braced himself for what was to come.

It wasn't much to start with. A slight tugging on the cuffs, as the rope tightened, the pressure on his wrists as the metal of the cuffs started to bite. Without making it too obvious, he let his mind focus on dissipating the pain, so that the effect sought by the Gauleiter and the Kommandant would take just a bit longer. Far be it for him to give them the satisfaction of a reaction that quickly.

Then the strain on his shoulders started. At first, it is nothing more than he would have felt from carrying something unusually heavy. But it is a different kind of stretch. The tendons between his pectoral muscle and his upper arms starting to pull. Then a pause. A tug as the rope was secured, and he was left hanging, leaning slightly forward, his feet still on the ground, but head tipped forward. A scrape of chairs on the floor behind him, and a slight creak from the wood, as both the Gauleiter and the Kommandant take a seat.

Interesting. The thought crossed Gavril's mind. Psychological, because I can't see you, and physical torture. Clearly they had a lot riding on obtaining a reaction.

"So, Herr Negrescu, shall we discuss these local legends which you and your ... wife mocked me about?" The Gauleiter opened the discussion. "As you know, legends generally have a base in fact. We could start with the death of your ... grandfather's former business partner, perhaps."

"He died in a hunting accident. Hunting wolves. It was one of the reasons the practice fell out of fashion." Gavril kept his tone measured, but gasped as the rope twisted slightly, pulling, knowing that the purpose of keeping him in this position was to make it difficult to draw breath, as well as the damage caused to muscle and tendon.

"Convenient, how that happened so soon after your ... Grandfather's arrival here, from Wales, a land steeped in its own legends." The Gauleiter's tone was insidious.

"Get to the point, Herr Gauleiter." Gavril commented. "I have an estate to run if you want to keep taxing it."

"Admit that the fiction about your grandfather is a fiction. Admit that you are the same ... man who came from Wales. Admit that you are not human. Admit that you are, in fact, Cŵn Annwn, a half man-half beast of Welsh legend." The demands snapped out.

One of the chairs creaked, and the Kommandant came to stand behind Gavril. His evil nature hung around him, miasma-like. "Admit you are not human, or you wouldn't be able to tolerate this." He hissed.

Almost without warning, the rope was yanked down, forcing Gavril's arms back and up, to an angle that was almost shoulder dislocation point, had Gavril been human. He did what he had to do and screamed.

His mind registered the enquiry from Bran, at his outburst. Sending his friend the mental equivalent of a grin, Gavril reassured his Pack Beta that it was to impress the humans. For the Kommandant's benefit, the scream was followed by muttered swearing in Welsh, "Chi esgus ffycin bastard am dynol!", roughly translated as "You fucking bastard excuse for a human."

The rope released abruptly, dropping Gavril down his knees. As he hit the tiled floor, he let his breathing sound laboured, before he answered the Kommandant's question.

"And if I wasn't human, if I was some creature of legend, don't you think I might want to kill you for pulling a stunt like that?"

"Oh, no, Herr Negrescu. The Kommandant and I are quite safe. If anything happens to us when we are known to be 'talking' to you, your wife and ... sister will both die. Are you prepared to risk that?"

He had a point, but he also didn't seem to realise that as soon as he told Gavril that, Bran and Owain knew to protect Aaleahya and Sandu knew to protect Kat.

"Well." Gavril's voice remained apparently pain filled and laboured. "I am going to have to disappoint you, because that fucking hurt, and given the choice, I wouldn't have hung around for the experience. Unfortunately, being as human as you are, I don't have a choice."

Gavril heard a 'snick' behind him. "There is one last thing, before we end this meeting today, Herr Negrescu." He felt a sharp prick in his neck. "You are going to give us a sample of your blood. One of our doctors is interested in the unusual and he has expressed the view that your 'true' nature will be apparent in your blood. You may have heard of him? Dr Mengele?"

There was no way that butcher was going to get his hands in Gavril's blood. It was a small thing to fill the syringe with the Kommandant's own blood. Let Dr Mengele make what he would of that.

His arms were released and Gavril was permitted to stand. Gingerly, he relaxed his shoulders, before rotating them carefully. Sore, but not disabling.

"It is fortunate for you, Herr Gauleiter, that I am a working estate owner, and not just a landowner, otherwise your little game would have crippled me." Gavril point out coldly.

"We shall see, Herr Negrescu." The Gauleiter's tone was equally frosty. "This is but the first of many discussions we intend to have with you. If you think to avoid them, perhaps we will discuss the same matters with your ... wife or your ... sister. It is interesting how your sister bears such a resemblance to your wife, Aaleahya, is it not. Your Roma wife, that is."

The threat was less implied, more a brick-through-a-window obvious. "I understand. I have no intention of avoiding my responsibilities to my family. My grandfather raised me better than that. I don't pick on women."

Yes, it was quite clear. Either he played along with their games or Aaleahya and Kat would be their targets.

CHAPTER 8: UPPING THE STAKES (JUNE 1944)

Each week, Gavril was escorted to that little room for a chat with the Gauleiter and the SS Kommandant. Each meeting, their methods had become progressively more brutal, such that, as a matter of routine, he had taken to hiding the scars and other evidence from Aaleahya. If his Mate saw what was happening, she would be torn between protecting their daughter from the attentions of a young Gestapo Officer, who is determined to bed her, and trying to protect him. Gavril knew he couldn't let her split herself in such a way.

As to why they have not dragged anyone else in for a conversation? Since they sent the sample of Gavril's blood to Dr Mengele, and it showed nothing abnormal, they have become more cautious about informing those higher up the Nazi 'food chain' about whether they have found a paranormal advantage which may be coerced into use for the benefit of the Reich.

All the injuries from their chats have appeared to heal as they would for a physically fit and healthy human. Gavril had been careful that when they prepared him for a 'discussion', those scars or open wounds that needed to be seen were there. Hiding them from Aaleahya and then 'revealing' partially healed wounds was draining, but it was necessary.

The Gauleiter and the Kommandant appeared to have reached the conclusion that Gavril was the only Cŵn Annwn in the area. He should have laughed that they didn't realise that the estate housed a full Pack, and that they had incoming and outgoing Pack both from Wales and from the USA, particularly on days when they were covering multiple evacuations of innocents.

Bran and Owain had been invaluable in hiding what Gavril had done from his Mate. It did not sit well with his two senior Sentinels that, rather than protect their Alpha, they were cognisant of him being injured.

Each meeting a different method of interrogation was used. Sometimes it was beating, sometimes it was electric shocks. They were trying to work out if pain would cause him to give some indication of his 'true nature', but at the same time, were wary of doing anything that might cripple Gavril permanently, and thus make him useless to their cause.

They had even tried to use the local population to force a reaction. Hoarding of foodstuffs, allegedly because of the black market potential, was severely punished with a public flogging. The locals may be considered close to subhuman, but they are productive subhumans, so killing them does not serve the interests of the Reich.

On this particular occasion, a group of teens had been arrested and charged with hoarding grain. Six of them. Teenagers but they were still children. The usual sentence of thirty lashes would have crippled them, if not killed them, given that they were human, and the fucking Gauleiter and his best buddy knew that only too well. They knew that, when Gavril found out about the situation, his own sense of duty and the need to protect those who look to him, would mean that he would offer to take their place.

Herr Gauleiter and the SS Kommandant decided that they would make a spectacle of the punishment, to 'discourage any repeat of the offence'. Believe that, and you will believe anything. So, what better day to hold their spectacle than the Summer Solstice, a day known for its pagan links, and thus, if anything was likely to stir a pagan-based creature like a Cŵn Annwn into revealing themselves, surely it would be on a day such as this. It was a shame they didn't realise that the opposite was true. Had they picked the Winter Solstice, then perhaps that might have happened. But Summer? When the powers were at their peak? It was certainly their loss and it would be Gavril’s gain.

Gavril had to use his Alpha's will on Bran and Owain to force these two, who as well as being his senior Sentinels, were also his friends. It was more important that they ensured that Aaleahya, Kat and Sandu were not present when he was punished. With the intention of the authorities being to make a spectacle of the whole thing, it meant that the majority of the German soldiers stationed in the area would be in the centre of the village, ensuring that the locals fully appreciated the show being put on for their benefit.

It also made the date perfect for increasing the number of evacuations through the cellars of the Hunter's Arrow, considering that there would be minimal 'guests' present.

A platform had been prepared. Could they have made this more packed of clichés, Gavril wondered? Platform? Check. Well-lit square with torches burning? Check. Ominous looking 'executioner'? Check. Bucket of water to revive the miscreant? Check.

Still, the key thing from his perspective was that it was Solstice. The Earth energies around him were there to be tapped, and he could use it to pull in the additional strength that he would need in order to ensure that not even his eyes would change, or that anything other than human sounds would be uttered when the lash broke his skin, as it was sure to do. The whole point of this evening's 'festivities' was to cause enough pain that it would force a reaction from him. On this occasion, it didn't matter if Gavril passed out, or was incapacitated for a time. They wanted to force the reaction, and they were not going to hold anything back, given this opportunity.

The six teenage children, the original accused, were made to stand, at gunpoint, where they could see every stroke of the lash. It was summer, so walking onto that platform without a shirt was no big issue.

Bran was the only Pack member present. He had all but begged his Alpha, on bended knee no less, to be allowed to stay at his side. Given the centuries that they had been friends, long before he became Gavril's Sentinel and joint Pack Beta, Gavril did not deny him his request. Bran knew he would need someone he could trust.

They had rigged a post on the platform, complete with manacles. Gavril stood, calmly, whilst his wrists were secured, before grasping the peg at the top of the post. The reason for the sentence was read out, and here was a susurration of protest around the square. Whilst the manacles prevented him from facing the villagers, Gavril cleared his throat before speaking.

"Byddwch yn dal i, fy ffrindiau. Mae hyn yn fy nghyfamod â chwi, ac yr wyf yma o fy ewyllys rydd hun." (Be still, my friends. This is my covenant with you, and I am here of my own free will.)

Let the Germans wonder why a village in Hungary would speak Welsh. Taking in a breath, and with it, the rush of Earth power that flowed around himself, Gavril waited for the lash to strike.

The first five seemed to follow in quick succession, measured, even, striking a different part of his back each time, the intent to tenderise.

The next five were spaced unevenly, to prevent him bracing himself. Ten down. Twenty to go.

The sixteenth was the first to break the skin. After that, there was a deliberate intent to cause damage. Gavril could feel the blood trickle down his back, under his trousers. The coppery tang filled his senses and he gripped the peg tighter. Gavril knew he could not release that grip, or risk hanging by the manacles.

At twenty-six, the angle changed, and the last four were swung at his legs. Protected as they were by leather working trousers, the lash would still leave substantial bruising.

At thirty lashes, the fiery pain across his back ceased. Gavril felt Bran's hand over his, a tacit signal that he could release his grip on the post. Facing his friend, Bran supported Gavril against his shoulder, while the manacles were released, giving his Alpha a chance to gather his strength. At his silent command, Bran stepped back, as Gavril turned to face the Gauleiter and the SS Kommandant.

"Ffyc chi, foneddigion. You failed." Gavril enunciated his opinion of them clearly, before turning and walking from the platform. How he felt was irrelevant. It was more important for people to see that it was not futile to resist. The Allies had landed in France earlier in the month. It was only a matter of time before the glorious Third Reich would fall.

Bran returned Gavril to the room he shared with Aaleahya. Gavril had known that, despite his best efforts, she had been in the crowd, and her proximity had meant that she had smelt his blood in the air. He could feel her struggle to control her wolf, her instincts screaming at her to tear those guilty of this attack on her Mate. Tinged with that, was anger, and justifiably, at him, that he had thought to keep this from her, and sorrow. Why had he not wanted her at his side? My sweet Mate, Gavril thought, I wanted only to protect you. Hell, his Mate was going to be spitting nails when she saw the state of his back. All he could do right now was stop her from acting in a precipitous manner otherwise this little show would have been for nothing.

With her focus on protecting their daughter and adopted son, the way that the authorities dogged their movements, following their daughter in the distance was tiresome to say the least. Aaleahya made sure she knew that Kat and Sandu were safe while they transported those poor innocent souls across the borders to others who had agreed to help these refugees leave and get them to safety aboard the ships that will take them to America. Her Mate, a perceptive businessman, had set up a fund to help those who have escaped the nightmare that Eastern Europe had become.

The day started out like any other, as Kat and Sandu went to the Hunter's Arrow to work. Heading out into the garden to check on the root vegetables, Aaleahya was conscious of her shadow guard following her. She was picking those vegetables that were ready and placing them in her basket, curious as to why Gavril had sent Bran and Owain with a list of vegetables to check on. She frowned, given that she could not help but feel he was keeping away from the house. A young village girl walked up to the soldier following her, flirting with him and soon they took off. As soon as they took off, Aaleahya made her way to the Hunter's Arrow to help with the evacuations. Sandu and Kat were busy handing out the papers with new identities and credentials to the escapees with instructions to keep to the woods and only travel at night as the soldiers seemed too preoccupied with local legends and have become afraid of going into the woods late at night. The refugees huddled with the small children. They were also instructed that someone will come for them when it is time, before they were led to the secret room that the pack had built under the floor of the basement which has comfortable seating and candles to keep the young ones from being afraid. This is where Aaleahya found her daughter, sitting on the floor telling stories about an angel, sent to protect them and who will one day allow the destruction of those who harm others. She could not help but smile as she heard the chatter of the small ones. Kat finished the story and then distributed drinks to the children along with some hoarded cookies. Watching the children enjoy the drink and cookies reminded Aaleahya so clearly of when Kat was that small herself.

Finished with the evacuations for now, Aaleahya selected some ingredients and supplies and carried them upstairs where her shadow was standing with his arms crossed over his chest and a smug smile on his face. Aaleahya acknowledged him and continued to the preparation table laying them out along with some herbs while she was at the garden.

"Frau Negrescu come with me now!" The officer's tone was abrupt, brooking no hint of disobedience.

Wiping her hands on her apron Aaleahya untied it and followed the officer to the village square where a platform had been erected, where someone was being beaten. She could hear the number of strikes and then the scent of her Mate's blood reached her nose. Her anger was palpable as she turned to demand of the smirking officer what was going on? She asked why her husband was being whipped in public, whilst at the same time, she fought to keep her eyes from turning to the Cŵn Annwn red. Aaleahya flinched, hearing the slap of the whip on her Mate's skin. Her eyes flashed with anger, not only at those who were inflicting this on him but at her Mate as well for keeping this from her.

Aaleahya noticed Bran on his knees, and she could feel the flow of supportive energy from Beta to Alpha, even as his own eyes mirrored the hatred that was showing in her own. She tried to move closer, to let her love know that she was there with him. Tears coursed down her cheeks, as on the outside she looked like a grieving woman whose husband was being punished for some unknown crime.

To Gavril's mind, such petty attempts as the public flogging were just that. Petty. But equally, there comes a point when it becomes impossible to ignore what is happening around you; when no longer can you say that it is best not to cause a stir. Gavril promised the locals living around and working at both Negrescu Hall and the Hunter's Arrow that he would protect them.

Rape is never a justifiable crime. Rape of a minor ratcheted the stakes up to a whole new level. When Gavril found out what had been done, again to try to provoke a reaction from him, he could no longer ignore the sly attacks and attempts. Regardless of what it might mean to him personally, when he became Alpha, he swore to protect.

They knew they had to find the right button to press. It was the only thing those bastards got right.

It was night when Gavril found out. Although the Pack were housed in the former servants' wing of Negrescu Hall, they had maintained the practice of keeping a Pack member on duty during the night. With the village a good five miles from the Hall, if they were needed, they had to be able to react quickly.

The light, almost hesitant knock on the kitchen door was answered immediately and in view of the reason for this particular villager seeking help, she was brought to Gavril's attention immediately. Leaving Aaleahya sleeping, he came down to the kitchen, pausing only to pull on some pants and boots first.

It was one of the women, whom he recalled from working occasionally at the Hunter's Arrow. She was crying, soft sobs of desperation. That, coupled with the fact that she had made the walk up here said that clearly something of fairly major implications had happened.

Sending the door guard out of ear shot, Gavril crouched down by her chair, in order to seem less imposing and quietly asked her to explain. Through her sobs, she told him that her daughter had been attacked. Her daughter was fifteen years old. What was it that they were picking on the teenagers, because this had all the indications of another of Herr Gauleiter's traps for him.

Several Gestapo soldiers had grabbed her daughter on the way back home. With the longer nights, it was possible to cover more work in the fields and with harvest approaching, its success meant improving the chances of everyone surviving winter. However, it meant that individuals were not necessarily coming home in the safety of groups.

They had grabbed her, and they had raped her, repeatedly, laughing at her screams. They had not been satisfied with 'just' that, but had forced her in all ways possible. By the time she had stumbled back home, this formerly innocent teenage girl knew the full horror of war. She was bleeding so badly, her mother said, and crying. She couldn't stop crying. She said they had ignored her pleas to be released, for them to stop, forcing her to service two at a time, one orally whilst another took her from behind. And, she said, laughing all the time, slapping her when she had gagged and forcing themselves deeper.

Gavril knew he had no choice but to investigate, and punish those responsible. This was part of the covenant between the village and the Pack. As Alpha, he had to respond. Even knowing that it was probably a trap, he still had to respond. This had been set up to be offensive to everything that he espoused. Without a doubt it was a trap.

Informing the door guard of where he would be going, Gavril helped the woman to her feet. In this instance, it would be better if he transported himself directly to the mother's house. The sooner he could attend to her daughter's injuries, the better the child's chances of recovering, at least physically.

"Advise Bran and Owain of my destination, but do not wake my Mate. It has been a busy day for her, as well and Kat and Sandu, and it will be a busy day tomorrow for them. Let them sleep."

The door guard hesitated. "My Alpha, what if it is a trap?"

Gavril had a half smile on his face, as he communicated mentally. "Of course it is a trap. The sheer brutality of the attack on this girl has been co-ordinated with the deliberate intent of making me respond, given that I took on the punishment of those teens last month. But a trap is only going to work if I didn't expect it."

Gavril had no doubt that the girl's mother had been sent to bring him, and no doubt that she had been told her daughter's life would be under threat should she fail to convince him to return with her. However, for what he wanted to achieve, the mother had to believe that Gavril knew nothing of a potential trap. So be it.

Turning to the mother, Gavril asked her to think of a room in her house, and plucked the image from her mind. Taking her by the hand, he transported us to the kitchen of her small cottage. The multiple clicks of guns being cocked confirmed that it was a trap. So be it.

"Before you think to try anything, Herr Negrescu, I suggest you look this way." It was the young Gestapo Officer, the one who had been following Gavril's daughter.

Turning to face him, Gavril took in that the girl now wore a belt loaded with explosive material, with a wire connecting her to a hand-held trigger held by the Gestapo officer. Gavril gave a small nod. "A dead man switch, I take it?" he asked calmly. The man nodded. "Very well. At least let me check the girl over. Unless, of course, you made her mother lie about the attack also?"

The officer laughed. "No, the fun with had with this girl was quite real. There is nothing like a young virgin for the screaming and the pleas. As if we were going to stop while she made such alluring noises."

This was the scum who thought that he would have Gavril's daughter, his Angel in his bed. Truly, the scum had no idea. "The villagers are mine to protect, and you and your superiors know that. You have my word. I wish only to make sure that she has not been damaged by what you have done."

Through this exchange, the girl's mother stood with her fist in her mouth, tears streaming down her face. Gavril knew that a part of her had hoped that her betrayal would result in her daughter's release, but she realised that the chances of that were diminishing.

"Unlike you and your ilk, I keep my word." Gavril snapped coldly. "Now release the girl so that I may check her injuries." The man was not one of his Pack, but the power behind Gavril's voice was such that his hand relaxed on the dead-man switch slightly. "I said, release her." This time Gavril's voice thundered in the confines of the small room.

The officer moved to disconnect the dead-man switch from the explosives, before he seemed to realise what he was doing. Sneering, he pushed the girl hard towards the 'creature'. Gavril opened his arms to her, murmuring words of comfort, even as she sobbed her despair. Gently, he disconnected the explosives from around her, and placed them next to himself.

"Child, look at me." Gavril spoke gently, much as one might to a skittish young animal of any species. Her tear-stained face showed the bruising of the attack on her. Gently, brushing her sweat-snarled hair from her face, Gavril placed his thumbs against her temples. There was physical damage and there was mental damage, both of which he could help her overcome. Of greater concern to Gavril was what else he felt, and he had a sad smile on his face that this child would face the choice of leaving childhood behind her forever, whilst never being able to forget what had been done to her. The bastards had chosen her as their target for a reason. Within her womb, the spark of a new soul glowed.

Gavril did not speak, but told her in her mind what he had found. She looked at Gavril, the shock in her eyes. She was of peasant stock. She knew how children were conceived. "Please, take it all away, my Lord. Please." She begged Gavril quietly.

He nodded. That tiny soul was not guilty of the crimes of the father, but it would forever remind its mother of what had happened. War leaves enough scars without her having to deal with the aftermath of bearing a child from her attack. As much as he hated to take such a young soul, it was better that he did so, rather than the child suffered with a mother who would hate the very sight of it for the memories that were not its fault.

Taking her hand, for all intents and purposes Gavril gave her fingertips a kiss. In actuality, he bit down, gently, breaking the skin sufficiently to draw blood, and to remove the small soul from her. Drawing his tongue over the small holes made by his fangs to seal them, he smiled gently.

"It is done, child." Gavril stroked her face. "Join your mother. You should bear no guilt for your part in what has happened."

"I am so sorry, my Lord." She whispered. "I should have been more careful."

Gavril shook my head. "No guilt, child. I mean that, whatever they might tell you."

His gaze moved to the gloating face of the young Gestapo Officer. "As I said, I keep my word." He reminded the German officer, stepping forward.

The Gestapo officer glanced at the girl and her mother. "Bring them both. Since Herr Negrescu came running at their call for help, they will prove useful to ensure his tractability."

Part of Gavril was relieved that the smirking officer had not suggested Gavril's Mate or his daughter for this purpose. For them, there was a strong chance that he would have done quite a lot to keep them safe, and hated himself for doing it. Whilst he felt responsibility to the woman and her daughter, it was not the same, and the look that the mother gave him told him that she realised this.

Placing her arm around her daughter's shoulders, she looked at her child. Something passed between mother and daughter, before she spoke.

"My Lord, do what you must and don't worry about us." She said quietly. "You tried to help us, and for that, we thank you. Do not compromise your standards for us."

The young Gestapo Officer's mind was full of the triumph he felt at being the one to 'trap' the elusive Herr Negrescu. His superiors, including the Kommandant, had known that there was 'something' about this local landowner, who looked down on them when he should acknowledge the might of the Third Reich, something that could be of use to their cause, but they had struggled to find a way to gain access to that potential advantage. That it transpired that the key had been to exploit his sense of duty to those who looked to him for protection filled him with scorn. To his mind, who could care more for others than themselves? Such a being was weak. As such, this sort of being only proved his inferiority to the might of the Third Reich. And now, he was glowing with his triumph. Mentally, Gavril shrugged. On the one hand he was inferior for caring for others. On the other hand, he was a potentially valuable advantage to be exploited by the Third

Reich. The officer wasn't quite sure how Herr Negrescu's abilities could be used, and it was that little detail that Gavril intended to exploit.

The fact is, when telling lies, it is best to keep as close to the truth as possible. Whilst one of the more fanatical, this was also not the first regime which Gavril had had to circumvent. He doubted that it would be the last.

They took the precaution of putting Gavril in chains, wrists and ankles bound in turn to a heavier chain around his waist. The mother and her daughter, in turn, were attached to the waist chain by means of a collar and lead. In procession, we were marched back up to the Hall and back into the little side room which Gavril had come to know so well. A further heavy chain was used to secure him to the wall. Clearly they wanted to take no chance whatsoever. Also clearly, they appeared to have forgotten that he had just appeared, with the mother, in the cottage in the village. However, for the moment, it suited his purposes to play along.

It would also appear that, for the moment, the fact that his wife, Aaleahya, and 'sister' had remained at the Hall, asleep, was an indication that he had kept this 'other side' hidden from them, thus rendering them of little use when it came to controlling him.

The girl and her mother moved closer to him, their fear clear. Whilst they were not Pack, Gavril was able to extend the calm and reassurance of Pack Alpha to them. "Be easy. You are safe whilst they believe you to be key to controlling me." he murmured.

The mother nodded. "Please forgive me, my Lord. They said that my daughter would be raped to death if I did not come to fetch you. I couldn't let them do that. Please say you understand, my Lord." Her voice had a catch in it, which spoke of her conundrum at having to betray one who had so far only protected her and her family. "I have lost my husband and both of my sons so far." She continued, her head bowed. "I couldn't lose my daughter too."

Gavril had suspected as much, and tried to reassure her on that score.

Perhaps half an hour had elapsed before the door opened, and they were joined by the Kommandant and the Gauleiter. Both wore looks of satisfaction, that, at last, they had Gavril where they wanted him: unable to continue to deny that he was 'other', not when a dozen soldiers had witnessed his reappearance in the cottage's kitchen.

"I am as human as you are." The Kommandant's tone was mocking. "Last time I checked, humans are unable to move themselves in a thought from one place to another over five miles away."

There was no point in denying it. Gavril let him continue. "The question is what other tricks do you have up your sleeve, Herr Negrescu?" He moved to stand next to the girl and without warning, pressed an eight-inch blade against her throat, under the line of the steel collar she wore.

His actions were to be expected. "I can move myself and anyone in physical contact with me. I am also able to heal injuries." The latter was the least of his skills and thus one that Gavril felt comfortable in revealing.

The Kommandant released the girl and came to stand before Gavril, the blade still in his hand. The contrast between his black uniform, and his prisoner's shirtless state might have been amusing. "Show me, then." He suggested, and with little warning, abruptly drove his blade into Gavril's right thigh, dragging it down slightly to cause the wound to bleed but leaving the blade hanging.

"Rydych yn bastard ffycin! (You fucking bastard!)" Gavril kept his tone even, but there was no mistaking his anger. "You will need to release my wrists, preferably before this becomes messy." He pointed out.

"And if I don't?" The Kommandant demanded belligerently.

"Then I bleed out over the floor, and you lose a potentially valuable asset." Gavril replied, calmly. "You choose." The fact that he was automatically knitting tissue and blood vessels together as he spoke was irrelevant. Gavril wanted him to think that he needed hands on the injury to be able to do anything about it.

The Gauleiter scrambled to his feet, and fumbled with the key to the manacles. Placing his hands in either side of the knife, Gavril appeared to complete the healing process, leaving a gash in what had been a fairly decent pair of working trousers. "You may remove your knife now, Kommandant." he suggested. "I have finished. Please feel free to check."

The Kommandant drew his Luger pistol, and indicated that Gavril was to stand, his hands raised. "Chain him up again." He ordered the Gauleiter. "Wrists behind his back."

Gavril resisted the temptation to roll his eyes at this melodrama. Considering he had just told the Kommandant that he could transport myself and anyone in physical contact with himself, did the man really think that the chains would stop him? Then the Luger moved to the mother and her daughter. "You will obey, Herr Negrescu, or they will die. Do I make myself clear?"

Gavril nodded, and pointedly stood back, extending his wrists to that the Gauleiter could reattach the manacles, before bringing them behind Gavril's back so that he could fasten them to the heavy chain around Gavril's waist. Let them think that they had the correct key to his continued good behaviour. For added good measure, the Gauleiter pulled the manacles back and attached them also to the wall chain. Only then, did the Kommandant replace his Luger in its holster and approach him.

Gavril stood still whilst he poked and prodded at his healed leg, "Stand on one leg, on the one you just healed, Herr Negrescu." He ordered. Gavril obliged, at least as far as the chains would allow, his leg showing no sign of weakness.

"Interesting. Very interesting." The Kommandant stepped back, indicating that Gavril could stand on both legs. "This is definitely something that The Reich can use. What is the limit to the number of injuries you are able to heal?"

Gavril shrugged. "Provided there is no major blood loss involved?" On that he was being honest. He had healed Aaleahya after she had given birth to Kat, but his preference was to heal injuries before they reached that stage.

The Kommandant smiled. "Yes, this will be something that we can use." Yes, Gavril thought, you could. It would be interesting what would happen when the Kommandant realised that those who can heal are also those best suited to take you apart.

CHAPTER 9: 'CAT AND MOUSE' (AUGUST 1944)

Have two weeks ever seemed so long? It had only been two weeks since Gavril let the Kommandant and the Gauleiter have confirmation of what they believed to be true. They knew he was not human now. They knew he could move himself around in a thought. They knew he could heal injuries, with the proviso that major blood loss had not been involved. Their conundrum was that they couldn't decide if there was more to be discovered about his abilities.

If they went to those higher up the Nazi command structure with their 'discovery', they would lose access to Gavril and lose influence. The war was now clearly not going their way. In addition to the Allies continuing success in Europe, the Great Bear of Russia under Stalin was making its way from their own borders, no doubt with an eye on how Europe would be carved up when, not if, when the war ended.

Such global concerns mattered not in their little part of the world, except from the perspective that the Pack continued to move innocents out of danger. Gavril knew that Kat and Sandu had built up an extensive list of contacts with their work on the Underground Railway. As Pack Alpha, he had that information also. But that remained his daughter's particular project.

Cat and mouse. There was no better metaphor for the game Gavril played with the local authorities, keeping their attention on him, so that his Mate and my daughter could operate with, relative, impunity. As Aaleahya continued to use her talents to ensure the Hall gardens remained productive, she was followed, but perhaps not as assiduously as they might have done, had they suspected that she, too, was Cŵn Annwn. Kat and Sandu were followed by the scum of a young Gestapo Officer who had instigated a teenager's gang rape, but as much because they were part of his extended family rather than being under suspicion for their own activities. For the time being, Kat was believed to be Gavril's sister. No, for the moment, the Gauleiter wanted to confirm just how much of the Cŵn Annwn Legend was fact and how much was fiction.

The walls of the small interrogation room were becoming all too familiar, as attempts continued to find out just how much of the legendary abilities of the Cŵn Annwn had a basis in truth. Each time Gavril was taken down to that small room, each time he was bound in chains, each time a new method of interrogation was used, he had to block his Mate from knowing what was happening. Gavril told himself that, if it meant that his Aaleahya, or his daughter and son were not made to suffer the same demands, then it was worth the pain.

Then came the day when the mother and daughter made a decision between them that would have far reaching consequences. Until that point, the authorities had used them to keep Gavril in line. With the threat made regularly that they could also be beaten, electrocuted or stabbed, his tractability was ensured. Until that point, there had been no attempt to extend that threat to others in the village, or others known to be close to him.

Each time that he was taken to that small room, they would also be brought in. They would be chained to the wall, and made to watch as each new method of interrogation was used. What had started as a desperate attempt to protect her daughter had become a mother's nightmare. Rather than protecting her daughter from the horrors of war, her daughter was made to watch what could and did happen. Her daughter had suffered gang rape, and now, she was made to watch as pain was inflicted, as Gavril was pushed harder and harder in an attempt to determine just how far they could go, and how much pain he could take.

The day came when both the mother and daughter decided that they had had enough. Gavril knew when they did it. Their souls, tormented, driven by what they saw and heard being done, begged for release. Their own religion would have damned them for taking their own lives, but his Goddess was not so unforgiving. When Gavril visited them, their faces both bore an identical look of peace. As he absorbed their essence, he realised that they had left him a note. Addressed simply to "My Lord Alpha.", the mother explained why they had taken this course of action.

[Letter] "For two weeks, my Lord, I have watched you suffer indignity after indignity, all because of what happened to my daughter. Had you not come to help her, they would never have found out about you. But you came. From the time I was a girl myself, you always came when a plea for help was made. You never hesitated and you never seemed to stop to consider whether you should come to help. You just helped. I can't do that. I can't sit back and not return to you the gift you have been prepared to give not just us, but everyone who looks to you for protection. If my daughter and I are no longer here, then we can no longer be used to force you to do as the authorities wish. Forgive us, my Lord, for taking the coward's way out. I can only hope that some good will come of this."

Gavril burned the letter. He knew that the woman meant well, but with her death, the indignities, as she called them, would not end. Rather, the authorities would find someone else. They would hold another life or lives over his head to ensure his compliance.

Gavril had managed to convince them that the only ability he had was to transport himself and to heal, but even now, as the tide of the war was turning, they were looking at ways to use him. Originally, they had intended to use his abilities, or whatever abilities they could discover, for the greater good of the Third Reich. Now, their plans had changed. Now, with the tide of the war turning away from them, their plans were directed at ensuring that they did not end up the losers in this conflict.

Gavril had laughed to himself in a humourless manner. After what the Kommandant, and his merry band of SS, and the Gauleiter had done, did they really think that they would be able to walk away? Not bloody likely.

It didn't take the authorities long to find someone else, whose life was under threat if Gavril did not comply. This time, however, they didn't insist that these individuals attend each interrogation. They had realised that there was more to be gained from Gavril knowing that, if he didn't comply, then the 'hostages' would pay the price. They realised that the mere threat that they held over these hostages would ensure that he would obey their instructions instantly. They knew that he would never, ever, let this particular group of individuals suffer because of his refusal to act.

In the dark of the night, Gavril would raise his head to the sky, and howl his frustration and anger. My sweet Mate, his soul would howl in pain, it was her life held over his head. Her life and that of their daughter.

May the Gauleiter, the Kommandant, and all of them be damned for eternity, because they had found the key to ensuring that they would have Gavril collaborating with them, for all intents and purposes.

They threatened to kill his family.

CHAPTER 10: DEATH CAME CALLING

When it happened. Gavril's world, and Aaleahya's world would be forever altered.

Somehow, he would have thought that the day that he and Aaleahya experienced the true cost of war should have started in some momentous fashion. But no, the sun rose, as it did normally. The, along with several others, managed to produce breakfast for 100 soldiers at the Hunter's Arrow. The faces may have changed even over six months, but the numbers had stayed fairly constant. One thing was noticeable. So many of them were younger now. Gavril knew from his contacts elsewhere that the war was certainly not going in favour of the Nazi regime, not now. The Allies had landed on the Normandy Beaches on 6th June 1944, a date which would be engraved in history. Slowly, but surely, the Allies were advancing across Europe. The true horror of the war, the extermination camps, were still unknown to them. These were the very places from which his family, his Pack had tried to save at least some. They had succeeded with several hundred children, but the majority were children would never again see their parents and other adult relatives.

Even knowing that the Allies were advancing across Europe, the Pack did not stop their efforts of evacuation of children. They had no idea at the time how long the Allies would take, or whether they would win in the end. The Reich was showing signs of disintegration. In July, the German leader, Hitler, survived the third assassination attempt on his life. His instability was becoming apparent even to his own side. Had the assassination attempt been successful, perhaps the war would have ended sooner? Or perhaps, it might have gone on for longer?

But in August 1944, such things were not the driving factor for them. They had the evacuations. They had the cat-and-mouse games they had to play with the Gauleiter and the SS Kommandant, both of whom appeared to be convinced still that Gavril was hiding something. So, they were right about that, but it didn't mean that he was going to tell them that they were right. They had the local population, dependent on them for the last eighty or more years, who still needed us to ensure that they survived the war. Root vegetables may not have been the tastiest of dishes, but it was food, and it meant that they didn't starve to death in the face of shortages. The penalty was instant execution for anyone caught hoarding food, and not giving the bulk of it to the regime. The Pack was able to secrete some of it away, and thus ensure that, by dint of taking care of them, the locals would continue to protect the Pack, with their campaign of whispers about vampire legends to hide the deaths that came from soul harvest.

But that day. Along with Kat and Sandu, Aaleahya had gone out. Whilst their daughter and adopted son handled the majority of the transports, Aaleahya also helped by ensuring that Kat's 'tail' as they had named him, the young Gestapo Officer who was determined to have their daughter in his bed, did not cause a problem. Aaleahya did not enjoy having to be in proximity to him, with his focus both on their daughter, and his attitude towards those whom he viewed as traitors to the Reich, but she did it, to protect their child. To protect their children.

Gavril had stayed behind at Negrescu Hall, taking the, relatively long, walk. up the mountain, rather than the quicker method, to continue to hide his true nature from the Kommandant and the Gauleiter. Arriving at the Hall, he had entered via the back door, the servants' entrance, and gone to the room off the kitchen which he used as his office to do the estate accounts.

As with all his Pack, Gavril kept a mental eye on Aaleahya, Kat and Sandu. It was akin to a series of lights on his consciousness. He felt no concern when the light that was Kat dropped out, nor when the light that was Sandu also disappeared. It would not be the first time that they had gone into a psychic 'radio silence' whilst they were working. Gavril could still feel Aaleahya, and beyond her usual level of concern for their daughter, nothing else seemed amiss. The hammering sound of running, booted feet changed that. The Kommandant himself barged into Gavril's little office, six armed SS soldiers accompanying him. Gavril was ordered to stand, and his hands cuffed behind him. Again, in keeping with the fiction of being human, he did not struggle, and complied with the order to go with them. He was pushed and prodded out through the hallways of his former home, into what had been the entrance way, with its imposing marble staircase. Part of him could not help but remember his daughter learning to climb those stairs, and her first descent in a ball gown.

More soldiers awaited them. The smell of fighting lay heavy in the air. Gavril was told to stop, the guns staying on him. Perhaps thirty SS soldiers filled that hallway. Then the Gauleiter entered, with more soldiers, who were dragging someone with them. Gavril's heart sank as he recognised Sandu. He was dead. The Gauleiter's mind was filled with triumph, as a second group of soldiers entered, again dragging a body.

"So, are you still going to tell me that you and your .... family are normal, Herr Negrescu?"

As Kat's body, his angel's body, was dumped before Gavril like carrion, another group entered, and this time, Aaleahya was forced to the ground before him. Alive still, but her beautiful face was streaked with tears at the sight of their daughter and her protector. Dead.

Their eyes met, and, as Gavril looked at the Gauleiter, the man's gloating words, threatening his Mate with the same fate unless he cooperated, stuttered to a halt, and his faced paled.

Following the young officer that seem fixated on Kat made Aaleahya's stomach turn as he attempted to pull her closer. Ever the protector, Sandu leapt between them putting himself between the officer and Aaleahya's daughter. The unexpected move and the sudden explosion of the gun that was pulled was so loud in her sensitive ears that it took a moment for Aaleahya to realise what had happened.

Her screams echoed those of Kat and soon they were surrounded by SS officers and soldiers. Ekaterina's eyes turned red and the officer who had been chasing her suddenly swore upon seeing the change in her and shot her also. Aaleahya sobbed, her anger pulsing through her as she was restrained. The Officer who killed her children gloated at his discovery and ability to prove that Kat was not the human they had pretended. Grabbing Aaleahya's chin he looked into her own eyes waiting to see if they would also change. Aaleahya fought the change, only possible since she had been around longer than their children. She was marched back with rifles and machine guns pointed at her, pulled and pushed to keep moving. The Officer called a halt and then punched Aaleahya in her face repeatedly, calling her foul names, telling her what all he intended to do with her and what the Gauleiter will have Gavril do for their cause. Brought into the house and thrown on the floor in front of Gavril, tears were running down her face. She cried not from the pain that was inflicted on her, but from the senseless loss of their children.

She looked up at Gavril as the Gauleiter and more soldiers surrounded him. The Gauleiter's pleasure that he was right about her Mate was clear for all too see. It did not matter than their daughter and their son had to die to prove his point. All that paled into insignificance, so pleased was he that he had been right all along about Gavril.

Angrily, Aaleahya implored her Mate through their link that this needed to end now. These men are monsters and needed to die, she told him, indicating the ones responsible for the death of Sandu and Kat. As she looked up her hair hanging down and her face stained with her tears, bruises forming from the blows to her face, she smiled incongruously. Her Mate's eyes were no longer the warm, welcoming chocolate brown that she knew was his peaceful side. Now, they were Cŵn Annwn red.

"All cultures have a variation on a theme, Herr Gauleiter." Gavril's voice was a low growl. "Ha játszani a tűzzel, készüljön fel kell égetni. If you play with fire, prepare to be burned."

Without taking his eyes from his target, Gavril called the Pack to himself. The low howl echoed around the hall, becoming a crescendo of sound. It was a call rarely used, because it connected him with his entire Pack, both those in this country, those in the USA and those still in Wales. All would come at the call. All bar two members, who lay dead on the floor before their Alpha.

"Whatever you are doing, stop now, Herr Negrescu. I am warning you. Stop now, or your Mate ..." The Gauleiter tried to sneer, "… your Mate will die." He pulled his handgun from the holster at his side, and pressed the barrel against Aaleahya's head.

Even as he spoke, Bran and Owain appeared, taking their usual places to his left and right. Their sudden appearance made the Gauleiter's hand shake. The doors leading from the Hall slammed shut, locking the SS contingent, including their Commandant and Kat's 'tail', the one who had fired the killing shots for both Kat and Sandu, in with the Pack. Gavril heard guns being cocked even as the whisper of sound around them, coupled with the rush of power of being surrounded by my Pack, told Gavrilto that the Call had been answered, and that the Pack had registered the death of two of their own.

Gavril heard Bran's quiet words. "Kat, Sandu and your Mate covered our escape with the last group of evacuees. We managed to save another sixty souls, my Alpha." It was small consolation, but at least Gavril knew that his daughter and her friend had died doing what was important to them. Sandu had died protecting Kat, and Kat had died because she believed that saving the lives of innocent souls was more important than saving her own life.

"My love." Gavril addressed his words to Aaleahya, her face now calm, as she begged him through their link to end the lives of these creatures who call themselves human. "Herr Gauleiter is your prey. Deal with him as you see fit. I will deal with the rest of the refuse."

Aaleahya heard her love's words in her head and the change on her was immediate. The one holding the gun to her head screamed as she called forth the power in her, as her own eyes turned red then black as soul she was about to take. The Gauleiter hand shook as he realized too late that Aaleahya was also Cŵn Annwn and his life was now in her hands.

The change to her wolf was flawless and in that wolf form she was quite large, perhaps not as large as her Mate but large enough and scary enough that her sensitive nose could smell the urine that stained the Gauleiter's trousers, the same neck that was now in her powerful jaws, the coppery salt of his blood trickling down her throat. The cries of the others dying filled her ears but paid no attention. She wanted this one's death to be painful; she wanted to him to see himself die, wanted him to suffer, as her claws and teeth ripped the flesh from him, strip by long strip, the blood splattering the walls and coating her fur.

Aaleahya could hear the gurgle of death as it approached this foul being. The strength of her jaws finally finished what she had started, snapping his neck as he breathed his final breath.

The one who shot the children was standing, being held by some of the pack Aaleahya circled around him growling snapping her teeth as she passed in front of him. At her mental command, he was released. In a panic he ran to the door, clearly thinking that there might be a chance for escape. Aaleahya lunged at him, sinking her teeth deep into his thigh until they hit bone, and then snapping it in half as if the bone was a toothpick. His screams bounced off the walls, as he pleaded that he was only following orders. Just as Aaleahya did with the Gauleiter, she started removing his flesh from his bones making sure he suffered with each swipe of her claws. When he was nothing but a bleeding pile of bones, she sank her teeth into his throat, pushing one last thought into the bastard's mind before he died. "You killed the ones I loved and threatened my Mate but it is you who will die and burn in the fires of hell."

Snapping the SS officer's neck, Aaleahya ended his life. She devoured his black heart nearly choking on the vile organ but her powers negated the effect of evil in seconds, such was the gift from their Goddess: the ability to absorb evil and destroy it with in her body.

As Aaleahya savaged the Gauleiter, her fury at the fact that he has threatened her Mate, and killed her children was obvious in the way that she ripped him to shreds. Gavril was only too well aware that it was not often that his Mate, his gentle and forgiving Mate, demonstrated that she fully appreciated that sometimes being gentle doesn't work. Sometimes, as with men like the Gauleiter, it would be execution, plain and simple.

The Gestapo officer who had pulled the trigger on Kat and Sandu fared no better. His screams were music to Gavril's ears also. His jealousy for Sandu drove him to kill a young, for Cŵn Annwn, male, whose only 'crime' had been his earnest desire to protect the daughter of his Alpha. Then, he killed the 'object of his desire', their Pack's 'Princess', and why? Fear. He saw Kat's eyes change to Cŵn Annwn red, and for no other reason than fear, he had murdered her.

Another throbbing howl to the Pack was the order to kill all non-Pack in the room, and to harvest.

Gavril's target was the SS Kommandant, the man who had invaded his home, and who had enjoyed their weekly discussions. He had not told

Aaleahya what transpired during those meetings. Suffice it to say that, as Alpha, the injuries heal. He had made the choice between ensuring that he was fully fit for the needs of his Pack over the temporary discomfort of burns, knife injuries and bruising from beatings. Gavril stayed in his human form, as his prey backed away from him, a glance at the remains of the Gauleiter and the younger SS officer and his sudden pallor making it clear that he knew what was coming. A shaking hand brought his Luger up, pointing it at Gavril. Gavril's smile widened as his snarl showed his fangs, leaving little doubt what he intended to do.

"You wanted to use me and my family." Gavril's growl was low but audible. "You thought we could be forced to support your cause." One hand transformed into claws, the length shrouded in the dark fur of his wolf. Flashing closer and pushing him up against a wall, Gavril held him by the throat in one hand. "Payback time, Kommandant." Gavril's clawed hand struck down and across the Kommandant's chest, cutting through the fabric of his uniform, blood gushing down his torso. He screamed, a high wail of pain. "Did that hurt?" Gavril purred. The claws struck again, lower, across gut and genitalia. "How about that?" He asked. The Kommandant screamed again, the German words begging, pleading for mercy. "Ah yes." Gavril smiled, letting him see fangs. "The same level of mercy you showed when we had our little discussions?" He laughed. Still holding the Kommandant by the throat, his clawed hand moved lower, and this time, digging his claws deep into the Kommandant's leg, into his femoral artery, Gavril raised him clear off the ground, feeling the gush of arterial blood flow. As the light started to fade, and the screams turned to whimpers, Gavril sank his fangs into the man's neck, drinking deeply, taking in his essence. This scum was even worse than his actions over the last six months had implied and the world was well rid of him.

Raising his head, Gavril dropped the remains of his prey on the floor, the blood from the Kommandant's femoral artery slowing and stopping even as his heart stopped beating. Around him, the sounds of fighting started to fade, as each member of the Pack dropped to one knee before their Alpha, offering Gavril a wrist that he might take the souls that they had harvested on Gavril's behalf. Thirty dead, but none of those deaths would bring back his angel. None of them would bring back the child his Mate had borne him, and again, his howl echoed as Gavril screamed his pain and rage at the senseless waste of her life and the life of Sandu, the son of his heart.

Aaleahya, still in her wolf form, padded up to him, the blood of the Gauleiter and the Gestapo officer coating her fur. "It is done, my love." Gavril murmured to her, as her tongue dragged across his hand. Gavril signalled to Bran and Owain, who shifted from their own wolf forms back to human. "Bring Sandu and Kat." He instructed them. Looking around the room, at the Pack in both wolf and human forms, he was aware of the fact that they all felt the same.

It didn't matter. Those who had murdered their own were dead, but it would not bring back Kat and Sandu.

"Return to the Hunter's Arrow, via the caves so that you may clean up. I will dispose of the evidence here. The authorities will be made to believe that a fire has occurred here, destroying the whole frontage of the building." He shrugged, Gavril's smile cold. "I warned them that keeping as much weaponry as they did here was a mistake."

Running his hand along Aaleahya's head, he murmured to her softly. "I will join you shortly, my love, and we will mourn together."

As the flames took hold of Negrescu Hall, the home in which his Mate, Aaleahya had borne their daughter, and they had hoped to raise a family, Gavril found himself reflecting on the events of the last six months, since the Nazis had invaded Hungary, and since the effects of the war really started to be felt in their corner of the world.

When their homes, both the Hall and Hunter's Arrow, had been taken over by the Nazis, the Pack continued their efforts to evacuate those at risk from the policy known as the Final Solution. They had tried to protect those innocent souls from the evil that they saw around us.

The cost to their Pack had been high. They had to face a constant barrage of being watched, of being followed. Aaleahya had had to take care to hide her accent, which may have revealed her origins as Romanian, and thus put her at risk of deportation. Their younger Pack members such as Kat and Sandu had had to be careful not to do anything which might have revealed that they were something other than human. As with the young of any species, this was far from easy. Kat may have lived for more than 60 human years, but it still meant that she was young in terms of being Cŵn Annwn.

Gavril had to face weekly 'meetings' with the Gauleiter and the SS Kommandant who now called his Hall their home. The taste of the Kommandant's soul, as Gavril watched his home burn, was no consolation. They had called the Pack animals and subhuman, but what this ... creature had done, in the name of the twisted politics that he held dear, that showed his lack of humanity.

Gavril had not told Aaleahya what had happened during those meetings. They were interrogations. They were weekly sessions intended to force a reaction from their prisoner that would reveal his true nature. They tried various methods: violence to the point that bruises would have been disabling had he been human; deliberately inflicted knife injuries, where fortunately, Gavril could slow the bleeding until he could attend to the injuries in a more traditional fashion. But he had to tread a fine line. Heal too quickly, and his captors would have had confirmation that he was something other than human. Leave himself disabled by their 'gentle handling', and he risked putting his Mate, and his Pack at the mercy of those who wished to use them to further their twisted politics. It was draining, and something Gavril wanted to share with his Mate, but could not. For some reason he could not.

CHAPTER 11 - FROM THE ASHES: AUGUST 1944

Diary Extract: Gavril Dracul Negrescu

The ashes that were all that remained of Negrescu Hall were still glowing. It would be a while before the remains of what had been the home I had shared with my Mate, Aaleahya, was even cool enough to approach. By then, any clue as to what had caused the conflagration would be impossible to detect. But, it wouldn't bring back what had been lost. My heart wept, knowing that nothing would bring my little Angel back. It wouldn't bring the son of my heart back to me either.

Why? Without my Pack around me, I felt that, at last, I could howl my sorrow and his despair. I had tried to keep my family and my Pack safe, and it had been for nothing. I had hidden what had been done to me from my Mate, the one with whom I should have shared everything, and it had served no purpose.

Not sure how it happened, Gavril found himself in Aaleahya's old cave, the cave in which they had consummated their Mating all those years ago. The furs had long since rotted away, chewed by rodents and other forest beasties. The plants still grew, but the walls were cold, bare, with no trace of the passion with which they had kindled their relationship.

His back sliding down the wall, Gavril sank to the ground. It did not help that he knew they had the legacy that Kat had left them. Hundreds of children who might have died in the extermination camps would live, and hopefully thrive in their new homes. But Gavril's own family? Gone. Lost to him.

With no one to see the truth, he could let go of what he had kept hidden from his Mate for the last six months. The scars from the burns. The slash marks left from knife wounds. The bruising that was still visible. Had his sweet Aaleahya seen any of this, she would have struggled to keep her she-wolf under control, and for that reason, to protect the one who was so precious to him, Gavril had kept it hidden.

But for what purpose now?

Her heart felt like an empty shell as Aaleahya went in search for the one being who could fill it once again. She passed the burning embers of what was once their home, the carnage hidden except in her mind. Lifting her head, she howled, low and long, all the sorrow and pain exerted into that single, painful howl. Tears coursed down her face at the loss of her baby girl and male whom she had considered to be like a son. She could sense her Mate was keeping things hidden from her, knowing that such things cannot be hidden from one's true soul Mate. She had been dogged every day by the Nazi officers wanted her to service them, taking perverse pleasure in defiling the local leader's wife and, always, she had refused taking the beatings instead, staying loyal to her Mate. Even now, she had not known how she had managed to keep her beast at bay, but she had. Her Goddess had come to her, telling Aaleahya to be strong, that her time of suffering would be at an end and soon she would be able to have her vengeance, but it had still been so hard. So very hard.

Clearing her head, she watched as the last of the embers smouldered into ash, before beginning to look for her Mate, her lover Gavril. As Aaleahya inhaled, she realised that his scent was strong on the air. Following it, she realised that it led to the cave where they consummated their mating, and where she had become pregnant with Ekaterina. Her tears and anger surged again, at both her loss and her Mate's loss, at what they had both lost, and, for a moment, she hesitated to enter the cave which held so many memories, buried in the smell of decay from the old furs she had used, when this little cave had been her home and shelter.

Grasping her courage, Aaleahya entered the cave, not sure what she would find, but knowing that Gavril's scent remained strong. She had not expected to see her Mate, lying on the dirt floor of the cave, naked, the cuts, bruises and burns covering his body. Putting her fist in her mouth to stifle her exclamation, she moved further into the cave, fearful, that on this day that she had lost her daughter and the son of her heart, she might also lose her Mate. As she approached, Aaleahya felt as if her heart started to beat again, as she realised that Gavril lay, not dead, but unconscious, his breathing soft, but even. He was alive.

Gavril may have been alive, but Aaleahya realised that he was weakened, his visible injuries being only part of the picture. Rushing over to him, she knelt at his side, stroking his hair.

"Gavril why didn't you tell me? I am here for you, love; let me heal you. I can feel the evil taint under his skin." Through touch and voice, Aaleahya tried to reach her Mate, wherever he had fled. "Gavril my love you need to rid yourself of this soul. Let me rid you of it." Shedding her own clothes Aaleahya gathered him in her arms, letting the dark evil to be absorbed into her own body. In her soul, Aaleahya gave thanks to their Goddess for the precious gift which in turn destroyed the evil absorbed by her Mate, as if it never existed.

Closing her eyes, she kissed his forehead gently, his skin hot and dry on her lips. Using her powers, Aaleahya manifested a carpet of soft moss to cover where he was laying. She whispered, "Gavril I am here for you. Let me in; tell me what happened. Tell me what they did to you."

Part of him could feel the relief that came from Aaleahya taking the taint of evil from him, and his skin welcomed the softness of moss underneath him, in place of cold, hard stone. But another part of him wanted to, not hide, but just not have to face what this war has cost him to date.

Gavril was the Alpha of his Pack. He had been the Alpha for several centuries, but this war? It seemed that there was no end, even though all the signs are there. The Nazis will lose, but they won't lose without taking far too many innocents with them first.

Gavril could hear his sweet Mate's voice calling him, begging him to tell her what had happened. He knew that she could, at last, see the scars, see the burns and bruises. And then, through their bond, he realised that, as much as he had been abused, she has had to fight her own battles, and instead of fighting side by side, they had fought alone, trying to protect the other from the truth.

Gavril's eyes opened, and his hand reached up to her face, stroking the side of her cheek. His voice felt old, dry, as if he had not spoken in too long. He had not. He had not spoken with the one who mattered most to him, the one who was and still is the other half of his soul.

"I should have told you, my love, but I wanted to protect you."

Aaleahya hushed his words, hating the tone of guilt in his voice that he had hidden the truth from her. "I know love; we have both had to fight our own battles. If I had known this is what the outcome would have been I would have begged the Goddess to let us destroy them sooner. Maybe then we wouldn't have lost what was so dear to both of us."

Tears filled her eyes again. Aaleahya had thought she had exhausted her tears, but seeing her Mates' scars brought forth some of her own that she had also been hiding. "I miss her Gavril. She was the light of my life and has such a tender good heart. I am proud of her what she was able to accomplish in her very short life; Sandu also. I think they were Mated, my love, given that he never left her side and I could see the love in his eyes for her and well as in hers. I am angry they didn't get the chance to discover this together like we were able to."

Aaleahya placed her hand on her stomach that will forever be barren of children, as it is not meant to be unless the Goddess sees fit to bestow that treasure on them once again. Snuggling against Gavril, his skin dry and hot, she let all her love she had for him flow through her into his body, healing his skin from that of dead skin to pink healthy smooth skin. Running her fingers across his body Aaleahya leaned in and kissed him fully on the lips.

As he relished the feel of his Mate's lips on his own, and the healing glow that came from her touch, her special gift from our Goddess to them both, Gavril find himself hoping fervently that what she said was true. The devotion shown by Sandu for Kat. Her bond with him. Yes, it spoke of them being Mated, and had they had a few more years, perhaps it would have been a mating which would have been consummated. But they would never know that now. Releasing Aaleahya's lips, he traced them with his finger.

"They are together now, my love. That is what matters. Seldom apart in life, and now together in their deaths."

Gavril's hand moved to Aaleahya's belly, and he remembered the choice he had to make: act quickly and with less finesse than he might have done to save his Mate's life, or take his time and risk that she might die from blood loss. Given the choice again, Gavril knew he would rather keep his Mate by his side than have dozens of young. This time, as he sat up, and pulled his Mate closer to him, Gavril took her lips, devouring, wanting to show her that her 'barren' state as she called it mattered not to him.

"Perhaps the Goddess will see fit to bless us in time, my love." As Gavril scooped Aaleahya into his arms, bringing her close to him, feeling her length against his, he felt also the final taint of the souls, harvested in the Hall, leave him, to be replaced by calm.

This was not the fierce passion of their Mating, but this was something more important. As he ran his hands down her shoulders, down her arms, her sides, her hips, before bringing his fingers back in a little dance up her back, her eyes half closed. The slight discomfort of her lying against him paled into insignificance.

Aaleahya knew they both need this mating to ease their hurts and sadness at the loss in their pack. She could feel the anger and sadness as well as the relief that they were no longer under the control of the Regime through the bond they had with their Pack. Many had loved their daughter and Sandu; they were as much children of the Pack as they were the children of their parents.

She could feel Gavril's hands as they traced her shoulders making a path down her arms all the way to her hips. Her body broke out in goosebumps as the skin rose under the little dance his fingers make up her back. She was moaning as, leaning forwards, she captured his lips with her own.

At Gavril's slight wince, Aaleahya pulled back. "Love I don't want to hurt you more than you have been hurt." Her whisper was soft. Her love for her Mate was surging within her, as they sought comfort in each other's arms. Aaleahya could not help but wonder if he could feel the scars on her back from the belts of the officers who found it amusing to use them on her when she didn't do as they thought she should. She felt him tense when he traced the scars to the left of her back where the beating broke the skin, shuddering when his finger lightly traced it.

“It seems, Gavril, that we have more than our outside scars to remind us of this horrible time in our lives but also the mental scars to go with them.”

Aaleahya sighed softly at the feel his fingers at her core which has moistened just for him under his ministrations. Her voice was a soft whisper, throbbing with her love for this male, as she nipped his ear. “I love you.”

The growl from Gavril’s anger at what his Mate had suffered also surged through him. He had wanted to protect her, and yet she wanted to do the same, by not telling him what had transpired, the indignities that she had suffered.

As his fingers wandered down, his hand cupped her mound, before gently parting the lips of her core, and feeling the moist, welcoming heat of her arousal. Gavril want to wipe from both their minds what they had to do, in their attempts to protect those dear to them, and to remain true to their service with their Goddess. The sigh of his Mate at his attentions drew his eyes back to her face, to the half-closed eyes, to the flushed cheeks, as she relaxed against him, the moss cushioning them both. Her head tilted back, offering him her throat, the pulse of life visible.

Gently, Gavril pressed his lips to her neck, laving the length, luxuriating in the feeling of being alive. Yes, his movements communicated to his Mate, we have lost a dear part of our lives, but we still have each other. His tongue swirled lower, to the dip in Aaleahya’s throat, and her soft sigh encouraged him more. Lower still, and tilting her body back gently, Gavril took one offered peak in his lips, sucking gently, his teeth grazing slightly, but his tongue swirling round, bringing the delicate little peak tighter and higher.

Lowering Aaleahya’s body, so that her head rested across his lap, Gavril transferred his attentions to her other breast, while his fingers played with both the aroused peak, and explored her core. One finger strayed higher, invading her, but Aaleahya’s slightly raised hips indicated it was a welcome invasion. Leaving her breast, Gavril took her lips again, savouring the softness.

"My love, my Mate." He murmured. Her half-opened lips beckoned to him, and this time, he did not resist the invitation. Gavril seized her mouth with his own, his tongue driving in, possessing, needing to wipe any memory of what others might have done to her. "Mine. Always mine." he murmured, lifting his lips for a moment, before devouring her mouth again, his mind repeating the litany through their bond.

Aaleahya’s eyes were half closed as her Mate’s fingers ran over her body. Her own hands were mirroring his actions. She knew that at the heart of his actions, Gavril had just wanted to protect her, ironically in the same way that she had wished to protect her Mate and her daughter. At the touch of his fingers, Aaleahya inhaled sharply, lifting her hips at his invasion of her core.

"Gavril."

Aaleahya murmured his name as her back arched, his mouth taking her nipple in his mouth, suckling on in until it became stiff with desire. She could hear him calling to her, her mouth half open, his tongue diving into her mouth possessing her wiping away the bad memories for at least for a moment in time. Those memories will remain with them, always and only in time would they be able to look back and remember the loss without so much pain.

The word, "Mine" flowed through their spousal link, sending ripples of pleasure throughout her body. Aaleahya repeated the mantra in her own head sending it through the link also. "Mine, Gavril, you are all mine and will be for always."

What started as a gentle reaffirmation of love for each other had grown. There is almost a desperation in his need to touch his Mate, to explore, to taste. He would never forget their loss, but they say that time will make the loss seem more bearable. For now, Aaleahya knew that she needed to feel one with the only other person who could understand that loss, and share the impact of that loss with her.

"My love, my Aaleahya, my Mate." Gavril's own litany formed a counterpoint to Aaleahya's chant down their bond, the words weaving together, delicate as a result of their shared loss, but strengthened through their love.

Lifting his lips from his Mate's, Gavril lifted her torso off his lap, bringing her face up to his, wrapping his arms around her, almost crushing her breasts against himself, the need to hold her, and to feel her overcoming any thoughts of gentle passion that he might have had earlier.

Aaleahya's legs parted, such that the warmth of her core was firmly over his own erection, the moist warmth telling Gavril how much she shared his need. As her hands wound through his hair, Gavril remembered their Mating, how she rode him. Raising her slightly, Gavril bring Aaleahya down over himself with force, sheathing himself in her warm core, feeling the muscles surrounding him as surely as her words wrapped themselves around my soul.

"My Mate, my Aaleahya, my one and only love..."

Perhaps now, with the loss of Kat and Sandu, the time had come for honesty. The time had come for Gavril to share with his Mate what had happened.

In the meantime, the work done by Kat and Sandu was not done. It would not be done until the war was over, and the threat of the extermination camps was over. There could be no better memorial for the daughter who had been his Mate's precious gift to him.

CHAPTER 12: FUNERALS AND FAREWELLS (AUGUST 1944)

They held the rites for Kat and Sandu at the end of August 1944. But that day, Aaleahya and Gavril bid farewell to more than just their daughter and son of their hearts. The day was made more poignant with the death of an old man, who was no threat to anyone, least of all those in an alleged position of authority. But, just as their children had been murdered in an act of senseless violence, so was the old priest, whose first act on arriving in the area had been their daughter's baptism.

Aaleahya's soul and heart ached with the loss of their daughter and Sandu, whom she loved as if she had borne him also. The pyres were decorated with symbols for each of them: Ekaterina's was adorned with flowers and Sandu's pyre was adorned with the weapons of the warrior he had become. She watched as the third pyre was built and the body of the old priest whose soul she had the honour to collect, was laid gently in place. Their Goddess had shared her own grief with Aaleahya, at the senseless nature of war, and the losses to them both, as she had accepted the soul of the old man. In times like this, it mattered not that he espoused a different faith to her own. All souls were united when the loss held this feeling of senseless waste.

Slowly, Aaleahya moved between the pyres, the roses she held symbols of each of those lost so recently: the red one for Sandu, a young warrior who paid the price of the love he had shown over years of protecting their lovely daughter; the white rose in Kat's hand for the innocence of life she gave her life for to protect from the evil of the Nazis; yellow rose in the hand the priest, showing the friendship he has shown their family over the years, protecting our secrets without scorn.

As Aaleahya placed the roses on each pyre, Gavril recalled the words of his Goddess. The time had come for the Pack to take retribution on those responsible for these three deaths which had taken so much not just from his Mate and him, but from their Pack. As the ruins of their home, Negrescu Hall, stood silent witness, some of those responsible had paid the price for their actions, but there are others. Some of those young German soldiers were not amongst that number, but too many of them were.

The panic engendered by the closing stages of fighting in any war led to more confusion. As the Allies advanced from the West, so the Russian armies were moving in from the East. And they had their own grievances against the armies of the, formerly, 'great' Third Reich.

The irony that Gavril acknowledged was that his geas to his Goddess meant that he would protect some of those boy soldiers of the

Reich, boys who had no place in war had it not been for the orders of a madman.

In the meantime, he would continue the work started by Kat and Sandu. The pace of the evacuations, if anything, had increased. Roma and Jews were being herded onto trains, their destination the death camps. The Final Solution may not be that in truth, but whilst they held power, the authorities were determined to send as many as they could to that end.

Coming to stand behind his Mate, as the fires were lit under the funeral pyres, he murmured to her. "I need to go to Paris, my love. I must meet with one of Kat's contacts, to ensure that those we evacuate find a safe route to America. His name is Nahuel Eskildsen."

Aaleahya felt a frisson of irritation thinking that her Mate had told her of this meeting as a prelude to saying he would go alone.

She whispered to him. “Remember love we are in this together from now on. No more apart. If you go to Paris, then I will be joining you.” Silent tears coursed down her cheeks as the pyres were lit to cremate the shells of their loved ones.

Pressing a gentle kiss to his Mate's head, Gavril murmured a response. "I wouldn't dream of not taking you with me, my love. As you said, Aaleahya, we are in this together now, as my Goddess intended. Paris is liberated now. It doesn't mean it is safe, but it will be safer than here for you."

"I don't know much about this man, but I know that Kat trusted him. It is enough of a recommendation that our daughter believed he held dear to her own principles. Still, I want to be sure. We are going to be moving whole families with his assistance, and that is no mean undertaking. I don't want to evacuate these people, only to expose them to more danger in another country."

As Aaleahya leaned into Gavril’s body, she had to agree with him. “I agree we would not want to move these good people to a new place to only be in danger once again.” She had a sad smile on her face, as Bran and Owain watch the funeral pyres burning, the smoke billowing high in the sky. Whilst it seemed strange in some respects that the villagers were also attending, Aaleahya realised that it was their own way of showing the support of love and concern for their paranormal protectors.

"Gavril, I only pray we are going to make the right decision for these people and wherever we move them to that their lives will fine.”

Gavril had a wry look on his face. "If only I knew the answer to that question?" Gavril found himself wondering the same thing. Yes, they were helping these families to avoid the death that awaited them at the end of a train line, but would life be any easier for them across an ocean?"

"I have made sure that there are sufficient funds with our American bankers that each family is given a grant to help them establish themselves. I predict that there will be a surge in food establishments after they arrive. It seems to be the most popular choice."

He told himself that it was the smoke from the funeral pyres which was making his eyes water, but Gavril knew he was lying to himself. "It is our daughter's legacy, my Mate, and I will do whatever is necessary to ensure that it is remembered for all the right reasons."

Aaleahya had reached up with her hand, gently wiping the tears off her Mate's rugged face, leaning into him and allowing him hold her close, both of them silent as they say goodbye to those who meant the world to them. She could feel the sadness echoing through the pack bond, hearing the whispered goodbyes of each member of the pack as they expressed their love for two of their own and one gentle soul. Her own tears were no less, as she too bid farewell.

Gavril's mind could not help but think about their forthcoming meeting in Paris. The capital city of France may have been liberated, but it was not yet free. The war still continued, only now, it is not just affecting those whom the Germans wish to exterminate. Already, there is the start of panic amongst the ethnic Germans living in Hungary, in the advance of the Red Army. The politics of this man, Josef Stalin, were as extreme as the Fascists, but from the other end of the scale. Having tried to keep his family safe through one regime, Gavril have no wish to go through the same process again.

The resolution came to him, to move his Pack again. Hunter's Arrow would be signed over to a 'workers' cooperative' made up from the local village, which will meet with the approval of the whoever retains power, since the lands and properties will be in the name of local Hungarians. The loyalty felt by these people will keep the Pack's former home safe, so that perhaps, one day, they might return to this place where his life with his Aaleahya started, and where their children were born.

But for now, their priority would be continuing the safe evacuation of those in need of their help. This would be their memorial to their children.

CHAPTER 13: A MEETING IN PARIS

Despite his agreement with Aaleahya that they would handle together the Underground Railroad established by Kat and Sandu, Gavril was reluctant to take her with him on this first meeting with Kat's contact in France. He had the name, Nahuel Eskildsen, and a description. But he had little more information. Given what had just happened at Negrescu Hall, when he had nearly lost his Mate to the machinations of the Gauleiter and the local SS Kommandant, Gavril had compromised in persuading her to let him meet this man alone, initially. Once Gavril was satisfied that the contact was not a danger to him, his Mate, his Pack, and those innocent souls they were trying to help, only then would Gavril let the contact meet his Mate.

Call him paranoid, or call him duly cautious. Gavril didn't care. Just because Paris was now 'liberated' did not mean the city was safe. Those who were considered collaborators were reviled. What he had to tolerate from the Gauleiter and the SS Kommandant came perilously close to collaboration, even whilst he had been smuggling both Jews and Roma out of Hungary and onwards to the safety of the USA via the Negrescu Cŵn Annwn pack base there. His efforts to date had saved several hundred children and young adults, and had cost him his daughter and son of his heart. But in the closing stages of the war, the need was now to move entire families, and that needed co-ordination.

Gavril had agreed to meet in a back-street café, one of the few that had managed to survive, which was a fairly good indication that it had 'links' somewhere.

Nahuel stayed in the background still not sure of this new contact. Too many infiltrators have tried to thwart their struggle to evacuate those in need so caution was paramount, especially with the Allied advances. A male he had not seen before entered the cafe with an aura of strength that stood out. The others eyed him with distrust but went about their activities so as not to tip him off. As he passed by Nahuel could sense something familiar and non-human about him. He had no doubt that this was his new contact and Nahuel eased himself to the stranger's table, sitting opposite him. "The coffee is rather good here if you don't mind the French brewing. It can take a little getting used to." The two males studied each other, each working to determine trust in the other.

As he entered the café, Gavril was aware of the suspicion towards him, wondering if these humans realise that suspicion has such a pungent odour, particularly to one who is part wolf. Scanning the room, he examined the nature of the souls huddled in their little groups or sitting alone. As his gaze settled on one individual, who matched Kat's description, his arm was grabbed from behind. Aaleahya, his Mate was clearly unimpressed that she had been left her behind at the boarding house.

Pacing back forth Aaleahya was furious that once again Gavril was trying to protect her. She had as much riding on this as those poor souls did. Moreover, she was determined that she would not have a repeat of keeping things from each other. Using her senses and finding her Mate in a cafe sitting with a large formidable looking male, her eyes were flashing her anger at her Mate as she grabbed his arm, hissing through their link. "Gavril whatever happened to 'never be parted'?" Turning to the male sitting with her Mate, Aaleahya smiled. "Good day to you, m'sieur. I am Aaleahya, wife to Gavril. I am pleased to meet you."

Nahuel watched with humour as the female clearly asserted herself with Gavril. He had always admired a female of strength. "Bonjour, Aaleahya, je suis enchanté de faire votre connaissance." Nahuel tipped his head to the as yet unintroduced male. "Well met, Gavril." The waiter approached their table and Nahuel order coffee pastry for his guests. That was his signal to the rest assembled to keep an eye out to protect their private conversation. "I've not received word from the usual contacts in your region. I hope there is no trouble and that you are able to get word to them. Changes have been made and our, arrangement has expanded to include larger deliveries. I will be happy to share the particulars with your assurance that this information will be delivered to my friends."

Gavril closed his eyes briefly at this Nahuel's mention of his 'usual contacts' in the Carpathian region as he waited for the requested coffee to be served. This 'man' is not a man. He may have been able to keep that hidden from Kat and Sandu, but there was a lot more to him than met the eye.

"Your usual contacts were my daughter and son. Unfortunately, they are no longer with us, along with the ones who thought to use them for their own purposes. My wife and I have taken over management of the local delivery network" Gavril took a sip of the coffee. "It is good that you are able to handle larger deliveries now, since that was our specific concern."

Through his link with Aaleahya, Gavril reassured his Mate that he was only being cautious. Having just lost Kat and Sandu, if he were to lose Aaleahya as well, Gavril knew that the madness that overtook his former Alpha, his own dam, on his sire's death would await him. There was too much riding on Gavril staying sane and in control to take that risk.

Placing her hand on her Mate's arm when Gavril spoke to the male, Nahuel, Aaleahya could also sense that there was more to this male than was immediately apparent, communicating as much through their Mating Bond.

"I know you are just being cautious, my love, but it goes both ways. I need to be at your side." She added, "I can sense this male's soul, he has evil with in him but it is overridden by good. How is this possible?

Nahuel's face did not hide his pain at the loss of Kat and Sandu. So many have lost their lives to this evil permeating the land. Humans consider themselves superior and yet display such depravity. "I am terribly sorry to hear of your loss. They became close friends of mine and their loss touches me deeply. You honour their sacrifice by continuing their work" He smiled briefly thinking of them. "She could be quite demanding and I always looked forward to our negotiations." Looking at Aaleahya then back to Gavril, there was a brief smile on his face. "I see now who she got that from."

His senses told Nahuel that their strength and conviction was such that they would have no problem with the mission before them. They were more than Kat and Sandu and it will be interesting to see exactly how. "It's not often I run across those whose powers can match mine."

"All right then. Down to business. A new evacuation route has opened up with the recent Allied victory in Provence. We'll piggy back onto the network devised to spirit Allies caught behind enemy lines. I worked hard to negotiate the addition of refugees as some felt it would draw too much attention but I managed to work my 'skills' into assuring that they will do everything in their power to see it done. The only snag would be getting them to the Provence region and that is what I had hoped to discuss with Kat and Sandu."

Nahuel leant back and sipped his coffee, wondering how much they would be able to reveal to him.

Gavril reflected that in some ways, the irony was that this 'man' needed their skills just as much as he and Aaleahya needed his network to take the families the Pack wanted to smuggle out to the coast. Once the evacuees were on board ship, and in Wales, the refugees could rest and recuperate before we took them on the next leg over to the Pack's base in New York State. The only reason for needing to use another network was to enable them to transport more people. While one group was on board ship, the Pack could be bringing another group into the Provence region. The shorter transport also meant that Gavril's Pack would not wear themselves ragged trying to move as many families as needed to be moved.

The Goddess knew they wouldn't be able to move everyone that needed evacuation, but with the assistance of this 'man', this Nahuel Eskildsen, the Pack could increase their efforts so far.

At the same time, Gavril was listening to Aaleahya's assessment of this individual whom they were going to trust on the basis their daughter's contact with him. Gavril agreed with her: the combination of bad, overlaid with good was interesting to say the least. He 'hummed' with powers which were of a similar strength to his own abilities as a Cŵn Annwn Alpha, and yet, it did not appear that he could work out who they were, any more than they could find his true nature.

"Bringing people into Provence is no problem." Gavril told the other male with quiet confidence. "Using that part of your network, up to the coast to bring the families close to the UK mainland, where my people will handle landing them, will mean we can double the number of evacuees our own network has handled to date." Deliberately, Gavril turned his head slightly to Aaleahya, using speech instead of their link. "Cariad, yr wyf yn meddwl y gallwn ni ymddiried yn y dyn hwn. Ni fydd yn peryglu y Pecyn neu'r rhai sydd yn dibynnu ar i ni. (Beloved, I think we can trust this man. It will not risk the Pack or those who are relying on us.)

It would be interesting to see what this Nahuel Eskildsen made of Gavril's deliberate use of Welsh.

Nahuel was trying to work out why the male before him was such an enigma. Just what his powers were remained to be seen but, for his part, Nahuel was content to know that the spirits on which he called had told him to trust them. He knew they had been conversing telepathically and though he didn't know what was said, Nahuel understood their need for caution so did not react. However, Gavril's use of the Welsh tongue elicited a smile and he faced Aaleahya. "He is correct; you can trust me." Nahuel met Gavril's eye. "I can appreciate your caution. Despite our true natures we have vulnerabilities. Those we help and most importantly those we care for. It would not do to let our guard down and risk any of them. That being said, I have faith in your loyalty to this venture and will give you the information you seek."

Nahuel signalled to Peter who in turn led his group in song to cover the conversation, knowing this couple could hear his soft words so he did not lean forward. "There are two routes that can get your people to ships heading to the UK, both run by the Maquis. The Avignon group will get them to a small port outside Bordeaux. Another group in Lyon travels to another small port in St. Malo. Both boats will deliver them to Plymouth and it will be up to your people at that point. Be sure the travellers are well fed as parts of the journey are taxing for hu...for them. Money is tight in the network so make sure they pocket food for the journey as well. The meeting place for each collection point is the hotel bearing the name of the city. They are to go to the kitchen door and tell who answers that Papa sent them for the day old bread. Each transport leaves precisely at 3 am on alternating Thursdays." The song ended as Nahuel shrugged and smiled. "Let us hope the need for this Underground Railroad ends soon."

Gavril relaxed, feeling slightly more at ease after this male had passed the first test. For this man to understand the Welsh tongue and specifically, the dialect of North Wales, told Gavril that he was not some infiltrator. Only a being of power, or a native of the mountains of Cymru would have understood his accent, given that his native Welsh was tinged with years of living in Eastern Europe.

Resting an elbow on the table before them Gavril tapped two fingers against his temple, raising a brow in suggestion that they continued to discuss specifics via a mind link. At the same time, Gavril placed an arm around Aaleahya, drawing her closer to him, and smiled at the man, Nahuel. "Your friends are very creative." he commented, to cover the lull in conversation from speaking by other methods.

Speaking to Aaleahya alone via their own link. "I want to find out more about who this man is. I have a suspicion that this won't be the only time we will work with him, and I want to know why."

Speaking vocally to the man sitting with them, Gavril nodded. "Food and other provisions will not be a problem. If funds are an issue, I have scope to assist with that also. The assistance of your friends will enable my wife and me to continue the work of our daughter and son and for that you have our gratitude."

Nahuel nodded, acknowledging Gavril's offer. "Funding is sometimes difficult due to the logistics involved. Not to mention they cannot draw undue attention by purchasing larger than normal amounts of food at the hotel nor explain portable food stuffs. We cannot be too careful."

Nahuel had seen Gavril's signal to speak via mind link and admitted to himself that he was impressed this stranger could do this outside of pack. He was certainly more than he appeared and Nahuel smiled, looking forward to having more time to research him. One never knows when a future alliance would be beneficial. "I take it you did not enjoy my friend's singing voice. I'll have to speak to him about that." Nahuel sipped his coffee and continued talking. "You are two of a very few that know I am not human and even those do not know I can converse like this out of a pack. So tell me, why am I putting myself at risk by doing so? For that matter, why are you? Wouldn't it be better to think that I took you for a regular wolf? I understand the Nazis have quite the bounty on them. Can you imagine what you or I would bring?" Nahuel studied them both for a moment before continuing. "I have my own reasons for trusting you and for the most part they have not led me astray before."

Nahuel smiled in personal enjoyment at how lightly he had dismissed the dark spirit's continued attempts to sway him. "I am rather intrigued at what I sense in you and more so that you have trusted me."

Gavril knew his mind voice sounded cold when Nahuel mentioned just how much the Nazis 'valued' creatures such as them. "The local authorities in my area have already tried exploiting my value." Gavril informed him, holding Aaleahya closer at the same time. He took another sip of coffee. "We both bear the physical and emotional scars of that exploitation, whilst we took the burden of suspicion so that others could move more freely." Gavril acknowledged that his beloved Mate had shouldered some of the burden of blame for others, even as he had been keeping suspicions focused on his own potential abilities.

"The authorities also had to learn the hard way that it was a poor choice, particularly when their actions cost us our daughter and son." Not just the Gauleiter, the Kommandant and the young Gestapo officer had paid. Even now, Gavril fought the need for revenge. Without his Mate, it would be too easy to fall prey to that desire.

Gavril's gaze was direct when he looked at the 'man', Nahuel. "You are more than a wolf, as you said, as are we. I, too, have been told you are worthy of trust, despite the shadow both of us can feel in your soul. The one who guides me, in all the years I have served, has not maladvised me, so, trust? Yes, I am willing to trust you with the knowledge of what we are. We are not that different, for all that I have my Pack and you?" I paused. "You have Pack, and yet you do not? Curious, indeed."

"Going back to our plans, may I suggest that in advance of evacuees, my people bring in supplies? Aaleahya has a particular talent in that regard, which we can share. That way, there is no need for purchases to be made which might raise suspicions. The war continues, and those who stand to lose will only become more desperate and more vicious the more that they stare defeat in the face."

Aaleahya nodded in response to her Mate's comments. "Just let us know how much ... extra provision is likely to be required and I will ensure that they are provided. I am happy to ... visit regularly, so that no comments are made about the sudden appearance of additional supplies." Aaleahya smiled. "After all, by working together, by using our abilities, a better result is certain to be the outcome."

Nahuel studied the pair before him, watching Gavril as he spoke of the hardships they had endured and understood all too well the emotional turmoil that had been involved.

"You are strong indeed to refrain from falling into the hell of revenge. I've walked the razor's edge myself on too many occasions. It seems too easy to just succumb to the frenzy, when the reality is that the eventual cost will be too high." Nahuel nodded to them both. "I commend you for that strength."

The male's smile was cold as he spoke of the darkness within his soul. "We all have a shadow of darkness within us, some are just closer to the surface. I do not wish to delve too much into that part of me, except to say that I have learned to harness what I need to accomplish what I must."

Nahuel leant back, studying Gavril and Aaleahya. There was so much at risk and yet he had found himself a bit chagrined to realise that within one hour, he had divulged more than he had to any living soul previously. "It is sufficient to say that we trust each other. But, I warn you not to trust anyone else with any non-human attributes. There are far too many desperate people out there to be truly comfortable. I will draw you a staging area outside both towns. I use them myself when speed is required." He paused for a moment, considering Aaleahya's veiled comments about her abilities, and her willingness to provide additional supplies. "I have put special wards on the two farms." Pulling out a paper, Nahuel inscribed some symbols. There was a hint of whether he was wise to trust Gavril, but he nodded, almost to himself before continuing. "You will be safe there and can use it to hide if needed. I will make the necessary adjustments to accommodate you."

Gavril looked at the symbols which Nahuel had drawn for them, the protective wards on the two farms that they would use to bring in the evacuees. He raised a brow. "Nordic?" Gavril looked at the man before him and at the image that he portrayed. "That is your background?" Nothing in the man's manner had indicated to Kat that her contact was 'other', and certainly not the English/American individual that he claimed to be. With Gavril's own Celtic background, at least it means that there was no likely clash. Whilst he served his Goddess, Gavril knew that there were other pantheons as well as her own, who may have their own views on appropriate actions. The carnage that he had seen on the battlefields of The Great War demonstrated to Gavril only too well that understanding the politics of those in 'command' of beings like himself was vital.

"Aaleahya and I are Cŵn Annwn, working under the Goddess Mallt-y-Nos. We are soul harvesters and a Mated pair. As you may have realised, I am the current Alpha." Taking the paper with the wards, Gavril traced his finger over them, memorising them for use when they needed to access the farms. He passed the paper to Aaleahya so that she could do the same. "We appreciate your understanding our reluctance to let others, those not like us, knowing anything about what we can do. They won't see it as evil, they wish to use any and all methods that might win them the war but we have been used before and we have no wish to revisit the experience."

When Aaleahya had finished memorising the symbols, Gavril summoned a small, discrete flame and reduced the paper to ashes. "If there is nothing else we need to discuss, I suggest we part company before any notice is taken of us" Gavril shrugged, speaking out loud. "Perhaps you might suggest some sights in Paris where I might take my wife while we are here."

Nahuel nodded at the question regarding his lineage, realising that for Gavril to voice, albeit mentally, who and what they are conveys a strength of trust that he could both admire and appreciate. "I am Meleki." He chuckled a bit and wondered how to phrase a response. "Even amongst my own kin I am a bit of a, how do they say it? Ah yes, misfit. I have spent a great deal of time on the spirit realm and with humans instead of hiding away. I feel that my 'talents' would be better served helping others and in that, I believe we are in agreement." Nahuel watched them study the paper and was satisfied that they would master the necessary steps to ensure that their anonymity and the safety of the way stops. "Yes, there are those humans who hate that which they don't understand as well as those that wish to harness the mystery. Personally, I do not wish to fall into either's hands. Or worse, have those entrusted to my care to face that. Silly humans go on assumptions and atrocities they can inflict they think they are right, rival the gods at times." He sat back with a shake of his head. "Forgive me. I become frustrated with all the waste and hardship and get carried away."

Nahuel nodded slightly and smile in acknowledgement at his smooth transition to verbal communication and to also pull me from delving into his own anger. "There are many romantic sites in Paris that would enhance the closeness that you two share. The usual tourist sites are beautiful but there is a small café behind the Hotel des Invalides. They have a superb wine selection and Pierre's sauces can make a grown man cry." Nahuel winked at Aaleahya. "Now what Mate would want to miss that?"

Aaleahya looked thoughtfully at Nahuel considering his words. Gavril smiled also, dropping a light kiss on is Mate's head, as he held her close. "I think, my friend, given the way that my Mate is looking at you, that it will not be long before you, too, will know what it means to find the other half of your soul." Raising Aaleahya's hand to his lips, Gavril smiled at the memory of finding his own Mate. "I had to travel from Cymru to the Carpathians to find my Mate and it is a journey I would make a thousand times over, for the strength and peace that our Mating brought me." Draining his coffee, Gavril stood in preparation for taking his leave. "Who knows? The next time we meet, we may have due cause to celebrate more than the end of the war."

As Gavril made his way back to the boarding house with Aaleahya, he pondered the meeting with this Nahuel Eskildsen, this Nordic Meleki. War can cause some strange alliances to form. Celtic and Nordic? If it meant that their promise to Kat and Sandu would be fulfilled, then it was an alliance that he was more than pleased to make.

CHAPTER 14: PEOPLE MATTER (OCTOBER 1944)

As the leaves changed in the trees, and the nights started to draw in, so the Pack increased the number of evacuations they carried out, utilising the route opened up to them by this Meleki, Nahuel Eskildsen. At the same time, they continued with the method they had used from the outset.

For those families where the parents had either been lost to war or to deportations, leaving children and adolescents, the Pack moved them directly to their base in Cymru. There, the evacuees had the opportunity to remember for a short while what it meant to be young. When they had recovered sufficiently, they were moved to the new Negrescu Hall, in New York State, where the Pack helped them to re-establish their lives. The older adolescents were helped with establishing business if that was what they wished. The younger children were placed with other Jewish families. Their new parents could not replace those that they had lost, but it gave them a structure to their lives.

One of the first things that they had to address was that, with the loss of Negrescu Hall, the only Pack accommodation was the Hunter's Arrow Inn, which was already having to accommodate up to a hundred German soldiers at a time. In addition, whilst the Gauleiter and the majority of the local SS detachment had met an unfortunate end in that conflagration, as Gavril knew only too well, the little shit still had staff, including equally officious assistants, who were both jockeying for his position and trying to protect themselves, with the daily knowledge that the Red Army was approaching. Similarly, the death of thirty members of the SS detachment in an unfortunate fire was also going to result in, at least a cursory, investigation.

Gavril was summoned to the administrative headquarters for their Region, following the fire, to explain what had happened. So, he had two options. One was to portray the outraged landowner whose fucking mansion had just been destroyed through careless storage of armaments. The second was, well, still anger at the destruction of his home through carelessness, but portray his horror at the loss of life.

The problem was that the second option would have made him seem to be in sympathy with the Regime. A collaborator. The thought of collaborating with this scum, bearing in mind what he had had to tolerate for the last six months, turned Gavril's stomach in the extreme. That he might be seen as a collaborator, when he and his Mate had just held the funeral rites for their daughter and son, would have seemed ludicrous under any circumstance.

But this is war. This is the war when the side, who thought they were winning, were now having to face the fact that defeat was a very real prospect. Do those in power try to consolidate, or do they start planning a retreat. If anything, the Pack was potentially at a greater risk of discovery of what they could do now than when the Gauleiter and the SS Kommandant had been holding the threat of harm to Gavril's family over his head.

Gavril chose a compromise of the two options he could have taken when summoned over the destruction of his home. He was outraged. After all, Negrescu Hall was not a small property, and the gardens and estate produced a lot of foodstuffs for the local area. That part had not been touched by the fire, and Gavril knew that Aaleahya would ensure that the food production was not hindered either.

Gavril was also the grief-stricken 'brother' whose 'sister' had been caught in the fire, given that she had been at her home, along with her friend, Sandu. When it was presented to him that Kat and Sandu had, in fact, been arrested on suspicion of being members of the local resistance, Gavril protested that the suggestion was ludicrous. His sister? His future brother in law? Where was the evidence? Where was the proof that they were guilty of this accusation? Gavril's mind may have howled with his continuing grief at the loss suffered by him and his Mate, but outwardly, he did not let this show.

Then, the bombshell. The Gauleiter's flunkeys had known that Gavril was being taken in for regular 'meetings' but what was discussed in those meetings was not known, although they had their suspicions given his interest in the paranormal. It seems that all the files on their discussions had been stored at the Hall. Damn shame. Of course, Gavril had regular meetings with the Gauleiter and the Kommandant. He had expressed my surprise that such an occurrence should be called into question. His estate was responsible for feeding most of the local population. He had to provide accommodation for a large cohort of the occupying forces. It stood to reason that he would need to have regular discussions with the Gauleiter. So what if normal protocol would have been for those discussions to be with someone further down the food chain, so to speak. Gavril had looked at them with all the arrogance of being, at least before the war, a wealthy individual.

"Please, don't tell me that you are going to also start on the local legends." He had stated in a bored tone. "It took me months to convince them that they were just that, stories." Gavril had shrugged. "I don't deny that there have been deaths, and that bodies were found with injuries that match the local stories, but are you suggesting that I was involved." Gavril had sat back in his chair, his legs extended, and crossed at the ankles. From the leather trousers, to the boots, to the open-necked working shirt under his jacket, nothing suggested apology. Nothing suggested Gavril had anything to hide. His body language was pure Alpha. Try it, you little shit. Try it and see if you can make the accusation stick.

On leaving the Assistant Gauleiter's office, Gavril nodded to Bran, who had accompanied him, in his guise at Gavril's 'Estate Manager'. Like Gavril was going to use Bran's correct title of Joint Pack Beta where these scum could hear him? Together they made their way out of the building, before he stopped. Shaking his boot, as if to loosen a stone, Gavril paused.

[ML to Bran] "There is a junior flunkey making a list which could cause a problem two offices back. I need to take care of him."

Bran nodded, knowing exactly what his Alpha meant about 'taking care' of this individual. Understand, if you will, the thing that many underestimate, in a time of war, with a regime as extreme as the Third Reich, is that it was not those in command who did the most damage to the local populations. It was the junior grade administrators, whose belief in the ethics and rationale of the regime was complete. They were the ones who prepared things like deportation lists. And there was an administrator whose soul called to Gavril. He had prepared a list.

His list was for a mass deportation of a group living in the Carpathian Region. An order had been given to round up and deport the Pack to Auschwitz.

Pulling a piece of paper from his jacket, Gavril showed it to Bran, as if asking him something. They re-entered the building, looking at the room numbers and glancing again at the paper. Gavril knew which room he wanted, but he was not going to barge in there. Gavril had learned from doing that earlier in the year. At the same time, along with a pulse of wordless love for his Mate, he communicated with her down our link to tell her what he was doing, asking Aaleahya to warn the Pack just in case an attempt was made to carry out the deportation order. Realistically, it was unlikely. The Red Army already 'controlled' swathes of the Carpathian Region, and it was only a matter of time before they arrived in the Pack's corner.

The irony was that, as well as rescuing those families who wanted out, Gavril had also been approached by some of those fresh faced young soldiers, looking for any means of escaping, without risking any family they still had in Germany.

This is the advantage of being able to read souls.

The admin clerk whom he sought was working at his desk when Gavril entered the room. The man looked up, and any possibility that he was innocent faded in that instant. His eyes flicked to one side, and Gavril smiled grimly, as he approached the desk, and picked up the file lying there.

"So, who gave the order?" Gavril asked quietly. "On whose orders were we to be deported?"

Aaleahya felt her Mate's mind link to her, warning her of the order for deportation of the Pack. She could not help but growl, wondering to herself what was it with these humans that they couldn't leave them alone. They have taken her home, they have taken her child, and now they want to take this little part of the world from them, when all the Pack wished to do was to help those around them? The sudden thought that she could lose her Mate also hit her, and the panic in her mind-voice was real, as she begged her Mate not to take any risks. Suddenly, she smiled to herself, as the memory of what her Mate was settled her panic. Woe to whomever crossed him, for Gavril would end the life of his enemy quicker than they might beg for mercy, particularly given what the Pack had lost recently. Still, she did as Gavril requested, and warned the rest of the Pack. The discord echoed back down the Pack link, with some wanting to end the lives of those Germans still in the village, whilst others checked packs and supplies should an immediate evacuation be required.

Gavril could feel the frustration within the Pack that they had been targeted again. Looking at the administrative clerk before him, he repeated the question. "Who gave the order to deport us?"

"The Gauleiter gave the order a week ago. He said that you have the means to turn the war back in our favour, with the right incentive. That's why everyone else was to be deported to Auschwitz, with you, as hostages for your co-operation."

Gavril raised a brow. "The order was given a week ago, but nothing has happened until now?"

"The Red Army will take Budapest if we don't do something to stop them." The man's voice had become shrill. "The Reich cannot fall."

His conviction that Gavril had some sort of obligation to stop the fall of a regime which had killed millions was ludicrous, but the clerk was no alone in that belief. Holding such a weak mind in his grasp was childsplay, as Gavril manifested a flame and reduced the file to ashes. "Is that the only copy?" He demanded.

"Y-e-es." Came the stuttered reply. "I haven't been able to copy and have it circulated yet." On that, Gavril knew the clerk was telling the truth. His regret that his tardiness might have cost the Reich an advantage coloured his soul.

Allowing his Alpha strength to flow around the clerk, Gavril prevented him from further speech, whilst telling Aaleahya that he needed to use a cave nearby, before grasping the clerk around the neck. "Your life is forfeit for your lack of conscience in sending people to their deaths." Gavril smiled. "He was right. I might have been forced, but it won't happen now." The clerk was trembling, his mind shrieking in fear. Gavril tilted his head thoughtfully. "Now do you understand how other people felt." He asked the gibbering clerk. All Gavril could read from the man was a desperation. Not a sign of remorse. His only regret was that his carelessness had perhaps cost the Reich a victory. He was acting for the Reich. He had failed the Reich. All that mattered to him was the Reich should triumph.

"There is no convincing some." Gavril murmured, flashing his prey to the cave coordinates supplied by Aaleahya. In the cool damp of the cave, he harvested the clerk's soul.

"My beloved." He linked with Aaleahya. "The Red Army will show those young Germans no mercy. If there are any worth saving, who are only here because someone in command sees them as cannon fodder, then we can't let them die." Even if Gavril wanted to hate anyone who wore a grey uniform, his duty to the Goddess was clear. The evil doers were his prey, not these children whose only crime was that they were sent to fight for a dying regime.

The clerk's body was just a pile of ash when Gavril and Bran left the cave. They would both remain on their guard, but he also needed to ensure the safety of those who looked to him. Hunter's Inn was quiet when finally, they returned home. For a moment, Gavril wondered if he was too late, that the deportation order had been carried out, but then he felt his Mate through their Bond and was reassured. He sent a pulse of wordless love down their bond, pleased to be back home. The soul he had harvested did not sit well with him, but it was there nonetheless, the sound of the little administrator whimpering about how he had failed the Reich. Knowing that, whilst he held the soul of an evil-doer within him, he would hear this barrage of protests of their innocence, Gavril had trained himself to ignore them, over the years. When the time was right or when he carried enough to make it worthwhile, he would visit his Goddess and transfer them to her keeping. For now, he had other things on his mind.

The administrator had spoken of the Budapest Offensive by the Red Army. Gavril knew that the Russians were making their way through the Carpathians, and it was only a matter of time before they arrived in the Pack's little corner of the world. His concern was not all those who wore the uniform of the Third Reich had the same attitude of the little administrator. Some of them, as Gavril had noticed, were barely young boys themselves. They were not old enough to be thrust into a uniform and sent to a front to face an army like the Red Army, keen to extract revenge for their own losses during the war. But, this is what happens in the dying days of a regime in war. As they run out of adults to send to die, they use the children. They were the children forced to join the Hitler Youth movement, told that their duty lay with protecting the Reich, but they didn't understand the politics. They wanted to be home. They were not conscienceless murderers, and they were not the sort who had robbed Gavril and his Mate of their daughter and son.

In short, they were innocent souls and that meant Gavril had a duty imposed on him by his Goddess to protect them.

He found them in one of the outside store rooms, the one where they stored the sacks of vegetables which would see them through the winter, and enable them to feed whomever they had to accommodate at the Inn. For the moment that was still German soldiers, but it was only a matter of time before Gavril envisaged their 'guests' being members of the Red Army.

The first thing that struck Gavril was their pallor. The second thing that struck him was their youth. There were four of them. One had an improvised bandage on his head, two wore their helmets, with one crying softly. The fourth just sat there, shaking.

As they realised Gavril was standing there, they scrambled to their feet, their pallor increasing as Aaleahya appeared at his side. The soft crying washed away any hint of the anger that she might have felt towards them as German soldiers. As Gavril knew, these were mere children. Approaching them, she dropped to her knees, speaking softly to the one with the bandage on his head, asking to see his wound. Looking at her Mate, Aaleahya sighed. "These are just babies with guns in their hands. They have no idea of what they ae doing and just want to go home. I am afraid if we send them home, they will be punished, along with their families, for not following their orders. What should we do, my love? I will not harm an innocent, and I know you will not either." She stood, taking her Mate's hand and giving it a gentle squeeze.

Gavril nodded. "They are only children. I do not make war on children, and I do not harvest the souls of children." Gavril knew only too well that if these boys were found, they would be shot as deserters by their own sides and as enemy combatants if found by the Red Army. Yet they were only children who had fled in terror, forced into an army and a war, when they should still be with their mothers. And to think that the Gauleiter had seen Gavril as some sort of monster?

"Take them to the caves, my Mate. Keep them safe. I will speak with Nahuel and see if there is somewhere that we can take them to keep them safe." Gavril could feel the mass that was the Red Army coming closer.

With such a body, driven part by vengeance against the faceless might of the Third Reich, these children could expect no mercy from them. Gavril approached the boys carefully, conscious that their souls were so full of their fear, both for themselves and for their families. Gently, he explained that he had no intention of reporting them to anyone in authority.

The oldest of the four boys looked at the others before speaking. “But Herr Negrescu, if you don’t, they will punish you.”

“The authorities might try to punish me, but they won’t succeed.” Gavril explained calmly. “For now, I need you to go with my wife. She will take you to a place of safety, while we work out how we can help you to find your families, without endangering them.” He hastened to add.

The boy who had been crying looked at Gavril, and then looked at Aaleahya. The gratitude in his eyes sealed Gavril’s intent to help them. These children were not the ones who had killed his daughter and son. They were as much the future of the wold that would come after the war as any of the Jewish and Roma children the Pack had saved so far.

Gavril touched Aaleahya’s cheek gently. “I will speak with the village council. We will sort out what needs to be done.”

CHAPTER 15: CHANGE FOR THE BETTER? (DECEMBER 1944)

The Red Army had finally secured the whole of the Carpathian Region, with the remnants of the Nazi Army in full retreat. Last ditch attempts were being made to hold on to Budapest to avoid it falling to the Russians, but there was an inevitability that it would not be long before the war was over. Still their Pack's lives continued. With the Nazis gone from the Hunter's Arrow and the front portion of Negrescu Hall a charred ruin, the majority of the Pack were quartered at the Inn. Bran and his 'estate management' team remained at the Hall, and Owain, the Pack's other Beta stayed at the Inn in his capacity as 'manager'. The village cooperative who were the titular owners of the Inn were happy for him to stay in charge, saying that his presence brought a feeling of normality.

Gavril and Aaleahya used rooms at the Hall for sleeping, but alternated their time between the two sites. With winter temperatures and weather, there was a keen need to ensure food supplies for both the Pack and the village. There had been some looting of their supplies by the departing Army and they had every expectation that they would be expected to 'show their gratitude' to their 'liberators' by feeding them also. Well, as long as they didn't mind root vegetable soups supplemented with the meat from the deer herds and rabbits they had maintained in the forests, then all would be fine. It still meant that Aaleahya's gift, combined with Gavril's control over water was needed, but the important that thing was that both the Pack and the village would survive.

Bran could not help but look at the ruin that had been Negrescu Hall and remember a happier time, when the sound of children's laughter might be heard through open windows. The entire front of the building had burned in the conflagration which Gavril had started to hide the true reason for thirty members of the local SS unit, their Kommandant and the local Gauleiter had died. Had they actually investigated the fire or for that matter, had modern forensic methods existed, then they might have noticed that whilst the smoke damage was extensive, the fire itself had not rendered the whole of the Hall uninhabitable.

As far as the village and the local authorities were concerned, Bran was the Estate Manager, and it was entirely expected that despite the damage to the house, he and his team would remain there, to try to gather what they might from the fields and orchards. Much of what they might harvest was due to Aaleahya's powers.

But then, the Russians came.

Owain was meeting with a group of the village elders when they heard the sound of running boots that presaged the arrival of armed force. It was a far from welcome sound. The tension in the villagers was almost palpable. All of them had had encounters with the occupying Nazi army and they had no reason to think that this new force of occupation would be any different. Whilst Owain's own abilities were not as refined as Gavril's he endeavoured to spread a generalised feeling of calm.

"Do you wish me to speak on your behalf?" Owain asked quietly. "I will introduce myself as being employed by the village to run the Inn." Silent nods were their answer. Sending a mind-link to Gavril, Owain advised his Alpha of the situation.

Gavril thought afterwards that if the Red Army had thought to catch them unawares, they were sadly disappointed that day. Throwing on some clothes that did no scream 'landowning bastard scum' to the Comrades, Gavril flashed down to the cellars of the Hunter's Arrow. Grabbing the clipboard from the hook on the wall, Gavril made his way up the stairs, pausing the listen. He could hear Owain talking, explaining that he was an employee of the workers' cooperative who owned the Inn. There were murmurs of approval at the language that he used. Gavril hid a smile, knowing that his friend and Beta knew what he was doing, implementing a strategy which they had planned for such an eventuality. Let the masses hear what they thought was important. Brushing against a wall to dirty his shirt, Gavril opened the door leading to the bar.

- x –

Bran had agreed with Gavril that he would remain at the Hall, given that a group seemed to be heading their way. The Hall was, after all, a prominent symbol of the capitalist exploitation that was anathema to the Comrades of the Red Army. If they could find an excuse to seize such a property, so that the impoverished masses might share in its bounty, surely this would be greeted with joy by the oppressed villagers. Bran smiled to himself. Such political bullshit was guaranteed to make anyone fall asleep.

Of course they had a plan for such an eventuality. Bran smiled. There was a reason why Gavril was their Alpha, and why the Pack had prospered under his leadership, surviving the worst of the Nazi occupation. Both the Inn and the remains of the Estate were held by the village under a co-operative ownership with the intention of giving them the means to support themselves, when the time came for the Pack to relocate to their New York base. So, when the Russians arrived, expecting to find some bloated capitalist lording it over his peasants, they found Bran, in his shirtsleeves, preparing the plough horses for work.

Owain affected a look of annoyance as Gavril pushed open the door from the root cellars, muttering that the potato stocks were depleted, trying to hide his grin as Gavril's voice trailed off as he seemed to realise that they were not alone. Turning back to the officer type addressing him, Owain continued his explanation that he was merely the employee of the village co-operative.

"And where is the previous owner?" The officer addressing Owain had a grating, guttural accent.

"That would be me." Gavril lost the look of the village idiot he had affected. "I am the previous owner who gave away this inn so that the village would have the means to support themselves after the war. Why? Do you object to the peasantry owning and operating such a wealthy and profitable business?"

Up at the Hall, Bran realised that there had been a sudden change of plan when Gavril broadcast his verbal conversation across the Pack link. It was a method that had been used when instantaneous communication was needed, generally because, as Alpha, he perceived a threat to the Pack which might require massed action. Given that they lived within a human community, 'instantaneous action' might mean revealing themselves as paranormal creatures. It was not a decision Gavril took lightly.

Along with his words came an image, and Bran realised what had prompted his friend to act as he had. During an earlier action, their scouts had reported the presence of Russian demons in the advancing Red Army, feeding off what had started as a not-unreasonable desire for revenge against earlier Nazi atrocities. The action of those demons had escalated. The humans used to call it possession.

Then came the message that was to Bran and Bran alone. "Protect Aaleahya, my friend. Protect my Mate."

Owain swore under his breath as he realised what was happening. As if it wasn't bad enough that Gavril had spent the last six months protecting the Pack from the suspicions of the Gauleiter and the Kommandant? Now he had a possessed human, who was acting not just on suspicions, but on actual knowledge. With the demon's assistance, this human was not just guessing about them. Just as the Pack could sense demons and other paranormal beings as part of being Cŵn Annwn, so this demon was providing information to the human. The question was how the human intended to use that information, because, unlike with the Nazis, this was not suspicion about the Pack's paranormal nature, this was certain knowledge.

The Russian officer's smile widened as Gavril confirmed his identity. "I have orders to arrest you as a Nazi collaborator." The relish in his voice was clear to everyone.

There was a swelling noise of protest at the accusation from the villagers present in the bar at that early hour. This would be why they had come early because the demon knew that the village would protect Gavril if they could.

"You have proof to back up this accusation? Considering the Nazis killed by sister and her husband, not to mention their use of me as a scapegoat for any infractions against their rules, I have an issue against being accused of collaboration." Gavril's voice was cold. The damn demons were after something, and Gavril suspected that it was the same potential seen by the Gauleiter and the SS Kommandant, to use him as a weapon by holding the lives of those dear to him over his head.

As he heard the accusation being made against his Alpha and friend, Bran dropped what he was doing. The other Pack members provided cover for his disappearance by encouraging the horses to move *en masse* out of the barn area, forcing the soldiers to back away. A mass of stampeding plough horses is not something with which to argue.

He zoned in on Aaleahya, who was in the garden, but running back to the house. Like him, she had heard Gavril's message. She glared at Bran, shaking her head, saying her place was at her Mate's side. They had sworn to face the future together.

Wrapping his arms about her, Bran shook my head. "If you go to him, they will use you against him, Aaleahya. He knows that. He needs to know you are safe."

"I can go invisible." Aaleahya fought to free herself.

"There is a demon there. Think, Aaleahya! He knows what we are. He will be able to sense you, whether or not you are visible. If anything happens to you, Gavril will be crippled. Please, stay here and let us keep you hidden. I don't know if the soldiers here are also possessed, but we can't let them find you. Please, Alpha's Mate."

Bran hoped that by using her title, he might persuade her to listen to him. He knew her link with her Mate was pulling her to him, but she had to fight it. Gavril needed a clear head to fight, and he needed to know his Mate was safe.

Owain saw Gavril's half smile as he heard Bran pleading with Aaleahya, trying to stop her from standing the with her Mate. No doubt he was thinking of the promise they had exchanged, after he months under Nazi rule and the loss of Kat and Sandu, that they would face everything together. But, Owain had to agree with his fellow Beta and Sentinel. If anything were to happen to Aaleahya, then Gavril would have a problem. Bran and Owain had both lived during the fallout caused by his sire's death and their former Alpha's descent into insanity. They had no wish to see that happened to their friend and present Alpha.

There was the sound of more booted footsteps and the sound of children crying could be heard. Again there was a rumble of anger from the few villagers with them. The Russian officer smirked at Gavril. "I hope Comrade Negrescu was not planning anything … heroic. Just in case he may want to reconsider. Bring them in!"

The main door to the inn was pushed open, and the children of the village, ALL the children, stumbled in, most of them half dressed, many of them crying, the older ones trying to look stoic but their fear showed in trembling lips and hunched shoulders, all of which was hardly surprising.

"Let me make things clear, Comrade Negrescu. Either you come with us … willingly, or we will find some way to persuade you."

"Yes." Gavril drawled a response. "It seems that the vulnerability of children is something that all sides in a war will exploit." Each time he had been flogged during the Nazi occupation, it had been because of a supposed infraction by a child or a teenager, completely out of proportion with the punishment. The only reason for those punishments was to push him and to continue to push him, in the belief that eventually, Gavril would reveal his 'true' nature. The fools didn't realise that Gavril's true nature was the last thing they wanted to see. However, what it did mean was that the Pack had contingency plans should anyone decide to try to use the children against him.

Opening his arms, silently, he called the children to himself, allowing the smallest ones into his embrace whilst the older ones placed hands on my shoulders and arms, reassured that Gavril would keep them safe. "Ydych chi'n cofio? (Do you remember?)", Gavril asked them quietly. Nods and tremulous smiles greeted his words.

"Well, Comrade Negrescu, what is your answer?" The Russian officer gave a bark of laughter, sure that he had Gavril well and truly trapped.

Up at the Hall, Bran still had his arms wrapped around Aaleahya, to prevent her from running to her Mate's assistance. Both heard Gavril's reassurance to the children.

"They are using the children against him, Aaleahya, because they know he will keep them safe. Think what they might demand of him if they had you, his beloved Mate, under their control." Bran urged Aaleahya to stop fighting his hold.

Aaleahya's eyes flashed in anger, one of the rare moments when her eyes shifted from human straight to Cŵn Annwn. "You can't go after them, Aaleahya." Bran reminded her. "Remember, we have plans in place to protect the children and Gavril will put those plans in action now. That's what he meant when he asked the children if they remember. They have all been drilled on what they need to do. Gavril has no intent of being used again, you know that."

Aaleahya's struggles to be released decreased some. Acerbically, she pointed out that she did know of the plans, but it didn't mean that she didn't want to be with her Mate.

Bran shook his head. "No, Aaleahya, I need you to stay in the caves, at least until we know they are not looking for you. It is too dangerous for you to be seen near the house."

Reluctantly, Aaleahya agreed with Bran. He breathed a sigh of relief. "Gavril has charged me with keeping you safe, Alpha's Mate. Let me do as I have been ordered, please."

Aaleahya gave a brief nod. She turned as if to return to the house, before shrugging, realising that she should go straight to the caves. Hopefully, the soldiers would not hang around once they realised they couldn't find her. It would make protecting her a lot easier, if she was not going crazy from claustrophobia.

Owain was seized with the urge to disembowel the possessed Russian officer. Whatever the human had been before possession by the demon, the fact remained that free will is everything when it comes to such situations. In the case of human, the demon would only have been able to take full possession if the human chose to let it in. From Owain's perspective, it meant that, as a Cŵn Annwn, it was now open season on the human's soul. The Pack had plans in place to protect the children, but in this instance, to avoid the risk to the rest of the village, Gavril was going to have to tread a fine line, to allow the Russian and his battle group to think that they had him in a checkmate position, when it was anything but that.

Much as Gavril wanted to wipe the smirk off the face of the possessed Russian officer, in as painful a manner as possible, he had to allow for the fact that he had sent part of his group up to the Hall and retained part of the group with himself, here at the Inn. Being demon-possessed, knowing what they were, he knew what they could do. Or at least, he thought he did.

The advantage for the Pack was that, as spectral hounds, rather than hell hounds, not all their abilities were known to the 'bad guys' and that was something that Gavril intended his Pack to maintain. Mentally, he shrugged. So he had just terminated thirty Gestapo, give or take a few. Now it was the

Russians turn. "It is interesting, is it not, the stories and tales that proliferate around here?" He commented, standing up, the children still clustered around him like little ducklings.

This was a means for him to determine just how many of this group were possessed and how many were still 'clean' souls. The clean ones nervously fingered their weapons, looking around as if they expected a vampire or werewolf to leap out of the woodwork. The possessed ones looked over confident as their eyes tracked around the room, working out who was human and who was Cŵn Annwn.

"Stories? Is that all you have to say, Comrade Negrescu?" The officer laughed. At the same time, his eyes narrowed. His words were for the benefit of the humans, just as Gavril's had been. The subtext was something completely different. He knew that Gavril was warning him: back off now, or face the consequences. Gesturing to the soldiers around him, he ordered them to load the children and Gavril into one of the lorries so that they might be taken down to the command post. The children looked at Gavril, and he gave them an almost imperceptible nod. At the same time, Gavril broadcast to the Pack:

[Pack ML] I have eight possessed humans at the Inn. Bran? How many at the Hall? [end ML]

Bran replied by the same method. "I have another eight here, and twenty 'clean' humans. Gavril smiled to himself. Forty humans in total and sixteen demons. He had ten Cŵn Annwn available to him at the Inn, and ten up at the Hall. The odds were in the Pack's favour, if he didn't care to conserve the humans. Unfortunately, he did.

Bran watched as the troops at the Hall continued their search. It was clear that his earlier fears for Aaleahya were justified, as he broadcast across the Pack. "The demons know our Alpha is Mated. I confirm that they appear to be searching for Aaleahya."

Aaleahya's wordless grumble down the Pack mind link confirmed that she had heard his message, closely followed as it was by Gavril's wordless pulse of love aimed at his Mate. If it had ever been doubted how important Aaleahya was to him, that was proof positive, Bran thought to himself. Knowing that she was as safe as possible under the circumstances meant that he was free to act or fight as needed without worrying for her.

"Are you satisfied?" Bran asked the possessed officer in charge of the group at the Hall. "Perhaps you wish to send your men to search the unstable parts of the building, although I won't be held responsible for their safety if you do."

"Where is she?" The officer's voice had a distinct guttural accent. "Where is the owner's wife?" He demanded. "Where have you hidden Comrade Negrescu's wife? Don't mess with me, dog!" He swung the barrel of his rifle at Bran's face, catching him. The scent of blood filled the air.

Owain watched as the village children were loaded into the lorry along with his Alpha. He heard Bran's report confirming the danger to Aaleahya. Gavril's mental order to both his Betas was clear. "Take Aaleahya to Wales. If they are looking for her, they intend to use her to force me to act for them. The children are a compromise only."

Aaleahya's protest was clear. She wanted to stay where she could support her Mate, and her fury that these demons might try to use her against her Mate was clear.

Gavril's order took Owain by surprise. "Dissonance, Owain."

He had been probing the demons whilst they were so busy gloating about how easy it had been to capture him. He had also noticed how uncomfortable they looked with the children's shrill sobbing. Whispering to one of the teens, who was known locally as a singer, he asked her to pitch her voice off key. The visible look of discomfort on the face of their captors had been clear. Gavril's order to Owain was for him to use his own particular talent against this group of demons: the ability to distort sound.

At first Owain's actions caused looks of discomfort and they tried to ignore it. The children followed Gavril's instruction to stumble as they were herded towards the waiting lorries. It started to become more difficult to ignore Owain's play with the sound, as he took the pitch to a painful level off the audible level of humans. The mother of the young singer provided Owain with his 'source', and he signalled two of the Pack members to protect her as he continued his 'games', varying pitch and tone. Only the demons were showing signs of discomfort and distraction. Gavril's brief grin was all that Owain needed to continue. Whilst the pitch rising to an inaudible banshee type scream was uncomfortable to the Pack also, they were used to Owain's tricks during Pack training sessions.

At that point, each targeted possessed Russian was relieved of their human soul, causing the host body to slump to the ground, each apparently supported by a Pack member. At Gavril's hand signal, the children scattered, the oldest teens grabbing their assigned toddler and melting into the shadows. Dropping the unconscious Russians to the ground, Gavril turned on the remaining human soldiers, his anger only too audible to them now.

"Who gave the order for my arrest? Who thought to target my wife?" He demanded.

The Pack mind link vibrated with the force of his anger. Bran could understand his rage. They were Cŵn Annwn. They were not hell hounds, taking pleasure in destruction and death. They served the Goddess and took their duty to protect very seriously. Yet again, they had been targeted by a group who thought to use them for their own gain. Just another tool. Just another weapon. How much more would this war cost, Bran wondered, both in personal terms and in the damage to those whom they sought to protect?

When Gavril had given the order to attack the possessed, those Pack members at the Hall had done just that. Bran himself took pleasure in seizing the officer who had named him 'Dog' for refusing to reveal where they had hidden Aaleahya. As with those at the Inn, eight bodies now lay on the ground, with the humans pointing weapons at the Pack members. Bran growled, but he did not attack. Protect the humans. Do not kill them unless there was no other option, even when faced with this level of provocation. To this day, he would recall how close the Pack came to taking another forty souls. Everything rested on the answer to Gavril's demand.

"He said the order came from the highest committee level." It was not a soldier with rank bars who spoke but one of the rank and file soldiers. "He claimed that you had the ability to ensure that the Revolution would be victorious." The soldier spat in the direction of the bodies. "He said nothing about making war on children."

One soldier. One man who, until the day he died, never realised how close he and his comrades had come to death. Had he not shown his revulsion in such a graphic manner, his body would have joined those on the ground. For the threat to Gavril's Mate and the threat to the Pack, Gavril would have given the order to kill. Better to silence the rumours sometimes than leave the evidence to be found. But that one reaction changed the outcome.

Gavril ordered Bran to bring the humans at the Hall down to the Inn, in a blatant show that, regardless of the guns held on them and the apparently superior numbers of humans, it was only because of the Pack's mercy that they lived. Did they prove their humanity? Several of the Pack members wrinkled noses at the sharp smell of urine from some of the transported humans, which Gavril supposed would be a natural reaction when you and a comrade feel your arms being grabbed and then darkness, only to find yourself reappear elsewhere. A temporary loss of bladder control was the least of their worries. There were murmurs aplenty from the group at the Inn when their fellow soldiers appeared in their midst. The Pack members took up positions around the courtyard, making it quite clear who was in charge.

"You have a choice." Gavril's voice still rumbled with his anger. "We protect this village and its people. For this reason, the village own the

Inn and the Hall, as a workers' co-operative." Gavril knew he would be classed as a capitalist, but in this region, in this time, this was the language and politics which worked here. "Threaten or attempt to harm them or us and you will die. It is as simple as that." A muted growling rumble acted as a strange counterpoint to his words. "The Nazis learned of that to their cost." He looked around the room. "There has been enough killing. Leave this area in peace and we will leave you in peace. It is quite simple."

The soldier who had spoken seemed to have been elected as some sort of unofficial spokesman. "You could have killed us but you did not. You killed only those who threatened you. For that, I say that my comrades and I should believe you. I, Sergei Vassilivitch Gorbachev, say we should believe this man." He shrugged. "I am a simple man. I want to go back to the collective farm in the Ukraine, which I call home, where my teenage son is driving a tractor instead of me. What say you, comrades?" The question was rhetorical.

"I say we report back that we could not find Comrade Negrescu and his wife, and that something made them …" He pointed to the corpses, "… go crazy and kill themselves. If we all say the same, they will have to believe us."

There was a murmur of assent from the other humans. Sometimes it is possible for them to be reasonable as a species, and this appeared to be one of those times.

Gavril smiled. "Then, we will let you live. Like I said, it is a simple choice."

CHAPTER 16: THE BEGINNING OF THE END (FEBRUARY 1945)

The siege of Budapest had ended. Budapest had fallen to the might of the Soviet Red Army and yet again, it was not those in power who suffered, but those who had tried to survive. The ethnic Germans who had made Hungary their home, who had never supported the Nazi Party were deemed guilty of collusion anyway. Deported from their homes. Returned to Germany. Not permitted to take anything of value with them. This was the cost of war. Bridges over the Danube were destroyed as the Germans sought to slow the Soviet advance, because now, the race was on. The race to Berlin. The race to end the war. What did the great politicians care for an ethnic German family in the face of their plans for a grand victory? Make no mistake. Not all of them were innocent souls, but a fair few were, and yet again, the Pack faced the dichotomy that they harvested souls from both sides of the war. It was a balancing act, because even as they worked, there were those, such as the Russian demons they had face only months ago, who wanted the violence, and the suffering. That was their 'food and drink', and they were only too keen to secure it.

They had tried to ensure that their former home and those in the village who had looked to them for protection during the war would remain safe, but it was far from easy.

The horrors of the concentration camps were now known, after the Soviet Army entered Auschwitz in January. But for the slow work of an administrator, Gavril was only too well aware that he and his Pack might have been one of the groups sent there. Or rather, the authorities might have tried to send them there. Somehow, he didn't think the Pack would have hung around long enough for them to experiment on them.

Either way, there was a certain inevitability in the air. Soon the war would be over. Soon, in theory, Europe would know peace. Harvesting the souls in the concentration camps had not been a task enjoyed by the Pack, for all that it was their reason to exist. They had not been able to prevent the suffering, not on the scale in which it occurred. All they could do was to clean up the mess afterwards.

After each harvest, Aaleahya and Gavril would hold each other close, knowing that they had been unable to help those souls in life. All they could offer them was the peace of death. Where they could, the Pack tried to time their harvests so that the final moment of death was not one that was felt. It was the least that they could do.

But, around their former home, there was at least for a while, some hint of the life that had existed before the war. The soldiers had gone back to their headquarters, and their story that Comrade Negrescu and his wife could not be found had been believed. It had been decided that the same account from forty humans was likely to be true, and thus, the village could, for the moment, breathe more easily.

There was no doubt in Gavril's mind that the Pack would relocate again. They had come from Wales to the Carpathians, and now, they would move again, to the area known as the Catskill Mountains, not least because of the proliferation of state parks, as the humans described them, where, to a certain extent, the Pack would have space to grow and thrive. There were some changes that had to be made which would not be immediately apparent to the village, but would be vital to maintaining the Pack's covenant to protect them.

To that end, Gavril found himself in Aaleahya's old cave again, contemplating the new decor, waiting for an associate of his Pack to arrive. If what he had in mind worked out, it would provide them with the means to maintain their protection, even from another continent.

A stirring in the air announced the arrival of his contact and Gavril turned with a wary look on his face, not entirely sure what his reaction was going to be.

"Well, Zarek, did you receive a response?"

-x-

There was no doubt that the cave had changed substantially since he was last there. Zarek meandered around the space, examining the lush vine growth that covered the formerly bare walls, the moss covered floors and formerly bare rock benches. Apparently natural openings had been made in the cave roof, to allow light in but the openings were screened from a casual glance. Pride of place had been given to a tall carving and it was this which drew his attention.

"Nice touch." Zarek commented, running his hands over the intricate stonework. Someone had taken a lot of care with this, and he was impressed, although at this stage, he wasn't going to show it. "And yes, the old man responded. He is willing to talk. He thinks your proposal may have some merit."

Gavril recalled the evening he had first encountered Zarek, son of Svitovid, when he came into the bar, just after their first encounter with the Russian demons 'riding' with the Red Army. He hadn't been sure of what to make of the tall male, whose build showed that he was more than used to fighting. His looks had put him in his third decade, much like Gavril himself and most of the Pack. That was the first indication that he was not all that he appeared to be. As it transpired, his father was the key factor here, and unlike most by-blows, Zarek actually had a good relationship with the 'old man', as he referred to his sire. That was probably just as well, considering that his father was the Slavic God of War and Fertility. Svitovid. And, to the Pack's advantage, it seemed that the 'old man' was a bit put out that some low level Russian demons were poaching on his territory, so he had sent Zarek to investigate.

This presented Gavril with an interesting way of ensuring that the village and surrounding area stayed safe. He had seen enough of this new political system, 'communism', to now that whilst setting up the Hall and Inn as workers' co-operatives, the time would come when 'wealthy' peasantry would be viewed with the same scorn as the previous 'capitalist pigs'. So Gavril knew that he needed to ensure that some other form of protection existed. Either something, or as it turned out, someone.

"My Beta, Bran, has a gift for working with stone, amongst other things and my Mate is talented when it comes to plants and other vegetation." Gavril explained. "We thought it might meet with approval, particularly since any … devotional activity will have to be concealed." Gavril replied.

Zarek nodded. Gavril's words were a tacit acknowledgement that, for the whole protection gig to work with his father, the village whom he was wanting to be protected would pay due observations to Zarek's sire. That said, given the political situation, they could not openly worship any form of deity, hence Gavril and his Pack coming up with the idea of turning the cave into a temple of sorts. They had done a fairly good job of it, which in turn told Zarek that Gavril felt quite strongly about protecting these humans. As a half-human, Zarek could understand that and he knew he would consider as a friend any being who was prepared to protect those in need as his first priority.

"Well, the old man was not impressed with either the attempt by that demonic scum to poach on his turf, nor with this politics, that 'religion' is no longer needed." Zarek shook his head. "Clearly, the rank and file have not realised that they are still going to be expected to give their devotion to something. It just won't be a god. Or rather, it will be a political god." Zarek laughed. "Politics won't line their bellies, unlike the old man's gifts to his followers." Zarek looked around the cave again, before turning to face Gavril. "So when are you planning to relocate your Pack? I am guessing quite soon."

Gavril smiled at Zarek's words. That was the amusing thing about working with the son of a god, even a little known and definitely parochial god like Svitovid. "We have not decided on an exact date. We wanted to be sure of the situation here first. My Mate, Aaleahya, and I have come to care for these humans and it would suit us ill if we were to abandon them."

Zarek returned Gavril's smile, hiding the fact that he had not really had to argue that hard with his sire to come to some sort of arrangement. Of course, he was not willing to reveal everything, not at this stage. Time for that would come. Without a doubt, the end of this conflict, what the humans would come to call the Second World War, was going to change the world, far more than any conflict to date. His sire had not survived and maintained his powers as well as he had by not realising how much the nature of war had changed, even in the last few hundred years. There was more. This political idea of communism. Great in theory: share things equally, but were humans actually capable of doing this? This man, Josef Stalin? Something about him set Zarek's mind on edge, and he realised that he could understand why Gavril and his Mate were so keen to ensure the safety of this little group of humans who had, in their own way, protected his Pack of Cŵn Annwn.

"The old man has decided that he wants me 'on the ground', so to speak. He was thinking that I might take up your old shed, Negrescu Hall, perhaps pretend to be a ghost or something." Zarek shrugged. "It would both keep people away, and bring them in, which in turn would benefit the Inn."

Gavril was surprised at Zarek's suggestion but it did make sense. The Carpathians were riddled with legends about the supernatural, so it made sense to capitalise on this, with a view to protecting the village. Since his Pack had moved there in the late 1800s, a mutual protection pact had evolved, with the Pack protecting the village and the village maintaining their silence over how they did that. Over time, they had hidden the fact that Gavril was the same individual, whose Pack had protected the village for nearly a century, claiming to any who asked that Gavril was his own 'grandson' or whatever relationship suited the gap of intervening years.

Yet now, the village would face a completely different threat, one which was based around politics and the effect of a new political system on their lives. It was a system which espoused everyone benefitting from local wealth, but as Zarek pointed out, were humans really capable of doing this? This was why the Pack had transferred ownership of their properties to the village.

"That sounds like a workable plan. Come. Let me introduce you to Aaleahya, my Mate and the village council, who are the technical owners of our former property. I am certain they will be pleased to know that the protection will continue.

Zarek grinned briefly. Gavril's earlier thoughts that his Pack would have the beginnings of a solid friendship did not appear to have been mistaken. Still, he could not help but notice Zarek's thoughtful look when he met Aaleahya. For his own part Zarek noticed the sadness in Aaleahya's eyes. This land was, after all, the land of her birth, and the land in which she had borne her child, only to lose their daughter to war. There seemed more to this pairing, Zarek thought to himself, more than just being mated or married or whatever you wanted to call a permanent union.

The old man had told him that the war had cost them their only daughter, but Zarek felt that their closeness was more than just that shared grief. It was as if they also grieved for the losses of those around them. Clearly living with others, interacting with humans, was going to be more difficult than his sire had given him to believe. Zarek shrugged to himself. He wouldn't be himself if he didn't relish the challenge.

CHAPTER 17: AVOIDING THE INEVITABLE (MARCH 1945)

It only lasted a week or so, but if anything showed the desperation of the once great Panzer Army of the Third Reich, it was the events of March 1945, in what was to be known as Operation Spring Awakening. What possessed the German High Command that the weakened Panzer divisions, who had just faced the Battle of the Bulge, would be able to advance against the Soviet forces, was a mystery to Gavril and to his Pack.

Of greater concern to them was the potential impact of the closing stages of the war on those around them. Zarek's suggestion that he should pretend to be some supernatural spectre inhabiting the ruins of Negrescu Hall was welcomed by the village council. Like Gavril, they could see that there would come a point when the wealth that would come from running an inn on a popular area for visitors would attract the 'wrong' sort of attention.

Human greed, plain and simple. It was the same mentality that saw Gavril's sire slaughtered all those years ago in Wales. Envy, jealousy, greed. The humans number those emotions amongst the deadly sins, but seem unable to overcome their drivers. Sooner than the Pack anticipated, they were to encounter the shape of things to come in their little corner of the Carpathians, and it made Gavril realise how valuable an ally they might have in the form of Zarek, son of Svitovid.

Musing to himself, Zarek considered that his home amongst these humans was not bad, by human standards, and by the standards of a formerly-travelling son of a Slavic god, it was fair also. In keeping with the whole image they wished to portray of the shell of Negrescu Hall being haunted, he had two sets of rooms. The old master suite was his 'official' residence, with heavy, dusty hangings, and intriguing little details like a part finished glass of wine, if it was wine.

His 'real' residence was on the top floor, and Gavril and his Mate had made sure that he would be comfortable. If anything, the care to which Aaleahya had gone to ensure that Zarek would not lack really showed that this Pack of Cŵn Annwn felt a significant responsibility to protect these humans. Yes, the old man had been right. Watching this interaction, and being part of it was sure to teach his son a great deal about the humans and those who protected them from harm.

It was inevitable, Gavril thought. They had the Nazis trying to steal the Pack's property. They had a load of demon-possessed Russians try the same thing. So, it was inevitable that a 'commission' would arrive, to 'assess' the properties in the area, with a view to 'appropriate allocation of post-war resources'. Goddess above and below, he thought, did these humans think that Gavril and his Pack were stupid? The plans that Gavril, Aaleahya and their Pack had in place for them to leave their former home in the Carpathians were well in progress when this human 'commission' arrived.

The same thoughts occurred to Zarek. 'Appropriate allocation of post-war resources' translated into 'what can we appropriate from the local economy before they wise up to what we are really doing'?

Spring has always been the busiest time of the year for Bran and his team on the estate, so having a group of humans arrive to assess how much they could steal before anyone noticed was far from welcome.

At least this commission could not claim that they could appropriate the whole estate, not when there was clear evidence that the place was owned by a co-operative already. Gavril had felt that there was an inevitability to the Russian-influence Communist Party, in some form, taking over the country's government. As a result, he had examined how property had been 'redistributed' following the Russian revolution, and had tried to apply the same principles to the Pack's properties, at least on paper. The humans knew that they were holding things in 'trust' for the Pack, but since it secured their own futures and their families' futures, they seemed to be in agreement.

So, back to the human commission. They arrived at the Inn first, and co-incidentally, Zarek was down there with Owain, 'learning the ropes' as they put it. The idea was that Zarek would be both a member of 'staff' in the Inn, but he would also live up at the Hall, pretending to be a cohort of supernatural creatures, providing ample reason why the village 'avoided' the 'haunted Hall' of the former landowner. Stories of how a whole troop of SS had died under mysterious circumstances, after the owner's daughter and son were murdered during the war were circulated as to the origin of the spirits that seemed to haunt the place.

One thing Zarek noticed about the human commission was that they were full of their own self-importance. The have come from the ... wait for it ... drum roll ...Government. They wanted to make sure that 'everyone' would survive the inevitable post-war hardships. Zarek had to bite his lip to stop himself laughing. Even with his relative lack of exposure to humans, Zarek was surprised that they had not come up with a better set of lies.

Since he was not, officially, a member of the village council, he had carried on working, whilst they had parked themselves in the Inn and consumed the food offered to them greedily. The avarice that came to their eyes when they realised that the Inn could serve a substantially meaty venison stew was apparent to all.

Of course, if you are from the towns and cities, and have had food shortages for a while, you might not realise that eating venison stew for a week straight was not all that it cracked up to be.

When the 'commission' arrived, it was perhaps fortunate that Aaleahya and Gavril were in the Hunter's Arrow enjoying some lunch. They, too, saw the greed with which the humans consumed their food. Looking at his Mate, Gavril observed that she had noted the same.

[Open ML] “How do you want to play this, my love.” [end ML] Gavril asked her with a smile in his mental tone.

Aaleahya gave a mental shudder in reply. The image she sent Gavril was one of the rose that used to grow in her garden at the Hall, and a pair of secateurs. Gavril smiled again in response, squeezing her hand in acknowledgement of her suggestion to nip any attempts by these incomers to seize the property owned by the villagers under the Pack’s protection.

Gavril stroked his finger across the back of his Mate's hand, giving her an imperceptible nod. He agreed with her, that, as always, their priority needed to be the villagers who looked to the Pack for protection, and whom the Cŵn Annwn had sworn to protect.

[Open ML] “The Communists have not managed to seize power in central government, as they wanted. I suspect this is a precursor to what they want to achieve. I think it might be an idea to see first what they hope to achieve. Remember, the village is protected by the fact that this inn and the Hall is registered both locally and centrally as being owned by a co-operative. Let's see if they actually know who we are first.” [end ML]

Nodding to his Mate, Gavril stood, collecting up the dishes from their lunch. After all, in a well-run co-operative, there would not be an expectation of being served at table. Leaving the dishes on the bar, he nodded at Owain, a glance telling the Pack Beta that Gavril was going to speak with the commission about what they planned to do. His Beta nodded, and took up the dishes.

Approaching the commission, Gavril took in the thoroughly cleaned, or rather scoured dishes. Glancing at Aaleahya, he posed the question via an open mind link.

[Open ML] “Is food really that short in the cities? Perhaps the question might be better coming from you. Less of a threat, I think.” [end ML]

Aaleahya’s smile was that of the gracious hostess, neither overbearing nor subservient, as she suggested that perhaps their visitors might wish for a second portion? As she placed the full bowls of stew before them, she asked if it was true as she had heard, that food was in such short supply in the cities, and thanked their good fortune that they had the resources around them to ensure the same was not here. The members of the committee nodded, and said that this was so, and that they were here to ensure that such bounty was shared equally with those in dire need, as decreed by Mother Russia.

Listening to the lies coming from the mouths of the commission, Gavril was struck by the fact that some of what they said, they actually believed to be true, that 'Mother Russia' will take care of them. Mother Russia might have done, but unfortunately, Mother Russia was run by humans. Humans, when presented with an opportunity for self-aggrandisement, are, sadly, unable to resist the temptation.

What the commission didn't realise was that Gavril had two key advantages over them. Firstly, he could see through their lies into their souls. Secondly they had the advantage of knowing what had happened in Russia since the Revolution of 1917, something which, had they truly been inhabitants of a small enclave in the Carpathians, they would have no idea.

Tipping his head in puzzlement, Gavril joined his Mate at the table occupied by the commission. "Excuse me, my friends, but I am confused. I thought that our government was Hungarian. I didn't realise that we now had Russian overlords."

He chose the word 'overlord' quite deliberately, with its connotations of power and lordship over lesser beings.

Watching as the members of the commission try to come up with an answer to his question, Gavril decided to prod them a bit further. Raising his voice, but allowing the calm that was his Mate's gift to infuse his being, Gavril ensured that his words were heard by all in the room.

"Please, do tell us. We have lived under Nazi occupation. We have lived under an invading force who claimed to be Russian, who tried to take everything from us. Please do tell us how you will ensure that this will not be yet another attempt to steal all that we have, and that we might hope to have, and put us back under the yoke of an absent landlord."

Yes, Gavril could play the game of making a political speech with the best of them, and this group of humans was far from the best.

"No, no, you misunderstand us, comrade." One of the commission spoke up. "Your government wants to ensure that all share the bounty of the country, but all must work together.

"Do you think us to be fools." One of the village council spoke up. "What you say? It is what all the others have said."

Listening to the men talk back and forth and when one of the village council spoke up, Aaleahya could not help but agree with him. "Very true sir." She said to one of the Commission. "It is what all the others who have tried to take from us have told us. Only fools would believe what the Government would say at this time as we have been through some hard times. Everyone in this building has been through tough times. We have lost many friends and family from the Germans. What is to say that will not happen once again?" The hard hitting words seemed at odds to the gentle, almost reasoning, tone.

Gavril knew that sometimes more is achieved by letting others speak for themselves, and he needed the village council to have the confidence to be able to take on those such as this 'commission', and be able to argue their 'corner', so to speak.

"My friends, let the 'comrade' from the city speak." Gavril used the word 'city' with the same level of distaste as he had implied with his earlier comments. "Perhaps he has some light to shed on why we should believe him over the lies of the Nazis and the lies of the so-called Russians." Gavril smiled, but his smile was cold. "Perhaps he does have a reason why we should not treat him and his friends in the same way as anyone else who thinks they can steal all that we have worked for in our village."

Watching the members of the commission attempt to find an answer to his questions yet again, Gavril nodded at the Village Council members present.

"My friends, it seems our city 'comrades' are not sure what we meant. Perhaps we should make it clear." His smile was cold, but he wanted the Council to take the credit for protecting themselves.

"I agree, friend." One of the Council spoke up. "The Nazis tried to take our lives, land and our livelihood. They are dead. The so-called Russians tried to take our children, to force half our village to travel as labourers elsewhere. They are dead." There was no laughter, as the villagers made it clear they were armed. "This is our land, our property and our people. Try to take it, and be prepared to die. Is that clear enough?"

Gavril was pleased that the Chairman of their village committee had taken it upon himself to be the spokesperson, allowing him to slip backwards. Standing against the bar, Gavril watched the interaction, prepared to step in if the 'talents' of the Pack were required.

"So, if you are not from the central government as you claimed first, where are you from, and what gives you the right to investigate what we have established here?" After the initial show of what he might be prepared to do, the Chairman sheathed his dagger at his side.

The members of the commission again looked around the room, their fear an almost offensively strong odour for Gavril and his Pack. "We are members of the Communist Party." One of them admitted. He stood up. "We may not hold the reins of power yet, but we will, mark my words. If you are sensible, you will side with us. We will be the power, the ones in charge."

"Strange, but that is what the Nazis said also. And where are they now?" Another member of the village committee took up the proverbial baton. "I thought you said communism was all about everyone reaping the benefits, and of there being no more 'masters'" He smiled. "And yet, I do believe, my friends." He addressed the rest of the villagers in the room. "I do believe that our city friends here have just threatened us. Either we toe the party line or we will suffer, and have everything taken from us."

He turned back to the commission members. "Did I have that right?" He asked, his smile polite.

Gavril hid a smile. Someone had been watching how he worked a crowd, and was a quick learner.

Approaching her Mate, Aaleahya threaded her arm through Gavril's, watching as the villagers took an active part in deciding what they wanted for themselves. It was strange how the ones who want to be in absolute power resort to threats. Aaleahya shared Gavril's pleasure with the villagers and with the fact that they were not going to roll over and just take the commission representatives at face value.

The chairman was asking questions and when the threat was made he took a stand. Through their link, Aaleahya told Gavril that it looked like the villagers learned a valuable lesson as they took a stand against what was wrong and standing up for what would be of benefit to the villagers. They had all learned a valuable lesson about governments seeking power and the lengths they will go to achieve it. More villagers trickled in the bar and were standing there backing up the chairman whom many would consider too young but also showed his burgeoning wisdom.

The memories of what happened to their Pack during the war were still too fresh, Gavril mused, not just for his Mate, but for the rest of their Pack. They had lost much during the war, not least of which for Aaleahya and himself was the loss of their beloved daughter, Ekaterina. Gavril tried to reassure her through their mind link:

[ML to Aaleahya] “We are going to relocate the Pack, my love, but I need to make sure that I am not leaving the humans unprotected. This area is going to change, there is no doubt about it. The son of a god who lists divination under his 'attributes' does not just appear conveniently. Something will be happening in this region which will have profound implications. I will not allow those who have looked to us for protection to be used in the games of the gods.”

As Gavril watched the young Chairman of the village council pose his questions to this 'commission' who came not from the government, but from the Communist Party, he saw the same degree of ferocity to protect that marked Gavril’s own species. It gave him hope. There were those motivated by sentiments other than greed. They may face an uphill struggle, but they were willing to take that chance.

Gavril noticed Zarek standing to one side, in the shadows, watching the by-play. What is your game, my friend? He wondered. What do you, and your sire, hope to gain from what will happen here, or is it something so momentous that it will have more repercussions? The world is only just coming to terms with the closing days of another world war. What is it that our Pack Associate, and his sire have foreseen?

Gavril laughed to himself. The chances of them finding out, until it was the 'right' time was likely to be zero. Paranormal creature he may be, but that did not mean he would be unaffected.

CHAPTER 18: A NEW HOME AND A NEW START

The house and estate that would become the new base of the Negrescu Cŵn Annwn was in the Catskill Mountains region of New York State. It was large enough that they had their own land on which to run, as well as being close enough to several state parks that they could run, and hunt, there also. Of course, they would, as was their habit, have their own deer herds on their land, which they would manage. After all, there was no point in running the risk of some gun-happy hunter thinking he was doing the world a favour by taking out the 'vicious' pack of wolves that seemed to have moved into the area.

Of course, there were other things that were a good idea when moving into a new area. One of the families who had facilitated the relocation of several of evacuated Jewish children ran a law practice. They were duly engaged to act for the Pack, since they understood the need for client secrecy, and had reason to appreciate why the Pack need a particularly high level of security.

Part of Gavril wanted to learn from their experience of dealing with the human authorities during and after the war in their former home. The last thing he wanted was for the American government to realise that a Pack of paranormal beings lived on their soil. There would have been no hesitation on their part in taking action, but that action would likely be on the lines of either you work with us, or we exterminate you as a probable danger to our 'way of life'. So, to that end, Gavril had decided that his liaison with the human world would be through the Pack's lawyers, and through agents acting with them to manage the stock portfolio which was being established to provide an income for our Pack.

There were several interesting companies: IBM, Jeep, Boeing. All companies who had thrived during the war, and were likely to continue to thrive in the post-war period. The Pack did not restrict themselves to considering only American companies either. There were others in the UK and in the Europe gradually being rebuilt, which also bore watching. The world was changing around them. Gavril knew that he had yet to figure out what it was that Zarek and his sire had on their minds when they had agreed to work with the Pack. Make no mistake. The gods do nothing for free.

One of the first things that the Pack did on arriving at their new home was plant a garden. Simple enough, given Aaleahya's talent for growing things, but there was significance to this particular garden also. Zarek had suggested to Gavril's Mate that it would ease the pain of the loss of Ekaterina and Sandu by having something in their memory, a place where they might feel close to the daughter of their blood and the son of their hearts. Thus the first of the memorial gardens came into being.

It was walled off by hedges, so that even the walls were alive. Aaleahya's beloved roses were encouraged to grow. Gavril and Aaleahya paid a visit to the rose growers in England, where with the end of the war, beauty could once more take over from practicality. Gallica roses, with their old fashioned double shape, and their rich, heavy perfumes, were their choice. They had some new varieties also, which might be encouraged to bloom as early as March, the first colour of the year. Mountain ash, the rowan tree of our Welsh homeland was another addition. The berries lasting into the colder season, providing colour and sustenance to the world around them.

The garden was the Pack's monument to their Alpha's daughter and the young male they saw as a son. It was a place where the pain of their loss did not seem as bad, and Gavril was certain that, in time, the pain would fade. It would never go. He may have harvested the souls of those who had murdered their children, but it would never bring them back. But in their memory, and in the memory of other friends and Pack lost during the war, he and Aaleahya planted their garden, and they made a solemn promise that they would protect those in their care. If it could be seen as a legacy, then it would be a good starting point.

Even if they were going to minimise the Pack's interaction with humans, to maintain their privacy, it was still necessary for the Pack to have some interaction. The easiest way to achieve this, as they had found in the Carpathians, was through running a business such as a workshop or a bar. The bar concept had worked well for the Pack before, so that was what Gavril decided his Pack would do.

With their interest in archery, the ideal combination was a hunting supplies shop, specialising in bow hunting, with a bar tacked in the side. We decided to name it "The Hunter's Arrow", the same name we had used before. The workshop and bar were designed to have the 'natural luxury' which seemed so popular here: lots of exposed wood, stained in warm tones; lanterns even though there was electricity, fireplaces. All in all, going for the 'log cabin' look. The bar had the same air: rough-hewn wooden furniture in a bar which was anything but rough.

And amongst all these arrangements, there was the question of what their Pack Associate, Zarek, wanted from them. He had been willing to ensure that the Pack could protect the village in the Carpathians, making sure that any 'incomers', be they human or otherwise, would not harm the legacy they had hoped to establish. The Gods never grant the benevolence of assistance without wanting something in return, and so far, beyond establishing a temple of sorts, the Pack had been asked for nothing. All Gavril had in terms of information was that Zarek seemed remarkably keen for the Pack to move to the USA.

Still, with Eastern Europe in turmoil after the war, with Stalin fighting it out politically with President Truman, without a doubt, there was more to come. Borders were shifting, changing, governments and their politics were jostling for supremacy. Caught in the middle? People, who like the village in the Carpathians they had recently left, who only wished to live their lives in peace.

As Cŵn Annwn, the Pack was no different. They also wanted time to heal, to be left to regroup, and to renew the bonds which make them Pack. Aaleahya and Gavril needed time to mourn their daughter and son.

Would they be granted that time? Gavril had no idea.

It gave Gavril great pleasure setting up their new home, the third home that the Pack would have since he had become Alpha. Whilst there were undeniable similarities, each one was different. One thing remained the same. Good old fashioned human curiosity.

The latest incarnation of Negrescu Hall, their new home, had been a near derelict when the Pack bought it during the war years, when it became apparent what was happening in Hungary, and that they would need a safe place to bring those whom they succeeded in evacuating. Transforming a derelict building into a luxurious home could not go unnoticed, despite the best attempts of the Pack's legal team. So, perhaps the large gates were a bit obvious. But the Pack valued their privacy and if there is one thing that will happen in America, the 'land of the free', it is that money will buy privacy. And they had plenty of the former to establish the latter.

A further detail that came with the Pack's new home was that training their next generation could become a more formal process. The war had meant that training had been 'on the job', and as Alpha, that was a far from ideal situation for Gavril. Losing a young member of his Pack because they lacked the training to control their eye change, as had happened with his little Kat, is something that should never have happened.

Gavril had discussed the matter with Bran and Owain, his joint Betas. What he wanted to establish was a formal training programme for those younglings who wished to become Sentinels. Not all were suited. Their Pack Healer, Angharad Lloyd, for all that she came from a line of healers, still had to fight during the war, but in return, she asked that Gavril might let her have time away from the Pack, so that the gentle side might also be fed. Of course, he granted her request.

"America." Angharad sighed as she looked at the vista before her and refused to start listing all that needed to be done in setting up her practice here. "Once again we start anew." Would she face the persecution of the human healers here as well or would they be allowed to practice their art without fear of being labelled witch? She had lost so many she called sister healers through the centuries and could only hope that human society had advanced enough to embrace the old ways.

-x-

Angharad turned back to look at their new home and sent a silent prayer to the Goddess that they would find comfort here. The loss and sadness they had endured from the old land still weighed heavy upon the Pack no matter their strength. Lost in the sad memories she bent to pick up a stick and swung it to and fro through the tall weeds and watched as the pollen floated through the soft breeze and thus, let those feelings sail away as well.

Despite her best efforts, Angharad's mind began to catalogue what needed to be done. She needed to dig and prepare a suitable root cellar. She needed to visit the local native American tribes and re-establish a relationship that she had let lapse. Their knowledge of local plant life and healing practices was most enlightening. Set up a workshop apart from the manor. Well, that would come later once they were established but it was necessary if Angharad was not only to teach others but to learn from them as well.

Idly, she scattered pollen and seeds once again as she contemplated their relocation, not only the excitement but also the sadness. A soft secret smile lit up Angharad's face when she thought of Zarek. The mysterious one. No doubt she would miss him too. "Ok, enough of that. There are things to be done that don't involve beating the local flora." Angharad threw the stick and trudged back to the house determined and with a plan of action in place. "First coffee and then I'll tackle my new workroom."

CHAPTER 19: AFTER THE WAR (DEATH AND REBIRTH)

Standing in the gardens of their new home, Aaleahya wondered how best to use her powers to create the relaxing ambience of their home without attracting attention to them being paranormal creatures. She smiled at the memories of how she could just lay her hands on the soil and the plants would sprout, before maturing to food bearing grain crops, vegetables and fruit. It had been easier then, with the villagers trusting them. But the wars had changed all that. They had to hide their abilities now. Now, Aaleahya knew that she would have to be more discreet, to avoid the risk of discovery and the fear of being hunted by those in authorities.

Another aftermath of the War was the way the struggle of the various governments to hold sway over others and impose their own version of the word 'democracy'. On the one hand, there were the American and British views, and on the other the Russians and their communist ideals, which even this soon after the war, had cracks showing. It would impact both on the Pack in their new home and on those they had left behind under the protection of Zarek, son of Svitovid.

Wiping the tears on her face, Aaleahya looked up, a hesitant smile on her face as she saw her Mate approach, asking her what she thought of their new home. She knew it would do her no good to wish that things had been different, that Kat and Sandu had not died in such a senseless manner. May the Goddess grant her the strength to deal with the pain of that loss. Answering her Mate's question, she agreed that the place had potential, and she was sure she would be able to transform it to resemble their former home.

Gavril had been drawn to his Mate, the sorrow in her heart calling to him, a beacon from the gardens of their new home. Even though he had been working on plans for the Pack's future in what would become his study and the heart of Pack operations, he could no more ignore her need than he could a scream for help.

Flashing closer to the gardens, Gavril had gone in search of his Mate, finding her in the part of the gardens which had been designated as the new memorial garden. For a moment, he and Aaleahya stood in each other's arms, taking comfort in the fact that they had survived the carnage of the war. They could also take comfort in those whom they had saved, even at the loss of two so dear to them. Ironically, many of them had chosen to settle close to the new Pack home, drawn by the similarities of their former homes in Europe.

In answer to Aaleahya's question of whether they would ever be able to return, Gavril shook his head. "I don't know, my love. Who knows what will happen?" He smiled. "Let me amend that. Zarek and his sire probably have a good idea of what will happen but they are not going to tell us. All we can do is learn from our pasts. Still, at least we know that he will take care of our former home. Perhaps, in time we may be able to return."

Wanting to take Aaleahya's mind from its sorrowful track, Gavril told her more of their plans for the future. "Bran, Owain and I have been working out how we are going to start training the younglings in a more formal manner. Our new 'Sentinel School'." He smiled, his fingers tipping the corners of Aaleahya's lips into an upward curve. "I will not lose another youngling to something we could teach them, such as controlling their own abilities and giving them the means to be able to hide amongst humans, without fear of discovery. For all their talk of freedom, the paranoia that this American government felt towards Communism will mean that, in time, they will be looking to ensure that they have the strongest deterrent an if that means making slaves of supernatural creatures, they will not hesitate to do so."

Taking Aaleahya's hands, Gavril pulled his Mate close to his side. "Come my love. Why don't you show me what you have planned?" Listening to her plans, Gavril explained his rationale for selecting this particular property.

"One of the reasons why I selected this as our home is its isolation, and the large amount of land attached to it, property which is of little interest to others due to its lack of commercial advantage. Forests are not seen as a cash crop to these people, so it is unlikely that others will investigate the changes that we are making around us. We will be able to live in privacy."

Gavril also explained some of the arrangements he had made to manage their resources. "The routes we used to settle the children we evacuated and the lawyers who were involved will act as our representatives to the outside world. We will not be the only affluent recluses in this area."

Gavril was also investigating how their representatives might also give them advance warning of any problems which might occur. What Aaleahya said was true. These people were so suspicious of the risks to their 'way of life', in their paranoia, they saw enemies all around them. "It is a fine line we must tread, Aaleahya, there is no doubt there, but this is our home now. If we had stayed in our old home, then we would have been used. I will not let that happen. Ever."

Resting her head against Gavril's shoulder, Aaleahya sighed. "I know, but all these changes will take time. I miss my homeland, not least because it was where I met you." Lifting her face, she smiled, caressing her cheek with the back of her hand. Looking around, Aaleahya realised that her Mate spoke truly. Vast woods did surround their new home, and he was right, they did need to do this. She knew only too well now that Gavril would do everything in his not inconsiderable power to protect his Pack, and could take comfort in that. Describing to him the way that she envisaged their garden, "I want this to be a garden all the year round, with different plantings to highlight each time of year."

It seemed to Aaleahya that she could almost hear their daughter's laughter in the air, and knew that Kat would have loved it here to. Gavril was right. It would be a fine line that they must walk, and if that meant becoming what the humans saw as recluses, then so be it.

This move was necessary so that the Pack might survive and heal. The dreams will continue to haunt them, and Aaleahya would always see the body of her daughter on that fateful day. All she could hope was that the image would fade, along with the anger that had boiled in her veins. The one who shot their daughter was long dead, and perhaps time would heal Aaleahya's own soul. It might have been hoped that with the defeat of the Germans, peace would rule her homeland again, but that had not allowed for the Red Army, who invaded their borders demanding the imposition of their way of life. Her thoughts were interrupted by an abrupt noise as a herd of deer broke through the cover and ran across the lawn, stopping as they realised the bounty that lay before them. It reminded Aaleahya that life did go on. The herd had faced hard times, but they survived as the Pack would also survive.

A sudden gunshot seemed to shatter the peace of reflection, as one of the deer fell. To their sensitive hearing the gunshot was like a cannon. Raising his head, Gavril checked for scents, and a low growl rumbled through him as he picked up a human's scent, a human on the land which he had assured his Mate was their land and safe for the Pack to roam. Releasing his Mate, he started to track the scent, momentarily confused by the smell of animal urine. Realising the two scents came from the same direction, it became clear that the human poacher had used the scent of urine to mask his approach on the deer herd.

As he approached the point at which the hunter had concealed himself, Gavril made a clear and obvious target of himself. "If you are planning to use that toy in your hands on me or my wife, I suggest you reconsider." He looked directly at the bush. "I believe local laws permit me to kill you in self-defence and your gun was discharged in my wife's direction. This is your final warning." Gavril's voice deepened with his growl.

Aaleahya shivered when she heard the lethal tone in Gavril's voice towards the idiot hunter. She had only heard that tone a few times, and knew that if the hunter chose to ignore her Mate, then he would be in for a … whole lot of hurt, as humans would say.

The poacher was in for more than a small reprimand as he made no move to emerge from the bushes. Aaleahya's mind voice matched his own anger, as she realised, when she checked the still warm corpse of the deer, that the flesh contained poison. Her own growl was soft, that she had found poison on their land, aimed at the deer. It had not been ordinary hardship that caused this herd to look deprived. The human was a murderer twice over as far as she was concerned. Still he had to be given due warning. "I can excuse the poaching if you thought the estate was not inhabited. However, the purchase of this property was registered in 1938. You have trespassed and vandalised my property as well as poached on my private herd of deer." Gavril's voice took on the tone of his Alpha strength. A shifter would have struggled against him. A human stood no chance. The bush rustled and an adult male emerged, covered in what passed as hunting apparel, looking like ex-military.

"I have a permit. It's deer season." He grunted. "It's my right. I have paid good money for my permit."

Gavril laughed. "Last time I looked, no permit issued by the local authorities permits hunting on private land or the use of poisons to destroy another man's property."

The human's eyes narrowed as he spat to one side, in casual disregard for this being 'private property'. Reloading his rifle, he raised it again, this time in Gavril's direction. "You can't do nufin' about it if yer dead." He grinned, showing yellow stained teeth.

Gavril smiled. Well, even the authorities would agree that having a weapon aimed at you was a threat, even without those words. His smile was because the human had no idea what was coming. Even as he thought he had the upper hand, an arm wrapped around his neck, and a blade was pressed to his side. Bran's deep voice with its hint of a Welsh accent was quiet but clear.

"Shall I dispose of the trash, sir?" Bran's face was cold. To his mind he had failed his Alpha during the war in not preventing some of the occasions when Gavril had been beaten. He would not fail his Alpha now.

With the hunter immobilised by Bran, Gavril approached him even as he struggled. Taking his weapon from him, Gavril examined it. It was well used and spoke of someone who saw his 'right' to hunt as a given. Small matter it would seem if his hunting took him onto private land or land retained by others.

"It is not deer season, not when the does are carrying young. As I said, even if it was, you are trespassing on private land. Since we moved back here, clear signs have been erected, indicating our boundaries, which you have chosen to ignore." Again Gavril smiled, but for all his hunting prowess, the human did not realise that it was the smile of a predator protecting his home range.

"If proof is found that you laid poisoned bait on my land, then I will request my lawyers to begin proceedings." Gavril watched the human for his reaction.

The sudden pallor gave it away. What was it with these people that the threat of lawyers scared them to such an extent? Gavril growled at his reaction. "You fucking poisoned my land. Poisoned the creatures living in what is a private game reserve?" His words carried on a snarl.

Transferring the gun to his left hand, Gavril's right hand seized the human around the neck as Bran released him, sensing his Alpha's intent. "If you were just poaching, I might have shown some leeway, but the use of poison? Perhaps I should make you ingest some of the same and you can tell me how that feels?" Gavril had his answer in the stink of fresh urine and the stain on the human's clothing.

Knowing that this foolish human had just soiled himself at the suggestion that Gavril feed him the same poison he had used on the Pack's land made him realise that the human was not worth the effort. Gavril resisted the temptation to smile at Aaleahya's suggestion that they take advantage of humans' current attitude to the treatment of alleged mental illness, but it was a simple one. The key risk was that Gavril did not want this American government, with their paranoia over the risk of strange, and thus, Communist behaviours, to place too much credence in the stories of half human wolves living in the Catskills. On the other hand, a short sharp shock might be all that was needed.

His pondering took a matter of seconds, before Gavril requested that Aaleahya and Bran both change their top half only to wolf form. Bran's mind linked laughter again made him want to smile, but equally, Bran shared his Alpha's concern. They had only just escaped with our lives from the machinations of the Nazis and the local government in the Carpathians.

[ML to Bran and Aaleahya] "Do it. Just a quick flash to wolf whilst I have my hand around his neck. He will put it down, hopefully, to a lack of oxygen due to my near throttling of him."

At Gavril's signal, his head and upper body changed to the black wolf form that was like a second skin to him. Behind the human, Bran did the same. Aaleahya followed suit, extending her nose delicately forward, as if investigating the human for supper.

Equally fast they all changed back. His hand was still holding the human as the male started to blubber. "What the fucking hell are you ... creatures? What godforsaken hell spawned you?" The human blustered, but the stink of his own urine gave away his fear.

"I am the landowner on whose land you have been poaching and trespassing, causing material damage to my property. As I was saying, I suggest that you leave my property, and never return, or I will have to ask my legal representatives to intervene." Gavril affected a look of puzzlement at his reaction.

For good measure, Bran bent the barrel of the human's rifle in a casual show of strength, before handing the useless weapon back to the man. "And, this will be your only warning." Gavril reminded him. "We have guards patrolling our estate borders. If you or any other human ... or person is found within our boundaries, we will utilise that right of the Constitution, to bear arms, and respond accordingly."

The human grabbed his useless rifle and ran as Gavril let him loose. "This should prove interesting. Either we have done just enough or we have done too much, as will be plagued by the local authorities. We shall see."

Aaleahya linked her arm through her Mate's, smiling up at him, watching as the hunter took off running, babbling about demons, in the woods. She knew the locals will scoff at him and that they already did not like this particular person, since he was a loud mouth know-it-all. It really seemed like an institution will be his new home shortly if he breathed a word of what he thought he had seen.

CHAPTER 20: A COLD WAR IS STILL WAR

It had been a couple of years since Gavril, Aaleahya and the rest of the Negrescu Cŵn Annwn relocated their home to the Catskills in New York State. When Zarek had first met the enigmatic Alpha of the Cŵn Annwn, it was because his sire sent him to find out who and what was poaching on his turf. The problem with the Carpathians is that every fucking paranormal wants a cut of the action.

Protocols, people. Protocols. Would a human just waltz into someone's home and set up shop? Some might, but normally no. So why do dumb ass paranormals think that doing the same thing is just fine? That was the question Zarek asked himself over and over again.

The agreement that he had with Gavril was quite simple. Zarek would live up at the partial ruin that was Negrescu Hall. The cave in which Gavril and Aaleahya had consummated their Mating had become a hidden temple to his father, which was appropriate given that Svitovid was a God of Fertility, Warfare and Divination. It gave Zarek a quiet place to make his observations, and also if any of the villagers wished to join him, they were free to do so. Thus, as the darkened of Communism extended its grip, that little cave became a place where Zarek's pagan sire might actually grow in strength where all the other Gods floundered.

What did Zarek do in return? Son of a God of Fertility? His role was vital as the incompetence of the local Communist party machine became all too obvious. Famine. An ugly word at the best of times, but when the food is available in the fields failed to reach those in needs, the situation takes on a whole new dimension,

That was one of the reasons why his help was needed. For all the years that war had gripped this part of Europe, Aaleahya had used her talents to provide food for as many as possible. Now the problem was slightly different. The Soviet Government refused to reduce the punitive harvest level required from the farms in this area. If anything the repression and punishment which was meted out only served to make the situation more difficult. When a peasant farmer must work on the State-owned farms every single day with no days off, how is he to provide for his own family and work his own land. But then, land ownership was seen as a hangover of their bourgeois past, and anathema to the Communist authorities. So, everyone had played cat and mouse.

Rumours were fostered of the haunted Negrescu Hall, caused by the mysterious death of a whole platoon as Gestapo, killed when the weapons cache stored they had gone up in smoke, the reason for the place being a virtual ruin. What it did was make the Hall a perfect hiding place for the surplus grain produced, on the understanding that all would benefit. The village was accustomed to working with the Cŵn Annwn so is was an acceptable progression for them.

It was still inevitable that another 'commission' would pay them a visit. The village had been cautious. They knew others in the area were struggling to meet their quota of grain harvest, and they had to play a balancing game of ensuring that they provided enough and close enough to quota that they did not attract attention, but at the same time, did not bring the wrath of the local administrators down on them for not providing enough. A balancing act indeed. The other thing Zarek had to watch was ensuring that those from his village did not look too ... healthy. A healthy appearance meant that they were eating properly. When all around them were facing famine, it would have clued an observant administrator that something was different about our local setup.

His sire's intent in having Zarek 'on the ground' was that he might understand more about these humans and what made them tick along with a few other … issues. This whole Communism thing. Great in theory. Share everything out. No one starves, but no one benefits more than anyone else. Like he said, great in theory. In practice? Whole different ball game. There was that little detail that everyone seemed to forget when coming up with their perfect system: human greed. It is part of their biological makeup, to want what someone else has. Aspiration or greed? The same or different? Winston Churchill, the great Prime Minister of the United Kingdom during World War Two described the actions of Russia's Stalin as if he dropped an iron curtain across Europe. These humans, many of them had hoped that Communism was their way forward, and now they were discovering the very opposite. The administrators, the leaders seemed to be the ones who reaped the benefits, whilst the general populace starved. And all in the name of politics.

The journals of Angharad Lloyd: 1942

My mother rushed into her workroom frantically searching for something and I knew enough to stay out of her way when she was in such a state. I put down the pestle and pushed the dried herbs and mortar toward the wall lest she knock them over. "Mam?" With a shout of exasperated triumph, she heaved her travel bag out from the cabinet. My mother may have been a brilliant healer but she was not very organized. Thank the goddess she had me. I took a breath to comment on her organization but the words died when I saw the torment on her face. I knew then that something bad had happened. She had a way of seeing things and sadly, it was never good so I stood to receive the news.

"Dod fy merch, mae'n rhaid I ni fynd." My mother, the Pack Iachawr or healer bade me follow her with no explanation but this time I would not fuss about it for the look on her face was sheer devastation. I grabbed my healer bag and followed her from the room. "Mam? What is it?" She firmly grasped my hand and said one word before we flashed away. "Lidice"

We arrived in a wooded area outside of the small Czech village of Lidice but we dared not move. The village was surrounded by Nazi soldiers and the smell of gunpowder and blood was heavy in the June air. Hundreds of male bodies were piled atop each other, dead from gunshot. My Mam and I reeled from the pain and fear emanating from the citizens as the women and children were torn from each other's arms. Their screams and begging tore at my heart as we stood as silent witness. The women and children had watched the slaughter of their men by the Ordnungspolizei and the SD, only to be told that they would be sent to concentration camps. My gut churned at the hateful words. "Mam? They mean to kill the children? But why? For what purpose?" My heartbreak turned to raw anger as I made to run down into the village square. I had forgotten the strength of my mother's arms until she held me firmly back. We struggled for a few moments before she flashed us home.

I threw my bag across the room, my rage so all-encompassing that reason was no more. "We could have saved those children! Children! We could have saved them Mam!" I cared not that I screamed at her or that my hands curved down into claws as I stepped forward. "We're healers and you just left them to die? What kind of..." Her hand landed across my cheek with such force that I crumbled onto the work table, the herbs that I so carefully protected earlier scattered everywhere. She wrenched me up roughly by the shoulders and shook me.

"Do you honestly think I don't bleed for them Angharad? You think I am cold and heartless? We would have been killed and would have accomplished nothing." She shoved me back with a snarl and turned away from me. But I had seen the pain in her eyes and since she shocked me into rational thought, I felt her pain as well. She still had not turned to me but her soft controlled voice reached me from across the room. "My young Angharad. I didn't know what we would find there, only that we would be needed. If I had known, I would never have taken you there. One of life's lessons you need to learn as a healer is to lead with your head, the heart will follow. We could not save them for we are not an army. You and I cannot combat such hatred and violence; we can only heal the wounds left behind."

Mam walked to the doorway and her tearful smile was so bittersweet it tore my heart open. "I'm sorry I slapped you merch but you needed to understand. Now I must find our Alpha and apprise him of this situation. I love you Angharad." By then I was crying uncontrollably and mouthed my love to her as I could not voice it through the tears. I sent a silent prayer to the Goddess and asked for the strength my mother had, to deal with such heart wrenching decisions as a healer so I could better serve the pack.

CHAPTER 21: TRAGEDY CLOSE TO THE HEART (ABERFAN 21 OCTOBER 1966)

It was the middle of the night when his Goddess called Gavril. When he realised what had happened, he had summoned all adult and fully trained soul retrievers in the Pack with the priority being for those who were Mated. This was not one for the younger Cŵn Annwn, not given the scale of what they had to deal with.

At 9.15am in a small town near Merthyr Tydfil in the Pack's own homeland of Cymru, death had come calling, when the slag from the nearby colliery started to slide, the mass turned into slurry by rainfall. Down the side of Mynydd Merthyr it came, above the village of Aberfan. All that stood in its way stood little chance: a farm, 20 terraced houses along the Moy Road, and the north side of the Pantglas primary school and the nearby senior school. The slide deposited slurry to a depth of over thirty feet deep, with many recalling afterwards that they thought a jet plane had come down. Parents arrived on the scene, digging frantically with their bare hands, but it was to little avail. By the end of the day, 2000 rescue workers had arrived on the scene, but no one was pulled alive from the debris after the first hour.

In all, the Pack retrieved the souls of 116 children and 28 adults. One hundred and forty-four souls.

It is times like this that barriers between faiths and religions disappear. The Pack are pagan. They serve Mallt-y-Nos, and when the souls they must retrieve are from their own homeland, somehow it seems harder. One hundred and sixteen children aged between 7 and 10 years old: almost half of the school's register. A village devastated in a way that had only been seen before in their homeland with the slaughter of young men on the battlefields of the 'Great War'.

Whilst it normally fell to Aaleahya to collect the souls of the innocent, Gavril knew that she could not have borne them all. For that reason, this was a Pack effort, and whilst the death certificates would show death from asphyxiation, or crush injuries, the Pack knew that they had acted quickly enough that the victims had died not knowing what killed them.

There were some Gavril would have liked to harvest who were not as innocent, such as the reporter who told a little girl to cry for her dead friends because it would make a better picture to sell his bloody newspapers. Was this really all that mattered to him? More sales, more money, more praise from his employer for 'hitting targets'?

Did any good come from this tragedy? Yes, there were substantial improvements made, not least was more attention paid to the siting of such spoil deposits. The one near Aberfan had been sited on an old river, known to both colliery engineers and mine workers, who had believed the safety underground was more important. Much was learned in the aftermath of the disaster. But as the Alpha of the Cŵn Annwn, that day would be etched forever in Gavril's memory.

When Gavril called the Pack together and briefly explained the dire situation in Aberfan. Angharad knew that there was no hesitation from any of them as they whisked themselves to the devastation. The cry of the souls would have made a lesser being crumble but their combined strength and the will of their Alpha provided the fortitude needed for the task at hand. Angharad stilled a moment to gather herself and to remember her Mam's words. "Lead with your head and the heart will follow."

Unseen, the Pack flitted to the tiny bodies buried under the putrid sludge. Warmth and comfort was flashed to their minds so that their last thoughts were not of pain and fear but rather of calm and peace. Angharad learned long ago that she could not save them all but she and the rest of the Pack could give comfort and that would have to be enough as their pure little souls were gathered so that they could be sent on.

A shout from a rescuer gave her hope and Angharad rushed to his side as he found a small girl hidden in a cupboard. The handles were made in such a way as to have provided a small breathing space. Still, she was barely alive and would not make it without help. Wasting no time, Angharad sent her mind into the child's still body. Her skull was cracked and she was bleeding internally. Time was of the essence so Angharad dwelled on the blood loss and then worked to bring the brain swelling down. It was difficult checking for further injury as they loaded her onto a stretcher but Angharad was able to float above her and sealed up a major blood vessel in the child's thigh. The rest will be up to the human healers as Angharad's work here was not done. She turned back to those still trapped but the other Cŵn Annwn had it covered so Angharad turned her attentions to the rescuers and mourners.

Walking unseen around those that dug tirelessly in the muck, ignoring the lacerations and injuries. One by one, Angharad laid her hand on them and pushed out the sludge from their wounds and healed them. When she came upon a mother, the woman was too tired and devastated to cry as someone tried to wash her hands. Her nails were gone, lost to the force of her digging for her child. Now is when Angharad's heart followed her head and she touched the grieving mother gently. She would not heal the mother's wounds except to remove the sludge from inside lest it set up infection and but she could reduce the pain. No, Angharad did not heal her for she could feel this mother needed the scars on her hands to prove she did all she could to save her child. Instead, she stood silent vigil over all that provided help in one way or another. All would carry this day in their soul forever.

Gavril let the Pack know it was time to retreat and take care of the souls now in their charge.

Aaleahya knew that as with the rest of the Pack, her memories would forever remain in the front of her mind. She had gathered as many as she could but there were too many and she had been grateful that she was not alone, that she had her Pack. Yes, the Pack came to help her and yes, they were able to rescue the children's souls before they could even understand what had happened. The screams of children were Aaleahya's one weakness and the one thing that made her angry enough to shift to her Cŵn Annwn which she fought very hard to not do. She looked on with pride as Gavril coaxed a few of the young scared souls to him wrapping them within his own being. The Pack had been busy that day but they came together as they always did, working as a whole unit. The harvesting of the souls of innocents and delivering them to their Goddess was never easy, but where there is evil, there will be innocent victims. She would protect and nurture them as she did their own child and her best friend. It was not just her duty as Cŵn Annwn, but her solace that she could help them find their rest.

22: WOODSTOCK – SEX, DRUGS AND ROCK 'N' ROLL

Owain and Gavril were discussing where and how to construct an obstacle course and training facility in the woods behind Negrescu Hall, when one of the younglings found them. Gavril waited for her to regain her breath, as she had run from the house with her message, keeping a straight face so that she did not feel the Alpha was laughing at her efforts.

"There is a human here to see you, sir." She was still gasping as she delivered her message. "Eira said it is the man who runs the farm for us, Max."

"Thank you, child." Gavril said politely. "Would you like a lift back?" She looked at him, almost horrified that the Alpha would give her a ride back. Shaking her head, she spun round and took off in the direction of the house.

"I think you scared her, Gavril." Owain was trying not to laugh, and once we were alone again, gave in and howled with laughter. "Big bad Alpha. Poor thing looked like she was going to freak out completely."

Gavril shrugged. He wondered what Max had to discuss, but it was not often that he would come to the Hall in person, preferring to use the phone if he needed to speak with Gavril with any degree of urgency. As the youngling said, Max leased the farm adjoining Negrescu Hall from the Pack, providing them with a tidy income stream, but at the same time, enabling them to avoid having to deal with the outside world, and answer those unnecessary questions about their unchanging, and non-aging, looks.

Eira had seated Max on the patio area overlooking the gardens, with her ever present coffee and pastries. Max had been a farmer in the Old Country, one of the older children whom the Pack had rescued and brought to the USA, and as such, whatever he might have thought in public, he never mentioned the fact that neither Owain nor Gavril had aged in the time he knew them. Perhaps it helped that he had been a child, since children allow for the 'unexplainable' much more than adults.

Smiling, Gavril shook the human's hand. "So, what brings you to the Hall, Max, that couldn't be discussed over the phone? Nothing serious, I trust?" he asked.

"It could be, Mr Negrescu. I was approached yesterday by a couple of guys. They gave their names as Michael Lang and Artie Kornfield. They wanted to know if they could organise a music festival on the upper side of the farm, but I told them I only lease the place, and would have to check with the owners." He spread out his hands. "So, sir, this is me checking with you."

Walking out onto the patio area, Aaleahya heard Max giving the location of a proposed music festival. Linking her arm through Gavril's, she expressed a concern. "That side is where we have younglings that like to run at night through the woods, some of them swimming in the pond that is located on that farm."

Pulling Aaleahya into his embrace was as natural a movement as breathing, as Gavril listened to what Max had to say. The plans outlined to him were that the two promotors were working with two others. They wanted to put on a music festival it seemed. It would only attract 50,000 people. At Max's words, Gavril felt Aaleahya's tension. Fifty thousand people on the land which the Pack owned, and from what Max was saying, around the pond which their younglings used to go for midnight swims 'without the adults knowing'.

"What else did they have to say for themselves?" Gavril asked Max, waving him to the seat he had been using, and taking a seat with Aaleahya on the bench opposite him. A youngling came out to refresh the pot of coffee and the pastry selection.

"Well." Max looked amused. "I heard tell that they had looked at other places, but the locals didn't want that many people around, so all kinds of restrictions were put on them. The plan is that they are going to sell tickets, so it won't be a free concert, but even so." He shrugged. "Part of me says it will be a good idea, because it means more income. The other part of me thinks what kind of mess will that many people leave. I might look like I am making money, but by the time I factor in clean-up costs? I could end up losing. Then, they might say it is all about peace and love, but, again, I don't know."

He looked torn between the options, and it was clear that he almost wanted the decision taken out of his hands, and to be made by someone else. Since the Pack actually owned the land in question, he was hoping that they would make that decision for him.

Aaleahya relaxed in the comfort she felt coming from Gavril's hand stroking arm. It seemed strange since she was usually the one to do the calming. She listened intently to her Mate discussing the pros and cons of such an endeavour.

After Max had left the Hall, Aaleahya made a suggestion to Gavril. "I have a thought my love. Why don't we send the Sentinels, as they would be about the right age? We could send Taren, Rhys and Cerys to attend this concert, letting them keeping a close eye on the attendees. and then around our perimeter we use the older guards in their stealth mode." Her fingers described inverted commas over the word 'stealth'.

Gavril smiled, and his grin widened as he turned to Owain. "Let's go for it. As my Mate suggests, it would a perfect exercise for the Sentinels in training, and enable them to study human behaviour in a different environment from the bar."

Angharad had gone out early, such that by now, later in the day, the basket of willow bark had become a bit heavy. Sitting down, she tilted her head up to the sun peeking through the trees. The breeze still held a nip to it but the warmth of the morning sun was the kind that made you glad to be alive. Her head dropped immediately when a twig snapped and the sound of someone walking slowly through the trees put her on high alert. She was not on Pack property and had no wish to run into some human hunter as they didn't always use their best judgment.

Before too long Angharad saw a female with a basket similar to her own working her way through the woods. The way she studied the ground let her know the female was no doubt a healer or herbalist herself. Her heart swelled a bit hoping that was true since she loved learning and sharing tricks and practices with others, especially if she was native to the area.

Angharad stepped out from behind a tree, intending that the female would see her from a distance and not be frightened. She was shocked when the female suddenly sniffed the air and dropped her basket, although Angharad couldn't tell if it was in fright or readiness. Her head turned looking for the danger just as their eyes locked and Angharad held up her hand in peace. "Hello sister healer." She made no move toward the female since she was clearly leery of her. To make herself less intimidating, Angharad stepped over to a log and sat. "I see so few healers and herbalists anymore and I would love to exchange notes with you." Her face lit in a hopeful smile. "Frankly, the so-called herbalists nowadays only concern themselves with marijuana."

The female planted her hands on her hips. "You may not want me to come closer and frankly, I'm not so sure I wish to either." Angharad frowned at her words trying to think them through.

"Surely healers share a bond that cannot be broken by feuds or so-called enemies. You may trust me. My name is Angharad."

The female pondered for a few moments and then made her way up the hill. Angharad sensed her nature as soon as she reached the crest and leaned back in caution. "Oh ho. Now I understand your reluctance. Greetings Hellhound." Angharad was smiling but also trying to determine the female's intentions. Their two species are not considered enemies per se but rather different sides to a coin that should not blend. Angharad's mind wondered at the implications of her presence.

Angharad was pleased when the Hellhound female's shoulders relaxed and her lip quirked up in a small smile. "Angharad, you have nothing to fear from me. I am merely a healer gathering items to treat my pack. I have no interest in politics. I am Alina." Angharad could see that she was contemplating the ramifications of this meeting and was carefully choosing her words.

"I am of the same belief Alina. I just love to help others and learn all I can." The two healers fell into silence, wanting to trust each other but unable to work past all that they had been taught since their youth. Angharad cleared her throat and smiled. "I come to this area hunting for willow and other such things every other day. Well, more for exercise and time away by myself. Perhaps we can meet again and talk shop over a small picnic?" Her eyes lit up with a smile. Healers are a bit different than the rest of the pack and always seem to be a little apart. Angharad didn't know the why of it but it was there none-the-less. Alina stood up and nodded. "I would love that Angharad. Perhaps on your next trip? I'll bring sandwiches. Now I will walk a bit more before I return. I will not mention this encounter to anyone."

"Neither will I Alina." Angharad paused a moment then voiced what was on both our minds. "Please don't make me regret that decision." She tapped her left wrist twice and tipped her head slightly. Angharad did the same to her before they parted ways. Long ago her mother taught her the secret sign between healers, from back when they had to hide their craft or be burned as a witch. Angharad walked slowly back to the Hall, her mind contemplated all that she had learned and what she may learn from the Hellhound female. Angharad still held a kernel of worry but the path had been chosen so all she could do was walk it. "I hope you are not making a mistake Angharad." She muttered to herself.

Listening to Gavril talking to Max, Owain's mind was already thinking along the lines of how they could send some of the Sentinel Trainees to this festival. Rhys was certainly ready, and that meant Taren could probably tag along. The question was Cerys and her sometimes abrasive attitude. Most saw it as abrasive. Owain saw it as a shield as she continued to try to prove to her parents and her older brothers that she could 'cut it' as a Sentinel, particularly in view of her unique gifts, which they had only recently discovered.

They were traditionalists through and through, seeing the female role to balance the male soul harvester. They forgot that their Alpha's own sire and dam had reversed that 'tradition', with his dam being the Alpha. It didn't mean his sire was weak by a long stretch. The Goddess knew that with the world changing as it was, they needed female as well as male Sentinels.

Owain was also considering the best way to organise the patrols for the core part of the estate. This 'Vietnam War' in which America was engaged had raised much anger, again tradition clashing with modern. The Pack had to be careful that their patrols were not seen as some form of military presence. To the traditionalist, communists in Vietnam were bad news. Their children did not see it the same way. The Cuban Missile Crisis was a distant memory for many, being over six years ago. A mere blink of an eye for the Pack, but a considerable time for humans. All their children saw were the photographs sent back, the stories of atrocities. Bran and Owain had both taken teams out there, harvesting, and it was not just the Vietnamese. It was the slightly older than WW1 but still boy soldiers mentally, the average age of 19 years old. How could they know politics? They saw dirt, disease, drug addiction. They saw friends dying and occasionally they saw kindness. But based on their sheltered lives before they left, they had next to no life experience. And then to come home, to be seen as a force of evil? The dichotomy of humans never ceased to amaze Owain. These hippies, who looked for the Age of Aquarius, of peace, and yet would cast their anger at the tools, rather than at the wielder of the tools.

Owain shook his head. He was in danger of becoming too involved in human affairs. Gavril had the right if it. Best that the Pack kept to themselves unless they had to go out in a harvest.

-x-

The young African American smiled at his wife. "Here baby, let me hold Jake Junior for a while." Grace, a slim, light-skinned, young woman handed their baby over to her husband as he woke up just enough to smile before nodding off again. "Hey Doug, how much further to this Woodstock thing?" Doug turned around and hollered to the back of the van. "A couple more days and we should be pitching our tents at the biggest event ever held for the flower children and heirs of the new world."

Jake looked over at Grace and rolled his eyes, she just patted his arm with a patient smile. "Baby, give it a chance. Even we need to feel free to be, well, free. Work will be waiting for us soon enough." She looked at her husband's hair and giggled. "I just hope to get that tension of yours to grow out as fast as that fro of yours." Jake snickered a bit and adjusted baby Jake in his arms. "It's hard to relax here on the road. Hell, I hate that we had to use an outhouse back there instead of the gas station toilet. That ain't morally right and I'm tired taking it but I don't want to do nothing that will put you or Jake in a bad situation. So what the hell do I do and still feel like a man?"

"We do what we must Jake, just like our folks did to make sure their children have it a little better than they did. Someday Jake Junior can go to college and be whatever he wants to be, eat where he wants and go to the bathroom where he wants. That's what we've been working for, that is what makes it worth it." Grace's voice was soft, accustomed as she was to trying to diffuse the frustration her husband felt being a black man in a white man's world.

"Grace baby, I'm going to make sure little Jake knows everything. Who and what our parents were, the things we been through and how far we've come. I'll make sure he accepts people for who they are, not what they are and to always hold his head high." Jake leaned over and kissed his son's head before kissing Grace as well.

Their private moment was cut short at another shout. "Hey Jake." Doug was once again yelling to the back of Moonbeam's van and woke everyone up. Jake raised his eyebrows to let his friend know he heard him. "I was meaning to ask you why you went to Vietnam and didn't dodge the draft. I mean, lots of guys did that." Jake took a breath and tried to word it so these hippies and their anti-establishment ways would understand. They're white so they had no idea how it's been and Jake also didn't want to dwell on the struggle too much either because it might ruin the group mood.

"My family and me did enough running and hiding for a lifetime Doug. I'm done with that and feeling like I have to turn my head to keep from making eye contact. My boy is going to grow up different. I want him to face challenges and fears head on with his head held high." Jake shook his head in determination. "Things are a changing my friend and if I couldn't face my fears then, how can I teach Jake to? Don't get me wrong. I don't agree with the Vietnam War but my number came up and I faced it like a man. Did what I had to do and glad of it. Things were different there. We were all soldiers and not so much the coloured thing. I liked that." Jake chuckled a little bit and looked at Nate. "Nate, I know you're tight with the Black Panthers and I respect that. Doing a lot of good they are. But they were a mite militant over in Nam and that didn't suit me too well. It fed some's prejudices in a way that Martin Luther King didn't. I like King's approach. He did things like an intelligent gentleman and that's what I hope to do." Grace's face was beaming at her husband and she shyly patted his hand. Nate nodded his head in understanding and then smiled. "Well Jake, while you were gone Grace organized half of Nashville to carry on the good Martin Luther King's work. She's pretty good at organizing things and keeping the peace. You're a lucky man Jake." Jake winked at his wife and nodded. "That I am brother, that I am."

Owain reviewed the plans they had in place for both patrolling around the estate and the venue itself. This was the perfect opportunity for them to test if the training programme for their younger Sentinels was on track. Rhys, Taren and Cerys would be at the festival. Given the undercurrent they were picking up, how it was considered 'chic' to be anti-war, forgetting that so many of those returning soldiers were younger than them, it would be interesting indeed.

The younger Sentinels had been children during the war, but still knew that the reason they had 'Sentinel School' was to avoid losses like Ekaterina and Sandu, for an inability to control an eye colour change. Cerys was not impressed with her hippy chick look, but Owain could see Aaleahya smile, given that it was a modified version of the gypsy dancer look which had ensnared Gavril all those years ago. She was the one who gave Owain the most concern. These 'free thinkers' were known to be free in their affections, but were still remarkably traditional in their outlook. Cerys was anything but, so it would be a test for her.

Already crowds were gathering. They had taken the decision to lock the gates to the Hall, making it clear that it was a private estate and signs had gone up around the boundary. Mind you, it was debatable if a 'stoned' human was going to be able to read them, but at least they tried. With Owain taking the lead on deploying the younger Sentinels under his training around the Woodstock Festival, Bran was 'taking point' on the patrols around the borders of the Pack's estate. He was in full agreement with his fellow Pack Beta on the nature of some of these 'hippies'.

Peace, love, the Age of Aquarius. Love your fellow man. And of course, let's not forget, smoke weed until you were stoned out of your tiny minds. Perhaps it is because he was Pack Beta, but leaving yourself vulnerable through addiction of any kind struck Bran as a very strange position for anyone to desire. Many a time, he had seen Angharad shake her head in dismay at how 'herbalists' of this era were more often than not just drug dealers by any other name. But the patrols. They had put up signage to indicate the boundaries of Negrescu Hall, and put up very simple wire fence boundaries since they did not want to impede themselves by turning our home into some kind of impregnable Fort Knox. It felt strange having to take these precautions, but when they had the first of what was to be many incursions, it became apparent that this was going to be a very long three days.

The queues of traffic were considerable. Hours in traffic queues had one very annoying side effect, which would only become worse during the festival. Human bladders and bowels have a limited capacity. That didn't mean someone else should have to deal with your waste products, particularly when that someone else has a very acute sense of smell. Thank the Goddess for the ability to burn such things discreetly, Bran thought. Perhaps it didn't help when it became apparent that some had not packed enough water, particularly with their drug taking resulting in extremes of thirst and hunger. Not all affected were to blame, and it left the Pack with little option but to provide food and water. Some were surprised that the ‘local landowners’ did so without charging for it. Others sneered at the Pack even as they accepted the simple food. They were parasites on the planet, preying on those less fortunate if they were part of an 'establishment' with the means to provide a free service.

But the incursions were more frustrating. The Pack patrols tried 'leaning' on their minds, something which was anathema to them, with their emphasis on free will, trying to turn them round, but if that failed, the Pack had to show themselves and let the strangers think the worst of them, that they were clearly uniformed and armed. More than one patrol was spat upon, with it being fashionable to hate war. The Pack was not anti-war, since that is something that humans do, and they were not human. However, after centuries of picking up the pieces, of bringing to justice those who wage war on innocents, it was hard for the Pack not to engage with these humans.

Perhaps it was not just the younger Sentinels who would learn from this experience?

Fane Anghelescu grinned at the sight before him: thousands of humans just ripe for the picking for his Pack of Hellhounds. Perfect fodder for them to exploit to the benefit of his Queen. It was a huge farm that the humans were holding this festival dedicated to peace. The opportunity, given its proximity to his Pack's new home, Anghelescu Hall, was just too good to pass up. As Pack members flashed into the barn they had identified previously as a rendezvous, the cattle, of the bovine persuasion, in their stalls just ignored the strange appearances. Fane cast a critical eye over his Pack.

It was absolutely essential that they blended in with the human cattle around them, and the clothing was designed for that. Tank tops, open cotton shirts for the males, flowing cotton caftans on the females. Flowers decorated the females' hair, and the males and females had left hair unbound. Fane's shorter hair was not ideal but at least his white tank top hid that he wasn't some soft human. All of his Pack carried a variation of a cotton canvas cross body bag, which held their daily allocation of goods for sale. It was good quality shit, as the humans would say: marijuana, coke and for those that wanted it and could afford it, heroin. They also had oranges, and a supply of ready-rolled spliffs. Everything their customers might want.

"Just remember, we want more anti-war sentiment flowing. I am going to work on some of the musicians. Absolutely key, you come back with everything sold. Half a million are expected. Way more than the organisers expected. If we can't shift this lot, then we don't deserve to be called Hellhounds, and I know I will enjoy assisting the Queen in making sure you understand that." Fane voice left no doubt in his Pack's mind as to his expectations.

He may have been Alpha for less than a decade, but in that time, the Anghelescu Pack had moved from the hovel that has housed them under Aurelija, to their new home. The supremacists loved the Hellhounds ready supply of weapons, lifted from army depots courtesy of their ability to flash in and out unseen. The hippies loved their product. And that age of peace was such a load of crock with the delightful negative energy Fane was able to siphon off and bring back to his Queen.

Yeah, life was good.

The noise of Woodstock faded as Jake walked with Doug and Grace in the woods just catching some time to themselves. Moonbeam had little Jake to get down with Arlo Guthrie. The music filtered through the woods and Jake found that he preferred the muted tone and fresh air far from the crowd. They paused at the sound of voices. "Fucking child killer." Those shouted words were followed by the sound of a fist hitting flesh and more curses. Jake knew immediately some Vietnam vet was getting his ass kicked. Been there and done that, man. He turned to Grace with a sad smile. "Gotta go baby." He didn't wait for her reaction and headed toward the fight. It was back in some trees but he saw three men beating another. Jake took no time to think before he threw them off the downed man and sure enough, his haircut said he was fresh out so Jake stood between him and the three attackers.

"Get outa the way nigger." Jake shook his head and braced his legs a little. "No can do man. You're gonna have to go through me. You see it's like this. You don't know what the hell you're talking about when you go calling Nam vets names and acting all stupid." The blonde huffed himself up and stepped forward like he was going to scare Jake away. "They're all baby killers and don't deserve to live." Jake laughed and shook his head at the blonde. Insulting yes but he was an idiot Jake hoped to make see what was right. "He stepped up like a man when his number was called, had no choice, man." Their sneers were making Jake mad and he no longer stopped to think before he talked. "Why didn't you go? Hid behind your mama's apron strings in college or did they decline you cuz your balls are too small?" Yep, that did it. They rushed Jake full force and he saw two more come out of the woods as the fists started to fly. "Fucking uppity nigger. You'll soon know your place."

Jake laughed at their age-old name calling. "It's clear you didn't go to college or you would have learned some new insults." His own fists began to hurt as bad as his body but Jake refused to back down. The vet was away, too hurt to help and Jake figured it only be a matter of time before he joined him. He heard Grace crying and yelling at Doug to come help but hell, Doug wasn't no fighter and was probably shitting himself about then. Somehow Jake was pummelled to the ground thinking that was it when suddenly the assholes were gone and all was quiet. His swollen eyes searched for the cause and saw two men dragging the unconscious attackers away. A tattooed man was left and holding his hand out to help Jake stand up.

Rhys' growl was the only indication that the situation he had first heard and then was witnessing was far from an 'ideal situation' for him.

"Cerys, hang back a few minutes. We're supposed to monitor and not interfere and having you go in and fight in that bohemian outfit would seem out of place." Cerys was as edgy as he was to watch that blonde male get beaten for being in the wrong place at the wrong time. "He doesn't act like a baby killer Rhys." Rhys shook his head but then motioned for her to move closer. "I've been reading the newspapers and some say the soldiers are wiping out whole villages of women and children in Vietnam but then I read other articles saying that stuff is just anti-war propaganda. People just don't know what to believe and as we've seen, humans can get worked up about things to where they close their minds to anything that doesn't follow their mind-set."

They stayed at the tree line and watched a dark human step forward to protect the fallen male. Rhys could not help but cringe when the … African American male goaded the other men into attacking. He reflected a moment that the music playing was in direct contrast to the fight going on. It seemed that all the hippie dogma of peace and brotherhood may have missed this spot in the woods. The dark man put up a good fight but they were not holding back and when one pulled a knife, Rhys felt compelled to intervene. He motioned for Cerys to stay where she was but Taren and Wynn joined him to make quick work of subduing the human attackers. "Take them off to the east a bit. Maybe they'll be cooled off by the time they wake up." Rhys stepped up to the African-American male and held out his hand to help him up, deliberately using human vernacular. "Are you alright, man?"

The man nodded but it was clear he was hurt and was having a hard time standing. His female rushed to his side and checked his condition then another male joined us. "Damn Jake, what were you thinking, man?" He looked at Rhys' face, then his clothing and tattoos. Again, Rhys was struck with the contrast between the 'public' image of peace and love from hippies and the harsh reality, as demonstrated by this male's reaction to his appearance. The human male shrugged, clearly uncomfortable with the image before him and how to react to the incident. "Uh, groovy moves, man. Thanks for helping my friend." He walked away a few steps then took a few to the right. Rhys could see right away that he was not used to violence.

Jake coughed, trying to hide his pain, knowing that Doug's exposure to violent situations was minimal at best, even if it was by choice and deliberate avoidance of issues. "Doug, I couldn't let them hurt him for something that wasn't his fault. It just ain't right. And let's face it, it's not the first time I've been beaten and it probably won't be my last." Jake laughed softly and grimaced. "Good news is that I think my ribs are building up a resistance." He tried to chuckle again but gave that idea up and turned to the strange tattooed man and held out his hand. "Thank you for your help." It crossed his mind that this strange man seemed military or at least has served time, but one thing Jake had learned is that you don't ask.

You never know when someone nearby was in the mood to spit on you or worse. He coughed again and the pain from his ribs took his breath away.

Grace of course was right there to comfort him. "Damn baby, I wonder if someone has some aspirin or something." The ever helpful Doug piped up. "We'll go back and light up the bong Jake, that'll take the edge off. Might have to dip you in the creek first though, you got blood all over you and Moonbeam will pass out in a second."

Jake groaned again as he tried to smile at Doug. He noticed the vet sitting against a tree just watching them. "Grace, please go check on that guy." She gave her husband a pointed look but went to check on him just as the vet's friends topped the bank, their hair and demeanour clearly marked them as fresh-out too. They quickly assessed the scene and rushed to his side. "Seth? What the hell man" Grace quickly explained what happened and their eyes zeroed in on Jake. "Thanks man, things have gotten pretty dicey here. I never thought it would happen but I think it's time we left this party." They looped his arms over their shoulders and walked him out. Jake would bet that they served over there together too. He was glad they were heading away from this festival and going home. Smart.

Cerys noticed the attention she was getting from the dark woman and introduced herself. It brought a bit of levity to the situation, making Rhys smile as Cerys tried to field questions about her clothing since he knew damn well she would rather be in fighting clothes. The dark woman pulled out a necklace of sorts and gave it to Cerys as a kind of thank you, Rhys guessed and was very grateful that Cerys seemed quite interested in the artwork. I turned to the man and assessed his injuries. "A friend of mine is a healer; she might be able to help you out." Jake shook his head and said he was alright, conscious that any professional healer would want money that he didn't have, but Rhys resolved to ask Angharad for something for his pain anyway. He risked his life to protect another and to the young Sentinel, that deserved the extra help. Rhys sent a quick mind link to Taren and asked him to bring something from Angharad. "Perhaps it would be best if you stayed in the crowd and not wander into the woods anymore." Conversation halted as a loud screech came over their loudspeakers to announce the next act, someone called Joan Baez and any thought of talking to a human was useless as the crowd went wild.

Taren ran up with a bag of herbs and told me the male needed to make a tea with it. Rhys nodded and then approached Jake's woman. "A friend of mine is an herbalist. Ah, uses natural medicines for healing. She has this herbal mixture that you steep for a tea. It will help with his pain and swelling." This woman's eyes narrowed from years of distrust ingrained in her and seemed reluctant to take it. "You may trust us. Your man is honourable and I would ease his suffering There's no charge for it." She silently eyed Rhys, her own eyes seeming to notice his tattoos, before nodding. "Thank you Sir." She rushed back to the two men and with a final wave; they went through the woods to blend back into the roaring crowd. "Come on Cerys, let's see what other mischief we can get in to. I'm picturing you dancing in that outfit later." Cerys growled at Rhys and mocked punched him, receiving an unrepentant grin in return.

Jake, Grace and Doug made it back to their little tented spot and Doug slowly lowered his friend to the ground, while Jake tried not to groan, knowing it would alarm both his friends and wanting to spare them the worry. "Jake, I've been meaning to ask you something." Jake would have rolled his eyes but they hurt too bad. "Doug? You always got questions. Always." he sighed in resignation. "What is it Doug?"

"Why is your last name Petersen? You don't look Scandinavian to me." Jake tipped his head back and adopted his best innocently confused look. "What do you mean I don't look Scandinavian?" Everyone got quiet and a little tense until Grace giggled and slapped her husband's arm. Doug cleared his throat and leaned forward all serious like. "Well, you aren't white, you're coloured." Jake tried hard to not smile given how earnest Doug looked, as if the reason for Jake's name was the be all and end all of the world. Despite how hard he tried, Jake couldn't keep it going because holding in his laughter hurt his ribs too bad, so he decided to put Doug out of his misery. "I knew what you meant man. I was just messin' with you Doug." Jake laid down and let Grace doctor him up the best she could while he talked. "My ancestors had many names through the years. A few generations back they decided to stick with Petersen." He grinned with one side of his broken mouth. "Besides, it makes people wonder. Now light that bong and give me my medicine."

As Aaleahya returned her horse Mystique to the stables at Negrescu Hall, she pondered what she had seen around her, both now that the humans had 'invaded' the farm, and in the build up to the concert. After much negotiation, it was settled that the large concert was taking place on the dairy farm the Pack owned on paper but was leased to Max and run by him. Gavril and Max had made all the arrangements. There had been considerable excitement around the compound with some of the younger pups wanting to mingle with the humans. Aaleahya had felt … not uneasy, but there was something about the whole event that had her watching the stages being assembled, and the gradual arrival of the hordes of humans. It became apparent very early on that the numbers quoted by the organisers had been a major under-estimate. The gentle slopes around the pond were crawling with humans, like so many ants when viewed from a distance.

Her horse had been one of the many gifts which Gavril had given her in this new land which they must now call home, so far away from the forests in which she had run as a child. To see the hordes of humans surrounding her had been difficult, when all that Aaleahya wanted to do was run and hide, to find a cave like the one she had used to call her home, hide and leave the humans to their games. But as Mystique ran, Aaleahya could not help but wonder how this … concert, supposedly dedicated to peace and love, would impact on the Pack. Would they be able to keep their secret, or would the humans prove too inquisitive?

Returning to the Hall, Aaleahya had entered the back door to the hustle of and bustle of the Sentinels as they reviewed their assignments. The plan had been that they were to mingle and keep an eye out for those whom might cause us problems making sure that the concert attendees do not cross over onto Pack property and cause them problems and also to keep the identities of Pack members hidden. Nodding her head at Rhys, and Taren and the others congregated around the kitchen, Aaleahya headed up to the room she shared with her Mate to shower and change from her ride.

The music had continued throughout the night the loudness of it making it hard to sleep, even more so with her knowing that Gavril was outside, keeping watch on the humans with the Sentinel Corps. Throwing the covers back, Aaleahya sat up in bed, hearing the neighing of Mystique. Grabbing her robe and pulling it on, she had run down the stairs. Aaleahya stopped dead in her tracks at the sight of some humans in their garden, the Memorial Garden planted in memory of her beloved children, Ekaterina and Sandhu. The humans were rummaging for food taking anything that is ripe and ready to be picked. A low growl erupted from her throat as she witnessed some of the destruction. The anger was clear in the mind link to Gavril, Owain and Bran, letting them know that the humans have crossed over to their property and are destroying the lovely garden. As she watched, some women were picking the wild flowers and placing them in their hair while others are climbing the fruit trees. Never, since moving to this country, had Aaleahya felt such rage. They despoiled this memorial without a care in the world. How dare they? How dare they?

Aaleahya clenched her hands into fists, taking in a deep breath as she caught the hint of a sweet smoky smell. The closer she approached the vandals, she could see their pupils were dilated as if they are under some type of influence and paused for a moment, wondering if she should approach them and let them know they are not welcome on this property. She was ready to do just that, when her ears picked up the sound of fighting. This was not supposed to happen in this country. The war was over.

The fury from his Mate was palpable, Gavril realised as he received her mind link. He recalled the care with which she had planned and then planted the garden in memory of their daughter, who had been killed in such a senseless manner. They had both gained much respite spending time in the garden, lost in their memories perhaps, but also coming to terms with the fact that their only child would not reach maturity. In another mockery of the so-called peace-loving hippy culture, there were humans close enough to the house that they were raiding and despoiling the gardens, both the food and the memorial gardens. His priority was making sure that the latter did not cause Aaleahya to act precipitously. That was the garden that she had planted, tending each bush, each flower with all the love in her heart, her sorrow at the loss of their children so apparent that Gavril's heart had bled each time, and yet he had known that she had taken solace in what she had created.

"Bran! Owain! Get your arses down to the gardens" Gavril's own anger matched that of his Mate. "Owain, bring a team down with you. Those fucking humans have pushed their luck." Love, peace and goodwill went straight out of the window. This was trespass, vandalism and theft, plain and simple, and Gavril intended to treat it as such.

[ML from Owain] "Brawd, I can't bring a team. We have some trouble on the border."

A string of cursing in Welsh followed, which gave Gavril an idea of what was happening had displeased Owain just a bit more than the destruction of the memorial garden. Seriously? These humans, these 'hippies' were supposed to be all about peace and love. Respect for your fellow man. Just not respect for your fellow man's property, it seems.

Gavril flashed himself to Aaleahya's side, and his Cŵn Annwn eyes picked up the numbers of individuals: the males in the fruit trees, not just picking what they needed, but in their lack of care shaking fruit loose onto the ground, which their friends in their drug hazes just trampled into the ground. The roses, planted for his daughter, had been all but stripped of their blooms, as the females danced around the garden, without a care for the delicate chamomile lawn, which had been planted for the Pack's observances to their Goddess. The garden was their memorial and their temple to Mallt-y-Nos, and this ... this vandalism was all the name of peace and love? Raising his head, Gavril's voice echoed in the Alpha's call to hunt. He had every intention of scaring the crap out of these people.

As much as his initial fury wanted to kill, Gavril's nose picked out that these humans were stoned out of their minds, to use human parlance. Swiftly Gavril amended the 'hunt and kill' order. Instead, the teenagers, those too young to be on Sentinel duty, but not pups, flowed through the orchard and gardens in their wolf forms, deliberately giving the impression of ghosts in the trees and around the gardens, their howls echoing his. No more than six adults supported them, their deeper howls an almost musical counterpoint to the younglings.

Holding his temper in check, Gavril instructed the younglings to start herding, having ascertained that he could smell no gunpowder on these hippies. Stoned they may be. Human they may be. But even by their own laws, they had committed vandalism and theft, and for that, they would know the wrath of the Alpha of the Cŵn Annwn.

The humans stopped in their tracks, their eyes dilating even further than they were already were. Their singing and frolicking stopped and nervous whispers filled the air. Inhaling deeply Aaleahya could smell the fear thick in the air. She looked at her mate whose face was a mask of fury. He wanted blood but also realized many of these humans were under the influence of drugs and, therefore, it might be claimed that they were not aware of what they were actually doing. Or were they?

Using the additional Alpha strength to add volume to his voice, Gavril's words thundered across the garden. "How dare you despoil a sacred place, a place of peace, a memorial to the dead of the war?" He wanted to see if they were aware of what they did or whether they were so stoned that it had not occurred to them that what they did was vandalism and theft.

One of the females gave a sort of 'eep' noise, snatching her coronet of flowers from her head and trampling them underfoot. Focussing on her, Gavril could see that her eyes were not as dilated as the others. On drugs, but not stoned like her friends. "Memorial to the dead? Murderers. Warmongers. Child killers. We do to your land what you have done to others. Retribution." Her voice was rising to an almost painful screech.

Goddess alive. Don't this generation know their history? Even allowing for them having been born in the USA, in the closing stages of WW2, they should have been taught about this in their schools, surely? But to name Gavril's beloved Ekaterina a child killer, when she and Sandu had saved nearly 1500 children from death? That was pushing it. The other females followed her example, such that the flowers they had picked with such abandon were crushed beneath their feet. It felt as if they were crushing all that the Pack had achieved during and after the war. These ignorant flower children saw what they wanted to see. They saw images from television and condemned all for the actions of a few individuals. Peace and love? As Owain would have said, "My arse." They wanted to live off someone else's efforts. Gavril was sure some of their type were genuinely about peace and love, just as not all in a war are child-killers, but this group here were bottom-feeding scavengers, hiding behind a guise. To him, it made them close to legitimate targets for soul harvest.

The children whom the Pack had rescued had gone on to find homes, and families. They had established businesses, as had been the case with Bran's acknowledged 'favourite' rescued child, Eliana. They had taken a tragedy and made something of their lives. They had not blamed others, but they had survived. The Pack had lost some, but the majority survived.

It was only that this group were but a sample of the peace movement that Gavril decided to not kill them, the only thing which saved them from death. They did not deserve the simplicity of death, when no doubt they would claim martyrdom in some twisted fashion. "Round them up, and lock them in the empty barn. No food. Minimal water at dawn. In the morning, we will hand them over to the local law enforcement, and have them charged under human law for vandalism and theft." The howls from his Pack told Gavril that they were not happy with this, but he was Alpha, and they would obey. As these fools came down from their drugs, they would face raging thirst and hunger. The Pack would give them enough to ensure that none went into kidney failure, but that was all.

Taking Aaleahya's face between his hands, Gavril used his thumbs to wipe the tears trickling from her eyes, as she looked at the devastation of the memorial garden. "You will rebuild it my love. The true memorial to our children lies within us, and that can never be taken away." Gently, he kissed her. "Come, let us return to our room, and sleep. I have a need to hold my Mate close."

With the interlopers secured, Aaleahya took a closer look at the devastation. How could they call the Pack baby killers when they saved many by sending to the United States of America. Aaleahya heard her mate growling inserting his Alpha strength as his voice thundered in the noisy air. There was no way those nearby couldn't hear him. Stepping forward towards the stripped rose bushes Aaleahya touched the bare limbs. She felt her Mate's arm around her, assuring her that she could, and would, take care of this with no problems. He was right, Aaleahya thought to herself and the first hint of a green shoot erupted from the stripped branch. The true memories are buried deep inside them. Yes, Aaleahya would have to use her special abilities and would have to wait until the human authorities had come and taken those whom trespassed onto the Pack's property. They would be charged under human laws, and some form of punishment handed down to them, but the unfairness of it was galling. This should not have happened.

As Gavril wiped the tears from her face, Aaleahya nodded at his suggestion that they go back inside and return to their beds. She wanted feel his arms around her and his body next to her own, chasing away the chill of the destruction that these so called peaceful humans caused. Laying her head on his shoulder Aaleahya let him guide her back inside. When they entered the house he picked her up, carrying her up the stairs to their room where gently, he laid her down on their soft bed. A shiver ran though her as she could see the passion and caring in his eyes. Wordlessly, Aaleahya reached for her Mate, needing to feel his length close to her.

Gavril's voice was soft. "My sweet Mate, my Aaleahya, the other half of my soul.". He could see in her eyes the pain that their memorial garden had been destroyed by a few careless individuals. Regardless of them being under the influence of drugs, their accusations were unjust. They might not know what the Pack had done during the war. Very few did, and even the children whom the Pack had saved generally only recalled strangers who came in the night, and took them, somehow, to a place where they were given food and milk by a young soft-spoken fair lady and her friends, before finding themselves, again somehow, in another country, with others who welcomed them with loving arms.

Gavril would never forget their sweet Ekaterina and all that she and Sandu achieved in their short lives, but that no one outside of the Pack would remember them was painful sometimes. That much he acknowledged. But his Aaleahya, who had been with him for over eighty years now, at his side, supporting him, bringing light into the darkness which might overwhelm otherwise, it was in her eyes that he saw the need for him to show her his love, to show her how much she meant to him. Each day, Gavril gave thanks to his Goddess for the precious gift for which he had to travel so far to find.

Stroking her face, Gavril leant forward, pressing soft kisses to her eyelids, around her mouth, along the length of her neck, and not least, to the silvery scar on her neck that was the Mating Mark, the sign of their union being blessed by the Goddess.

"My sweet love." He breathed the words against her. "I thank the Goddess for you, and that you stay with me."

Gavril slipped Aaleahya's casual robe from her, and beheld his very own Goddess. She shivered slightly, and he ran his hands down her shoulders, down her arms, before bringing both her hands to his lips, and kissing each finger in turn. One hand held her hands above her head, as his head dipped down, and he paid homage to the still full breasts.

"Roll over, my love, and let me worship your body as you deserve." Gavril whispered to his beloved Mate.

Leaning her face into his touch, Aaleahya felt his strong fingers stroking it.

Bringing her left leg up she draped it over Gavril’s leg, running her toes up and down, both exploring the muscle definition and eliciting a reaction as she reached behind his knee. Lifting her head, she brought her lips to his nipping at his bottom lip. Moaning in the pleasure with which her love plied her in an effort to help ease in the pain in her soul from the vandalism of their sacred garden.

Her breath felt like it ceased when Gavril told her to roll over, his voice deep with the passion he felt for his Mate. Once he has released her hands from over her head she moved as he had asked. Her hand cupping his face, she stroked it as if she was blind, her finger lightly tracing his eyes, nose, and lips. Her fingers were feather-light as she followed his chin down to his neck and the Adam's apple before allowing her hand to trace his chest. The hardness beneath her fingers as she followed all the ridges of his muscles across his wide shoulders was exquisite. Her eyes opened once again as she stared into the depths of his chocolate-brown eyes, the sensation of drowning in the passion mirroring the passion she felt for him. His low growl ringing closely in her ear as he nibbled and laved it.

The curve of Aaleahya's back, to the dip just above her backside was silky soft, and Gavril was conscious of the contrast of her smooth skin to the roughness of his hands. The last few days, putting up the barrier fences and signs around the estates had been hard physical labour, and it had been for nothing, given that Owain, Bran and the other Sentinels had to use aggressive persuasion to protect the estate, and even then, it had not been enough.

Mentally, he shook himself out of his own darker mood. He had harvested today, a veteran from the war. It made the human sound old, calling him a veteran, but he had been a boy, only twenty years of age, but old enough to serve when his number came up. His soul had wept at what he had witnessed, what he had been ordered to do by his commanding officers, of the things about which he could not speak when he came home, because he had arrived at the airport, still in uniform, and a woman with her daughters had been waving an anti-war banner, and had spat on him. Perhaps that was why he was in such a black mood, Gavril pondered. The young human male should have had his whole life ahead of him, rather than ending it with a gun he had bought in a backstreet pawn shop.

But Gavril had his Mate, and he had his Pack. Pouring some almond oil scented with that flower child favourite of patchouli into the palm of his hand, he allowed the oil to warm from his own body temperature, before spreading it over both hands, and starting to massage it gently into Aaleahya's skin, the soft scent filling the immediate area as the oils warmed further. Slowly, gently he massaged the oil into his Mate's already soft skin, enjoying the feel of her beneath his hands, enjoying the soft murmur of encouragement, enjoying the gradual relaxation of tense muscles.

"You stole my heart, my beautiful she-wolf, inima mea." Gavril's whisper was for her ears, a confirmation of his love for his Mate.

Feeling Gavril straddle her back, Aaleahya whimpered as her knotted muscles loosened under his gentle but firm touch. She heard his words, swallowing the lump that formed in her throat as he told him Mate that she was his heart.

Sighing in contentment while he continued to rub the fragrant oil into her skin, his touch leaving her feeling like a shivering pile of liquid mush, Aaleahya yearned for more than his touch. She wanted to feel his very soul inside her for her to hold, cherish and protect. Knowing that her Mate had harvested a soul today, she murmured under his all too talented hands. "Let me take the burden of that soul from you, my love, as our Goddess willed."

Rolling Aaleahya onto her back gently, Gavril continued the slow strokes of the massage around her breasts, down her sides, before lifting her hips and pulling her close to me. "Inima mea." he murmured. Those two words "My heart." The unvarnished truth since without his Mate, Gavril would be dead. The fate of his dam would have been his own.

Spreading the lips of her core, he inhaled the sweet scent of her arousal, before dipping his head down and teasing her with his tongue, swirling around the small bud of nerves, her soft voice only serving to encourage him further.

It did not matter how many times Gavril was able to taste his Mate, he thought, rising above her, he would never be sated. As he sheathed himself in her welcoming warmth, Gavril paused for a moment, before kissing her lips, savouring the love communicated through their Mating Bond.

As her own hips lifted to welcome him, Aaleahya welcomed her Mate. She could not help but be aware that the love that there were no words to describe the love she held for this male. Their bond was unbreakable; they were mates for eternity and she would have it no other way. Their love making has always been special but tonight it felt as if there was something more. The hippies, the fact that Gavril had to harvest a soul of a former soldier driven to suicide. As Aaleahya accepted the soul of the solider that he had harvested into her keeping, she acknowledged what her Mate had seen, that it was a good soul not a black one. A troubled soul indeed. May the Goddess take good care of him.

Gavril felt Aaleahya take charge of the soul of the young soldier, and felt the relief that he would soon find rest. Maybe not peace immediately, but he would at least find some rest. It was never easy taking a suicide, particularly one such as this one. As with all wars, who was the victor and who was the loser seemed to become almost irrelevant. Perhaps it was only the politicians who won?

But, the feeling of relief also meant that he could focus his mind on his Mate, on his precious Aaleahya. The surge of love that travelled across their Mating Bond, like a wave of emotion. Humans measure a long life together by having reached fifty years. They had surpassed that by another thirty, and would be together until the Goddess called them to her, which would be many years from now.

Holding himself still, Gavril savoured the taste of his Mate's lips, before nibbling around her mouth. The sight of the silver scar on her neck drew him, and gently, he laved this very visible mark of their love for each other. So many years since that night in a cave in the Carpathians. So many years with both loss and gain. The feel of his Mate's heartbeat under his tongue, as he lapped the scar, wove its own siren's song. Raising his head, Gavril felt almost drunk with the pleasure he was feeling, of being held by his Mate.

Later as they basked in the afterglow of their passion, Gavril wondered at the task set him by his Goddess: protect the innocent and harvest those guilty of evil on their fellow man. As one of those protest songs said, times were changing. Did the Cŵn Annwn still have a role to play as a Pack and as an entity? Yet, even as he asked the question of himself, he thought of those who did still need their help, and as he and his Mate sank into sleep, he knew that, at least for now, their path could be nothing else.

- x -

"I got him sugar. You just relax and have fun. I need a break from the crowd anyway." Jake hefted a fussing baby Jake into his arms and worked his way through the people and hoped like hell the smell of all the unwashed bodies would someday leave his nose. "Come on little man. We'll find us a nice smellin' place to sit. I'll even make sure there's no shit nearby." Jake chuckled and held his son closer. "Just don't tell yer ma I said shit." The youngster's little oh-oh made his father laugh and as he sat down at a tree, and reflected on the good things he had going, like his wife and child.

He heard someone step up to him and raised his eyes to see that tattooed fellow from the day before. He tipped his head like he wanted to sit so Jake just nodded while scooting little Jake to his other side. "How ya doin?"

Rhys saw Jake, the dark man from yesterday and something about him made Rhys curious so he walked up to him. Jake didn't smile but he did greet Rhys. A good sign. "I'm doing rather well now that Jefferson Airplane is playing. The name's Rhys, by the way." Rhys actually preferred that Santana music but he had noticed Jake nodding his head to the beat and he wanted a conversation lead-in. "You look like you're healing up pretty well." Rhys' eyes darted to the child then back to the male before he sat down. "You did a good thing stepping up for that other male. Not many would do that." Jake shrugged he and his son both eyed Rhys, unsure of why this stranger was talking to them. Rhys had read and heard things about the human prejudices and this man had his colour and the war to deal with, so he could understand the reticence.

It was clear that Jake came to a decision when he tipped his head. "Jake." He introduced himself, not recalling whether he had done so before with everything that had happened. "Where you from? I can't place your accent." Rhys grinned and leaned back on his elbows. "Europe. I've travelled around there for a long time and decided to check out America." He turned his head to Jake and smiled. "The jury is still out on where I prefer. They both have good points and bad."

Jake had to agree with what Rhys said. "It was the same in Vietnam and back home, boring, good or fucking bad. Kinda messes with a man when you both miss and hate it." Jake huffed a quick laugh and allowed little Jake to walk around him. He shot the stranger a look knowing he knew not to mess with the toddler but having to give him the look anyway. "Grace wants to move here to New York, says she can do so much more for equal rights here but I got a decent job in Nashville. That messes with man's head too. I know I don't make much but it's decent for a black man." Jake frowned a little wondering why in the hell he was telling him this shit when he hadn't even said anything to Doug.

Rhys pulled out an apple from his pocket and raised his eyebrows to Jake before offering it to little Jake. The boy's father nodded and Rhys handed the apple to the child. "This area is a good place Jake. Good people, clean air and lots of nature nearby. I also hear things aren't as, um, tense as further south." Jake looked at Rhys hard then wondering what he was up to and then shook his head. "I'm a mechanic, a damn good one. If we were to move north, it would make sense for me to go work at one of them car factories in Detroit but she said she has a feeling. Damn women and their feelings." That brought out another oh-oh from little Jake and he caught Rhys smiling at the apple-juiced face of the little boy.

Afterwards, it struck Rhys that he and Jake had sat for hours talking, in which he learned a lot about the soft-spoken African-American man and his quiet determination for equality. It was clear that he had a keen mind but was most comfortable with a hands-on approach to which Rhys could truly relate. His son fell asleep nestled in his father's arms when the music stopped for the night. The crowd was still active but there seemed to be a more subdued atmosphere in this area. His friends had checked on him from time to time, never approaching but they were clearly watching. This too told Rhys a lot about the man's character.

"Jake, if you could do anything, what would you do?" He looked at Rhys a bit strange but then quirked up his lip and leaned back to look at the sky in thought.

"What would I do…." Jake let himself dream. Why the hell not, it's only talk and this fellow was easy to talk to. As rough around the edges as Rhys looked, there was something deep in him like an old soul. "I'd like to open my own repair shop. Big engines, small engines, it don't matter. Hire me a couple a brothers, put Grace in an office with a new adding machine and a typewriter." Jake looked at Rhys and grinned. "She's a cracker-jack in an office. Types faster than I can read too. She could do her secretary stuff for her group and maybe take on some extra stuff while keeping up with the garage papers." Jake laughed a little. "Give me something greasy to fix and I'm fine but I don't have the head for billing and stuff." He sighed and got deep into his dream. "For folks that can't pay then I reckon we would barter. Everyone has something they can do but don't always have the money. For a fella like you this may seem foolish but that's what I'd do."

Rhys smiled at the other male's dreams, dreams he had quite clearly thought long and hard. "It sounds like a fine plan Jake. I hope it happens for you." They silently watched the crowd as Rhys thought of the Foundation Gavril started in memory of Ekaterina and Sandu. It wasn't his call on who benefits but this man had impressed Rhys somehow and he was almost driven. Rhys knew that, like many in the Pack, he had become a bit jaded with humans so this feeling had him perplexed. Perhaps he needed this reminder that he too couldn't lump all humans together. Prejudice can be an ugly thing.

Rhys stood and reached out my hand to Jake. "Thank you for speaking with me Jake." He shook Rhys' hand and nodded. "Do you and Grace have a place to stay until you find work?" His quick nod quelled Rhys' worry over them sleeping in a tent. "That we do Rhys. Grace has some friends at the Liberty Baptist Church and they have a small house out back. They're good folks." Rhys dipped his chin at him and smiled. "Give my best to Grace and your friends." He turned back to the woods and the Hall, planning his request for Foundation funds for Jake.

It struck Gavril, when Rhys came to see him, that the thoughtful look on his face somehow out of place on this young Sentinel who always tried to find a bright side. The events of the last few days, the invasion of the estate grounds had unsettled him and had him questioning whether humans were all on the 'take'.

"Come in, Rhys." Gavril held open the door to his study, closing it after him. While Rhys took a seat, Gavril handed him Eira's magic potion in a steaming mug, along with the ever present pastry. It said everything that Rhys put both plate and mug on the side table.

"So, Sentinel. What is on your mind? I have not seen you turn down food, I think, ever. So something must be on your mind. I suspect it is something to do with all the patrols we are have to run and these recent incursions by humans. The festival will be over soon, and hopefully things will be back to normal." Gavril's lips quirked in a smile.

He had only just finished talking to the local State police over the group who had vandalised their memorial garden. The police were very apologetic when Gavril pointed out that the garden was a memorial to his daughter who had died in the war, but there was little that could be done. The group had no money and could not make recompense. Gavril's voice had been hard when he said that they could work off their debt. The fruit harvest could still be salvaged. The vegetable gardens, even with Aaleahya's encouragement, still needed hard labour for digging and preparation. Gavril had pointed out coldly that if these hippies cared for the land, then they could give back to the land what they had despoiled. If that happened, Gavril would refrain from having his legal team press charges.

He came to sit near Rhys. "So what is in your mind, youngling?"

Rhys glanced at the coffee then faced Gavril. "I met this man at the festival. The one I told you about when he defended a stranger." Gavril nodded for the young Sentinel to continue. "He has a quiet integrity about him even though life has saddled him with obstacles." Rhys leaned back in the chair not knowing how to voice his thoughts. Like Jake, he was a hands-on individual. Maybe that was why he identified with him. "He wants so much more for his son and has uprooted his family to move here hoping to accomplish that." Rhys shook his head then gazed at Gavril. "I find that I want to help him somehow but not with a hand out. That would insult him. He's what they call a working man but because he's a negro, he has to take what he can get. He's a good man with a good wife. I was … I was going to ask about Foundation funds for him. To maybe set him up in his own repair shop."

Rhys couldn't believe he asked for this, especially for someone he didn't know but deep inside he knew it was the right thing. He could only wait to see if Gavril felt the same way. Jake wasn't displaced by war or forced from his home for any reason other than to give a better life to his son. Would that be enough to be considered? If not, then he would think of some other way to see he had the chance at his dream.

This was the first time that Rhys had come to Gavril with a request like this, and it was a good indication that his abilities as a Cŵn Annwn were maturing. Such maturity occurred at different times for different individuals, and having that 'feeling' that a person was 'good' was a clear indication. From Gavril's own perspective, he knew there were reasons why that son of a God of Divination, Zarek Svitovidson, had wanted the Pack to move to the Catskills and Gavril could not help but wonder if this was one of the reasons why.

"Rhys, congratulations on your first full soul reading." Rhys looked at Gavril, surprise in his face. "Not all whom we help have been displaced by war or forced from their homes. For some, the chance to make more of their lives is the driver. Had he left for less savoury reasons, you would have known this. However, you saw an essentially good man, dealt a hard hand. However, instead of saying "Woe is me." He is trying to change his circumstances. How much would you feel is sufficient?"

Gavril took a sip from his own mug of coffee. "You have my permission to contact Abe Micula, the lawyer who administers the funds. He will approach this individual and act as our intermediary. Our standard condition is that he does not know anything more than the Foundation name and he may not tell anyone about the grant, not even his own family. I suggest you find out from Abe when he will contact this man, and report back to me, after you have observed the meeting, invisibly of course. Are you happy with that?"

For Rhys, it seemed as if suddenly everything clicked into place and he stared at Gavril as his mind raced. He had thought he would not have the ability to truly read a soul so he had thrown all his energy into being the best Sentinel possible to compensate. Rhys gave a breathy laugh and dropped his head. "Late bloomer I guess."

Rhys tried to tamp down a feeling of pride as he continued speaking but it felt good to know that he was helping someone in this way. It made him feel like he was actually contributing to something bigger than himself and the pack. Great, now he was turning into a female youngling and the next thing you know he'll be crying. Rhys growled internally and found his Sentinel face for his Alpha. "Thank you Gavril. I will speak with Mr. Micula for his suggestions. I do not know the human prices but I believe he will know best." Standing, Rhys dipped my head low to his Alpha. "I will make arrangements to meet with him Monday as I believe it is their customary work week and will report to you when done. Now I will eat before joining the perimeter guards." Rhys nodded his head quickly and then with a grin, he took his coffee and pastry before leaving Gavril's study.

As Owain went for a run the morning after the little incursion into the estate by the human hippies, he contemplated how going for a run was preferable to an almost instinctive need to physically tear into the hippies he had encountered. They had ignored the signs and the very basic fencing, and just decided that they might wander where they wished. The Pack tried to herd them back, but they would not listen. Then, because his team were in clothing which resembled uniform, they had decided that the Pack members were 'child murdering scum' like the other military and were to be reviled and attacked, made to suffer as they had made others suffer.

Where do these humans find these opinions? Owain had killed and he made no bones about it. He had killed some of those responsible for trying to force the Pack to collaborate with the Nazi invaders of the Carpathians. He had killed other tyrants in wars. But to be accused of killing children? He had come so close that night. His junior Sentinels did him proud that night. They controlled their tempers. They controlled their shifts. But, Owain thought, shrugging his shoulders mentally, others had gone for a run this morning, not just him, even though our reasons had been similar. But they didn't kill. They came too damn close, and all down to a group who claimed to be peaceful?

As she sat back in the bus, trying to not show her distaste at the smell of bong combined with unwashed bodies, Stefania Anghelescu pondered events of the last few days. Woodstock. The place where people came to exchange their love, passion and questionable taste, in music, poetry, drink and more often than not drugs. So naturally she was there, sampling the human world as a human to the naked eye. It was hot, the temperature only encouraged the crowds to swarm in and there were bodies everywhere doing all sorts of passionate things. Although most people where peaceful individuals, you did get the odd fire starter who seemed to be the sole owner of causing mischief and it was in one of these incidents that she found myself escaping the law and heading towards the back of the festival where the lucrative goods were on sale.

In this instance it was drugs. She had known before she even looked at him, he was a Hellhound. She knew because she felt an instant connection with him and for the first time in years, she felt ashamed of not being part of a pack. She hadn't seen him before so he was obviously not from the pack she had abandoned in hope for a better life but still she felt a wave of familiarity wash over her, a hint of a pull. If it had been that easy to go over and just ask to join his pack, she would have but that's not how Hellhounds work. For all she knew, this could have been Aurelija's lover, since there was every likelihood of him being from her birth pack, given the location of the Woodstock festival. In her moment of casual thinking, she had realized that if she could sense him, he could sense her. His head had snapped up and she darted into a group of passing humans, shielding her scent from him.

She had half expected him to come looking for her, and part of her, a secret part of her, wanted to watch him and the others work. They were selling drugs, which didn't surprise her at all. Hellhounds weren't really fond of humans or their lives, where Stefania had grown quite attached to them, but then she was not exactly a standard Hellhound. A weirdo if you like. Deciding her deadly attraction obsession with this Hellhound would only end in one way, she realised that it was safer if she avoided this part of the Festival. Her certain death being the likely outcome of him finding her, she put as much space in between them as she could, making sure to use her innate ability as a Hunter to mask her scent at all times in case he wanted to investigate what he thought he has sensed or even seen earlier.

Unavoidably insecure Stefania found herself wandering around the festival, searching for something amongst the humans she had not yet witnessed or found. She wasn't sure what it was she wanted from the lower race. Did she want love? That feeling of unbearable hurt, pleasure, intensity, of bonding to another person? No she just wanted to be accepted that was what she found with a small community of people. Their eyes didn't judge, their hands didn't seek anything from her and their kindness made her feel like she was part of a family. No not a family. It was like being in a pack. A pack of her own.

CHAPTER 22: ONE WALL DOES NOT A PRISON MAKE

"Grace? Hey sugar, do you know where I put the new wrench?" Jake was lying under a small tractor hopin' like hell to get this contraption working again and maybe word would spread at what he could do. It had been a week since Woodstock and jobs were few and far between so he needed all the work he could find. Soon he heard her steps in the grass get near him. "Jake honey? You mean this here bent piece of metal something?" Jake peeked out and saw that she had the wrench he made and smiled. "Yep, that's it darlin. I made that myself." She looked dubious but handed it to her husband and he got back to work. "Jake, Little Jake and I are going over to the meeting, so if you need any more of those tools then you'll have to get them yourself. Love you, babe." Jake's voice went soft as he gave his love to them both in return then he returned to the thorny problem of a non-working tractor.

Jake heard a car pull up but then the nearby church was always busy so he ignored it as he put the last piece in place on the tractor. Jake shouted out in joy when the homemade replacement part fit like a glove and shimmied out to give the engine a go. After tossing his tools on the ground he noticed a fellow all suited up standing there and he swallowed his nervousness when he saw the briefcase. Past experience had demonstrated that white men in suits very rarely brought good news with them. "Can I help you?" The man smiled and Jake noted his kind eyes crinkling at the edges. "No young man but I can help you. My name is Abe Micula. May we go inside and talk Mr. Petersen?" Jake nodded curtly, as much to hide his surprise at being referred to as 'Mr Petersen' without a sneer on the speaker's face, and showed him into their little kitchen. "Have a seat. I'll wash up and get us some ice tea." Jake heard him sit at the tiny table and his mind tried to make sense of this man and what it was he wanted but hell, he couldn't wash his hands forever so he dried them and reached out for a shake. "What can I do for you?"

After exchanging hand-shakes, the older man pulled out some papers and an envelope then turned to Jake with that smile again. "Mr. Petersen. May I call you Jake?" Jake nodded and Abe continued. "I am the administrator for the Negrescu Foundation. They provide grant monies to help deserving individuals." He turned the papers toward the younger man and sure enough Jake's name was on them. He looked at Abe then back at the papers and began to read. "Five thousand dollars?" Jake flopped back in shock. "Is this sayin' you're going to just give me five thousand dollars?" Abe's smile was kind as he nodded.

"Jake? How about some of that ice tea you were talking about." Jake nodded and absently got them both a glass of tea while he mulled it over. "Jake, I did some research on how much it would cost to set up an automotive repair garage. I know of a garage that closed down when the owner died. I'm friends with the family and they agree to lease it to you for $1,000 down and then $100 per month in a land contract. That means that you are making payments toward owning your own building." Jake continued listening but all the time he was wondering what good deed he had done for the Lord to bless him so. "Also Jake, I priced a motorized lift and the tools you will need to get started plus licenses. I'm afraid there won't be any left for hired help but that will come in time. Now, my family and I will help you with the contracts and purchasing of the tools you specify. Any questions?"

Jake barked out a laugh. "Questions? I have about a hundred running through my brain right now. I can't wait to tell Grace. She been prayin' for a miracle and here it is." Jake stopped short, puzzled at the shake of his head. "Jake, there is a stipulation." Jake closed his eyes. He thought they must be some kind of criminals out to use him. Dayam, He'd have to turn it all down. "I ain't gonna do nothin illegal no matter how nice this all sounds. I'll make my way by the sweat of my brow." There came Abe's smile again.

"Jake, the stipulation is that you tell no one where the money came from, not even your family. This Foundation is a closely held secret but I assure you, there are no nefarious activities involved." Jake saw him acknowledge the pain in the younger man's eyes at this rule. "I don't lie to my Grace Mr. Micula and I ain't about to start now." Abe appeared to ponder this a moment before another smile split his face. "Mr. Petersen? I have a plan. As I said, my family and I will help with your acquisitions. You will only need to sign a few papers to obtain ownership. You will then be able to say that Mrs. Mosenfelder offered you her husband's garage on a lease to own land contract." He smiled and sipped his tea. "All of that is true and all the equipment will be standard for a garage so there should be no need to question." Jake thought long and hard but found no problem with that. It seemed that by some miracle and a helping hand, he was able to climb up and over the wall he thought would remain in his path forever. Then it was his smile that lit the room. "Can I get an adding machine and one of those typewriters?"

Rhys could hardly wait to report back to his Alpha on the initial meeting between Jake Petersen and Abe Micula. At his soft knock on the study door, Gavril bade him enter. "Gavril? Mr Micula met with Jake this afternoon and everything is set." Rhys' smile was a contented one as he sat before the large study desk. "I also think the two of them will have an ongoing friendship. Once the meat of their conversation was done, they talked of family and common goals for their children." Rhys began the chuckle outright. "When they visited the site of the garage, I had to go outside to keep from laughing. Jake was like a youngling when Eira's been baking, and you could almost see the shop design in his eyes as he flew around planning." Rhys' smile became just a tad nostalgic. "Abe was deeply touched by all of this as well. I think the act of helping someone, bestowing a kindness, as he does with the Foundation …" Rhys paused for a moment, trying to recall what he had heard, "… Abe called it something. Ah yes, a mitzvah. It pleased him." Rhys caught Gavril's eye. "So in a way, the grant has benefited them both." Rhys stood again, once he had delivered his report. "If you need nothing further, I will head to the kitchen." Rhys grinned and wriggled his eyebrows. "I can smell cake."

As Rhys left his study in search of the promised cake, his pleasure at having been able to help the human, Jake Petersen, was quite clear. Once again, Gavril found himself wondering if that had been the intention behind Zarek's insistence that it was a good time to relocate the Pack to the Catskills' area of NY state. The games the Gods will play with those creatures who serve them, and Gavril's Pack, for all their supernatural abilities, were no different in that regard from humans. They were servants of their Goddess. Still, it begged the question. He went in search of his Mate, his Aaleahya. Since the destruction of the memorial garden, she had been overseeing the replanting of both it and their vegetable gardens. Those hippies, once they had come down from their drug highs, had been surprised indeed to discover that their reparation work would be supervised by a relatively soft-spoken female, who did not look any older than they did. Well, she was soft-spoken until three of the males tried propositioning her as a means of avoiding labour. Gavril smiled. He was not sure but he doubted that they enjoyed having to fork out the manure from the stables of Arabian/Paint cross horses that were Aaleahya's hobby, not when that blasted stallion of hers was prone to trying to take 'love bites' out of anyone he didn't know.

Owain had also approached Gavril. It seemed Zarek had a plan over an issue that was becoming more acute in Eastern Europe, caused by a more physical version of Churchill's described Iron Curtain. The Berlin Wall, a symbol of the imprisonment behind said Iron Curtain had gone from being just a border crossing to something much more than that. Gavril had instructed his Beta to begin talking to Zarek. If assisted evacuations of those trapped in an untenable situation was likely, it was not that different from what the Pack had done during the Second World War, and thus, seemed a good way of training the Sentinels and enable them to practice their control techniques.

One thing was certain. Life was far from boring.

As she watched the hippy vandals who had despoiled the memorial to her beautiful daughter, Aaleahya had a small smile of satisfaction on her face at the sight of the sweat pouring off the backs of the males who had tried to proposition her to evade their work. They even seemed to be taking pride in what they were doing, which went a small way to mollifying her anger at them. Yes, she could have just used her Goddess-given powers to bring the garden back to life, but she wanted these humans to understand what they had done. The police had suggested that, to make the 'punishment' fit the 'crime', they should be worked from dawn until dusk, with a bus arriving to drop them off and return them to the local jailhouse for as long as it took them to fix the damage they had done. A generous donation to the local law enforcement welfare fund had ensured that they had no problem with this arrangement, even though it was not an official punishment.

As the sun dropped in the sky, tools were returned to the shed, and several dropped to the ground, their exhaustion evident. Aaleahya folded her arms as one of the young women approached her. It was the one who had named them 'child killers', which left Aaleahya less than inclined to like her. "Ma'am, I just wanted to say how sorry we are for what happened here. You must have loved your children very much to grow such a beautiful garden in memory." She paused. "I wish I hadn't listened to some of the others when they went and found it, and I wish …" She dipped her head, and her voice was almost a whisper, "… I wish I didn't call y'all baby killers." She looked up. "I see now how wrong I was."

Aaleahya looked at the young human female. "Wynter, isn't it?" She asked her. "I am sure your own family love you just as much." Wynter shook her head. "No, I think you are wrong. They are mad at me right now, because …" She looked away, "… they have different opinions than I do. You see, I don't understand why our men and boys have to die in a useless war." One of the males called to the young woman, as the bus to take them back arrived. She smiled again at Aaleahya before running off. Aaleahya watched the bus pull away. Turning back to return to the house, she paused at where the newly turned soil was and dug her hands into the rich soil, planning the seeds of the two rosebushes that she had planned for this section. Her powers ensured that the seeds would germinate and take root. Feeling the earth accept the nascent growth, Aaleahya stood and brushed her hands clean, before heading back to the house in search of her Mate.

Meeting him just inside the house, she listened as Gavril related the conversation he had had with Rhys about Jake Petersen. Could there be a greater contrast between the two? One was a man who wanted to improve his situation and was not afraid to work to do so. On the other hand, was a group whom, it could be argued, were only working hard because the alternative was prison. Her ears pricked up at Gavril's next words.

"How would you feel about a trip back to Europe, my love." He asked his Mate.

Aaleahya smiled, wrapping her arms around Gavril. "I think that would be lovely." Her smile widened at the thought of seeing some of her old friends again, assuming that they had survived the incoming Communist authorities. "I would like to see what changes have taken place. The gardens are almost finished. One more day should see it finished. Do you wish us to go that soon?"

Gavril smiled at Aaleahya, before continuing their conversation by mind link, outside of the earshot of others. "Zarek has identified an issue over which he needs our help and our experience in organising an underground railroad to smuggle people out. It seems the authorities is what is now called the Deutsche Demokratische Republik or what the Western world calls East Germany, have built a physical wall partitioning their quarter of Berlin off from the quadrants controlled by the former Western Allies. In effect, there are people in East Berlin trapped in what is as much a prison as anything else, complete with the secret police, which is not very secret, but which terrorises neighbours into reporting their own friends."

It was surprising, Gavril thought. They had thought that with the end of the war, there would be no need for people to be desperate to leave their homes and flee to an uncertain future. They had been wrong. They had not taken into account that the Soviet authorities knew that not everyone liked their ideology and had an aggressive policy of preventing cross-border travel. As their influence spread over the whole of the area that had become known as the Warsaw Pact countries, so the desperation of people to leave increased. There had been an anomaly in that with three quarters of Berlin controlled by the Western Allies, it had been possible for people to 'escape' via Berlin. That had changed in 1961, with the building of first a wire fence and the tearing up of roads between the Soviet controlled quarter and the others. Now it had become even more acute as the authorities built an almost impregnable concrete wall: a mental and physical barrier preventing their own citizens from having freedom of movement and cutting off what had been the only hope for many.

Gavril could not help but remember the last time the Pack had been in what was now Eastern Germany, when they had acted en masse harvesting the souls of children killed by their own mothers, who had been terrified of the oncoming Soviet Army. War had not ended the struggle it seems. It had only made it more acute.

\- x -

Aaleahya found herself besieged with images of her memories of this place, which had been home for many years even before the Nazis had wrought their destruction. She could see Kat and Sandu standing hand in hand in the gardens, still children themselves by Cŵn Annwn standards and thus not ready to make the commitment of being Mates. She saw the rose garden as it had been the day that Kat had been born, not as the overgrown tangle that it was now, it had to be now to fit in with the fiction that the fire-damaged Negrescu Hall was haunted.

But then, she also saw other images, other memories. The Nazis had spilled blood here, both her own family's blood and the blood of others. She remembered images from the war, of children crying out for their parents as they were taken from their homes and shipped to concentration camps and work camps, of fragile lives snuffed out for a twisted ideology, and here, now, another twisted ideology was putting those for whom she cared in danger.

Smiling at Gavril, as their soft footsteps traced a path up to what had been their first home together, she asked him where there were to meet up with Zarek.

Gavril had smiled back, lifting her hand to his lips. "Technically, we shouldn't be here." They had flashed to their old home. Even after all these years, the landmarks were still the same. "We are in theory citizens of an Eastern Bloc country." Gavril knew that his Mate needed to visit their former home, but this was not where they were to meet up with Zarek. "His suggestion was that we meet on the East side of the Country Wall." Gavril referred to the Berlin Wall as it existed out of the city. Where once it had been possible to cross to the West via the thick wooded countryside, that was changing, as the East German government tried to keep its citizens from flight.

"From what Zarek has said, we can slip through Checkpoint Charlie in the American Sector provided that we remain invisible. The other side of the wall has a minefield and he believes they have seeded even the countryside to deter crossings. The checkpoint is safest, since not even we are immune to being blown up. There is a cafe near the Brandenburg Gate where we can meet, once we are through."

Gavril could not help but think of those people from Poland and Czechoslovakia who had fought on the side of the allies and yet now, were separated forever from their families by a regime as intolerant of dissent as the Nazis had been. If it was within their power to help them, then he and the Pack had an obligation to do so.

He recalled a report he had received from Angharad, their Pack Healer, and her horror at what she had found on receiving a call for help from an old friend. She had been trying to attend a meeting held in Dessau regardless of the fact that it now fell on the 'wrong' side of the border. Her main concern had been the rise in illnesses in areas now cut off from modern medicine, because it was an idea from the 'decadent' West. It should have been the opposite, but the insular mentalities of some countries, particularly those under the control of those who held onto their power through fear, plus political prejudice had widened the divide. Communism had not brought equality for all, but rather had widened the divide between the 'have' and 'have not' sides.

When Angharad had arrived in Dessau and the meeting, she had been pleased to recognise many familiar faces. How some of them had managed to travel into the DDR was a mystery and the healer knew better than to ask. Greeting one of her friends using a traditional herbalist recognition symbol, the older woman had pulled Angharad into her arms, almost sobbing in relief. She had towed her down to the street to the old apartment building in which she lived, the poor upkeep apparent to anyone. Angharad was shown to an apartment with her friend explaining that the whole family lived here. In contrast to the hallway leading up, the place was clean and smelled fresh, given that the windows were open. The old healer had needed Angharad's advice on one patient in particular: her eleven-year old granddaughter.

"She had been training for the Olympics." Angharad told Gavril afterwards. "Gretta said that she started to change rapidly both physically and mentally, but the worst was when jaundice set in. She could treat the symptoms but not the cause. Chemicals and steroids, specifically anabolic steroids had been used on a child." Angharad spat out the words, her disgust apparent. "Her granddaughter and the family, when they were allowed contact, were told that it was vitamins and her mother didn't think to question the coaches and trainers."

There was no doubt in Gavril's mind that Angharad had been fuming after the event. She had been angry, and the Pack had walked very carefully for several days. Never anger a Healer, Gavril thought to himself, because they can take you apart just as soon as put you back together. But he could understand his Healer's frustration. She might be able to help one girl-child but she was one out of many being poisoned in this way, just to 'prove' that the Communist way produced sterling athletes better at winning than their Western counterparts.

With Zarek's instructions in mind, Gavril decided to involve one of the other Sentinels, particularly as Cerys had acquitted herself so well at Woodstock. He did make a point of checking with Bran and Owain first, not least because the latter had identified that Cerys had a particular gift which needed specialist training. Was it a good idea to risk her in this way, or was it better to keep her in reserve for emergencies where her talent might be put to good use. In the end, the decision was to give Cerys the choice, knowing that she also wanted to prove to her parents that she had not been wrong in her determination to join the Sentinel School, which had been established after Kat's untimely death.

Cerys' nervousness at the summons was apparent from her rapid heartbeat, but Gavril was at pains to put her at ease. Deliberately, he chose to stand at the fireplace with Bran and Owain, a mug of coffee in his hand, to demonstrate that what caused her to be summoned was nothing bad. Owain had done his best to reinforce the relaxed atmosphere.

"Come on in, Cerys." He had smiled, standing and indicating that she should take his seat by the fireplace. "There's no need to look so worried."

Gavril had laughed at their attempts to relax the young Sentinel. "Child you are anything but in trouble, I assure you. If anything, we wanted to give you due accolade. You passed all your exams with flying colours and are now a fully-fledged Sentinel. Congratulations." He informed her.

He could not help but smile as he felt Cerys' mental reaction to the news. "Omigosh! I had done it. Really, I've done it. I passed my exams. Omigosh! I proved I could do it. Mam and Dad will be blown away. Omigosh!"

Gavril laughed again. "When you have calmed down, perhaps we can discuss the reason we needed to see you." His face looked serious. "We have a job for you. Your first job as a full Sentinel will be working in Europe with Zarek. He needs some help with, I believe, a jail break."

Cerys' eyes widened, as Owain picked up the details. It seemed the Chairman of the village committee in which the Pack had lived in the Carpathians had been arrested by the local authorities, along with other members of the committee. Cerys shook her head. "Seriously? The guy was what, 25 years old when we left the area after the war. He must be close to 60 years old now. What kind of threat did the authorities think he might pose?"

Gavril nodded in agreement at my scepticism. "Exactly. However, the fact is that he has been arrested and he is seen as some sort of threat, so we need to ensure that he is not seen in that way. Your role is this. Zarek will need a distraction. He will need you to ensure that the coast is relatively clear for him. As a Cŵn Annwn, you have ability to escape from danger if necessary, but as a female you can provide a fairly decent distraction." Gavril gave Cerys a wry smile, which she acknowledged was only too true.

And that was why when, a matter of days later, Zarek was thrown in the back of the truck, Cerys didn't look up or acknowledge him in any way. But as Rhys was prone to saying, "Game on."

Zarek had suppressed a grin at the guttural voice behind him and the ominous click of an automatic weapon behind him. "Stop!". Had he been human, he might have had cause for concern, but that was how these people remained in control, how they ensured that the local population were too frightened to cause trouble. Even the corner of the Carpathians in which he had made his home was affected by the repression of the Communist authorities. How did they even think that they could claim that their 'way' was better, when fear and intimidation was used to ensure that their will was done without hesitation?

"I said stop!" The order came again. Even though Zarek did not resist, even though he stopped himself from raising his hands to fight back, he knew what would come next. The whistle of the baton, the bruising impact which, again, had he been human, might have broken his arm.

Zarek dropped to the ground, as they expected of him, and there was coarse laughter. "Take him to the truck" was the next order, as his arms were grabbed and he was dragged to the waiting truck. Several others were already being held at gunpoint and they resisted the temptation to look at him, even though the subtle glances told him that the humans were watching as he was pushed into the truck, prodded by their weapons, just in case he might be foolish enough to resist.

Zarek had briefed Cerys that they knew the authorities were rounding up 'dissidents', although what the hell they thought an old man like the village committee chairman might be doing beggared belief. He and the other members of the council had been rounded up, and taken to the town to be incarcerated in the offices of the local police. What made the matter significant was the discovery that several individuals had come down from Moscow to speak with them.

This could not be good. To date, Zarek had managed to avoid anyone outside of the village noticing that he had not aged since he had arrived. The village knew why this happened and given the benefits from having him on site, they were more than happy to help Zarek with his subterfuge. He had used his gifts from his sire to ensure that in return, they had food, regardless of the demands made of them in terms of wheat quotas, and they appreciated it.

The Hunter's Arrow Inn had become well known, given its location in relation to the Carpathian range. It was a popular base for visitors to the area, although they tended to be more the ranking sort than the workers. Strange how that happened, Zarek thought. When there were people who might pose a problem, Zarek stayed over at the old Negrescu Hall, with its local legends of being haunted. But then this had happened. People had been rounded up. Specialists from Moscow had arrived. There was only one reason to take a group of older human males into custody and that was to force the hand of whoever was believed to be 'helping' them.

The truck stopped and the sound of boots could be heard along with the sound of weapons being readied. The canvas flap at the back of the truck was raised and the soldiers who had been travelling with the prisoners jumped down. They turned to face the occupants of the truck, weapons at the ready. Eight occupants of the truck and perhaps twenty of them. Zarek nodded to himself at the 'balance' which clearly indicated that they believed they had something to 'fear' from one of the occupants of the truck.

Ironically, if the authorities had truly wanted to round up the local dissidents, then the group in the truck were the ideal targets. The difference was that each of them had volunteered to be detained this time. The four humans, along with Cerys and Zarek were there because it was their fathers who had been taken. Each of them knew that, if they could, Cerys and Zarek would ensure they escaped also, but there was no guarantee. The important thing was that they had to ensure that the reason for these 'specialists' travelling down from Moscow was determined, and that they were made to believe that there was nothing to be found.

Gavril had warned Zarek that this would happen. For a being without any form of clairvoyance, he was surprisingly perceptive, Zarek thought to himself. But Gavril had said that he had seen this obsession with the paranormal with the Nazis, he had seen it happen with the first wave of Russian 'liberators'. It was part of that drive to gain ascendency in this pathetic 'cold war' between East and West.

With the weapons trained on them, the group in the truck were ordered to dismount from the back and then stand. In turn, they were told to extend their wrists and manacles were attached. Then they were formed into a single file column and were marched into the building. Down to the cells and as each door was unlocked, one 'prisoner' was pushed in and the door slammed shut, the grate of the key in the lock intended to add to the finality of the sound.

Cerys was the last but one prisoner, and as the guard shoved her towards a cell, he groped her breasts in a very deliberate insult. Cerys hunched her shoulders round as if trying to avoid him and ducked her head, giving the impression of a cowed prisoner. Zarek had to smile. This was the difference between a trained Sentinel and Gavril's late daughter. Zarek was not surprised that he didn't end up in a cell. Now, he thought, they would find out what this was all about.

Cerys was feeling quite pleased with herself as she prowled around the cell. She had remembered her training when the little shit of a guard had groped at her. This was the sort of thing that the Sentinel training was intended to allow, such minor insults intended to force a reaction, but the training means that they didn't. In short, she reacted as a human woman might when surrounded by guns, having watched each of her friends shoved into cells. Hunched shoulders, lowered head and definitely no sign of her eyes changing colour that indicated she was anything other than human. She heard Zarek's mental laugh at her acting and that reassured her. First things first. Manacles? What manacles? It was just a case of a short hop, but first she checked around herself, very thoroughly. It was all too easy for there to be some form of recording device in the cell, ready to pick up the sight of a human female disappearing and reappearing.

She did appreciate that Zarek stayed in mental contact with her, and she could hear his running commentary that he was being taken elsewhere. He definitely had a strange sense of humour, Cerys reflected in the way that he viewed the attempt to intimidate as comical. But then, he was the only son of a god of warfare, fertility and divination, with that rather neat little immortality clause inherited from his sire. As a result, Cerys knew that he had been taken to a room where three human males waited. Something akin to an old fashioned barber's chair was in the room and it was quite clear from the image that it was intended to restrain a prisoner.

Cerys smiled. This was going to be interesting indeed.

- x -

After meeting with Zarek at Checkpoint Charlie, Aaleahya and Gavril had repaired to a small café from where it was possible to watch the Eastern side. The barbed wire was thick and deadly. The view was dank and dark, as is to emphasise what was waiting one the other side.

Aaleahya knew that the plan was that Zarek and Cerys would allow themselves to be accused of being dissidents, allowing the Communist authorities to imprison them with a view to finding more information about the ongoing situation. They wanted to rescue those who had been imprisoned before and also to determine what the authorities had in mind with this sudden change of tolerance towards the village.

The reality of the situation in East Germany was brought home suddenly to Aaleahya as she became aware of the shade of a soul close to them, pacing back and forth. The East German border guards had shot him as he tried to escape, hitting him in the pelvis, his body becoming entangled in the deadly wire, his body shredded as it hung there. Aaleahya sent a quick message to her Mate, letting him know that she intended to absorb the soul to convey it to the Goddess. As her own spirit approached the lost soul, Aaleahya realised that it was a teenager, caught between being a child and being a young adult, the repression of East Germany too much for him to bear. Speaking to him in his native language so that there would be no mistake in what she was saying.

"I mean you no harm, dear boy. I am here to help your soul find rest. Our Goddess will make sure that you live in peace and in freedom. All you have to do is take my hand."

The boy reacted in fear, spouting question after question. "What are you? Are you an angel? Why should I trust you?" Aaleahya knew that she could have lied to the spirit, but that was not the way that she worked.

"No I am not an angel. I can sense your unrest and came to help you find the peace and freedom your soul seeks. I am Cŵn Annwn. Our Goddess guards the gates of the Underworld. Not Hell." Aaleahya hastened to point out the key difference. "Our Goddess can feel your pain and she wants to comfort you. You don't have to trust me, but I can see your soul is kind and good. For that our Goddess will reward you with what you desire most in the afterlife."

Reluctantly, the young spirit took Aaleahya's hand, and she was able to absorb him into her being. She could feel the peace that radiated from him, now that he was no longer tormented by the image and sensation of being speared by the barbed wire. As her own spirit returned to her body, Aaleahya nodded to Gavril to let him know that she had succeeded in retrieving the lost soul, and would deliver it to their Goddess when possible. As she allowed herself to look around, she knew that the hopelessness in some of the faces waiting to enter the Eastern section, to see relatives torn from them by politics, would stay with her.

- x -

"Well, comrade, it seems you have screwed up royally." Zarek did not think the three worthy individuals who had come all the way from Moscow to investigate the 'anomalies' reported to them expected him to smile. Shake, look concerned, maybe even soil himself in terror at the sight of the chair with its restraints and the tray of vials and syringes.

Guttural Russian voices had barked out orders to secure him. Zarek decided that wasn't for him and he was quite happy standing where he was, so when one of the guards had approached him, he wrapped the chain of the manacles around his neck, pulling the guard against him. Human shield time and whilst Zarek hadn't soiled himself in terror, the same could not be said for the guard.

"Damn, did you have to do that." Zarek muttered in Russian under his breath. Zarek heard the sound of weapons being cocked behind him and to his side. The clear leader of the three wise monkeys smiled coldly. "Release him or you die, comrade." He ordered.

Zarek grinned in response. Decision time. Release him and let them play their games, or give the game away that those silly little projectile weapons that they had pointed at him would only irritate him. He sent a mental message to Cerys, asking if she had found everyone who had been taken previously.

Releasing the guard and pushing his malodorous person away, Zarek spoke calmly, his very attitude bleeding arrogance over them. "Royal screw up, comrades." Zarek repeated. "I was placed in this pathetic wilderness prior to my mission. You have blown my cover." He smiled, a cold smile as he looked at each one in turn.

"I hope you like Siberia." He added. Each of the three wise monkeys looked at each other, dawning horror on their faces. Of course, they had no way of knowing in Zarek spoke the truth, but his attitude reduced them to the mindless flunkies that they were in truth, for all that they came from Moscow.

"Have us all returned to the village and I will say nothing." Zarek looked at each of them in turn again, his foot tapping impatiently. "I am waiting."

The three of them glanced at each other, almost as if they were unsure on who should take the lead. "Do you want to answer to my handlers for screwing up an operation that has been years in the planning?" Arrogantly, Zarek stalked forwards before resting both of his hands on the table behind which they sat. "I am waiting, comrades." He barked at them.

One the three stood up, clearly trying to avoid being intimidated by Zarek leaning over him. "We have no proof of what you claim. We would have been told if the village was being used in this way."

Zarek laughed. "You think, comrade? Really? You are nothing but low level bureaucrats." He snorted, his posture and actions highlighting his disgust with them, mere paper-pushers compared to his own active service of the Motherland. "You know nothing of what is being planned."

Listening in on the conversation, Cerys was hard pressed to not laugh herself. She had a lot to learn from Zarek and the way that he was pushing his 'captors' into the course of action that he wanted.

Zarek had noticed that the trick with the various levels of bureaucracy involved in the 'Party' apparatus was that much rests on who can appear to be the bigger fish in the pond. He didn't need to act arrogant. He could be as arrogant as the next demi-god. Oh yeah, that's right. There's not many of those around Eastern Europe. The fact was that every time someone had sex on his old man's home turf, he and his sire received a boost to their powers. Not a bad deal if he had to say so himself. Definite home team advantage.

Anyway, little Wise Monkey in front of him thought that he would be able to bluster his way through this. "Let me make this quite clear, comrade." Zarek infused his tone with scorn. "Either you release all of us from the village now and I mean fucking all of us, or I will have to file a report with my handlers. And here's something more for you to consider. Why do you think that a little village in the middle of the Carpathians has as good a phone system as we do? Come on, borscht for brains. Think about it. Why do you think we don't worry about food production quotas being exact?" Zarek stood back, arms folded, tapping his boot impatiently. "Are you really that desperate for an extended stay in Siberia. This operation has been twenty years in the making, setting up critical work for Mother Russia."

The Three Wise Monkeys huddled together for a moment, before their apparent leader stood again. "Very well, comrade. We will take your word for now and release the villagers. But don't think for one moment that we won't be checking your story."

"Damn, but you must really want to see Siberia, you fool." Zarek shook his head. "You don't get it, do you? Secret operation. If the fucking Americans get even a sniff of what we are doing, years of work will be lost, and all because you want to make yourselves look good."

Zarek shook his head. "My advice to you is to shut the fuck up about checking my story, because if you do, you will either be locked up as insane or sent to Siberia …" Zarek grinned, as if relishing their potential fate, and wishing he could be involved. "At least until other more permanent arrangements may be made to ensure your silence."

Listening in on Zarek's conversation, Cerys relaxed her muscles in preparation to act, quite willing to demolish everything in their path once the signal to move was given. The dripping pipes outside the cells gave her the potential weaponry that she needed. And damn, the authorities probably thought that the constant drip-drip served only to prevent the prisoners in the cells from being able to sleep. The sound of combat boots reached her sensitive ears and she heard the click to the lock of the basement. The clattering of the boots echoed off the walls. Again, it was a cheap method of making prisoners wonder? Was that echoing signalling their end?

The guard who had groped her returned with a scowl on his face, muttering under his breath. Poor, poor baby, Cerys thought to herself. You won't be able to come down later and become 'better acquainted' with the female prisoners as you had planned. He eyed Cerys with disdain as he unlocked the cell, whilst muttering under his breath that she was free to go and something about "I'll be watching you." Cerys snorted in laughter at him, until he tried for one last grope. Snarling, she grabbed the hand on her breast, applying pressure to his wrist and bending his hand and then forearm backwards until she heard a loud snap as the bone broke. His scream made her smile, but she remembered her training, and her eyes stayed 'human', even as she replied to his comment. "Watch all you like, tovarishch. You only need one hand to pleasure yourself. Unless you want me to make the damage permanent, don't try manhandling me or any of the other female prisoners again, borscht for brains." Throwing his hand away, Cerys stalked out of the cell.

Mind-linking to Zarek, she let him know that they had been released and were waiting to be taken back to the trucks that brought them in the first place. Advising him that she would meet him there, she followed the rest of the villagers out to the waiting trucks.

There was a thumping on the door of the room in which Zarek was 'in conference' with the Three Wise Monkeys. A guard entered, cradling his hand. "The bitch broke my wrist. She shouldn't be able to do that. She's not human." He protested.

"I bet you grabbed her breasts, you fool." Zarek retorted. "I told you we are preparing for our mission." He shook his head as if in dismay at the sheer stupidity around him. "What do you expect if you try touching up a trained operative?"

Strangely enough, it was Cerys' actions along with his words which seemed to convince the Three Wise Monkeys that he wasn't messing around.

"Escort him to the trucks and get him out of here." The middle Monkey snapped, desperately trying to regain some face in the situation.

"I don't need an escort, comrade." Zarek's stress on the last word was heavy with irony. "I am sure I can find my own way out. Just keep the fuck out of my operation, and everything will be just fine." Rudely, he shoved the guard out of the way, swung the door open and used scent to track his way back to the exit. Still bleeding with arrogance, Zarek flipped the canvas on the back of the truck out of the way. "Everyone here?" The acknowledgement he wanted was from Cerys and the chairman of the village council. Receiving a nod from both, he grinned. "Let's blow this joint then." He suggested, deliberately using American idiom to emphasise his story about an undercover infiltration mission.

Zarek waited until the trucks had left before joining everyone in the bar of the Hunter's Arrow Inn. Locking the doors behind him, he smiled. "That went better than I had hoped. However, we need to make arrangements to move those in the most danger out of here." He nodded to the village chairman. "It will fit in with what I have said if several people disappear from the village. It will be assumed that they have been 'deployed'." Cerys nodded at his words. Whilst it was easier to flash people out, particularly if they were not being observed, this slower method of evacuation by road would fit in better with their story.

"I have spoken with Gavril." Zarek explained. There were murmurs of surprise as some who had been children when he and the other Cŵn Annwn had left after the war, looked at each other, at the fact that they were old men with grown families. "We have arrangement, as you know. Tonight, those who are most at risk will go. We will meet up at the old kitchen at the House." He told them, referring to the ruin that was the old Negrescu Hall. Gavril and several of the others will be waiting for us." He explained.

"Cerys!" He called the female Sentinel over to where they were talking. "There will be some new faces, Cerys amongst them, in the village. I want to give the impression that this is some sort of staging post for an infiltration operation of the West. That way, new faces will appear, who will be 'new operatives', but will be Cŵn Annwn Sentinels like Cerys here."

There were nods from the humans with them. The chairman smiled. "Gavril promised that he would watch out for us. He has not let us down."

Later that day, it was with mixed feelings that Gavril flashed into the old kitchen of Negrescu Hall. After all, this was the place from which he had gone to the aid of a woman in the village which had let to the unlamented Gauleiter and his friend, the Kommandant, trying to force him to do their will at the risk to the lives of both his beloved Aaleahya and his daughter, Ekaterina. As it transpired, none of his efforts had saved his little Kat, but that was, as they say, water under the bridge.

He nodded to Zarek, who was waiting for them, along with several members of the village council. The old chairman had tears in his eyes as he came forward. They were cloudy eyes, his vision fading with the lack of healthcare options open to him here. Wordlessly, Gavril smiled before embracing him briefly.

"You did not forget your promise to us. On behalf of the village, I thank you." The chairman's voice wobbled with his emotion.

"I promised that I would not forget my covenant to you, my old friend. I would never break such a sacred trust." Gavril assured him. "As now. As Zarek has explained, we have a plan which will mean that there will be no questions asked about those who must leave. To the authorities, it will seem that some have died in their foolish attempts to leave, perhaps, rather than let anyone think that this is a viable escape route to the 'decadent West'.

He turned to Aaleahya, who had accompanied him. "You remember Aaleahya, of course?"

Aaleahya nodded, and took up the explanation. "Gavril and I will detonate the hidden mines along the Country Wall causing multiple explosions. The authorities in East Berlin will assume that the offending escapees have perished, but instead other Sentinels will take them to safety."

The old chairman and the other members of the village committee opted to stay behind. They pointed out that their whole lives had been in this small village in the Carpathians and whilst they wanted their offspring to be taken to the relative safety of the West, them themselves would stay behind.

Zarek could understand that. Humans built up memories of a place, which seemed to mean more to them, perhaps because of their relatively short lives. The undeniable advantage was that it would also reinforce the story he had concocted on the spur of the moment in the faces of the Three Wise Monkeys, that the village was some sort of training camp for infiltrators of the decadent West. That said, things were changing. There were hints of a particular outcome which might actually come to pass, but still, so much depended on human free will. Yet, who would have guessed when Gavril let a Russian soldier live just after the war, that this could ever be the potential result?

The road was bumpy making for an uncomfortable ride in the back of truck which Cerys was driving later in the night. The canvas flapping in the back as they drove down the desolate road was the only sound to be heard. Their destination was a section of Country Wall where previous escape attempts had left trucks jammed in the breach in the fence, the machine gun traps triggered already. It offered the potential for several people to squeeze through the barrier, not that they would, but the authorities must be made to think that it had been their intention. The truck hit a hidden deep rut, throwing it to the left side of the road. Grabbing the wheel, Cerys cranked it furiously, keeping the truck from hitting the ditch. Mumbling to herself, she cut the lights so she could see the ruts in the road clearly without the glare of the lights. She yelled over her shoulder to check her passengers were not injured by the rough journey and was reassured by one of the males.

As the two trucks rattled to a halt, Gavril could hear the murmur from the passengers as they picked themselves up. The authorities had left the road in a poor state of repair on purpose, a simple but effective method of discouraging 'desertions' from the 'utopia' of the DDR. It always seemed curious to him that the Communists used words like 'democratic' implying rule by the people, and yet here, it was a dictatorship. Their leader may be an old man, but he was still a dictator, with his power base bolstered through fear of the Stasi secret police.

The twelve individuals were all children born since the end of the war, where the world of soviet state was all that they knew. Yet, they could not accept that this was their lot, any more than their fathers would accept the tyranny of the Nazi regime. So, they made their choices known and as a result, had to flee their homes, leaving fathers and mothers, with no knowledge of whether they might ever see them again. Yet times change. Politics change. A boy who drove tractors during the Second World War was becoming noticed both by his own people and by the Western World. Perhaps this would be a temporary separation, Gavril pondered. They could but hope.

The plan for escape was simple enough. Lodging awaited them in West Berlin and the provisions by the East Berlin authorities against 'desertions' would be used to their advantage. What did it matter if such scurrilous dissidents were killed in their foolish attempts to flee? The scraps of bloodstained clothing would be sufficient to demonstrate that it had not been animals which had caused the explosions.

And then, one day, perhaps they might be able to see their parents again.

Zarek's part in the plan was relatively straightforward. Whilst Gavril and Aaleahya set off the mines which had been planted with a callous disregard for human life, Zarek and Cerys would transport the twelve individuals over the border. These people were marked by the authorities now, regardless of Zarek's little story. At least this way, they would have their lives, something no longer guaranteed at home. This way, their disappearances would be excused by them being heroes of the revolution, who had sacrificed their chances of remaining with their families for the good of the state, to infiltrate the decadent West and prepare for the new revolution.

In the meantime, when the East Berlin local authorities came running in response to the mines being exploded, all they would find would be scraps of humans remains with enough trace evidence to be able to confirm the remains were human. As the Dylan song of the hippy age said, times were a-changing, Zarek mused. Attitudes were changing. Another revolution was coming. That much was true and those who thought oppression would keep them in power would be able to do nothing about it. The corruption of the communist idea, the restrictions, the lies in the name of a discredited political system would all become more and more apparent. Another revolution was coming. That much wold be undeniable.

But that would be in the future. The present was ensuring the safety of twelve men and women, who though they knew it not, had a key role to play.

As the trucks emptied, Aaleahya walked over to the crates which had been stacked to hide them. The crates held a crucial part of the plan: twelve human cadavers that had been on their way to an incinerator. The operator of the facility was more than happy to off load them to Gavril, when he had produced papers purporting to claim that the cadavers were their extended family who should have been buried on a family plot.

Nodding to Zarek and Cerys, she watched as they began to walk through the death zone, keeping their footing careful. As soon as they were at the breach in the wall, the first young adult came through, until all had made the crossing safely. Gavril gave e signal and the bodies are dragged to the death zone and placed near the ground. Another signal and the bodies themselves were used to detonate the mines, ensuring loud and very messy explosions. Going invisible, the Cŵn Annwn waited as the soldiers and border guards came running, machine guns at the ready, stopping only when they saw the dismembered corpses and blood pieces of clothing in the sandy dirt. Aaleahya could hear them commenting on the stupidity of these people. A brief discussion ensued before they decided that the mines had done their job and the risk of actual escape had been eliminated. Such was their preoccupation with the graphic evidence left so deliberately, that they didn't think to check the old breach in the fence.

Leaning into her Mate with relief, Aaleahya was grateful to the Goddess that they had the means to help the villagers from their old home. Too many had died in the closing years of the last war, so many shipped to Auschwitz, that being able to save even this dozen was truly a reason for gratitude.

CHAPTER 23: TIMES THEY ARE A CHANGIN'

New York State, 1975

Jake smiled down at his young son and at his darling Grace. "You ready Grace? Jake?" They smiled at young Jake's nod and took each of his hands as they walked the last block to the Elementary School. "Remember son, hold your head high and be kind to those that need it." His heart swelled so much at his son's firm nod that Jake felt about to burst. He didn't dare look over at Grace because he could hear her sniffles from here and his boy didn't need to be seeing him cry too. "Now Jake, they started something called desegregation busing so you won't be the only coloured here like in Kindergarten. They won't be from your neighbourhood so you watch out for them best you can." Little Jake continued to nod while his eyes scanned the crowd gathered. "You have friends here that you know so it's cool." Jake Junior stopped walking and looked up at his father in exasperation. "Cripes dad, I'm going to school not the lion's den." Jake smiled, so proud of what his son was able to do in such a short time. Leave it to his boy to cut the tension. He just had the knack to put folks at ease.

Jake Jr. let go of his parents' hands to walk up the steps to the school as Grace bumped her husband's shoulder with hers. "He gets it from me babe." Jake snickered a bit then turn back to the school to watch the parents milling about watching the kids go in. A few were eyeing Jake but he ignored them all and turned back with a smile and short wave. They had met a lot of people because of the garage so things should be a problem but old habits die hard. Suddenly his son stopped when he heard his name called by little Elizabeth. She ran to his side and talked excitedly about how well they would do in first grade and all the new friends they would find. Their little voices were drowned out by the bell ringing and we turned toward home.

Elizabeth's parents, Martha and Isaac Levin, were standing at the corner waiting for Jake and Grace to join them. "Good day Jake and Grace." Isaac reached forth to shake the other man's hand. They had become fast friends with their family ever since Abe Micula brought them here from New York City. They were distraught after the tragedy of losing a brother in the 1972 Olympics so moved their jewellery store here to start over. Some would think their friendship was because their peoples have something in common but Jake liked to think it was just good folks finding good folks. He and Isaac talked business while the ladies discussed Rebecca's health issues. Jake didn't listen in as women stuff is women stuff and none of his business unless Abe needed his help.

Their talking was interrupted by the sound of spitting behind them. Bert Carlson. "It was bad enough to have one nigger in the school now we got more and Jews besides." Jake kept his calm face on even though he wanted to lay the man out as he stepped between him and the women.

"It's a brave new world our kids are facing Bert and I gotta admit I envy them." He snorted in derision as Isaac stepped forward. "Bert, I was sorry to hear that store you were working at closed down. I sure hope you find work soon." Jake really wanted to be nice and keep things cool but Isaac sometimes brought out the game in him and picking on the town asshole was just too easy to pass up. "Hey Bert, if you're needing work I think I can fit you in at the shop. Know anything about engines?" Grace slapped his arm as Bert spun on his heel and walked away. "What babe? I was just being neighbourly." Jake looked innocently at his wife, before his grin gave away the small pleasure he had just given himself.

Africa, 1975

"Kafi! It is good to see you again." Angharad walked to her spice stand for a warm embrace. "Angharad, you do not age." The Cŵn Annwn healer laughed it off and sat on the small woven stool next to her friend. "It's only been two years since I've been to Africa. Look closer and you can see the wrinkles forming." Angharad leaned back and looked her over. "You look well Kafi." That was not true as she noted the deep fatigue and slower than normal movements. "Here, let me pour the tea Kafi." Angharad studied the human woman closely and was pleased to realize that she was just tired and did not suffer from some malady. "So Kafi, tell me what has been happening with you."

"Oh my friend." Kafi sighed deeply and sipped her tea. "Do you remember that strange disease Zai mentioned when last you were here? The wasting disease?" Angharad nodded as she thought back to what Zai had told her. At that time, she did not investigate as Africa is like a birthing place of life, be it animal or viral. Actually to her they are the same. A living force wanting to propagate and it all evolves as time progresses. Angharad paused in her musings and listened to Kafi tell of the sickness hitting the area hard. "Angharad, I firmly believe it spread here when they came with the inoculations to help us combat malaria. I have been keeping a journal on those infected and most of them received the shots. Zai spoke with the authorities and they deny fault but I tell you now, they change needles for each patient now." She leaned back smug. "That alone tells us that they know the spread is partly their fault." She cleared her throat and poured us each some tea. "We know it isn't airborne and now it is just through bodily fluids so that is something. I just hope it doesn't change again." Angharad nodded her agreement on that.

"Kafi, are you treating these infected people?" At her nod Angharad continued. "May I visit them and perhaps obtain a sample of their blood? I don't know that I can help but I would like to understand it more." She smiled and patted Angharad's knee as a customer arrived. Angharad watched her expertly measure the cinnamon and complete her transaction. She suddenly remembered her reason for being here. "Before I forget, here is a list of the spices I will need on this trip." Angharad yelled to a young boy and handed him the list. "Just have him bring it to my hotel room when he's ready. Tell him I have a treat waiting for him there, wrapped in white paper." The boy's eyes lit up as he quickly worked on the healer's extensive list and she leaned toward Kafi. "Yes, I brought you some chocolate bars and ink pens too." Two older boys arrived just as the sun was setting to help her friend close up and lock away the open spice baskets so Kafi took her hand.

"Come Angharad, I'll show you someone who is suffering with this terrible disease."

She took the Cŵn Annwn healer to a small apartment and the choking smell of death was thick in the hot air. Angharad knew her species was immune to human disease but she always studied the new strains that came forth. An old man once said "even a blind squirrel will find a nut now and then" when explaining a strange quirk of fate. She had never forgotten that and so she had been vigilant in her studies to keep from complacency. You never knew when something evolved enough to get past their immune systems. That was why she was there, gazing upon a wasted male covered in sores. The infection running through him had weakened his body beyond repair so he sadly waited to die. Angharad pretended to take his pulse as she delved into his body to see what she could find. His white blood T-cells were all but wiped out for some reason. "Kafi, please ask if I may take some blood for analysis." Permission was granted and Angharad drew a few vials. It seemed her trip here would be cut short so that she could test this against her own blood.

Angharad hated to cut her trip short but she arrived back home with the varied spices and herbs and most importantly, her blood samples. She let some of the younglings bottle the spices while she made her way to her workroom. She held up a vial of the victim's blood and let her mind wander inside. She saw the strange cell with its little suckers sticking out and wondered how it worked so she thawed and warmed up a bag of donated human blood to see. The virus cells quickly attached themselves to the T-cells and shot the infection inside. Angharad was amazed at how fast it worked and hoped the humans got a handle on this before it spread outside of Africa. To confirm her own immunity, Angharad withdrew her own blood and added the tainted sample to it. Again the virus was drawn to her T-cells but bounced harmlessly around the perimeter. She kept checking hour after hour until she was secure in the knowledge that the Cŵn Annwn would be safe from this disease. Only then did she incinerate the tainted samples.

New York State, 1977

"Rebecca. I'm so glad you could see me on such short notice." Angharad followed Rebecca into the living room where Abe was waiting with a clear look of apprehension. "Relax you two. I have some interesting news for you and a chance to make a choice." Rebecca absently placed the tea tray on the table, completely forgetting about it as she sat next to Abe and clasped her hand tightly with his. "I travel quite a bit in my healing studies and therefore meet a lot of people with varying areas of expertise. I was recently in England and met up with a friend, Robert Edwards who is one of the leading physiologists on human reproduction. He's on the verge of a great breakthrough. I also met his colleague Patrick Steptoe who is a forward thinking Gynaecologic Surgeon. I have to be honest; I'm so excited to share this with you."

"Angharad, you know that I lost my ovaries to cancer a few years ago. I cannot conceive." Angharad nodded as her smile widened. "Yes I know Rebecca but this is a chance for women who cannot conceive on their own to carry a child. It's called several things but it is in vitro fertilization. They take an egg from the mother, in your case, from a donor and fertilize it in a petri-dish. Two or three days later the fertilized egg is placed within the mother's womb and everyone crosses their fingers that it stays. Now it's not fool-proof and it's still in the testing phase but Rebecca, Abe, you have a slot in their trials if you want it."

Angharad leaned forward and poured them all a cup of tea while they stared into each other's eyes. "I don't need an answer right this minute. You have until the end of this month to decide or they will fill the opening. They want the initial part done by December and the births to begin in 1978." Just then a young boy entered the room wearing a policeman's badge and sunglasses. He stopped short when he saw Angharad and grinned. "I'm sorry, I forgot you had company."

Abe rustled the boy's hair and sent him into the kitchen for a cookie before turning back to me with a smile. "We're watching him for a friend of ours." Rebecca beamed after him. "His name is Jake Junior and he fancies himself the next Ponch." She noted Angharad's confusion. "That's a policeman on a show called C.H.I.P.S. So don't panic if Jake should run through here sounding like a motorcycle." The healer turned to the kitchen in time to see the child grin and go out the back door. If the doting look they gave to someone else's child was any indication, Angharad knew she would be setting up an appointment in England quickly. "Ok, I'm going to leave now. You have my number if you have any questions."

"I have one Angharad. You said a donated egg. Would I get to pick the donor?" Angharad thought a moment and answered. "That can be arranged. Either a friend of your family or perhaps someone from my family. You would need to think on future implications should you choose someone you know. It's a changing world and this is all new. Sometimes a little anonymity is a good thing." She stood up and gathered her bag.

"We'll do it." They both jumped up and said it together which pleased Angharad so much. "I'll let them know and give your contact information to them." They weren't listening closely but instead whispering, so Angharad walked to the door and went to the porch to give them time.

"Angharad? Would you and Owain choose the donor for us? I don't think we want to meet her but we trust all of you enough to know that your choice would be wise." Their faith in their Cŵn Annwn friends was humbling. This was no light decision but they trusted the Pack to keep their best interests in mind. "I'll contact Owain. Now, enjoy a night of celebration and hope. Good day to you both." After a few hugs she left for home feeling good about life.

New York State, 1978

Angharad was startled from her book when Eira rushed into her room. "Angharad, Abe Micula just called." She was absolutely beaming with joy and wringing her hands so the healer knew what she was about to say. "The baby is coming and they're on the way to the hospital." Angharad jumped out of the chair and threw her arms around Eira. "It is a good day Eira! I'll be at the hospital with them in case anyone needs me." She was about to flash herself there but thought it best to arrive in a car. Besides, human birthing can take a while.

When she did arrive, she was shown straight to the Delivery Suite, as soon as she introduced herself as the Miculas' private physician. "Rebecca, you look beautiful." She laughed quickly at her attempt at humour but there was no sound from Abe. Angharad looked him over and leaned over to Rebecca. "But Abe looks a little peaked it seems." He just groaned then grimaced when she clutched his hand through another contraction. He was trying to tell her to breathe but it just came out garbled. That's when Angharad decided to let her mind slip into his body and calm him down just a bit. It would have been a shame for him to pass out at the birth of his own child. She was pleased to see his colour return and some of the adrenaline to wear off.

"Angharad." Rebecca struggled to catch her breath in order to talk to me while Abe was attempting to feed her ice chips. Angharad giggled when she glared at him and he meekly put the glass of ice down. "Yes Becca?" She reached out for my hand. "Angharad, will she know?" Angharad knew instantly that she was asking about the woman who donated her eggs. A Cŵn Annwn but Rebecca didn't know that. How would she answer that without making her wonder who the donor had been? "I'm sure she will hear about it and be joyous in the birth. For you, not herself. She is a giving and caring female so of course she will be happy for you." Becca's breathing sped up as another contraction began. "Angharad. Tell her thank you."

Her labour progressed normally and now that Abe had gotten a handle on things, he was doing quite well also. Angharad watched him as he stood near his wife's feet to see the baby's crown appear and as was the case with all births, Angharad's eyes misted at the miracle unfolding. Even the LPN from the *in vitro* study taking pictures and dictating into a recorder couldn't take away from the sheer joy they found in their new daughter. A perfect little girl. The LPN's voice caught as she recorded the news for Robert Edwards. "Born 3:45 pm EST on October 8, 1978. Female child." Later she recorded the weight and height for the test-tube studies but that was all ignored by Becca and Abe as they whispered soft words to the infant. “Hello Avigail our little miracle.”

New York State, 1984

Last period was let out early so Jake knew had time to go home and get something to eat before heading to the garage to help his father. His savings account was growing slowly but surely and by the time he started to attend college he would have food and gas money maybe even a little extra for some fun. His mental calculation of funds stopped short when he turned on to Jade Street and saw little Avigail trying to talk down a group of boys.

"What in the hell are the Lawsons doing on this street?" He wondered. They didn't hear his mumbled question and as he drew closer he saw the Henderson kids cowering behind Avigail. "Shit" They're bigger than Avigail but their little spitfire didn't care. He was close enough now to hear her firm reprimand.

"It's not fair of you to judge them by what they wear and it's time you boys went back to your own neighbourhood." She crossed her little six-year-old arms and stood smug as you please in the face of the teen bullies. "Now would be a good time to move along and leave these kids alone." Jake's presence was announced as he snorted out a chuckle and all eyes turned to him. He made a show of looking at the kids before he turned his eyes to the Lawson boys. "Picking on little kids now? What? Did ya run out of high school victims? Oh that's right the guard patrol stopped your lunch-money shake-down."

Luke sneered as he jabbed his finger in his chest. "Just another thing that pisses me off about you…boy." Jake faked a big yawn. "Is that really the best you can do?" The boys moved to take Jake on and damn, he thought, if Avigail didn't get between them wagging her finger. "I told you to move on and leave us alone. That includes my friend Jake too. It is against the law to harass people you know and if you hit him you can be charged with assault." The shocked look they gave her would have made Jake laugh but he didn't want to offend Avigail, so he leaned forward a bit. "Avi, why don't you get the Henderson kids home then go home yourself? Okay?" She didn't budge so Jake picked her up and put her on the grass before turning back to the Lawsons. "I need to know that you three are safe. Please go." She nodded quickly in understanding and with a sad look; she took the kids in hand and ran down the sidewalk. Only then did Jake turn to the boys. "Ok, now where were we?"

Luke threw the first punch and Jake would have hit the ground but Lee punched him in the kidney which broke his fall. He managed to get a few good hits in when old lady Johnson came out with a broom and began to hit the boys in the head, he was pleased to note that not only was he still on his feet but that even they wouldn't hurt an old lady. He spat blood on the pavement and stepped up to Luke. "You leave those kids alone Luke and my best advice is to stay in your own neighbourhood. We've organized a neighbourhood watch and I know your daddy wouldn't want to come bail you out." Miss Johnson chose that moment to pipe up. "I already called the police station and unless my hearing aid is whistling, that's their siren right now." The boys swore up a streak as they ran down the sidewalk and Jake turned to Miss Johnson. "Thank you, ma'am. You aren't hurt are you?" She broke into amused laughter and patted the teenager's shoulder. "I'm fine young man. I know those Henderson kids. Their momma is having a hard time since their daddy died. It's not right to be picking on little children when they're facing home troubles too."

The police car pulled up to the curb and Jake's eyes flared when he saw their sharp uniforms and badges. Someday he was going to be a cop and then a detective like Tubbs on Miami Vice. So while he answered their questions, he watched everything they did so when he graduated from college and became a cop, he could be just like them.

New York State, 1995

Gavril was smiling as he opened the post which Bran had brought up to the Hall when he returned from his patrol. Way back in 1980 whilst combing through various investment options for the Negrescu Foundation funds, one had caught his Beta's eye. It was a company set up by some 'geeks' in California, who had some fairly interesting ideas on how technology would develop. They were floating their company at the considerable sum of $22 a share. Bran was certain that this was going to be an interesting investment.

Gavril had given his approval when, on one of his infrequent visits to Negrescu Hall, Zarek had a half smile on his face. God of Divination agreeing with an investment choice? Gavril had also gone with another company start-up, which had come about because IBM had decided not to patent the idea of the 'PC', the personal computer, seeing a time when these devices would be in every home. Again, a fairly imaginative concept at the time. So, he had authorised the investment in the second company in 1983.

Now in 1995, he was being invited to the launch party for their new software version. The event would be on 24 August 1995, and the product would take part of its name from that year. Gavril had put the letter to one side, intending to ask Aaleahya if she would like the trip to this launch party. It was one of the few events where they might attend and their relative youth would not be seen as abnormal or out of place. Technology was the realm of the young and imaginative, it seemed. For no other reason, it meant it was a potentially enjoyable trip.

That early investment in 1980 had not done too badly either. Suffice it to say that the Negrescu Foundation funds would not lack and that in itself was satisfying. The greater the bank balance, so to speak, the more people the Pack could help.

It was a fitting memorial to his lost daughter, Ekaterina.

Gosselin Compound Canada, 1998

Turning 18 is a milestone for anyone, and when you are a wolf shifter sired by the Alpha of one of the pre-eminent Packs on the North American continent, then even more so.

Casimir Gosselin knew he was seen as the dutiful second son. He was the 'spare' in the 'Heir and Spare' pairing, with his brother Laurent being the Heir. He knew this. He didn't appear to have a problem with it, because Laurent was too busy being Beta to his dear sire's Alpha, that both failed to notice what the humble 'Spare' was doing. How very silly of them.

It is true to say that Casimir did have to prove himself to some when establishing his own business interests. After all, he was a callow youth, untried, untested. Until they tried to challenge him. He had to allow himself a small smile at the recollection of their abject apologies when they realised that they had underestimated their alleged prisoner.

And now, as the time came for him to celebrate his 18th birthday. His father has given him full access to the Pack's bank accounts, instead of having to pass everything by him first. So trusting of him, and again, Casimir had to smile that his sire believed firmly that he was loyal to him and to Laurent. If only they knew. If only they knew.

Meticulous planning would take him where he wished to be. It was a simple as that. There was nothing that could stop him, provided that he anticipated all likely problems correctly. The Shifter Council? Please, Casimir thought to himself, don't make me laugh. They are so focused on maintaining their positions that they don't care what is happening to the ordinary shifter on the streets. A powerful Pack must be a well-led Pack. After all, power begat power. And the mythical Cŵn Annwn? No one had heard of them in decades. They are a myth, a legend. And a myth that no longer cared. Nothing would not stop Casimir Gosselin in achieving the plans that he had been building for so very long.

New York State, 1999

In retrospect, Bran supposed it was not surprising that he enjoyed this 'new' technology which meant that he could accomplish a lot of the Pack's financial affairs without actually having to talk to anyone.

Gavril had agreed to convert a room downstairs in the Hall for him to use for the servers and individual stations which they used more and more to manage bank accounts and to search or investigate situations in which they may have to intervene. It was so much easier now to drop Abe Micula an e-mail than it was to arrange to meet with him in his offices. After all, he would joke to Bran, he wasn't getting any younger, and appreciated not having to trek out to meet with him. For Bran, it should have been no big issue, since at worst he had to drag his bike out of the garage, dig out his safety gear and travel the forty or so miles to his office.

The thing was, given his sentiments about the chances of him finding a Mate, Bran could not see the need to interact with the outside world as much as those who thought that possibility was still there for them. He had accepted that is was his punishment for failing to protect his Alpha and his Alpha's Mate during the war. Owain was far more sociable than he was and more to the point, Owain was happy to run the Pack's bar, the Hunter's Arrow. Just as they had kept the name of the Pack home, they used the same name for their bar business. Now, as the new millennium approached, as humans measured their years, all the talk was of the Y2K problem, the risk that computers would seize up due to the problem of changing from 1999 to 2000. There was still time for the problem to be resolved.

Bran found himself thinking of another major event, celebrating its tenth anniversary now, that he was certain Zarek knew was inevitable. All those young adults whom they had relocated to West Berlin, finding them homes and employment in Cŵn Annwn sponsored businesses, had a role to play and then some. One night in 1989, the might of the people had spoken. By the time they made themselves heard, the impenetrable barrier which had been the Berlin Wall had fallen. People power and sledgehammers had torn down this symbol of division.

Ironic then that now, Bran thought, he was opting to lock himself away behind the anonymity of online banking and share dealing, using e-mail instead of face to face meetings. It was easier. No one would know that his features did not age. A wall it may have been, but as the year 2000 drew closer, it served the purpose of enabling the Pack to keep their secrets and let the Cŵn Annwn become creatures of legend once more.

Gosselin Compound Canada, 1998

It was late one night; a noise had awakened Alix. At first she thought it had been the storming raging outside her window. The wind and thick raindrops plastered the window relentlessly, but that had not been the noise that had disturbed her slumber. Another ka-thump followed by something heavy dropping on the floor and then a howl. Gooseflesh crept all over her back and my arms. Alix knew that howl ...

The following morning when she went down for breakfast Alix looked at her mother as she sat with her cup of Earl Grey with a twist of lemon. She was playing with a cranberry swirl scone. Usually her mother devoured those scones in an instant. Today her mother seemed to be more interested in making crumbs than eating. Alix was only ten years old but she would never forget that morning. The morning when the veil had been lifted and she saw her mother for what she truly was, a victim, but also strangely enough, a survivor.

She concealed her bruises as best she could but had either been in a rush or had not noticed the bruising on the back of her shoulder blades. The bruises were already healing, but Alix could tell those had not come from messing around with your mate. Those bruises were deliberate blows with a hard object. The sharp edges and the deep colour in the middle of the wound indicated the force it took to deliver that blow. Alix's mind recalled the noise she had heard and her eyes instantly watered as she went to her mother to hug her.

Alix's mother held her arm to stop her daughter, knowing that if she had not, Alix's sire would have seen them embracing. He would have seen his daughter cry, and that would have been even more disastrous. Alix held her mother's gaze as she supplicated with her eyes to contain her emotions. She was bespelled by her mother for she remembered nothing more of that day except her steady gaze and the warmth she felt emanating from the flesh to flesh contact as she held her at arm's length.

That was the end of Alix's childhood. She was no longer ignorant of the abuse her mother endured. From that day on she no longer walked with blinkers. She faced life head on doggedly determined to make her life better and more meaningful than what her mother had chosen for herself.

Gosselin Compound in Canada, 1999

Almost a year had passed since Alix's eyes had been exposed to the truth. By the age of eleven she had suffered countless torments from her older brother Laurent. On the rare moment when she was alone Laurent would play a wicked game of hide and seek with his sister; it was his life's mission to abuse her every chance he got. The 'game' always began the same way, Laurent would speak in a loud voice across the hall from my room "Come out, come out where ever you are little Piglet". It was his idea of fair warning, since he would always say in a reproaching tone so that she had had plenty of time to find a good hiding place. Laurent knew she had no place to hide but her room because he never gave her enough time to go hide somewhere else. Every time she heard that taunting voice she shivered with fear holding onto the one thing that gave her comfort: a little grey wolf that she had found abandoned in the park one day. It was only six inches tall. The little figurine was sitting on its hind legs with his head slightly tilted to one side. There was a strange look of affection and love emanating from his stare. It was the same wolf she had dreamt of all her life. That grey wolf was always there. Sometimes Alix would run together with the grey wolf, revelling in their wolf forms; sometimes he protected her, like it did so many times during these brotherly 'games' with Laurent.

The small wolf figurine made Alix feel safe, powerful and for some odd reason protected and loved. She never questioned its power. Without that little grey wolf she felt that she would never have survived what Laurent did once he found her. Tears would always stream down her face when Laurent eventually found her, he always did. The wounds he would inflict upon her small body would not be visible. He always made sure of that, but the scars he left in her mind would haunt her for a very long time. It was only recently that Casimir seemed to interrupt his games, but he made sure that Alix knew she should fear him also. Two brothers. Same sire and same attitude to those they saw as powerless to defend themselves.

Alix knew that she had to do something. After all, as much as Laurent and Casimir shared a sire, so did she. She had seen how her sire looked at her and Alix knew what would be expected of her. If her older brothers and her Papa had their way "The Gosselin Princess" would be forcefully mated where they could gain the maximum benefit. Her thoughts and feelings were of little to no consequence. If the mating would be advantageous to her sire in one form or the other, so be it, but it would seal her destiny to a life very much like her mother's. Her mother was powerless to save her from a life of torture. Alix had to save herself. She needed a plan.

Alix had sworn to herself that somehow, and she didn't care how, but somehow she was going to escape from this prison that her father called their Pack home. She didn't know how, but she would. Actually, she had formed a plan, and the irony has to be that it was after she realised that her father was beating her mother on a regular basis. She knew he was picking on the baby of the family, her brother, Adhémar, or at least her older brother Casimir was doing their sire's dirty work for him, but she thought he was just strict with her mother. But that year that she turned ten years old, she noticed that the careful make-up hid a different story that the cold, proud woman that her mother had always appeared to her. She noticed the bruising, perhaps because her father hadn't been quite as precise. But she knew, instinctively. She knew that a person didn't develop that sort of bruising from rough bedroom play. She saw the kind of wolves her father kept around him as his enforcers, as Alix came closer to puberty, she realised that they were looking at her in a different manner.

It was one of the few times she would admit to being scared.

There was nothing to stop her father mating her to one of his supporters. No one would know, and if they did, no one would question her father's rule. He was the Alpha of the Gosselin Pack, now that Gran'pere was dead. His word was law. So, that was when Alix knew she had to make plans.

Thank the gods for computers, that's all she could say. She could research ways that she could escape legitimately from the Pack. Alix started with school. Her grades were good, but she needed to start making career choices, assuming her father didn't have in mind to have her mated to someone as soon as she was capable of bearing pups. She had to plan this really carefully, and Alix sold the idea to her father on the basis that, with how well the Pack was doing, and the way that people respected him, it would look even better for her to educated in a fancy boarding school for girls, so she could mix with the daughters of politicians and people who could be useful to him. He liked that, he liked that a lot. Said she was proving her genes and thinking well.

So, come her eleventh birthday plans were put in place to pack her off to Miss Porter's School in Farmington Connecticut. It was not the most expensive school in the country, but he chose it based on the emphasis on languages. He wanted his daughter to be seriously multilingual. She could speak English and French anyway, and she had learned Filipino, Chinese and Spanish from the various visitors whom they had to the compound. It didn't matter to Alix. What mattered was that she was escaping out of the Gosselin compound, away from all those staring eyes, watching her, waiting for her to be old enough.

Alix felt really bad about leaving Adhémar, but she had to choose between staying behind and trying to protect him from Laurent and Casimir, or making sure that she had the means to survive on her own, and when she was old enough, break away from the Pack.

If she expected to live to adulthood, she had no choice.

Adhémar dreaded coming home from school, now that it had been decided that Alix was to be packed off to Miss Porter's School. Ten years old and all that was passing through his thoughts was that he didn't want to be with his family right now. He knew he was different from the rest of my brothers and sister Alix, who was the pride and joy of their father's eye. While he was tall and gangly with his hair a bit longer then Casimir's and the others, he wished he could remain invisible. He came to a stop as he entered his room. Everything had been destroyed: the mattress shredded, his clothes thrown on the floor, the smell of urine was strong in his nostrils. As he stumbled forward to examine the mess, Casimir came to stand in the doorway smirking. The look of satisfaction gleaming in his eyes told Adhémar who was responsible for this.

"Adhémar what happened? Qu'a tu fait?" Growling the younger boy leapt at his brother's throat only to be thrown down on the floor, just about managing to roll in before Casimir's kick to his stomach could impact. Rolling his body into the foetal position in an effort to protect himself, he tried to suppress the whimpering on hearing his father's footsteps and Casimir's laughter. Adhémar wanted beg but he knew what would come next: his sire's anger at the destruction and the inevitable punishment his brother's hands for his latest 'transgression'. Casimir was always the one to dole out the punishment, but he knew it was on their sire's orders. "I won't tell. Please Casimir, I won't tell." Adhémar knew that the urine was their elder brother, Laurent's, that he had trashed the room, with the sole intent to have Adhémar punished again.

Casimir grabbed his brother by the hair jerking the younger boy's head up. His eyes seemed large and black, some said like the soul that resided in his body. It was the thing that marked Casimir as being different from his half-brothers, the dark, almost black iris around his pupil. "You dear brother are a weak piece of shit" he yelled, knowing their sire was within earshot. A slap to his head, his hands grasping the thinner arms, bruising them, before he dropped his brother on the floor and swung his leg once more at Adhémar, whilst, snarling at him, "Tu es un morceau pathétique de merde." Another whimper escaped Adhémar's lips once he was alone.

"Adhémar?" The youngest sibling heard Alix's voice through the haze of pain his body was fighting. He lifted his head gingerly, groaning at the pain it caused. Alix knelt next to her brother, gently touching his bruised body. "Adhémar who did this to you?" Adhémar heard her quick intake of breath then she hissed as she exhaled the name Casimir. "Oh Adhémar why do you allow him to these things to you?" She cradled her brother's head brushing his longish hair off his tear-stained face. Adhémar felt like such a loser as his sister crooned to him soothing him. Only his sister would stand up for him against the others. "Alix …" Adhémar's voice shook as he pushed her hands away. "Papa is going to be here soon. I am sure Casimir went to tell on me even though he knows that Laurent is the one who did this destruction. I don't want you to get caught in the aftermath." Alix didn't budge.

He cringed when he heard the heavy footsteps of his father approaching. Adhémar knew deep in his soul this was not going to turn out well for him. His father bellowed "What the hell happened in here?" Adhémar was going to say to his father that this was the work of his precious Laurent, when Casimir appeared behind their sire, making a slashing motion with his hand across his throat. Adhémar swallowed his explanation and kept silent. Unfortunately, Alix did not. As she blurted out that Laurent ruined all her brother's things, Adhémar closed his eyes knowing what would happen next, what always happened next. His father crouched down on his haunches, his fingers under Adhémar's chin as he lifted his head and saw the blackened eye.

"Well Adhémar is this true?" He asked his youngest son, his tone deceptively quiet. Adhémar shook his head, denying that it was Laurent. His father's reaction came fast, a swift punch to his son's face. Alix screamed trying to hold on to their sire's arm to keep him from hitting her younger sibling again. Casimir had a grim look on his face, as if to say "I told you to shut up, brat." as the blood poured out of the younger boy's nose where their sire had punched him, breaking the cartilage. The elder Gosselin screamed at his son to pick up the mess and to toss everything out in the trash. Since he couldn't appreciate having a proper bed, he would have to sleep on the floor, and borrow Casimir's clothes since he couldn't care for his own. Pinching his nose to stop the bleeding, Adhémar made a solemn vow to himself. He would leave as soon as he could. He muffled his whimper as yet again, he felt Casimir followed up on his sire's abuse by resetting the broken nose, ready for it to be broken again. He knew his scars would be minimal in a few hours and by the next day the will be completely healed. How this happened he didn't know, but he could only guess that was the 'joy' of having shifter blood. The only scars he would carry would be inside his soul. Picking himself up off the floor again, Adhémar began the laborious process of gathering his ruined furniture, bedding and clothing and stuffing it into several garbage bags. Soon the room was empty bar a blanket which had been left against the cool air. It was either leave the window open or suffocate on the stench of his eldest brother's urination. Crawling to the corner Adhémar's anger seethed, as he marked his time to when he could finally leave his dysfunctional family.

"Adhémar?" He looked up, hearing the soft voice of his mother coming into the now empty room. "Oh my poor baby," She tipped his bruised face up for inspection. "I am fine Mama. I will be alright." Pulling her son into her lap she hugged him to her breast, the tears trickling down her soft cheeks. "I am putting an end to this. No little boy should ever have to endure this!" Adhémar looked up into her kind eyes and a shiver wracked his body. He knew if his Mama went to his father he would beat her. "No Mama I deserved this. I…I got on the wrong side of father."

He didn't mention Casimir or his role in all of this. His mother sighed, and Adhémar heard her murmur the name of his second oldest sibling, before she told him not to worry; everything would be put to rights. When she stood, leaving Adhémar in his barren room, he crawled back to his hidey hole looking for the magazine with the advertisement for models in it. Clutching it to his chest, Adhémar flipped to the dogged eared page and memorize the number. As soon as he could, he would be calling them to see if he could perhaps have the talent to model clothes. Won't that be a kick in the head for his sire but Adhémar didn't care. The Alpha hated him already, so what was one more mark against him.

New York State, 2001

It was always going to be one of those events in history where he would remember exactly where he was when it happened. They didn't have a television in The Hunter's Arrow, only a radio, and even then, it is just for the amusement of whoever was on bar duty when the place is opening up. Once the regular crowd start arriving, the juke box is hammered into action. But that day, it was quiet, and Owain had the radio on whilst he was cleaning up, in preparation for opening up later.

8.46am. The time was ingrained on Owain's mind, as he was brought to his knees by the impact of that number of souls being lost in one instant.

The repercussions of that first impact echoed through the Pack, with even the younglings being hit. Close on that echo through the Pack came Gavril's order to stay put. Do not react. Do not try to help at the scene. Owain could hear the howls of protests and wondered at his friend using Alpha will to enforce his order. On a tight mind-link to his old friend, Owain asked him what was happening. In response, he asked both his Betas to join him immediately in his study.

When Owain did, it was to see the last person he expected to see, Zarek Svitovidson.

Gavril had also not been expecting a visit from Zarek. The demi-god had flashed in, where Gavril was just working on some training assignments, unsmiling, which for this Associate of their Pack was unusual enough.

"Gavril, you need Aaleahya down here now, and you both need to protect your Pack." His tone was clipped, almost curt. "Do it now."

Gavril had known Zarek for long enough to realise that he wouldn't be acting like this without a damn good reason, so he asked Aaleahya to join him. She flashed in, responding to the urgency in her Mate's mind-voice, concern on her beautiful features. Holding out his arms, Gavril pulled her close, and using the combined strength of his bond with his Mate, he instigated a protective shell around the Pack. Something told him to protect the younglings, those not able to shield themselves, those most at risk to external events.

And at 0846, it happened. The pain from that many souls, not just the ones on the plane in that first strike, but in the floors above where the plane hit, the ones who realised suddenly that they had no way to escape death. Gavril felt Owain's reaction, as he sent out the mental order that the Pack could not respond. Zarek was adamant that they must not respond, and Gavril knew that if the whole Pack had tried to help, it would have raised more questions than anything. They had to operate in the shadows. That was how they could help people because no one knew they existed. Had the Pack helped, then the secret would have been out, with all that entailed. They would be looked on with suspicion and with hatred because they could never hope to save everyone, and yet, in that moment, Gavril could hate the fact that he could do nothing.

From Zarek's perspective, there are times when being a God of Divination was a real bitch, not least because as the timelines before him unfolded, he could see further and further. The instincts within him were to help and he was not alone in that, which was why he flashed himself into Gavril's study and told him to establish a shield over his Pack.

"You and your Pack cannot be involved in what is to happen, other than to mop up. The events of today will have repercussions that most will not be able to contemplate, let alone understand."

As Gavril and Aaleahya started to build the shield around their Pack, Zarek hoped that it would be sufficient to protect their young. They were the ones at risk, the future of the Pack, the future that the Cŵn Annwn could continue to fulfil the geas put on them by their Goddess. It was a measure of the friendship and the strength of the Cŵn Annwn Alpha that he did have the shield up in time, no questions asked, but even then, the vibrations could be felt.

As if the initial impact was not enough, there was the second impact, the strike at the Pentagon, the actions of individuals avoiding a further strike. And then there was the collapse of the buildings in New York.

This was the world of Man, and mankind would react. Some would react with as poisonous a hatred as had inspired the attacks in the first place, in the true biblical 'an eye for an eye'. Others would seek to move forward. Zarek watched as Gavril and his two Pack Betas, Bran Cadwgan and Owain Cadwaladr started working out how they could help. Bran's laptop was open, and his fingers flying over the keyboard as funds were diverted and apportioned, to help those for whom this tragedy meant the loss of not just a loved one, but the loss of their family's main source of income. This was how this Pack of Cŵn Annwn could help. Whilst they could not reveal themselves, they could help in other ways. They could help to pick up the pieces. Small comfort it is true, but it was something.

"Rhys! What the hell man." Rhys didn't stop punching the bag even when Taren got in his space. In fact, the young Sentinel didn't even acknowledge his friend's presence or his angry stance. That was why Rhys missed the change in Taren's expression before he tackled Rhys to the ground.

"Leave it Taren." Rhys' eyes narrowed but Taren completely ignored the warning. "Get. Off. Me. Now." His body was jittery with repressed anger but Rhys didn't want to hurt his friend. And hurt him he would if Taren didn't let go. That horrible rush of souls compounded by the visual on the television was more than Rhys could take. He knew he was supposed to be removed from the humans but he found them so fascinating that he spent more and more time interacting with them. All those thoughts flew through his head and a surge of anger hit him once more so he head-butted Taren. "Now get the fuck off me."

"Not gonna happen Rhys. We're all upset over the terrorist attack but you've lost it. Tell me what's wrong." Rhys braced his feet on the floor and twisted to easily flip Taren off himself. He knew Taren let him do it but the freedom to move was all that mattered to him. How could Rhys explain to his friend that he was mad at their Alpha's decision to insulate themselves, the abject failure to protect those weaker than him or any other number of things flashing through his angry brain? His bloody knuckles once again attacked the punching bag in impotent rage. "Just let me work it out on my own Taren. I just need to ..." punch "... work ..." punch "... through ..." punch "... it."

Aaleahya had just arrived back from collecting more souls for their Goddess. Gavril was with her, beside her and she could feel the darkness surrounding her mate. She reached out to him, taking a hold of his hand. Slamming her lips to his, she used her power to absorb all the negative dark taint that was left behind, feeling the burn of darkness as her light fought to negate it. It felt like it was almost too much darkness but she knew that she had fought more darkness throughout all the years she had been helping her mate, that their Goddess gave her the power to syphon off and negate this flip side to what her Mate had to do. Aaleahya could feel his arms around her middle as the dark taint left his body. His own lips were as demandingly firm on her own as he deepened the kiss giving her the boost of energy Aaleahya needed to destroy the last bit of darkness.

Her skin that had grown cold was now warming up, as the last vestige of darkness left her. The television showing the smoking buildings and the concrete that fell to the ground. The black smoke, thick and choking. She and Gavril had just returned from collecting all the souls that perished today. No sooner had they finished at the New York site, when the call of many souls cried out in anguish as their light was extinguished in fell swoop. Both had flashed to the cries. The wreckage of the plane was everywhere, the smell of airplane fuel permeating the air. Thick black smoke covered the air in a deep choking blanket. Aaleahya had reached the first soul, a woman who was part of the crew. She told of how they fought the terrorist and how the pilot fought to keep the plane in the air and away from the White House, the home of the human American President. Her soul told Aaleahya of the passengers and how they all fought back, reaching out to loved ones before they died. Aaleahya had taken her ghostly hand in her own, allowing her soul to enter Aaleahya's body, feeling the truth and the strength within the young woman which told of her determination to prevent the terrorists from succeeding in their twisted goals. Their Goddess would make this soul a warrior in her army of soul collectors Aaleahya could feel it, even as she wondered what the future might hold that she could be so certain that more warriors would be needed. Aaleahya could sense her Mate and the others gathering souls themselves, with Gavril taking the darkest, the terrorists, his own abilities able to cage the poison of a warped interpretation of one of the monotheistic religions.

Later, as they bowed before their Goddess, the harvested souls were delivered to her for judgement. Aaleahya could feel the anger of her Mate as she reached for his hand knowing it was the taint the terrorists left behind. His hand was cold and his eyes were as cold. As she syphoned off the taint, their Goddess placed with her hand on Aaleahya's shoulder giving her an extra boost of confidence as well as a boost to her own ability. Their Goddess spoke, the sadness in her voice apparent, she told her Alpha and his Mate that they had done well, and as a result, she would bless them with enhanced powers. What was becoming of mankind when fathers kill their children in order to keep them away from their mother, or vice versa?

The television was filled with murders and crime amongst the human race, which only seems to be growing more intense every day. Aaleahya's heart felt heavy with the many lives lost today and in a way which seemed to be growing daily. The crusades of history where one religion fought another for their interpretation of 'peace' were flaring into life again, but this time, mankind had far more deadly weapons at its disposal. Leaning her head on her Mate's shoulder, Aaleahya could begin to understand why Gavril wanted to distance the Pack from humans.

-x-

"Car 14 on the scene." Jake clicked off the radio and exited the car reluctantly. No doubt this was another meth lab gone wrong if the explosion was any indication. His steps slowed when the breeze blew a tell-tale smell of victims caught in the blast and the still burning fire, a smell guaranteed to put him off roast pork for life. "Christ I hate this shit." Jake walked over behind the fireman manning the hose and barely caught his warning before he stepped on a body part lying on the wet ground. Jake froze. He froze as a wave of déjà vu came over him. Suddenly he was back in New York City on that September 11th.

That day would be forever etched in his mind. He was like the others, watching the scene unfold on TV when the call came in for volunteers to go help New York City. Hell, they had to fight to be permitted to go. Not a damn one of them had hesitated and he was lucky to be chosen. So he thought. He had arrived there just as the second tower fell and hell descended on them all. "Search and rescue, more like search and…."

Back to present day, and Sergeant Jameson gave him an odd look. Jake realized he had spoken out loud so he waved his hand and shook his head. He needed to get his head in the now and not back picking up dime size pieces of people amid the smell and ash. And he couldn't even describe the smothering pall of sadness among the police and fire departments. He shook my head once more and approached the Sergeant.

"Ok Sergeant, where do you need me?" His nod was curt as he pointed back to the street. "Quick response time as usual Petersen. Now go on out and help Smith keep the street clear." Jake stood straight and nodded. "Yes sir" He turned on his heel and jogged out to the street. He was no rookie but on this scene he and Smith were the low men on the pole. One more year and he would have his Master's degree and enough street-cop cred for advancement. And when he made it, he would know it was because he had worked for it and not who he was related to.

New York State, 2002

2002. "Jeez Dad, you even bought a new suit?" Jake's parents walked into the receiving hall with eyes bright and proud. They never knew that their pride meant more than his new badge.

"Not every day that my son makes Detective in the New York State Police, now is it?" Jake's father's eyes were bright as he grinned proudly at his son.

Mom slapped him lightly on the arm. "Besides, that November wind is cold and we couldn't have him show up with that old moth eaten winter suit of his, this was merely the perfect opportunity for a change." She stepped up to Jake and patted her son's cheek. "I'm so proud of you Jake. I know how hard you worked for this and now here you are: thirty-five years old and already a detective."

Jake linked his arms with theirs and steered them into the auditorium. He took extra care with Mom since she hadn't been feeling well at all, making a mental note to check out other doctors in the area. He thought a second opinion was called for. Shaking his head to stop his mental meandering, he smiled. "Enough with the compliments, you'll make me blush and ruin my tough reputation." As expected, they chuckled and that thankfully removed the moisture from their eyes. If they started, then Jake knew he would get all sappy too and he didn't want that to happen today. "Here's the seats I saved for you. It should start any minute now." Jake kissed his mother's cheek and looked at her with playful sternness. "No Hallelujahs, okay Mom? I don't think I'd live that down."

"Jake Jr. you are a bad boy, now get." He winked at his father and walked up to the other two new Detectives and took my place.

The ceremony was relatively short and the photographer made sure to get his job done quickly so the small reception could commence. The Captain of Jake's new division walked up and clapped him hard on the shoulder. He already told his parents that he would not introduce him except by saying Captain since his name wreaked havoc with Jake's mouth and he didn't want to mess it up before he had even started. He had heard he hates that.

"Petersen, welcome to the BCI. We're proud to have you." He turned his eyes to my parents and smiled. "Your son will make a great addition to my unit. I asked for him specifically you know. Not many make it into the New York State Police Bureau of Criminal Investigation. The most we've ever had was one thousand in the whole state. That right there shows how hard he's worked for this." He slapped Jake's shoulder again and he couldn't figure out if the Captain was trying to hurt him or just forgot his strength. Either way Jake's father was the only one that caught the brief hint of pain and of course laughed about it. "It was nice to meet you folks, now if you'll excuse me, I have some crowing to do with Vice. They wanted your boy too." He nodded and walked off and Jake turned to see my parents all misty eyed again.

"Stop that you two. I worked hard for this just like you guys worked hard for what you have. So let's celebrate. When we leave here we can go down to O'Malley's. My treat."

Gosselin Compound in Canada, 2004

Alix couldn't believe that five years had passed so quickly. Five years she had been a student at Miss Porter's. The drawback was that at the end of each term she had to go back to the Gosselin compound. The formalities of Christmas, Easter and then the six-week hell of the summer break was not her favourite by any stretch. She would listen to some of the other girls talking about going home, and yet all she could feel was dread.

With her enrolled at Miss Porter's, there was one good thing and that was that her sire could not just whip Alix out of school without questions being asked. She made sure that she made friends with a lot of the girls: daughters of Congressmen, daughters of Senators, daughters of captains of industry, girls who would happily invite their Canadian friend on weekend trips to their homes, to meet their parents. Alix made a point of maintaining her grade average. She didn't do too badly at sports, and overall, ensured that if he were to try to take her out of school so he could mate his daughter to one of his allies, that questions would be asked. And when Alix did go home, she made sure to talk about all the girls with whom she mixed, and what they had done, and the plans they had for the following term ... yada, yada, yada

Alix knew she was sailing real close to the wind. She could see the tension in her father's face, and the look he exchanged with his coterie of followers, his enforcers. So, she implemented Stage 2 of her plan. The look on her sire's face when she brought home the letter from the New York State Police College was a sight to behold. Sixteen years old, and her grades, her aptitude, all her volunteer work in the community, her desire to help other people had been noted, and she was being put forward for a college scholarship to take a Pre-Law course, followed by Criminal Law as a major. The only way now to take Alix off their radar was kill her, and she was the Gosselin 'Princess', of value to him, and that value would vanish if she was dead.

He had looked at his daughter, and for a moment, Alix had held his gaze, before she had dipped her head to hide the hatred in her eyes, and said that she hoped he would be pleased at the advantages of having his daughter being in the New York State Police and being seen as a rising star.

For a moment, Alix thought he was going to lose it. Then he had laughed. "You win this time, little girl." He had come round his desk to where she stood, her hands folded demurely in front of her, her posture not challenging. As he lifted her chin, Alix swept the hatred for him from her face, smiled, hesitantly. "Just remember, my little Princess, you are only of value to me for as long as I say you are."

"Yes, Papa." Alix understood. You bastard, I understand only too well, she murmured in her own mind. If she could get into college a year early, she would, but failing that, as soon as she graduated, she was enrolling for summer school classes, and making sure that she had no reason to return to the compound.

New York State and New Orleans, 2005

The quiet and solitude of the workshop in Angharad's little shop was like a balm to her soul after the hectic pace of the Negrescu Hall, especially trying to hold the attention of the younglings during their lessons. The August sun broke through a patch of clouds and bathed the table in warmth almost to emphasize the bliss she was feeling as she crushed herbs, the room redolent with the complex aromas. The only mar in the peace was the quiet droning of the television.

She set aside the mortar and pestle as the news posted an update on that hurricane Katrina that moved through the Gulf of Mexico. She had many sister-healers in that area and some had planned to ride it out since the intensity of the storm had diminished. Angharad had tried so hard to dissuade them since the bayou area is sensitive to the storms, no matter how small they are but they had lived there for many years and ignored her concern. Katrina had moved inland so the first pictures of the aftermath were being broadcast and they chilled Angharad to the bone. So many stayed behind in areas already below sea-level but when the storm surge broke the levees, they became completely submerged. She could only watch in fascination as clip after clip showed people clinging to their roofs and huddling in the sports arena.

Her herbs were forgotten as she sat mesmerized by the devastation, helplessness and anger being broadcast. Her chest constricted in a deep need to go down there and check on Marianda and Lucinda. They were the only two healers so deep in the bayou that they may not have received warning of the unusual storm surge. "Gavril, I wish to speak to you about the Gulf coast and hurricane Katrina."

The three almost simultaneous deaths somewhere south of their home alerted Gavril to something unusual. They were the souls of older people, so not the Pack's usual category for harvest, but it was the way that they departed. A cry of pain which reverberated through the ether. Old they may have been, but it was not their 'time' to die. Then he heard Angharad's call.

[ML to Angharad] "I have felt something down there, Angharad."

Flashing over to her shop workroom, Gavril noticed the television and its rapidly changing images as the severity of the storm's impact became more apparent. It should not have made a difference, this Katrina as the storm was being called. It had been downgraded to a Category 3 by the time it hit Mississippi and New Orleans. Still the news programme showed the sight of the huge casino ships moored at Biloxi being forced ashore into the homes along the Biloxi-Gulfport shoreline, destroying the homes which lay in their path as if they were made of paper or the matchwood they became.

"You have friends down there, don't you, Healer? Other healers?" Gavril could see Angharad was almost vibrating with the concern she felt for her friends.

"Yes, two dear old sisters who live deep in the bayou. Most of the others have made their way inland or to sturdy shelter but with this..." Angharad's hand waved helplessly at the screen. "It's hard to tell where safe really is." She realized belatedly that she had begun to pace the floor, internally torn in two. "Gavril, I'm having an attack of conscience. I understand why we have stayed apart from the humans as a whole but I've kept my contacts through the holistic network and I feel a strong need to be of assistance down there."

Her eyes held his as she tried to gauge his feelings. Gavril was a caring soul but his first instinct was to protect the Pack and the Goddess knows they had faced too much turmoil at the hands of the humans. But after the planes crashed into New York City and elsewhere, her need to nurture and heal almost overpowered her so that she had spent more time overseas than at home. How would he react to her request? That was an answer Angharad wouldn't know until she asked. "Gavril, I must go to New Orleans, if for no other reason than to check on my friends. If you have limitations to my involvement in this calamity, then please let me know."

Technology had become both the friend and the bane of the Pack in this age, Gavril mused. It had enabled the Pack to function more in the background, using the power of the computers and the 'geek squad' run by Bran, but at the same time, the increasing proliferation of camera phones meant that it was becoming too easy for photographs to be taken of Pack members, photographs which would show their lack of aging, and might even show their ability to flash in and out on a 'now you see us, now you don't' basis.

Yet, when it came down to it, the Cŵn Annwn were under a geas from their Goddess, which included the need to protect the innocent. They might not be able to save everyone affected by what would become known as Hurricane Katrina, but they could help those who would have a role to play in protecting others. So Gavril made his decision.

[ML to Owain and Bran] "Join me in Angharad's shop. We need to deploy Sentinels to the Mississippi and New Orleans area."

If the Pack worked under cover of darkness, with the inevitable power black-outs which would occur, then they might be able to do some good. Gavril knew he could not ignore the cries of those whose only 'crime' was to lack the financial ability to take themselves out of danger.

"Healer, go, but be sure to work under cover of darkness. Be aware that we cannot allow humans to catch us on their damn phone cameras. I will sort out a team to go with Bran and Owain."

Casimir smiled to himself, as he watched the news broadcasts from the safety of his rooms in the Gosselin compound. There is a special kind of pleasure when one sees a project come to fruition, but even so his smile lacked something. Some you win, some you lose. This particular project was going to be a very profitable win for the Gosselin Pack and he knew his sire would be delighted.

It started with working to ensure that the shoring up of the levees was not seen as a majority priority. It was on the work-plan, make no mistake, but there were other things that required the limited public money and there will always be politicians, both local and national, who will lobby for a particular approach in return for donations to their 'campaign funds'.

Humans. They pride themselves on morality. These politicians who pray to their Christian God, who hold themselves up as paragons of virtue and good intent. Yet, if one of the Cŵn Annwn of legend were to read them, they would find a soul so black that it made them a target for 'harvest'. But that was legend, not reality. Reality was a crooked politician or two, who had delayed public works. It was only a matter of time before a storm surge would cause a problem, and when it did, the private engineering company in which Casimir himself had invested, unbeknown to his sire, would be on hand to effect repairs ... at a cost, of course.

Owain had been in the break room with the other Sentinels when Gavril's mind link call came through. For once the games consoles and the good natured ribbing that went with them was silent. All eyes were watching the unfolding situation on the television. They saw the devastation of landfall along the Gulf Coast, and the confidence that damage would be minimal, with it being 'only' a Category 3 storm.

"It's not the storm." Cerys' voice was a whisper. She had proven to have a strong affinity for the ocean currents and as such tended to do a lot of water-based rescue. "There's a tidal surge coming in." She spun round, grabbing Rhys. "Check your damn computer. The levees. The surge is coming now, and it's big." Her eyes took on a distant look and she started to shake as she fought a battle the others could not see. The distance was immense and Owain knew that to do her best work, she needed to be on the scene.

"Cerys, Gavril is sending a team down. I need volunteers." Hands shot up. "We are going to have to be bloody careful. Damn camera phones." Owain turned to Taren. "Brief Eira. We will need high energy food for us, but also for those who are stranded." Clapping his hands, Owain gave the order. "Move, people. And remember your training."

Angharad didn't realize how tightly her muscles were clenched until Gavril said those simple words. "Go, healer." The relief washed through her with such force that she reached to him for support. She was not normally a demonstrative person, sometimes needing to maintain a healer's distance to be objective, so when she wrapped her arms around him for a hug of thanks, it shocked them both. "Thank you Alpha. I'll prepare now." Angharad pulled back with a facial shrug and no little amount of embarrassment at her display of emotion.

The nod of her head was slight as I forced herself back on track to quickly revert back to a professional demeanour. "I'll head deep in the Eastern area of the Louisiana bayou to search for someone. I'll wait and coordinate with the others before moving into the more populated areas." She had been stuffing her travel pack as she spoke which took little time since she was always prepared. Angharad only needed a few things from Eira before leaving. "I'll be careful Gavril."

In the break room, Rhys' fists clenched in and out in a steady rhythm as the feeling of something bad coming overwhelmed him. He had learned to trust his instincts and so he couldn't ignore the impending doom of something. Surely the hurricane was not to blame. It was downgraded to a Category 3 but even telling himself that didn't stop the feeling that something was coming.

Cerys' intense whisper ratcheted up the sense of doom so that he felt it run across his skin in tingles. He didn't answer her request except to snort out a huff of air before spinning to his laptop. "Come on, come on." Hell, Rhys didn't know where to check first. "Hey, turn it to the Weather Channel and I'll check the local police channel in New Orleans." They had become adept at patching in places and working around their firewalls so he became very frustrated when there was nothing. "I think New Orleans is down for the count. I can't hack into their public safety system. It's like it's not there."

He decided to bring up the schematics and information on the last inspection by the Corp of Engineers to at least figure out if the levees could withstand a strong storm surge. "Damn." His softly spoken curse had Cerys at his back in an instant. "Look at the reports. Some of those levees couldn't handle a dog pissing on them, least of all a surge." He threw his arm around her trembling shoulders for his own sake as well as hers, when Owain made his announcement. There was no surprise at the number of volunteers. The younger ones knew they had to remain to guard the border and he could see the look of yearning in their eyes. If they thought like Rhys did then they felt the urge to make a difference. Use the Pack's extra powers to help those in need. This time he would get his chance.

Angharad flashed herself immediately to the home of Marianda and Lucinda but purposely remained invisible. They knew she was more than a shifter but she had never told them just what exactly so she clung to a tree and surveyed the devastation. Their stilted home was no more and Angharad's heart broke at all the years of work that has been lost. She could only hope they were alive so that she could share her sympathy and help them to rebuild. So many relied on their old remedies and special gifts and if she could help them, then she would.

Angharad didn't sense the presence of her old friends, alive or dead, in this area so she floated slowly in the direction the wind took in case they had been blown further inland. As she moved, she took in the wildlife tentatively coming out of their hiding places, the birds flying back to land and survey the area. She chuckled at the alligators and the sense that nothing fazed them. They're an ancient species that has weathered too many storms to give this one but a passing thought.

"There!" Angharad scented Lucinda right before her voice caught the Cŵn Annwn's ear and she hurried in their direction. The other woman held the body of Marianda and she was softly singing the spirit chant in an attempt to tether it to her weakened body. Angharad reappeared behind a large tree and softly called to Lucinda before emerging from the marsh. "Lucinda, I'm so glad I found you. I feared the worst when I saw your home." Her shocked eyes slowly changed to hopeful ones as Angharad waded toward them.

"Give her to me Lucinda and let me check her out." Such was the trust of fellow healers that she did not hesitate and Marianda was nestled in Angharad's arms. Quickly she checked inside and fixed the tear in the female's lung. She could not heal her completely or there would have been too many questions so Angharad concentrated on the major problems. Once her lung was repaired she found the head trauma and repaired the broken blood vessels inside. The rest she would have to heal on her own. "Her breathing seems shallow, perhaps the wind was knocked out of her. You are her closest friend so if you breathe gently into her it might help." Lucinda stopped her singing and did as Angharad asked. They both sighed when Marianda's breathing improved greatly.

"Angharad. How on earth did you find us?" There was no guile, only true astonishment at finding what would be considered a needle in a haystack. Angharad grinned mischievously and squinted one eye. "Well, the two of you don't exactly bathe daily you know." As she had hoped, this elicited a loud guffaw and we laughed the fear and sadness away, if only for a few moments.

Back in Negrescu Hall, Cerys watched as Rhys wheeled his chair towards his computer. All reports from NOA was that the storm, or as the humans called it a hurricane had been downgraded to a Category 3. However, Katrina was still a force to be reckoned with. The vision along with her own sense of doom hit her hard. Her whispers filled the air, as Cerys' body began to shake when she heard the soft curse spill form Rhys' lips. She knew this going to be bad. Looking over the male's shoulder, she read the reports quickly. The levees were at full capacity and there was a huge storm surge heading straight for New Orleans. The need to try to hold back the surge filled her with dread. The whole pack was humming with the need to stop this from happening. None of them like the feeling of helplessness, not least given that it was all but a part of their souls to help those in need through no fault of their own.

"Rhys, we need everyone on this. This surge is too big and it will be total devastation when it hits New Orleans." Cerys felt Rhys put his arms around her quaking shoulders as if to calm his fellow Sentinel. The vision of this surge when it hits if they could not minimize it, plagued Cerys. There would be parts of New Orleans that would cease to exist. All the buildings would be washed away and potentially millions of lives will be lost. The reports were coming in faster now and the need to act was becoming critical. When Owain's call for volunteers went up, Cerys' hand shot up with Rhys'. She knew that whilst she had some power over the element of water but she had to be closer if she was to make a difference.

As soon as the instruction to proceed was given, the Pack flashed en masse to the weakest point of the levees. Cerys' focus concentrated on the huge surge of water heading towards them. She couldn't stop it completely, but she could work on slowing its progress, giving the human authorities the additional time they needed to organise evacuations. With some of the streets flooded with water just from the storm, the human authorities were working under pressure. Cerys continued to work on making the surge smaller; inevitably, there would be flooding but there will be no help for that. There will be destruction however but not on the scale of what would have happened if they had not intervene.

Other members of their Pack were standing by to bring in supplies to those who have made it relative safety. As she felt Rhys' arm around her shoulders, Cerys murmured that they needed to move to higher ground. She had tried to mitigate the force of the surge, but they needed to move now. The surge was coming and the levees would breach. There was nothing more she could do. Rhys' grunt acknowledged the truth of the matter as he flashed them both to another area. All they could do now was wait and watch as the levees burst, as the water rushed through the streets, stores and homes, an unstoppable force of nature.

Rhys didn't claim to understand what it was that Cerys did, but damn he could feel it as well as the cost to her. Gavril had taught the Pack that nothing comes for free, everything has a cost. You either pay up front through sacrifice or pay after with interest and with Cerys' gift it was always the after with interest. That's why he had stayed near her, ready to catch her when she was done as he knew that something of this magnitude would take its toll.

Her weak whisper of warning was his signal that she was finished and needed to replenish her strength. Wrapping his arms around her, Rhys flashed them both to a higher elevation, keeping them invisible until he found a place not crowded with fleeing humans. "Cerys, we're safe now." He brushed the hair from her face and smiled. "You did good and saved many lives, now it's your turn to rest. I'll guard you while you eat and hopefully take a nap." Rhys sat with his back against a tree and held her as he rummaged in his pockets for the energy supplements Eira packed. "Now eat. The others have everything in hand thanks to you." She quickly ate the bar and they shared an energy drink. Both of them knew that nothing would give her the energy to jump back into the game. Still she fought the drain on her system, so intent on seeing if her powers helped in any way but it sapped her completely dry. Rhys' finger traced her jawline as he smiled and rocked her gently. "Your part is over for now. Sleep my friend."

Cerys could feel the desperation of all the humans still trying to flee the surge. Some were climbing onto their rooves others trying to cross the many bridges that would take them out of town. Even though she was close to exhaustion, Cerys knew there was still more to do. Supplies needed to be taken to those whom survived this storm that Mother Nature had wrought. Her voice sounded broken as she whispered, "Rhys I couldn't stop it all it was too massive."

Out in the bayou, Angharad was relieved when Marianda woke finally but she was incredibly weakened from her injuries. "Lucinda, we need to get her to your pack." She puffed up her chest and adopted her usual authoritative attitude. "They are not our pack; we are separate unto ourselves." Angharad rolled her eyes into a sardonic expression. "Your superior attitude has lost its zing when you're all covered in swamp slime." Her eyes narrowed but she said nothing. "Will they not take you in?"

"Oh they'll take us in and try to convince us to stay with them. Then we'll be inundated day and night with slivers and diarrhoea complaints." Marianda huffed out a weak laugh. "Don't forget Dante's boils." They both shivered dramatically and Angharad decided it was probably best to avoid asking any questions about Dante. "Well you can't stay here, your home is gone. Just stay in the village long enough to recuperate and then I will help you rebuild and restock your supplies. Ok?" They both agreed rather reluctantly and Lucinda helped Marianda onto Angharad's back. They did not need to know that, as a Cŵn Annwn, Angharad was able to use her powers to lighten the female's weight as they trudged through the mangled swamps.

Despite the slow progress, they were able to arrive at their pack encampment which had escaped most of the storm's fury. The guards stopped them before they got close and despite the healer's injuries, the young males seemed petrified of the females but bade them follow. "Please tell me you didn't threaten them with some made-up spell." Marianda began to snicker at Angharad's neck. "We have to do something to keep them from wanting to bed us hoping for power." Angharad snorted out a laugh and trudged on. "Well keep your legs together until you heal. As soon as I get you settled I must go and help the others. I promise that I'll return and work with you."

Angharad inclined her head slightly to the Alpha, aware that he knew she was more than she pretended and thus was not expecting her obeisance, and set Marianda down on a cot. "Good bye for now my friends. I have work to do." Her body blocked the view from the pack members as the three of them exchanged the secret healer signal. With a final nod, Angharad shifted to her wolf and ran far enough out so that they would not see her flash to New Orleans. "I'm coming Rhys." She yipped at his terse response to her tardiness.

It had been hard for Rhys to leave Cerys even though he knew she was fine but the Pack had to transport the boats out to the outlying homes still deep under water. "Angharad, where are you? We're in boats." He sucked in a startled breath when the boat rocked violently due to the smiling Angharad now seated in front. She turned to him with a smile. "I popped back to the manor for more medical supplies. What's the plan?"

"We've been delivering food and water to those trapped in their homes." Rhys spotted something white ahead. "Taren, over there." Quickly, he pointed to someone waving a white sheet. "It's good that the moon is out so we can see." They pulled the boats up to the partially submerged home and tied off to the guttering. "I'm sorry that we can't take you with us but we have food and water. Is anyone injured?"

"My wife got a bad cut on da leg and it doan look good." Angharad was already climbing from the boat with her bag. Taren gave her a leg up to the roof even though she could have flashed up there but they were all being careful to not tip off that they were anything but concerned citizens. Taren climbed up after her and Rhys tossed food and water for the family. He saw a small girl child peeking through a window so tossed a small stuffed wolf up too. Taren looked at him strangely until he jerked his head to the window and the other Sentinel smiled softly before turning to her. Leave it to the younglings to have thought of the children and instinctively know that even the smallest thing would help them cope. That's why Rhys' boat has a bag of toys along with the other supplies.

Angharad and Taren made their way back into the boats and they waved their farewells. "Hey Rhys, he said there was shouting straight ahead today. He thinks there is another family trapped." I nodded and fired up the trolling motor. Each of them checked the homes that they passed but so far nothing. "That house has a sheet on the roof." They pulled up as Taren began to call out to those inside. Soon a head appeared in the window and they tied up once again. They may not have made a large difference in the disaster as a whole but at least they knew that they had made a big difference to those they found. After the frustration of what was being called '9/11', it was enough to salve Rhys' conscience for the moment.

Back at Negrescu Hall, Aaleahya was making efforts in the gardens, picking all the vegetables and fruits then using her powers to encourage produce close to ripening to full readiness to help fill the boxes they were preparing to ship out for those in need.

As much as she wanted to be on the scene helping, she knew that her greatest impact was here, preparing the supplies. Gavril had also stayed at the Hall, perhaps because with the memorial garden and its link to decades of rituals, it was a source of power that he could tap and feed through to the Pack. Either way, the Pack was helping those in need and that was what mattered in the end.

Negrescu Hall, 2006

2006. Ordinarily, Gavril would not watch human television. He might enjoy going to the occasional movie with Aaleahya, since even when you have been together for over 100 years, it never hurts to have a 'date night' with your Mate. But, his attention was drawn to a particular series of rants on certain sides of human media services, with the caveat that they were known for pushing their own very slanted agenda.

When he had relocated the Pack to the Catskills, it was for several reasons. They had a property, purchased in 1938, which they had renovated to form their home. They had space to run. They had space to grow. Several of the children whom they had rescued had also settled in the area, America itself was all about freedom.

Cut across to 2006, and Gavril was walking past the younglings break room when one of them was flicking through the TV channels. The rant in question was on Fox News. Definitely not the most balanced view, but the younglings were able to watch it for that very reason. As Cŵn Annwn, they have to harvest the souls of those who would do evil. Evil is different things to different individuals.

It was a movie. A story. Not real. And yet, the way that they spoke on Fox News made it sound as if America was under threat for some heinous threat which would cause all to die in pain and agony. Having seen battlefield deaths, more than he suspected the television presenter had had hot dinners, Gavril had shaken his head. This movie, Brokeback Mountain, was hardly the end of the world, but it did deal with a story of growing 'concern' to some parts of society.

The choice of one's partner, be it someone of the same sex or not, was not really the business of anyone other than the couple themselves. Yes, for the Cŵn Annwn, that usually meant a male/female pairing, but it was not unknown for the pairing to be male/male or female/female. They had both within the Pack, and guess what? They could still perform their duties and the Pack had not splintered as a result.

This situation caught Gavril's eye for one reason. The sheer intolerance that was becoming more apparent. How was this world of humans changing? During the floods of Katrina, there had been the divide between the 'haves' and the 'have nots'. During the Woodstock concert, they had seen the irony that their memorial garden to their own war dead was desecrated by a group of 'peace-loving' hippies. This was not just in America, but world-wide.

Could his Pack still stay involved in the world and still be able to fulfil their duty to their Goddess? That was a question growing in Gavril's mind. Was the Pack still relevant and still needed in this modern era?

- x -

Later in the year, Rhys stood leaning against the tree watching the large Samhain bonfires send their embers to the black sky. There is beauty in fire and how the smoke reaches for the stars. A wiser man would draw a parallel with their hopes and dreams but sadly that man is not him. Rhys preferred to focus his mind on the here and now and let others dream of the future. His musing was interrupted when he caught sight again of young Nesta skirting around the shadows. She's been shyly dogging his steps all day which was surprising since even as a toddler, she had jumped recklessly into his arms. She would be about thirteen years old now. Coming into her own mind about now and perhaps that has her confused. The Pack matured a little faster than humans but females are females and have always confused him. And that little one is more confusing than most. When most little girls were frightened by Rhys' tattoos and hard look, she found curious humour in them, taking every opportunity to interact with him.

"That's it." He shoved himself away the tree to go in search of her. Her spying on him had kept her from enjoying this night long enough. "There you are; I've been looking for you everywhere Nesta. You look quite lovely tonight." The poor child turned beet red and she made a strange choking sound so Rhys stepped forward to comfort her. "Are you ok Nesta? Has anyone bothered you?"

"No, no. Nothing like that. You just scared me is all." She quickly brushed her hands down her dress and reached into a pocket. She was so still and quiet that he held myself back from saying anything, letting her set the pace of our conversation. He just hoped he could figure out what was wrong with her. Rhys was not prepared for her rapid fire words as she shoved something into my hand.

"Here, I made you this for Samhain since we celebrate and remember those we've lost and well the bonfires and all the special stuff that...well. I made that for you in needlepoint. See? That's you and that's your parents watching over you and it's all in the Samhain theme. Like I said and here I am repeating myself. And well. Now I gave it to you and I hope you like it and I'm going now. Bye."

Rhys didn't have time to process her words before she ran away into the darkness. Only then did he look down at the small tapestry she had made. A lone wolf stood before two pillars of flame. One larger and one smaller. She even stitched the fire's glow onto the wolf's pelt. "Nesta made this for me." Rhys' heart lurched at the childlike sweetness of such a gesture.

He vowed then and there that he would watch over her and the Goddess help any male that tried to take advantage of her.

Gosselin Compound Canada, 2006

Life is not a straight line. It has curves and obstacles, hills and valleys. It takes you through panoramic views then all the way down to the devil's den. Alix had managed to convince her sire to enrol her in Miss Porter's School. She had spent seven years of her life there. It had become her home, her sanctuary and true to the school's motto it had empowered her to become self-sufficient, confident and resourceful. Alix loved the new person she had become. No more the Gosselin Princess, a mating prize and little more than that. She knew that she had it within her to become a female of worth.

Looking at her own reflection, she smiled at the image before her. Her sire and her dam were coming to her graduation. They had never come to see her at the school. In seven years, there had not been a single visit. Modern technology had helped her mother clear her conscience by Skyping with her only daughter once or twice a month. They had come reluctantly but the Principal of the school had insisted and had explained the importance of attending during a personal conference call with her father. She explained that Alix would be the only girl graduating without her family present. They would be here only for the ceremony and leave soon after. Alix didn't care at all, they meant very little to her. Through her years at Miss Porter's school, she had gone home for the holidays and only for the holidays, and when she did, she had felt more and more like an outsider.

The last time had been her eighteenth birthday party. Her sire had invited all the available men, but by the end of the night she had managed to chase them all away. Her sire knew her resolve and for some reason or other he was allowing her to continue. Laurent had tried to intimidate her, but had failed. Alix may have given him his due as titular Beta, but her wolf had made it clear: she was no longer prey. However, Casimir was the same pain in the arse as always. In his mind, it seemed, his sister remained nothing more than a brood mare. Money was wasted on her. He made sure she knew that every chance he had. After all a brood mare did not need an education to breed pups. Casimir's views bordered on Neanderthal. Barefoot and pregnant, that's all females were good for and nothing else according to her dear brother Casimir. One thing was certain, she did not belong in Gosselin Manor. She belonged to herself, and that was perfectly fine.

Hurricane Katrina hit in the summer of 2006, with the school's proactive attitude, the girls were encouraged to volunteer to help. Alix had joined those going to New Orleans eagerly. The devastation the hurricane had done was apparent in every corner of the city. People walked with overwhelming dread in their eyes. Horrid conditions were evident everywhere. The fetid stench of stagnant water mixed with human waste and rubbish was at times difficult to bear, but she believed in what she and her fellow students were trying to do. Alix had been one of the first volunteers to come and one of the last to leave. Helping to clean up the stadium was a lesson in humility and mankind's determination to survive.

They were a group of six volunteers from Connecticut. She became friends with Sandy Dudek, from New York. Her father was associated with the University of New York. When Alix had confided in her, of her dream of going to college and becoming independent, she had never noticed the twinkle in her eye. She was instrumental in setting her friend up for an interview for a scholarship. All her hard work and dedication was paying off. As she stood in front of the mirror looking at herself with her graduation cap and gown, Alix decided that she liked what she saw. Turning her back to the mirror, she knew was not only leaving the school. She was leaving her old life behind and starting anew.

Amazon Rainforest, 2006

The letter had arrived at Negrescu Hall, causing no end of curiosity. The anonymous, relatively, sender coupled with it being from an area which Angharad was not known to frequent gave the younglings sorting the post a chance to tease the Pack's Healer. "Angharad, you have an Airmail letter from someone named "V". Do you have a secret lover? Hmmm?" She had pulled the letter from Eira's hand and smacked her on the shoulder to the giggles of the younglings watching the exchange. Angharad had widened her eyes and wiggled her eyebrows mysteriously. "A lady never tells." Then she had flounced into her workroom and ripped open the seal after looking at the return address. "V… Valentin." Her soft sigh was only audible to herself. Not even Valentin knew how Angharad felt about him. Because he was a shifter and she was Cŵn Annwn, not to mention he was a lone-wolf and she was pack oriented, a relationship would only bring heartache if pursued. "Enough of this, read Angie." She had glanced at the letter and grimaced, wondering if anyone could read this chicken-scratching. She hoped for his sake that he was writing on the back of a monkey with a tree bark pencil.

Dear Angharad. I am finally settled in with the Urarina here in the Amazon. No more moving about for me. You must come back to the Amazon. This new area is stimulating and I am with a group fighting the advanced deforestation. I have found the most startling information on ancient medicines used by the indigenous tribes. You would also love prowling about the pristine geoglyphs that have been covered by vegetation all these years. Don't bother writing back for I will not get the letter. Besides, I would much rather see you. I know you will find me, you always do.

Best Regards,

V

"Oh I'll be coming Val but it isn't because of the ancient glyphs or the medicinal knowledge." Angharad left a quick note for Gavril as he was away at the moment and grudgingly allowed Eira to pack her up with food and water. She acted like Angharad was going to walk there. "Thank you Eira. I'll be home when I can." All kitted up, she flashed to her usual starting point at the jungle village but stopped when the marked difference in smell hit her. The lush earthy scent had been replaced by diesel and unwashed bodies, a sense of sadness hurried her steps to the village store for directions.

It took quite a bit of persuasion to decline a guide and transportation but finally she escaped from the helpful merchant. Now? Her heart thudded in her chest as she saw the vast emptiness in front of her. Five years ago she had stood at this same spot on the outskirts of this village and touched the jungle. Now there was machinery and smoke from the burnt trees. A lone tear fell unchecked as Angharad mourned the beauty that was lost in the name of progress. A part of her wished she had followed the villager's directions and flashed straight to Val's location and bypassed this terrible sight. But in reality it helped her understand what he meant by fighting the deforestation. "Stupid humans are their own worst enemies." Angharad stepped into the shadows and flashed to the general area of the Urarina peoples to begin her search on foot.

After hours of walking both as human and her wolf, she caught his scent and quickly followed it to a small clearing. Angharad leaned back against a tree and watched Valentin putter about his little hut. He was truly in his element. He was all student and content to pass on what he learned but not enter the world to put that knowledge to practice. There lay the largest obstacle to them becoming a pair. She admired his firm backside as he squatted by the fire and grinned widely when he finally acknowledged her presence.

"Are you going to stand in the brush all day or come and join me Angie?" She barked out a laugh and stepped forward. "I was admiring the view." Her smile was challenging as he worked through what she said. His eyes widened in shock when he realized that since he was dressed only in a loincloth, his butt was on full view to her. Angharad stifled her sigh when he donned that sheepish grin that always made her melt. "So Val, are you going to hug me or just stand there in your Tarzan outfit?" Her smile turned a bit smug as she saw him register the change in her behaviour towards him. But she had thought long and hard about keeping her distance and decided that if she couldn't have him all the time, then she would take what she could get. He must have thought the same as he stepped forward and drew Angharad into his arms and sighed. Her heart pounded hard against his as she nestled her head into his neck. "Angharad." That one whispered word spoke volumes.

He drew back and looked her in the eye, assessing and questioning. She watched as his face registered a decision before he spoke. "If I kiss you right now, I'll never get to show you what I found." His eyes followed his finger as it traced along her lower lip. "Ah hell Angie. It'll be there tomorrow." He said no more as he pulled her face to his to show her that he too wished for more between them. Angharad moaned softly and melted into his embrace to lose herself in his lips. Their movements became frantic as they worked to remove her clothing, neither caring that they were outside. Her head dipped back as she groaned at the skin on skin contact and his heated mouth exploring downward to her swollen breasts. Angharad quivered in abandon as his teeth grazed her tightened nipple before he sucked it deeply into his mouth. Her fingers dove into his thick hair to anchor herself lest she fell down but she shouldn't have worried as his strong arm held her about her waist. Slowly, almost gently he laid the healer on the grassy knoll so that they could both give in to their desires.

"Angie. I can't wait." Angharad grasped his hips firmly and pulled him into herself. She had wanted and waited for so many years that she couldn't wait either. Their lips and tongues tangled as he made love to her, there on the ground in his beloved Amazon. "Val" Angharad thrust upward to meet his movements then still as the wave built and she let it crash through her. His groan of release almost sounded like a sob as he pulsed inside her sensitive body, both of them trying to catch their breath and no doubt both wondering about their future. His hands framed her face as he looked deeply into Angharad's eyes but whatever he was about to say was lost as he quickly kissed her and rose to his feet. "Come my Angharad, let's wash and then I'll show you what I have found." Angharad was a little confused at his change of attitude as she gathered her clothes and followed him to the stream. Perhaps it was best if she didn't ask. She recognized the look in his eye as one Gavril had for his Aaleahya and she knew she could not give him that.

It had been a week of pure heaven working side by side with Val during the day and skin to skin at night. How could her heart and soul be so divided? She would miss lying in his arms, relaxed and sated as they drifted off to sleep but she had to leave before the National Geographic reporter arrived. The large exposé on the effects of deforestation was important but she couldn't be involved. Val knew this but was harbouring hopes that she would change her mind and would remain.

"Angharad." He kissed her neck then slowly drew his lips to her ear. "Stay with me. Be my mate. Please. I love you." She worked hard to regulate her breathing as her chest constricted in pain but nothing could stop the tears that coursed down her cheek. "Oh Val." Angharad's voice broke so all pretence of strength was lost. "I cannot survive without my pack. It's who I am and what I am. I love you too Valentin but I cannot live here with you." His head rested heavy on Angharad's as he breathed deeply, his wet tears dropped onto her neck as he pulled her closer. "Angharad." His soft sob broke her heart but she could not change. "Val. I can come back and visit you but I cannot stay or put the strain of a mating on you and be absent."

He rolled Angharad onto her back and cupped her face gently in his hand. "I only ask one thing of you Angie. Don't come back unless it's to stay. Just don't come back." They both cried as he entered her, knowing this would be their last time together. Their combined tears brought a saltiness to their kisses and their lovemaking became desperate, almost trying to brand each other into their skin as they loved each other through the night.

Val was relaxed in slumber as Angharad carefully untangled herself and prepared to leave. She knew instinctively when he woke even though his eyes remained closed and she allowed him the safety of pretending. For both their sakes it was be easier this way. She gathered her belongings and stood over him, drinking in the sight of his beautiful face until the pain was too great to control her sobs. “I’ll always love you Valentin.” With that, she flashed home and locked herself in her room, hoping she could someday harden herself to prevent falling in love again.

Negrescu Hall, 2007

2007. Grabbing a coffee from the kitchen, Bran headed for his own sanctuary, the computer room from which he ran the research facility for the Cŵn Annwn and the business side of the Pack. With the growth in broadband internet, there was less and less reason for him to physically meet with the individuals running the companies in which they had invested in order to increase the Negrescu Foundation funds held and utilised to help others.

His day started in a way that, increasingly, was becoming the norm. Flicking on his e-mail programme, he took a sip of his coffee whilst he contemplated the size of his Inbox. Perhaps it was easier when communication was by mail, handwritten or typed communications, after all, Bran thought with a wry laugh.

Some things made him smile. There was a message from old Abe Micula, still overseeing the Negrescu Foundation to a certain extent, but this message was a picture: the photograph showed Avigail Micula's graduation, her parents proud that she had been the one giving the valedictorian speech. She had grown to a lovely young woman, there was no doubt, and she was clearly going to follow in her parents' footsteps with her plans to study law.

Some things were not so good. The advantage of having been around for a few years meant that Bran could not help but track the changes in the stock market. Bran had lived through the Crash of the 1930s and the subsequent depression, although living in the Carpathians at the time, it had not had a huge effect on them. Watching how the massive gains were progressing, Bran's cynical thought was that he would see the same thing happen again. As then, it would not be the corporations who would suffer. It would be the ordinary man and woman. He made a note to speak with Gavril about it. They would need to be on the lookout for those driven to kill themselves in despair, just as people had thrown themselves from buildings after the Crash.

There was one soul harvest which had been of significance for him this year: Barzan Ibrahim Al-Tikriti, the former Intelligence Chief and half-brother to Saddam Hussein of Iraq. Executed by hanging, and it could be argued that the fact that in a split second, he went from being a 'human' to a 'soulless corpse' as Bran harvested that particular piece of putrid spirit was a lot easier for him as a way to die than it had been for his victims during the time that he had been in power. Bran swore the Pack needed to have shares in companies manufacturing heartburn remedies. What made it worse was that he was just one in a regime. And the 'good guys'? They were not so good all the time. There were those who saw opportunity at the fall of the regime, to grab, to steal. A quick buck could be made by selling the treasure of a looted museum. It was legitimate situation of 'spoils of war' surely?

No, Bran contemplated the memory and recalled the relief he had felt on off-loading that particular harvest on Gavril. What he had seen in Iraq was not isolated to that country by any means. The world was definitely changing and he could not help but think that it was reflected in the increased birth rate amongst the Pack. There was only one reason for the Goddess needing more Cŵn Annwn, and it did not bode well.

Negrescu Hall NY, 2010

Aaleahya had been called to collect the souls of the innocents that perished unexpectedly. Far from calming, the situation in the Middle East held rising tensions, and as always, it was the innocent who were caught in the proverbial crossfire. Standing before her Goddess, Aaleahya shared the Goddess' disappointment with the humans. It seemed all they seemed interested in was what they could gain for themselves and not willing to the help those that really needed it. Returning to Negrescu Hall, Aaleahya found Gavril in his study with his two Betas. She stopped outside the door hearing the sadness in his voice, as he discussed with them that he was considering how to pull away their association from the humans,

Even as he was discussing disassociating the Pack from the human world, Gavril remembered the lives they had saved during the Second World War, even though it had been at a significant cost to the Pack: Ekaterina, Sandu, the parents of Rhys Jones and others in the Pack, all gone as they endeavoured to help others. It was not as if they might be mourned either, not by those whom they had helped. In some respects, it felt as if their efforts were not appreciated, but Gavril knew that such a sentiment was unfair. They could not tell humans whom they helped, so how could they expect them to care what happened to the Pack?

As Aaleahya joined them in the study, it was curious how her own thoughts echoed his. They had seen world changing around them. Apart from the issue of humans not knowing of the Pack's work around them, there was also the change in attitude. It had always been the case that 'worth' was the word used to measure an individual. How often was a conversation between two strangers started with "So how do you make a living?", or words to the effect of what do an individual did to make money. There had been more demand recently on the Negrescu Foundation funds, not that they were at risk, even with the plummeting stock values of the 2008 crash. It had made a dent, but not enough that they were wondering if they could continue to support those in need of their financial or material help. The Pack measured 'worth' based on the individual's soul. That was what mattered to them. But that was not how humans viewed their fellow man. Time and time again, they would see 'good God-fearing' humans, both men and women, who would turn their backs on those in need because of their lack of cold hard cash. How was that a good thing? Should the Pack continue to work in a world where worth was measured in this way?

Gavril rubbed his face against Aaleahya's hand, taking solace from the close contact with his Mate, explaining to her why he was even considering this decision. "Can we continue to serve the Goddess and fulfil the geas she has placed on us when mixing with those who care not for their fellow man? Should we keep ourselves separate, so better to be able to judge when necessary? It is a decision that will be difficult for the younger members of our Pack, but I must consider the whole Pack." He answered the question. "We may continue to help, but from a distance, rather than involve ourselves in the lives of those near us."

Bran looked uncomfortable, and Gavril knew that this was partly due to his interaction with 'his' children, the ones whom he had saved from deportation when we had operated in Eastern Europe. "The other thing you need to consider, my Alpha, is the rise of technology. More and more people will have camera phones. It is becoming too easy for people to take a photograph and not be noticed. The next thing you know is the picture is uploaded onto the internet, and people are asking how someone has not aged."

"And even worse, we end up with some damn cosmetics company thinking they have stumbled on the next 'blockbuster' anti-aging wonder." As humorous as Owain's words seemed, he had not been smiling. He had already made his thoughts clear on the greed of these large companies, both in the USA and abroad.

"I have not made a decision, my love." Gavril told Aaleahya. "However, a decision will be needed soon."

Aaleahya had listened to what they were saying and it was true the world was changing at a fast pace and it was becoming harder to keep what they were from the masses. The humans did not believe in what they could not explain. The fact that they never seemed to age was one risk factor that they have faced since their creation.

Mankind was not about hard work anymore but they were looking for the easy way to riches. Aaleahya nodded her head as she agreed to was being discussed. The Pack would continue to help those were worthy of their help but it would behind the scenes. Returning her Mate's caress, she told him that she would back whatever it was he decided.

New York State, 2011

Alix was meant to be free, to be her own person and rule her own life. University was an enriching and fulfilling experience. In Miss Porter's school she had become independent, in college she became a fierce competitor, winning debates, awards and excelling in her studies. Her communication with her family had slacked off. At first her mother made the effort to contact her daughter by Skype once a month, but with her busy schedule and extracurricular activities it became less and less convenient for Alix's mother to hunt her down and talk about the day to day activities of Pack with whom Alix had begun to disassociate herself. Thus, the chats became less frequent until they only managed to say hello during a holiday or a significant event. Alix had no doubt her sire was keeping close tabs on her: she was still the only female child of the Gosselin Alpha, but for some reason or another he had been discreet about it. She still received a steady cheque from the Gosselin Compound. That cheque went directly to a savings account that she had not touched since she began to work and go to school at the same time. That cheque was a monthly reminder of her sire's hold on her, and not having to depend on that cheque was her way of breaking that hold one month at a time.

Sandy, her close friend from school, had been developing her own career, before she became a journalist for the Times Herald for Middletown New York. Alix continued her own studies in criminal justice and forensics, landing a job as a traffic enforcement agent commonly known as 'meter maid' with the NYPD in the spring of her junior year. The uniform Alix wore resembled that of a police officer. With the new ordinance passed in 2008, assaulting a meter maid and or preventing her from issuing a parking ticket was considered a felony in New York State. It was a job, her first job and she was proud of it.

She had made a reputation for herself, and even though a meter maid was not what she had liked, Alix knew that diligent work would mean that she would slowly move up in the ranks. People tended to underestimate a fragile looking female like she appeared to be. Many a times motorist had attempted to dismiss her, based on her small physical stature, and destroy her fine. She had developed thick skin and perfected a menacing look using her shifter eyes. Most humans never noticed, and those that did would dismiss it as a figment of their imagination. As she moved up the ranks, Alix continued applying for a street cop position every time one became available.

After nine applications she was given the opportunity to try out for a motorbike cop. The NYPD Highway Patrol had many different designations. If accepted she would be investigating accidents, doing sobriety testing, traffic enforcement or stand watch in antiterrorist checkpoints among other duties. She had passed the written exam with a perfect score. Her psych evaluation was top notch, their only hesitation was once more her smaller physical size. She had to prove to the committee that a 'little female' such as herself could handle a motorcycle. The candidates for the selection had been assigned by rank. She was the senior ranking candidate of the all, so she was to be first to mount her bike and manoeuvre an obstacle course. She felt like she was walking the green mile as she passed each of the nine candidates. Through her peripheral vision Alix saw a few smirking at her, elbowing each other as she approached the beast of all beasts … so they thought. The Harley laid on the ground. The test was whether she could to pick up the nearly five-hundred-pound bike, mount on it and ride the course at speed chase speed.

Needless to say when Alix finished successfully the obstacle course in record-setting time, everyone was speechless. As she walked back to formation, Alix made a point of looking at the two bozos who had elbowed each other and smirked at her earlier. She winked at them and straightened her shoulders walking just a little bit more proud of herself. Sure, it could be argued that she had cheated a tad, using her additional strength as a shifter to complete the assigned task. Their eyes however could not deny what they saw. The looks on their faces would forever be in her memory, that much Alix did know. Boy was she going to enjoy being a motor cop!

Madrid, 2011

Daniela contemplated that had been a while since she thought she had left her dear family behind her. Now, in 2011, they mattered squat to her. "Daniela Acosta!" That name, that voice. It couldn't be.

She dropped the man whose life she was squeezing out, gasp by gasp, and turned to face two people she thought she would never see, ever again. She was face to face with her father Lorenzo and her older brother Diego.

"Hello sister." Diego greeted her as if he has any right to speak.

"Call me that again and I promise you will regret that Diego." Daniela replied coldly. There was venom seeping into her voice. "Neither one of you has any right to call me anything! Why the hell are you here?" She snapped at them.

"Well when we heard that someone going by the name of Daniela Echeverria was killing off my mob members I felt like I needed to put a stop to it! Why are you here *mi hija*?" Daniela sneered at the older man's words. Since when was she his child? Their relationship was an accident of biology, nothing more than that.

"I am here because you kicked me out of your precious little house *Pendejo*." Her response was curt.

Her eyes turned to Diego and she watched him lunge at her. Apparently he didn't like his little sister calling his idol by such a coarse name. Almost without effort, Daniela slid into a fighting position knowing she would have to fight her way to freedom.

When Diego attacked he was pretty straight forward about it, lacking imagination or flair. He didn't try anything to try and catch his opponent off guard, no doubt recalling the child she had been so very long ago. Dumbass. Daniela's thoughts were scornful as she easily countered his attack and threw him to his ass. Drawing the sword from its back-sheath, the weapon that had become the trademark of her kills, she inclined it at him so he couldn't get up.

"Try me Diego!" Daniela hissed, increasing the pressure of the sword to his throat fraction by fraction.

"Enough *Angelo della Morte*!" Daniela stepped away from her brother and back in front of her boss, who happened to be a ranking Capo in the Cosa Nostra. “May I ask what is going on and why my dear Daniela is so worked up?” The man places his hands on her shoulders, calming his pet assassin.

“Family dispute." Her father stated. “She is my daughter, he her brother. May I ask what it is you called her?” My father wondered.

“Angel of Death. It is very fitting for her.” Daniela smiled a little still holding onto her weapons. “Do you wish to kill them my dear?” Daniela simply nodded her head once, giving him the answer he sought.

“Very well *Angelo della Morte*. Enjoy your fun.” The man who was behind her vanished from sight although Daniela knew he wasn’t far away.

“If you kill us Daniela you will have not only the Spanish mob after you, but many of our allies as well.” Daniela was unsmiling as her sword rose again, singing in the air, to Diego, who was still on his back in fear.

“Let them come.” She slammed the blade through Diego’s throat decapitating him as she went. “I will cut down any and all people who threaten me or anyone who allied themselves with you!”

Wiping the blade of the sword casually on the clothing of her now headless brother on the ground, she sheathed it again, before taking a few steps past her dead brother. “You deserve this!” Her weapons left her hands faster than most humans could blink. The daggers found their way into her father’s chest and throat. He wasn’t dead yet, but he would be soon.

She walked over and knelt down beside the dying figure of the human that had sired her. “Maybe if you would have protected me you wouldn’t be dying right now. If I can kill you and Diego without hesitation, I can kill anyone who tries to get near me!” Daniela down at him with a sweet Madonna-like smile. Leaning forwards, she whispered in his ear. “Enjoy hell.”

Retrieving her weapons and cleaning the blood carefully on the clothing of her victims, she smiled again, an expression at odds with the coldness in her eyes. “Farewell.” She stated as she walked away, cleaning a last drop of blood on one of the daggers.

A reputation as a cold blooded killer. A psychopathic assassin. Different people had different career goals, but reputation was everything.

New York City, 2011

It was a beautiful Sunday morning on the Tenth Anniversary of 9/11. The streets had been cleared and all potential threats had been dealt with. New York had planned a series of events that included a memorial service at Ground Zero, what was once known as the Twin Towers was now a memorial to us all. The names of all who perished on that day were forever marked in bronze within the walls of the two pools where the Twin Towers used to stand. Alix was stationed at the corner of 48th and 8th Street where there was to be a memorial for all the firefighters that had answered the emergency call on that day. All fifteen firefighters gave their lives and were now being remembered by their families. This was a private ceremony. Her task was to keep the flow of traffic moving. She had been on her feet for nearly five hours and had not had a break at all. The precinct was shorthanded that day since the events were spread through the city, but it was all worth it. The brave men and women that went inside that building to try and help others were true heroes in her heart. Standing without any breaks was a small thing compared to what those people had done on that day.

As she waved the traffic away from the ceremony a Harley zoomed passed her completely ignoring her gesture to turn left. The guy had not even acknowledged her presence. "The arrogance, the gall of that biker to disregard me!" Alix muttered as she climbed onto her own Harley and gave chase. With her brows furrowed she was mentally going through the procedure of giving a citation. This guy was going twenty-three miles above the speed limit crisscrossing through cars like a bat out of hell. Alix didn't want to turn on her sirens until she had cleared a couple of blocks and then she let them be heard. They hurt her sensitive hearing but she had to make sure the biker wasn't going to cause an accident. She caught up to him on a red light. How would have guessed? The biker obeyed traffic signs. Alix motioned to him to pull over with her now famous look of 'fuck with me and you will regret it mister.'

When he pulled over, the male did not get off his bike. His shoulder-length, straight, dark hair was being blown by the small breeze and revealed a chiselled face and excellent posture. He didn't seem affected by the cooler air: his sleeveless 'cut' had Celtic design embroidered on it, surrounded by words she didn't recognise. Incongruously, he wore gloves, when he could have done a helluva lot more damage to himself with the lack of covering over his heavily muscled arms. Alix parked her bike in front of his. Her face was red with fury as she heard a slight chuckle coming from the male. She was sure he thought Alix had not heard him since she could tell it had been muffled somehow. Dusting herself off, Alix removed her helmet. Her hair had become undone and now waved freely framing her well irritated face which was glowing with shame. Without further ado she approached the male "Are you aware that you were going twenty-three miles above the speed limit." She informed him with triumph in her voice "And not only that, you ignored the block signs and went right by me as I was directing traffic to veer to the left." She never made eye contact with him.

Alix was too involved with the citation and her own embarrassment. When he spoke, he spoke with a foreign accent, his words had a lilt to them, like there was music hidden in his voice? The stranger was well versed nonetheless on the norms of such citation. Alix listened to him politely, feeling his stare on her. Unable to avoid it any longer, Alix made eye contact as she issued him his speeding citation, slapping to paper into his gloved hand, pulling her own ungloved hand back sharply as the arc of static electricity between them. She held his gaze for the briefest of moments and broke eye contact when the blaring horn of a dumpster truck sounded in front of her. Shaking her head, she replaced her helmet trying to make a makeshift bun out of her long hair. Turning round once more to the biker, Alix reminded him to make sure to pay for the citation and to drive safely. Getting on her bike Alix went to see what all the fuss was about as people gathered on the side of the dumpster truck.

That night Alix dreamt once more of her grey wolf. The one that had protected her as a child. This time however he was not in wolf form. He was a male. A tall male with enigmatic eyes that smiled at her. She felt a sense of peace and safety surround her like a warm blanket. Lost in the dream, Alix smiled as she hugged her pillow. Her dream took her to that clearing up on a grassy mound. She and her grey wolf were together, the way it will be, at least her own wolf was sure of it. She woke up the next morning with a grin on her face as she went in search of that six-inch figurine of her grey wolf. It was on top of the mantel where it always had been since she had moved to New York. Taking the figurine into her hands, Alix sighed as she remembered the sweet caress of her grey wolf, still so real across the side of her face. Placing the little figurine carefully on its resting place Alix went to work with a smile on her face.

Bran had chosen to be 'on duty' in New York for the 10th anniversary of the event which had seen the loss of 2,977 souls in one attack and its aftermath. The event was likely to be fraught with significance, and if a similar group had planned something to commemorate the attack for the wrong reasons, then Gavril had several of the Pack standing by to read the souls and thus intents of individuals, and if necessary, the instructions would be to harvest on the spot, if that would prevent even more deaths becoming associated with this particularly tragic point in the human memory.

Of course, it was essential for the Pack to blend in. Some were mixed in with the crowds. Bran himself was on 'mobile' duty. Courtesy of the growing number of Harley Davidson bikers who would accompany things like military funerals, the formerly reviled bikers were gaining a level of acceptance for their patriotic duties. For Bran, it meant that with his jacket in the classic style of Harley rider, he could pass for an accepted individual to be at an event such as this. His jacket was decorated with a stylised snarling wolf in the Celtic style and the irony of a logo incorporating elements of him being Cŵn Annwn. If only the humans realised what rode in their midst?

There was considerable police presence, not least because they had to control traffic. As he had come past the junction of 48th and 8th Street, where the memorial to the firefighters was to be installed, he had noticed a slender figure in the uniform of a motorbike cop. The hair in a bun gave away the fact that she was female. It had only caught his eye because underneath her uniform and protective gear, it was clear that she was quite a small figure. Bran had shrugged mentally. She must be able to do the job, or she wouldn't have been stationed there. He knew that many saw such duties as an honour, as their way of paying back the sacrifice done by other emergency workers, and it was all to the good. It was times like that which gave them pause for thought, that maybe the human race was not headed downhill as they seemed sometimes.

Still, cop or not, she was in his way. Didn't want to go left, not least since one of their younger teams needed him to check something that was causing them concern. They didn't want to harvest, because it might just be a grieving relative wishing to hurt those who had not lost someone. Weaving through the traffic, it registered that the female cop was following him. Glancing down at the speedo, Bran realised that he was doing ... 23 miles over the limit. Bugger! He pulled over, knowing that he would be the butt of humour when he returned to the Hall. It wasn't the speeding that would be the issue. It was the fact that he was caught speeding.

Clearly the cop was annoyed. Bran could hear that much from her surface thoughts as she rehearsed what she was going to tell him when she read the proverbial riot act to the "Hell's Angel" she was pulling over. Then it happened. Somehow, her leg became entangled in the stand of her bike, and she ... Bran believed the term is 'face planted' on the road. His snort of laughter was inadvertent, and he stuffed his gloved hand over his mouth to camouflage it. As she yanked her helmet off, her neat bun of hair had come undone, leaving her long dark hair around her shoulders. Not bad close up, Bran thought, before he realised that he was supposed to be serious about this. So, he composed his face, and when she asked Bran for his details, he gave his name, and his address, using the town address that the Pack held on record rather than Negrescu Hall. It made things a lot easier, if they listed an apartment address. Accepting the citation from her, Bran nodded at her stern instruction to pay the citation fine promptly, but his mind was already on the call for assistance by another team.

Bran knew he had best move if he was going to check both promptly. It wouldn't do to be given another citation for speeding. Two in one day would be just too much

New York State University, 2012.

August 2012. Her senior year. Caroline grinned at she realised that she had made it. She, Caroline Jane McKenzie had made it to her senior year of college and was on her way to the job that she dreamed of doing since she had been a kid. All her work had paid off and now here she was, standing in front of the college she had grown to call home. It just brought her so much joy to know she had it. She had made it to her last stage before becoming what she always wanted to be. Her professors have been so helpful these past years and she owed them everything. It was a great accomplishment to be a college senior here. Her parents were proud of her. They should be. She had never given up hope on her dreams even after the incident her sophomore year. She had been pretty shaken up and had even considered leaving but she had convinced herself to stay. She had worked her ass off to get here and nothing was going to make her back down now that she was so close to graduating. All she had to do was survive one more year.

Preferring to use her mornings more productively, Caroline had made sure not to schedule any morning classes. She preferred using mornings for studying and workouts. She still had to gain her black belt and she felt very motivated in the morning so it made sense to schedule her training with the morning timetable that I had. It only seemed reasonable with the energy she found she had in the mornings.

Arriving at the library, and swiping her pass-card at the door, Caroline waved at the librarian It was still thirty minutes before the library was supposed to open but she had become good friends with the lady who worked there. Moving to an empty table near the back of the sitting area. Whilst waiting for the laptop to start, Caroline pulled out a granola bar, holding it in her mouth, as her fingers moved over the keyboard once the laptop was ready. She wanted to check out some new martial arts moves for her training session that evening. Silently, practising the hand and leg motions, Caroline smiled to herself. What happened in her sophomore years was behind her, and wasn't going to stop her from living her life.

Paris, 2012

The years had flown by for Adhémar since he had left home. His new home in the trendy side of Paris suited his career in the fashion industry, with the side streets and their little cafes and galleries for amusement. Finally, he had a degree of security, away from the rule of his sire and crazy assed brothers. Yes, he missed Alix, but she had made out well and was now a police detective. Adhémar couldn't be prouder of her. The photoshoot directors are more than pleased with what he had done to date, the producers likewise and he was a firm favourite with the designers, with his looks seeming to fit with the mood of the moment.

Still, he couldn't help but smile knowing that the old man would have a coronary if he saw his youngest son at the moment.

His next gig was in Paris itself. As Adhémar was talking with a few of the other models, he heard his name being called by one of the body guards. Getting up, he walked to the door where he noticed an older man behind the guard. "Hey Adhémar someone is here to see you." He grinned, as he moved aside and Adhémar could understand why, when he saw his father standing there.

The look on his face was one of hatred and disdain. Rather than greeting his son, the elder Gosselin snarled. "You goddam pansy." Adhémar grinned, "Then, why don't you just tell it like it is, Papa." His father tried to push him as an Alpha, ordering him to return home. Adhémar rubbed his chin as if he was contemplating it, before growling his response. "No way in Hell. You want my help or presence then you can fucking beg for it." Adhémar smiled, as if he had just given the opposite response, knowing it would anger his sire even further.

That really wound up the older Gosselin, as he went to grab his son's throat, all thoughts of polite or restrained behaviour leaving him. As the bodyguard intervened, Adhémar saluted the old man who was huffing and puffing with indignation, at being stopped from laying his filthy hands on his youngest son.

Returning to the dressing room, Adhémar's mood was restored when the smiling designer informed him that she wanted him to wear the show-stopper outfit. Adhémar admitted to himself that the encounter had shaken him. He had thought he was free from the asshole but it seems too far from the truth. Still, this was his life now. Time for him to strut his stuff in front of all the reporters and buyers in the audience. This was what it was all about, the glitz and glamour and it paid very well. He didn't need his family's business. He was like his sister Alix, free finally of the abuse and corruption that surrounded them. If he told himself that often enough, he would believe it.

New York State University, 2012

Christmas break had come around and it looked like Caroline would be spending it alone on campus. That never bothered her anyways. Christmas was for family and loved ones and beyond a few close friends, Caroline didn't have anyone that counted.

The librarian came over to her cubicle to point out that library would be closing soon. Caroline thanked her and smiled, going back to her reading. It was just getting dark, as she left the library and walked through the campus towards the street. Realising that there was a definite scarcity of taxis, she decided she might as well walk back to her apartment.

She heard jogging behind me and then a male voice was heard in my ears. "Need some help?"

Caroline turned to see a male jogging closer before he slowed to a walk. Caroline raised a brow and looked at him. She recognized him from around campus and nodded. "Uh, yeah. These damn taxis never pay attention to people flagging them down. It sorta drives me nuts on nights like these." She sighed, rubbing her hands together trying to get some warmth in them.

"Well here, maybe I can help. Sometimes you have to do more than just flagging them with your arm." He smiled at the young woman before walking to the side of the road and he placed his thumb and pointer finger in his mouth and whistled. He waved his arm and a taxi slowed and stopped beside them. He turned to her and smiled. "See, what did I tell you."

Caroline was impressed. "Wow. Impressive. I guess I'll have to try that." She looked at him. "Well, I'll see you around..." She felt clueless. She didn't know his name and felt rude for not asking when she first spoke to him.

He smiled and looked at Caroline. "You know, we can share the taxi. It would be easier for the both of us. We will split the price and you can get out of the cold. What do you say?" He opened the door to the cab and flashed her a smile. He seemed like a cool guy and it would be nice to not have to walk home in the cold tonight. "I'm Logan, by the way."

"That sounds like an awesome idea. I'm freezing." Smiling, Caroline walked towards the taxi and climbed in, sliding over so Logan can get in. Once he was in, he shut the door and turned to look at her. Caroline smiled. "I'm Caroline by the way. Thanks again for sharing the cab. It means lot." And it did. She hated the cold and she would have walked home if he didn't offer to share.

Logan smiled and looked at her. "Oh, I know who you are. I've seen you around campus and library a lot." He looked at the driver and then looked back at Caroline. "Would you want to get a coffee before you head home? I figured a coffee would be the perfect thing to warm those chilly hands of yours." Caroline agreed to the coffee and he told the driver where to go.

"Oh really? Yeah I like to spend a lot of time there because I just love to read." Caroline looked at him as she rubbed her hands together, trying to keep them warm. "So Logan, what were you doing on campus. I mean, it is Christmas break. Shouldn't you be home with family?" She brought her hands up to her mouth and blew some hot air onto them, her eyes never leaving his. Useful trick from her martial arts classes. She wasn't going to be caught out again, like in her sophomore year.

Logan smiled at Caroline and reached forward, grabbing her hands and rubbing them gently as he gazed at the young woman. "Well, to be honest, I've been waiting for you. You see Caroline, I've liked you for a while. You are just so cute and kind. I've seen you help out the freshman all the time. I also think you are so smart and your laugh, it's just so adorable."

This came as a complete shock to Caroline. No guy had ever shown any sign of interest in her and when a guy did, they simply tried to get in her pants. But here was Logan, who seemed completely different. It didn't matter though. She would never fall for a guy simply because he was giving her compliments, even if they were sweet and meaningful. She smiled faintly and looked at him, pulling her hands away from him and placing them in her lap. "Oh, well um..." Caroline was at a complete loss of words. "So, how about that coffee?"

Logan chuckled. "Alright, I get the picture. You're new to this. It's fine." He looked at her and then looked out the window. They just pulled up to a coffee shop. Logan smiled and motioned out the window. "The coffee is inside... Come on." He climbed out of the cab. He walked around and opened her door up for Caroline and even offered her his hand. His hand seemed to have snaked up and was now resting on her lower back. Pointedly, Caroline removed it as they reached the counter.

Over coffee, they chatted about family, school and life in general. No rush, no fuss and Caroline admitted it was kind of relaxing. As they finished up, Logan smiled, tossing his coffee in the trash. "Alright, well let me walk you out, make sure you get a cab." He looked at Caroline as she stood up, smiling. "I had a great time Caroline. We should do this again soon." Caroline nodded. It was nice to get out and just talk. She might definitely consider meeting up with him again. Or maybe not.

"Logan. You are sweet but I am really not looking for a boyfriend or anything like that." He looked down at her a bit disappointed in the rejection. Hearing footsteps approaching, they both turned their attention to three guys walking towards us and it was easy to see they weren't friendly. Logan instantly placed himself between Caroline and the offenders. Dropping her bag to the ground, Caroline held her arms loosely at her sides and waited to see what was going to happen.

The three guys came over and looked at the two of them but Logan stood firm. The guys were asking for all their money, the biggest guy there had a knife and Logan noticed it right as Caroline did. "Caroline... Get in the cab. I'll take care of them." She raised a brow and looked at him. He could take care of them? Who did he think she was? Some small town girl who can't fend for herself? Hell no. Caroline wasn't going anywhere. Her days of running were over. And she was going to make sure Logan and the three guys here knew that.

"I'm good right here, thanks." The three guys kept urging for the money. Logan looked back at her and yanked her bag off the pavement. He was seriously going to give into these guys? What the hell is wrong with him? Caroline couldn't believe what she was seeing. He is lucky she didn't drop him right there on that sidewalk.

Logan pulled out her wallet from her bag and started to fish through it, trying to extract all her money. He glanced back at her. "Seriously Caroline, this is no place for a woman." That was it. Caroline lost it. She hadn't spent hours and hours of martial arts training to be told that it's not a woman's place. She was so fed up with men thinking it's their damn job to protect her. She was a strong independent woman and she could protect herself just fine, and that is exactly what she was going to do.

The three guys started to threaten Logan, telling him if he didn't hurry up, they were going to have some major problems. Caroline couldn't believe this, how easily Logan was going to cave in. "Oh for fucks sake!" She kicked her leg out and hit Logan behind the knees. As he fell to his knees, Caroline planted her hands on his shoulders and jumped over him, snapping a sidekick at the middle guy with the knife, catching him under his chin. He stumbled back and dropped the knife. She moved forward, kicking the knife out to the street. As one of the others tried his luck, Caroline ducked as he threw a left hook towards her head. As she dropped her stance, she sent a swift right punch to his side before shooting upright again to send a forward kick to his chest, resulting in him stumbling back into his two buddies. She looked at them and narrowed my eyes. "What are you waiting for? Get your asses away from me!" The three guys exchanged a look before turning running off.

Caroline turned back to Logan, who was still on his knees, wide eyed. Walking over, she bent down and retrieved her bag, wallet, and money that fell from Logan's hands. She looked him right in the eye. "I do not and will not be protected by any man. I can do that myself. Be sure to remember that." Moving towards the cab, she climbed in and left Logan behind, too irritated right now to deal with a man.

New York State, 2013

It has taken less time that Alix had thought possible. Chance it seemed meant that she was able to be noticed by the right people, able to take the right exams, so that the day came when New York BCI had accepted her transfer. As she walked the stairs up to the precinct for the first time Alix couldn't help but reminisce all the great moments she had experienced in college and her career to date. Her petite stature notwithstanding, her look was going for mature and responsible looking female. Checking her reflection on the glass doors she sighed and opened the door to her new job, her new future, her new life.

The precinct was a labyrinth of halls. Announcing herself at the front desk she was escorted to meet the "Captain." The female officer gave her a once over. By the harsh look on her face, she had assessed me unworthy of such position. According to her, Alix should not be disappointed if the Captain dismissed her on the spot. Arching a brow at her, zipping her mouth and curbing her temper, Alix kept a non-committal look on her face. She had spent all her life being underestimated by her sire and her beloved brothers, apart from Adhémar. If Laurent and Casimir would have had their say in her life, she would be nothing more than a brood mare. Any thought of a career would have died a death.

As they approached their destination Alix saw two men in a heated argument. One of them was blaring down hard while the other bit his lip and replied in short but even staccatos while the former stopped talking to catch his breath. To Alix's dismay they stopped in front of the two males. Officer Valdez introduced her simply as Alix Gosselin, not giving her the title of Detective that she had worked so hard to earn. Shrugging off the officer's lack of professional courtesy, Alix extended her hand not sure which one was the infamous "Captain."

Her heart fell a mile deep when the male that had been arguing at the top of his lungs introduced himself simply as "Captain." She waited for him to say anything else. Precious moments extended into an uncomfortable silence, as it became apparent that any other name would not be forthcoming. Clearing her throat, she introduced herself. "I am Detective Gosselin reporting for duty, sir."

Both men chuckled at her remark. The Captain looked at Alix as if to say she didn't fit the description of what he was promised. His reply confirmed her assessment of the situation. "There must be a mistake. Cadets training is on the third floor. Go... Run before you are late for your first class, hun." Alix stood her ground and cleared her throat once more repeating her previous sentence with a bit more emphasis this time on the words detective and reporting. Perhaps her upbringing at the tender hands of her brothers had served a purpose in that she was willing to stand up to 'authority' when necessary.

The Captain burst into a guttural laughter that resonated throughout the room. "Petersen, am I being punked?" The Captain asked the male that had been standing next to him arguing just moments before. "No sir, not that I am aware off." Peterson looked at Alix with pity in his eyes so briefly that she doubted it was meant for her to see, but she had seen him and it had moved her to have an ally in this battle that it seemed she was about to face. The Captain turned his attention towards Alix. "Well then missy, it seems that I must have gotten the short end of the stick with you. Tell you what. Since both of you are here and I have no desire to babysit a newbie Petersen here will show you the ropes." Turning his attention to Peterson the Captain said with a smirk on his face. "Petersen meet your new partner."

Jake had been furious when he had first received the Captain's request to discuss his new assignment to the Vice Division. Storming into the Captain's office, he had managed to compose himself just in time. "You can't be serious! You know how hard I worked to build my street cred! I'm Homicide, not Vice dammit!"

"We're one heavy in this department and Vice requested you Petersen so suck it up." Had been the Captain's terse reply.

"Suck it up? They want to partner me with Johnson!" Jake's voice hissed through his clenched teeth. "Johnson's a 'hey world look at me' asshole!" Jake swung his arms in the air, vaguely noticing some girl in the doorway but not caring. "If you let them pair me up with him, I won't be held accountable for my actions." Jake pounded his finger on his desk for additional emphasis. "I'm not kidding."

"That ain't your call now is it, Petersen. Maybe I need to remind you of which side of this fucking desk you sit on!" His bellowing voice should have cowed the other man but Jake was too intent on getting the orders changed to care much. That's when the Captain noticed the girl. She introduced herself and Jake couldn't help but check her out. Her eyes were sharp but he could sense a desire to prove herself and that never bode well for the newbies. At least she looked like she had the cojones to live through that learning process.

Just as she was enjoying the thought of the older detectives breaking in a new one and a female at that, the Captain announced he was the sucker training her in. Jake's head spun to him with mouth hanging open. "Seriously? I thought I was going to Vice with asshole." Jake nodded to woman in deference. "Sorry, I meant Detective Johnson." His lip was still curled from saying the asshole's name when Jake turned back to the Captain's grin. Jake knew right then and there that the Captain was loving whatever he was about to tell his flustered Detective.

"I already told Vice that they couldn't have you, they get Lane instead, so suck it up Petersen and get back to work."

"Then what the hell was this all about?" Jake was so shocked that he couldn't even yell. It made no sense arguing for nothing. The Captain just grinned and leaned back in his chair as he sat. "It's like this Petersen, my wife pissed me the hell off this morning and since I can't yell at her like I want, I bring it to work. You were…. convenient." He made a shooing motion with his hand and turned to look out his window. "Now get the hell out of my office and get to work. Both of you."

Jake turned to his new colleague and shrugged. He guessed there were worse partners. He just hoped she didn't get him killed or mess up his life in any way. "Ok, Gooseling is it? Like a baby goose?" Jake jerked his head down the hall figuring she could talk and walk.

Like she hadn't heard that joke about her name before. Alix smiled sweetly at the Detective, thinking that her teachers at Miss Porter's would have been so proud of her. It was her passive aggressive look that she had mastered through the years of holding her tongue with her sire. Keeping pace with her new partner, Alix observed his body language. He was miffed at the Captain. A fact that was completely understandable, but Detective Petersen was also not surprised that he had been saddled with her. The look he had given Alix told her he would not cut her any slack, which was perfectly fine with her. His long strides took two or three quick steps of hers. Alix wished now she had chosen a sturdier pair of shoes instead of these pumps that clacked as a sprinted after him.

Arriving at what she assumed was his desk the phone was buzzing. Alix saw him pick it up and answer in a fastidious way. Petersen had no way of knowing that Alix could hear both sides of the conversation going on. Apparently a body of a young woman had been found in Lover's Peak. The operator was giving Detective Petersen the 411 on the case. Alix noticed he didn't write anything down. Apparently he was not planning on sharing any information with his new colleague. Instead of acting childish and crossing her arms and tapping her feet, Alix sat on the chair in front of his desk and amused herself with the little nic-knacks he had on top of his desk. Alix took a perverse pleasure in touching everything and leaving the various items just slightly askew or in the wrong place just to see how her new partner would react. Alix smiled to herself as she saw a picture of him and what she assumed was his father, since the resemblance was evident.

Waiting until her new partner had finished his phone call, and smiling sweetly Alix suggested they get started. “I have my badge and my gun. I don't know where my desk is, but I'm sure you won't mine sharing. I don't take much space after all." Alix was about to add a snarky remark about the nic knacks on his desk when a young pretty thing approached them. Once more Alix was scrutinised and deemed non-threatening because she just simply ignored the younger woman’s presence all together. "Jakey-poo when are we going to go for that drink you been promising me? I keep asking you and you keep ignoring me." The female said rubbing her ample bosom on the side of Petersen's shoulder. Alix could not hold a chuckle as she saw his face. She should have not laughed, since it probably made matters worse, but it was just so funny. Seeing that woman throw herself at Petersen when she had seen him just a few moments before butting heads with the Captain.

Containing her laughter to a small sigh of mirth Alix made a mental note to ask Detective Petersen for the Captain's name, not least because the Captain hadn’t introduced himself. So, she waited and wished she had popcorn so that she could better enjoy the show that was about to unfold before her eyes.

Jake didn’t mind the thought of a new partner but a young pretty woman was going to add a new wrinkle to his work on the streets. Developing those connections had helped unravel a few crimes and homicides through the years. Jake certainly didn’t want to have to bust their balls for pawing her and losing that edge. He sighed in resignation. He didn’t have much choice and she of the clacking shoes seemed intent on wedging herself firmly in the Unit so what the hell.

The phone was jangling when they reached his desk and instead of ignoring it, he answered it when he saw Dispatch’s line was lit. They only called directly when it was something hot that needed their attention so Gosselin could cool her heels for a few minutes while Jake took note of the deets. He didn’t respond much as they told him of a female body, already scavenged by animals up on Lovers Leap. Jake’s mind was divided by what details they had and the fact that his new partner was messing with the shit on his desk. She met his eyes and all Jake could do was raise an eyebrow to let her know the point was taken. Hanging up the phone, Jake was about to light into her for rearranging his stuff when Ellen walked in.

“Jakey-poo …” Jake cringed and wondered what planet she lived on to think that was even remotely attractive. To make matters worse, she had him trapped against the desk rubbing those padded boobs on him. Christ, give the woman a pole. Since she was hired in the clerical pool, she had worked her way through the ranks in this Department looking for a sugar daddy and there was no way he would dip into that pool. “Ellen.” Gently, he removed her hands from his arm with a half-assed smile. “Gotta work girl and you." Jake tapped his finger on her nose. No sense pissing her off since she was cousin to the Commissioner. "You need to behave. I'm having to walk the straight and narrow here and you look like trouble to me." Jake grinned wide and gave what he hoped was a resigned smile. "Oh, there is something you could do for me though. We need the paperwork on my new partner squared away. Names Gosselin." Jake pointed to Gosselin. Hell, he admitted to himself, he didn't even know her first name yet. "She needs a desk of her own too." Jake stared sardonically at Gosselin and jerked her head to the door. "Come on partner, we need to go."

Ellen sputtered a bit then shoved her fists on her hips. "Don't you think that is Captain Szczepkowski's job to order that stuff? Hmm?" Well hell, now Ellen was pissed and Jake had no wish to listen to her hissy fit. That's when a thought crossed my mind and he smiled widely. "I just wanted to catch you before Johnson comes up with another request for your time. You know how much he likes you and monopolizes your time." Her eyes lit up at the mention of Johnson's name and Jake could see her mind at work thinking his dismissal was in deference to the fame-hungry fool from Vice. Damn Jake loved that shit. "Gotta go Ellen."

Alix and Jake walked quickly from the room and Jake smiled at his new partner. "I noticed your face when she said the Captain's name. It's probably the only time you'll hear it too because he hates when you butcher the pronunciation. It's easier to just call him Captain. Hell, it's bad enough that we have to spell it on the reports." They reached Jake's unmarked car and he stopped to eye her over the hood. "Need your name too. Full name if you please and then I'll fill you in on where we're going." Jake slid into the driver's seat and waited for her to answer.

Ok, Alix decided, she had to give props to Detective Petersen. He knew how to get himself out of sticky situations. He had handled "Ellen" as a pro without ruffling her feathers and Petersen even managed to get her to find her a desk. Very smooth and very effective. Her enthusiasm didn't last too long. Petersen sprinted out of the precinct like his ass had caught on fire. He just assumed Alix would be his obedient dog and would follow him. He assumed correctly. Alix made a mental note to buy some cross trainers, considering the pace at which her new partner walked.

When they reached his vehicle Jake said something to Alix about needing her full name with a promise to fill her in about their first case. Alix almost smirked at him. She had heard everything that had been discussed on the phone, but of course she had to pretend she was clueless. As Alix fastened her seat belt, she made a point of introducing herself properly, giving Jake her name and making sure she enunciated her last name in her native tongue of French. "Alix Gosselin. Do you need me to spell it? It's French. I know some Americans have difficulty pronouncing French words."

After her little speech Jake was true to his word and updated her on the crime scene that they were about to investigate.

Jake took the time to turn a droll stare her way during the lesson in French as they drove to the crime scene. He thought it odd that her eyes didn't register surprise at the information but mentally filed that away for later. "Ok, I'm sure you know the drill." Jake hopped out of the car and flashed his badge. They knew him but rules are rules. Besides, Jake didn't want them to have to ask Alix for her creds. It's ok if he gave his new partner a hard time but it didn't mean that anyone else could take the same liberty.

As a shifter, Alix was accustomed to seeing bodies in many stages of decomposition, but seeing a pretty young girl in her mid-twenties, mauled and left in a pile of rubbish was something that she knew would stay in her mind for all eternity. The victim had been fully clothed. Her face was intact and you could see the look of surprise still frozen in her features. The attacker had come from behind and from the massive wound on her neck he had severed the artery. This had been a kill bite, and Alix knew immediately it was from a shifter, although she couldn't pick up a scent no matter how hard she tried. Of course, humans made up their own stories to explain bizarre wounds like this one. Alix listened to her partner as he analysed the crime scene. However, her mind was thinking why would a shifter kill a female? Females were cherished.

The victim's name was Emily Chavira. She was a college student and had been missing for ten days. Her family said she was a quiet girl and did not have a boyfriend. With very little leads the case went through the routine initial investigation. The police department was convinced it had been a wild animal attack. Even forensics had confirmed the cause of death was from an animal bite to a major artery. In their minds the case was solved. In Alix's mind it was not, so she began to snoop around some of the cold case files, wondering if this wasn't just one of many similar, and as easily dismissed attacks.

Alix and Jake walked the scene perimeter as the medical examiner finished with the corpse. "Whatcha got for me Doc? Doctor James stood and shook his head sadly.

"Hey Petersen." His eyes landed on Alix in question so Jake waved his hand in her direction. "This is my new partner, Alix Gosselin." Jake leaned forward with a small smile. "If you need help with French, she's the one to ask." He didn't give Alix a chance to pipe in before pointing to Doc. "This is Doctor James, Coroner and Medical Examiner deluxe." Due to the circumstances, they didn't shake hands before he went on with his report.

"What bumfuzzles me is that the wounds don't look post-mortem." He stopped for a moment in thought. "Something about this reminds me of another case a few years back. You worked on it Petersen." He exhaled loudly and shrugged. "Hell if I can remember what it was though. I'll know more when I get her back to the table. Now move, we're pulling her out." He zipped up the body bag and stood back as they wheeled it out from the crime scene.

Alix wandered around the area and checked things out. Jake wondered if maybe she was coming down with a cold as it seemed she was sniffing a lot. She didn't show any signs of crying, thank God. Jake had gone through that with a rookie about five years ago and he never recovered from the teasing. This kind of work was not for everyone and Jake was kinda glad she did so well. Now they would see what kind of detective she'll make.

Alix recalled afterwards, stuck in the cubicle of an office in which she found herself that sometimes life takes a body into a journey of self-discovery and sometimes your boss drives it into fast forward in an instant. Her first few weeks as flatfoot were as normal as any rookie detective would expect. Detective Petersen still kept being stern with her; even though she had caught him once or twice giving her a nod of approval when she had proven to be of use. She was slowly fitting into the groove of things. Alix had been given a desk tucked away in a corner, something she did not mind at all. With her sensitive hearing it was easier for her to disconnect from the rest of them and concentrate on her obsession, investigating on her own all those cases which were classified as missing person followed by cause of death being 'animal' related.

Ellen came that morning with a smirk on her face "Captain Szczepkowski wants to see you in his office IMMEDIATELY." She said the last word loud enough for everyone to drop what they were doing. A pregnant silence and the glare of each detective, secretary and visitor that was present followed Alix as she made her way through the maze of desks and people. Petersen was giving her a 'what the fuck' look. Alix shook her head and smiled at him. He could tell he was not buying her calm cool and composed act, but Alix wasn't going to panic, after all, what's the worst that could happen?

In truth, Alix felt like she was walking the green mile into her doom. The Captain was at his door. His face was red and his body language and scent told her he was beyond pissed. As a shifter, Alix knew the importance of eye contact. She had promised herself once she left the family home that she would not prey so her gaze never faltered as she approached the Captain "You needed to see me Captain?"

The Captain motioned for her to walk into his office and sit down. I heard him say to someone "Hold all my calls" and then he quietly shut down the door. "Detective Gosselin." He began as he dumped a stack of files in front of her. "I've been told you have had so much spare time in your hands that you have taken it upon yourself to reopen cases that have been solved. Since you seem to know your way around and think that you require no permission from your superior, I have made a new position that I think will fit you perfectly."

Whilst Alix smiled at him, she admitted to herself that she didn't have a clear understanding what he was saying. To her, his words sounded like she was being awarded a special position, but his scent and body language told her a totally different story. She had occasions to experience such duality from humans before. Sometimes humans said something totally different then what they really meant. A sense of dread filled her as she realized what the Captain was telling was not good news at all.

The Captain snapped his fingers in front of her "Gosselin pick those up and follow me." The Captain motioned to the stack of files. She rushed to pick up the almost two feet tall stack of heavy files. For a human female such task would have been difficult, for her it was no big deal. She had finally bought shoes that would allow her to walk quickly without clacking, so she had no problem following the Captain down a labyrinth of poorly lit hallways and a flight of stairs into the basement of the precinct. He stopped at the end of the hall and unlocked the room. A heavy smell of mould and dust assaulted her nostrils and Alix sneezed loudly. The Captain said nothing. Turning on the light the Captain motioned her to walk in. The room was filled with boxes of all shapes and sizes. There was an old wooden desk with a chair that had seen better days. The lights flickered off adding to the ambiance of this musty old room.

"This is your new office Detective Gosselin. You are now in charge of a special unit. Here are all the cold cases the precinct has not been able to solve. I expect a report on my desk by the end of each week. Make sure you don't disappoint me." Tossing the keys on to the desk he left, slamming the door behind him.

Negrescu Hall, 2013

Aaleahya had been summoned for another soul collection, her heart breaking for this innocent soul, a month old infant, left in a city parking lot while his mother partied the day away She was a drug user and never took into consideration that the infant would overheat in a locked car and effectively boil to death. Aaleahya could hear the tiny soul's screams as it was cooked alive. She had flashed to the car the infant sitting in, ironically strapped into a good quality child seat. He was a handsome boy, his expressive eyes looking at Aaleahya, first afraid, then his bright blue eyes changed and the look of trust entered them.

She was able to coax the tiny soul to come to her, and watched as it floated towards her, towards her outstretched arms. She felt such anger towards a mother who could leave a defenceless child in a car in the city with temperatures reaching well over 100 degrees.

Aaleahya had cradled the tiny soul against her chest, then absorbed it into her body for safe keeping. The silent cries changed to coos of contentment, whilst the feel of the tiny arms clutching Aaleahya's own soul seeking love and comfort reminded her only too well of her own lost child. Aaleahya's soul comforted the tiny one she had been honoured to collect for her Goddess.

As she was about to leave the scene scented with the infant's death, she heard the sobs of the woman the police now had handcuffed and were escorting to the back of the police car. She never looked towards her own car to see if her baby was alright. She was so hopped up on whatever type of narcotics she was using that she had no concern for anyone else other than the fact that she got caught using.

Aaleahya heard a policeman remark that this was her fourth arrest in three months, and that he hoped the judge would throw the book at her. She could see several policemen peering in the car where the body of the baby boy was still strapped into his car seat. Some had tears trailing down their cheeks and others were shaking their heads. She was glad she was invisible now, as she saw several people milling around taking photos with phones; it looked like what Gavril and the others are concerned with was now coming true.

When she delivered the tiny soul to our Goddess, Ekaterina and Sandu appeared. Kat took the infant from their Goddess and held him close kissing his forehead. The child looked up at her, his eyes intent. Aaleahya could see the love shining in her daughter's own eyes. The Goddess looked from Ekaterina and Sandu, seeing exactly what she was and smiled at them both, telling that that she was giving the child into their care. "I am sure you will be good parents to this tiny soul. He is yours to take care of and love. As I had given you to your own parents, I am now bestowing this child's soul to you, to nourish and cherish. Take him and keep him safe Ekaterina and Sandu."

Aaleahya watched with tears in her own eyes, watching as her own children who were taken away from her in a vile manner, became parents in the realm of their Goddess. Gavril would be happy when she told him this news. Aaleahya inclined her head to their lovely Goddess and vanished from her realm back to Negrescu Hall.

She could hear her Mate and his Betas still discussing what their intent was to protect the Pack. Now she could understand why Gavril was contemplating such a drastic move. She was in full agreement with him that they should pull back from any contact with the humans and hide their existence, the better to help those they felt are worthy.

Humans had changed so much in a matter of a few years. The Pack had to change also, or they risked failing in their sworn duty to their Goddess.

Winter Solstice 2013

In the feeling of 'being Pack' that seemed to permeate the very fabric of Negrescu Hall just after the celebration of the Winter Solstice, Gavril realised that it seemed strange that he would be making the announcement that he had decided was now necessary.

"It is with regret that I have reached a decision. From tomorrow, the Pack will withdraw from face to face interaction with the human world, apart from running the Hunter's Arrow bar. The bar will remain essential so that our young might learn how they must behave and interact with humans, since by and large, our customers are not the dregs of humanity whom we must harvest."

He felt that he needed to explain further.

"The world has changed. What used to be known as the Seven Deadly Sins seem to be more virtues rather than sins." Gavril gave a bark of laughter. "Of course, one can go to Church or the temple or the mosque, and all is forgiven." He shook his head. "Our Goddess calls upon us to harvest those who commit evil on their fellow man. Yet, now, people carry camera phones. It is too easy for us to be filmed and for us to be traced, which would hinder us. The last thing we need is to be accused of being some sort of vigilante organisation. If our faces become unknown, then our work will be less prone to risk. This was not an easy decision to make, but we must maintain our ability to serve our Goddess. We must be able to protect the innocent. We must remain true to being Cŵn Annwn."

Gavril knew, as he pulled his Aaleahya close to him, relaxing in the feel of her arm around his waist, that only time would tell if he had made the right decision.

\- xxx -

Read on for a sample of Volume 2 of "The Diaries of the Cŵn Annwn": Beta

ABOUT THE AUTHORS:

Jo Pilsworth, the Lead Author of The Hunter's Arrow Ltd, found that too many nights away from home resulted in needing to find a hobby, and joining an online role-play group based on Sherrilyn Kenyon's Dark Hunters universe, was the answer. As a result, she became friends with some of her fellow writers, Tracy Andrews and Donna DeBoard, who joined her when she started what was known in the role-playing world as an 'own character' group. Thus The Hunter's Arrow and the worlds of the Anghelescu Hellhounds and the Negrescu Cŵn Annwn were born.

Currently, The Hunter's Arrow team includes authors from around the world, most of whom have contributed to the subsequent volumes in the series. All of them met through the 'role play' worlds of Facebook, and despite the best attempts of Facebook and Internet trolls, have managed to produce several novels between us. Currently, they are planning the ninth volume of The Diaries of the Cŵn Annwn.

When not planning further stories along with the inevitable research, Jo works full-time in medical equipment sales, covering a substantial part of the United Kingdom as her territory. She is supported in her writing endeavours by her wonderful husband of more than 25 years, David, and her son, David Junior, who has been an invaluable advisor when motorbikes or archery were involved in the stories.

"Chains of Perception" was the first story Jo wrote, starting when she was still in school. Were it not for her friends' encouragement, she might not have considered that others might like to read it. "Bound" is the first in the "Diaries of the Cŵn Annwn".

Jo and her friends hope you have enjoyed reading this story, and that you will feel encouraged to check out some of the books they have planned for publication under the name of their co-operative, The Hunter's Arrow.

ABOUT THE HUNTER'S ARROW LTD

Currently, the authors involved in The Hunter's Arrow Ltd are as follows:

Jo Pilsworth (UK), Lead Author
Tracy Andrews (USA) Senior Author
Donna DeBoard (USA), Senior Author
Bethan Thomas (UK), Author
Gabriela Collazo (Puerto Rico), Author
Laura Livermore (USA), Author
Melissa Keyza (USA), Author
Katlyn Stone (USA), Author
Aiden Williams (Australia), Author

Friendship has no borders … Not when the Internet is involved.

DISCOVER OTHER TITLES BY JO PILSWORTH AND THE AUTHORS OF THE HUNTER'S ARROW LTD

The Diaries of the Cŵn Annwn
Alpha (planned publication May 2016)
Beta (planned publication August 2016)
Yr Ddraig (planned publication May 2019)

The Hellfire Pack
Cysgodion (planned publication Summer 2018)
Merysekhmet (published Spring 2017)
Toho (planned publication Spring 2018)
Medved (planned publication December 2018)
Ma'iitsoh (planned publication early 2019)

and now … what is planned in the world of THE CŴN ANNWN

BETA: VOLUME 2 OF THE DIARIES OF THE CŴN ANNWN

Bran Cadwgan, Beta of the Cwn Annwn, always told himself that his failure to protect his Alpha and the Alpha's Mate during the Second World War would mean he was fated to never find a Mate of his own. His fate was to die at the hands of his Alpha when the madness that resulted from harvesting evil souls became too much. Still, he continued to serve his Pack. One evening, his fellow Beta tricked him into singing with the in-house band in the Hunter's Arrow bar.

Alix Gosselin had grown up under an abusive Alpha, her own sire, before being able to flee, pursuing a career in law enforcement. One evening, she agrees to accompany her colleagues to their new 'favourite' watering hole, some bar in the Catskills. One drink, she promised herself, but her life is about to change.

Owain Cadwaladr was the joker of Gavril's two Betas. He was also fascinated by humans, and fed his fascination by being the barman at the Hunter's Arrow. Just before Christmas 2014, he starts talking to a lonely young woman.

Merida Davinier had been alone for so many years in seemed, plagued by a nightmare reliving the death of her parents in a road traffic accident. Christmas was coming, yet another year of being alone. In desperation to avoid that sensation, she decides to go to a bar out in the Catskills, and starts talking to the barman. He seems normal enough, but is he?

Two Pack Betas, loyal to their Alpha since the childhoods in the hills of Wales. Two women from completely different backgrounds. Friendship and love can come from unexpected quarters and lead to even more unexpected outcomes.

Available on e-book retailers. Read on for a sample

NOT A PROLOGUE

Extract from the personal journal of Bran Cadwgan, Joint Beta of the Negrescu Cŵn Annwn

So, in his search to make us seem more approachable, and to reintegrate with the world of humans, Gavril's next task for me was give you all something from my history. Now, I don't know if any of you noticed the necklace I was wearing at the Pack summer picnic, but this is the story behind it. This is why the Beta of the Cŵn Annwn will always be wearing a Star of David necklace, because it is in memory of a young Jewish girl called Eliana, and the woman that she became.

Up until the summer of 1944, Hungary itself was allied to the Nazi regime of Germany. In theory, it meant that the Jewish population was safe from the depredations that became known as the 'Final Solution'. Only, they were not. Perhaps they might not all have been shipped to Auschwitz, but a fair few did have that fate. The 'easier' option of the labour camps was also a destination, but the result was still the same: families were torn apart, parents lost their children and children who should have been protected and loved, instead found themselves alone and forced to fend for themselves. The very fact that the deportations occurred, that families were torn apart was the reason why Gavril had decided that, as a Pack, we could not stand on the side-lines.

As Cŵn Annwn we had abilities open to us which made us different. After all, the geas placed on us by our Goddess requires us to carry out her work, and that means the harvesting of those who would do evil. To do so, we must be able to travel quickly. We must be stronger both physically and mentally than those we seek to bring to justice. We are not just killers though. For all the killers, there are victims, and sometimes it is the victims whom we must bring to their rest. But the thing is, we can't save them all. We have to take into account that sometimes, even with the abilities granted to us by our Goddess, we might not be able to save them all. But what we can do is that we can try.

The ones whom Gavril thought we stood the best chance of saving were the children. He called them the hope of the future. They were indeed that. They were the hope that from the nightmare of war, some good might come of it. Some might find a way to forgive and for their spirits to thrive. It was a dream; it might be said, but it was a dream that as Cŵn Annwn, we had a chance to ensure became a reality. However, to do so, we had to save as many of those children as possible.

The majority of our own version of an Underground Railroad was handled by the daughter of Gavril and Aaleahya, Ekaterina, and the young male whom in retrospect was probably her bonded Mate. They had been together as children, and perhaps in a more peaceful time, they might have become Mates in truth, but that was not to be their fate. When Gavril had first proposed the scheme, he had known that Kat would insist on playing a major role, and to give Kat her due, she was a combination of her sire's fairness and her mother's passion to help others. It could be said that she could have taken no other path.

Gavril had enlisted the help of an old friend of his, a Catholic priest, whose first introduction to the Cŵn Annwn had been his attempt to baptise the daughter of the local landowner, who had shown her displeasure at the cold water by 'flashing' from his arms back to her mother's arms. Aaleahya and Gavril had laughed at Kat's actions, and had taken time to explain to the young priest that he was not crazy. Over time, Gavril and the priest became close friends, with the priest proving to be one of those individuals who could appreciate that other faiths and belief systems existed in this world. They had passed many an evening over a glass of wine, discussing the finer points of philosophy. The priest's very open-mindedness was the reason why Gavril approached him about setting up the routes to help the children find safety away from the war.

The priest had directed Gavril to another friend of his, a Rabbi. Like the priest, the rabbi was not a young man anymore, but he could see the dangers to his congregation, and was not intending to turn down the assistance of an individual who might save even a small number of those who looked to him for guidance. The problem was that not all were as open minded. For this reason, it was a careful process, to introduce Gavril to those whom the rabbi thought might be willing to entrust their children to a stranger, and a young looking stranger at that. Gavril was a stranger who spoke still with the slightly lilting tones of our Welsh homeland, albeit his accent was tempered by Aaleahya's own Romanian accent.

The outline plan was that the groups of children would be assembled at a safe location: either the home of the rabbi or at the home of one of the sets of parents. It could be called a prayer meeting or a Shabbat gathering, even though celebration of the latter was becoming more difficult as the war progressed. The horror that would become known as Kristallnacht had been but a start of the animosity fostered against one race. Depending on the number of children needing to be transported elsewhere would determine the number of adult Cŵn Annwn who would meet them there. Out of necessity we dressed as most of the population, and yes, that meant that as the deprivation of the war became more significant, so do the way that we dressed, all the better to avoid the attention of the authorities. Sometimes these transports would require just Gavril, Owain and me, and sometimes it would be more. That was a danger in itself since the gathering of that many people would be open to an informant noticing our activities and for the sake of some small gain, reporting us to the authorities. Had that happened, then yes, we might take steps to protect ourselves, but it damaged the chances of us being able to help these people. Make no mistake, as the war progressed, that desperation became great indeed.

But these were the days before people realised just how far the Nazi war machine was prepared to go. The authorities knew, but the individual man on the ground? It was easy to fool one's own conscience that your neighbours had chosen only to move away from the area, rather than to think that they had been deported. The stories of the camps were just that surely? Stories only. How many lives have been lost over time because neighbours turned their backs on those who might have been friends in other circumstances or perhaps even more worrying because they wished gain from denouncing a neighbour?

My apologies, I am known to be the more thoughtful of Gavril's two Betas, not that it makes Owain somehow slow or less able that I. He has his strengths and I have mine, and together we support our friend and Alpha.

When we had determined the number of children to be transported, either we did so between the three of us, since we might transport them as long as they had skin to skin contact with us, or we took them in relays. Our initial destination was the cellars of The Hunter's Arrow Inn. Yes, I know, it seems strange that we brought the children there, but it could be argued that it was the last place that might be expected to be used as a relay point.

It was one of the early evacuations after the Nazis had invaded Hungary. They had commandeered our home, and they had commandeered the Inn, forcing our Alpha and his Mate to accept the invasion of their home by people who were anathema to us all. It was either accept them, or everyone would suffer. Not just the Pack, but the village also, and if there was one thing that Gavril would never allow, it would be for those who looked to us for protection to suffer. We are paranormal beings. We have more means at our disposal to survive being starved, beaten and ridiculed. Humans have no such resources. For us to not use the gifts given to us by our Goddess would have been a betrayal of everything for which we stood.

So, this evacuation. I had been sent to collect a young girl. She was an only child, and her parents were dead. The neighbours had hidden her, but the net was closing. She had to be moved or, the 'authorities' having the mentality that they did, the whole street would have been made to suffer. She was perhaps 12 years old, slim, pale skinned as were most of her race, and big, dark eyes that saw into the soul, as much as my own abilities allowed me to do.

The house was in a quiet suburb of Paris, and if one closed one's eyes, it might almost be as if the war was not real. But then things would stand out, not least of which was the lack of children playing in the streets. War was a real and present thing, even in this quiet street, and here, the war against the Jews was in earnest. What was yet to become the norm in Hungary was happening here.

She had not said much to me when I arrived. She was old enough to know why I was there, even if her former neighbours had not told her. One of them waited with her, smoothing the child's braided hair, and I could see the fear in the older woman's eyes, and the sure knowledge of what might be her fate if it was known that she had sheltered 'an enemy of the regime', a child. She wore a dark dress, no different from any other child, apart from one thing: a yellow star sewn onto her dress, the symbol on which the authorities insisted to mark her as Jewish.

I was conscious that my size and my height in comparison to the girl's slender form. Crouching down, to bring my head closer to her, I had given her a half smile, trying to put her at ease, even in these difficult circumstances. Her face was thin, showing the deprivation that was becoming the norm for people here. She had no coat, so I had pulled off my jacket to give it to her, even though it meant that the damning yellow star was concealed, an act which might have meant even more trouble for both her and the family which have given her shelter. Given my size in relation to her, the jacket had swamped her.

She had smiled shyly. "Thank you, sir." Then she had looked worried. "I have nothing to give you in return."

"Nothing is required, child." I said gently.

"But my Mama said I must always give my thanks." She looked thoughtful, before she reached inside her dress, and pulled out a long chain. "This was my Mama's but she gave it to me ... just before." Her voice broke slightly. "I want you to have it. Will you wear it?"

I looked at the chain, and the small pendant that she placed in my larger hand. I knew that her faith was passed down the matrilineal line. Giving me this link with her mother was more than just thanks. This was a gift of considerable value, and one which I had to acknowledge.

"I will wear it so that one day I might return it to you, little one." I promised her softly. She had smiled, and placed a light kiss on my cheek.

"Then we have a deal." She had whispered to me.

We left the building, walking some way down the street, before we slipped into a doorway, and I was able to transport her to the cellars at Hunter's Inn. Kat and Sandu took over from there. As we had for others of her age, a family were waiting to welcome her in the States, and she would travel there via Wales.

After the war, even though I had never said as much to my Alpha, I could not help but watch over those children whom I had helped escape from the carnage of war. So many had died, and in comparison, we had managed to rescue such a small number. When they came to the USA, it was a far from easy process. We were conscious that this was the land where a boatload of Jewish refugees had been turned away, and forced to return to Europe, where many perished. Fortunately, we were not without our connections. As the children grew to adulthood, the Negrescu Foundation, established for reasons of sorrow within our own Pack, provided them with grants that they might establish businesses, attend college, build careers and in some way demonstrate their gratitude for the fact that they lived when so many had perished.

This girl, Eliana, thrived in her new life, yet it seemed that she did not forget either. Despite my best attempts to conceal my identity, she knew who I was. I would see her flash a quick smile in my direction sometimes, or when she stood from the bench in the park on which she had been reading a book, she would leave something, a thoughtful look on her face. It might be a poem or a story, handwritten. Always it would be dedicated to "My Angel". I felt a sense of guilt for the way that each of these tokens became precious to me, a reminder of a small light that had burned in a time of darkness. As each beautiful piece of calligraphy was stored with the others in a carved box in my rooms, I would smile. Much had been lost in the war, but this one girl, she reminded me that light can come from the darkness.

I had not forgotten my promise to her. I wore the necklace she had given me, but each time I saw her, when I might have returned it to her, it was strange, but she had shaken her head, almost as if she had divined my intent and wished me to keep her gift for the moment. I lost track of her when she married, not realising that the man who would become our public liaison for the Foundation was none other than her son. When I found Eliana again, she was an old woman, dying from cancer. Still, that smile was there, when she recognised me.

"Have you come to take me home, my friend and protector." She had whispered, a combination of the morphine and her own fatigue.

I nodded, unable to speak initially. "I looked for you, as I promised. I said that at the very least, I would do this for you." I held out the gold chain and its little pendant, perhaps a bit more worn from my wearing it every day. Gently, she had folded my fingers around it.

"Keep it safe for me." She whispered. "I have lived a long life, full of love and laughter, but you? You still grieve, my angel and protector. Keep it, and perhaps one day, you too will know love and you too will be able to laugh again."

She had given a soft sigh, as I absorbed her soul, her life fulfilled. In her memory, I will continue to wear her gift and I will treasure the memory of a young girl who hid her fear and maintained the purity of her soul in house in Paris whilst the insanity of war raged around her.

xxx

As I watched Eliana grow, I used to wonder what it must be like to have someone, just one person rather than a Pack, with whom I might share my life. What might it be like to hold my own child in my arms? What might it be like to be held by another, the closeness acting as a shield against anything the world might throw at us? Yes, I had seen that closeness between my Alpha and his Mate, a love that continued to grow, and continued to thrive despite the loss of their only child during the war.

That was not for me. I had betrayed the trust that my Alpha had held for me, when I had failed to protect him and his Mate from the attacks of the Nazis who had invaded our home. For me, this was as close as I would come. My lot was to witness the affection and support of a couple, but never to feel it myself.

Perhaps, if I had not failed my Alpha and his Mate, my life would be different, but it is what it is. This is the will of my Goddess, that I atone for my failure. I accept that.

But, I can't help but wonder, as I watched that girl, now a woman, with her husband and children. What if things had been different?

CHAPTER 1: A CHANCE MEETING

It started with a letter, just like it would in the best romances, so Bran had been told. Except, for him, it was not a romance. Romance had no place in his life, for all that he was a member of a species dependent on finding a predestined Mate if they were ever to have young. That was not for him. He had resigned himself to the fact that, as payment for failing in his duties to his Alpha and his Alpha's Mate during the war, he himself would have no Mate. Thus, he would never hold his own child in his arms. So be it. Bran knew he should have taken the beatings that were meted out to both Gavril and Aaleahya. That is part and parcel of being the Pack Beta: ensuring that his Alpha is physically fit and able to lead them. If that means he had to take injuries upon himself, he would do so willingly, knowing that it is for the good of the Pack.

But the fact remains that he didn't protect his Alpha and his Alpha's Mate. He didn't take those beatings and punishments, and so, he would pay the price for it. He had long since accepted his punishment.

There are, after all, other ways, when he might at least enjoy something of the sensation of having a Mate of his own, and young of his own, not least of which was something he had never really told either Gavril or Aaleahya. After the Pack's arrival in the USA, when the Pack relocated at the end of the war, Bran continued to watch over those Jewish and Roma children in whose rescues he had played a part. This included a young girl who had given him the sole link that she had with her deceased mother: a Star of David pendant which Bran wore to this day. Her name was Eliana, a name meaning "God has answered me".

Eliana was found a home with a Jewish family living in New York, ironically not that far from where the Pack would make their new base in the Catskill Mountains. Perhaps this was one of the reasons why Bran would look in on her more often than others. It was a relatively short ride on his Harley to the area of New York City in which she lived. With his features hidden by his helmet, it was easy for him to watch from a distance, as she thrived in this new home, growing into a lovely young woman. Somehow, she knew she was being watched, but although she might smile when she caught a glimpse of that watcher, she did not speak to him. Instead, Bran would find pictures she had drawn, poems she had written. On one occasion, she left him a copy, typewritten, of a short story she had written on how she had escaped from the death camps. She called her rescuer an angel: a man who had given her his jacket to keep her warm, and to whom she had given her mother's pendant. Her description of Bran in that story was surprisingly accurate, one of the reasons why he kept his face hidden. He would never grow old, but as he watched Eliana's life develop, Bran knew that she would, just as he knew that, one day, the time would come when he would harvest the soul of someone for whom he had come to care a great deal.

So, a letter. As one of the Pack Betas, there was a lot of correspondence. Bran would reflect more than once that whoever said that computers would mean the end of paper correspondence was, quite frankly, talking out of their behinds. It would have been very easy to miss this one, had it not been for the unusual detail: white envelope, good quality paper, and the address handwritten in fountain pen ink no less. The letter itself had a scent to it that said a female hand had penned it.

Why would a woman write a personal letter to him?

Owain had managed to persuade Bran and some of the others to take part in some print advertising for The Hunter's Arrow recently. With the winter approaching, there was all the scope of gifts to be bought. So several members of the Pack were made to put up with Owain ordering them into different poses using the different types of bows sold in the Pack's business. They also used it to showcase the bar, which was part of the store.

Anyway, when the letter arrived, Bran had put it to one side to start with, intending to read it when he had a bit more time. He nearly forgot about it, so it was with a touch of guilt that he settled down with a cup of coffee to see what it was all about.

Bran nearly sprayed his coffee out on reading the opening paragraph. A copy of the advertisement for The Hunter's Arrow accompanied the letter.

"My Angel." The letter said. "It is a long time since I have seen you and you have not changed one bit. I don't know who else I can ask for help, and I need help desperately."

"As you know, Abe and I had a daughter, thanks to Angharad putting us in contact with the pioneers of in-vitro fertilisation. We were blessed with our beautiful Avigail as a result. You would be so proud of the woman she has become, a fighter against injustice, particularly when it involves women."

Her letter continued, explaining that with her mother as an example, Avigail had become involved in helping at a shelter for battered wives, offering support where she could. More recently, the shelter offered assistance to trafficked women: women who had been kidnapped or tricked into a life of prostitution, and sexual violence. Her daughter, as a qualified attorney, had defended many of these women in court, fighting to protect them. Clearly she had been too good at her job, because six months ago, her daughter had been kidnapped. The kidnappers had made no bones about being responsible. If her family had any hope of seeing her alive again, they would stay out of the kidnappers' business.

Eliana's daughter closed her letter by saying that, if it was at all possible, she begged Bran to help her. The police had all but closed the file on the kidnapping. They had other priorities. Please, she had begged.

How could Bran turn down this plea for help?

He told Gavril that he had some personal business to which he needed to attend. His friend had raised a brow at this, knowing that for Bran, 'personal business' usually meant checking on one of 'his' children from the war. Bran let him think that, because, quite frankly, he had no idea where this meeting would lead.

Bran rode his bike to the address on the letter, arriving in the early evening. It hadn't crossed his mind that it was a Friday, not until he knocked on the door. Realising that this was not a good day to call on a Jewish family, Bran had turned around, intending to come back another day, when the door opened.

Rebecca, the wife of Eliana's son stood there, her fist in her mouth, as she saw his face, tears streaming down her cheeks.

"May God be praised." She whispered. "You came. You came."

Bran's hand was taken up in her hands, and she pulled him into the house. Her husband, Abe, stood at the entrance to their dining room, and his eyes widened when he saw their visitor, before he started to shake his head. He had grown old, this man whom Bran had known for so many years, but he remembered Bran only too well.

"They said we must not interfere." His voice quavered slightly. He knew about the letter his wife had written and he knew that, on the insane chance that the letter would be answered, they would have to face the risk that it might be too late.

"I had to try." His wife's voice was firmer, but even so, she could not help but glance at Bran. He knew she was trying to work out how he could be the man, the same man with whom her husband had worked. Bran realised that he had to stop that train of thought, before she convinced herself that he could achieve something beyond realistic.

"Please, I will try to help, but I can't promise anything. I am but one man." Bran wanted to ensure that by coming to their home, he had not raised their hopes beyond realistic expectations.

She didn't need to know that he may be 'one man', but he was also joint Beta of the Cŵn Annwn. Bran may not have the skills and talents of his Alpha, but he was not without a few tricks of his own either.

The woman's hand crept tentatively to the open neck of his shirt, where the chain was just visible. "You are the man who saved Abe’s mother, and you still wear this?" She asked gently. "I know she bade you keep it when she died. You did, and you still wear it. She has been gone five years now, but still, you wear her gift."

Bran put his own hand over her hand, remembering again that little girl in a kitchen in Paris.

"If I can help, then I will." He said quietly. As he stood in the doorway of the room, he realised that the table was spread for Friday Sabbath, and stopped. "I have come at the wrong time. Let me return at a more appropriate time."

"We would be honoured for you to join us." The husband spoke. "With that gift of our family that you continue to wear, you are family. Join us, my son."

And thus, Bran spent his first Sabbath. A Cŵn Annwn. A Son of the Goddess. But, that night, Bran was a member of another family.

Printed in Great Britain
by Amazon

40114793R00165